The Pursuit of Alba

C. B. Nash

Brazenhead Publishing, LLC

Cover design and illustration by Mike W. Chovanec, Chovanec Art. www.chovanecart.com

Published by
Brazenhead Publishing, LLC
PO Box 61872
Fort Myers, FL 33906

Printed in the United States of America
First Paperback Printing March 2013

Library of Congress Control Number: 2013932389
ISBN 978-0-9837994-2-9 (paperback)
ISBN 978-0-9737994-3-6 (eBook)

About the Author

Christian B. Nash is a reclusive curmudgeon who makes his home on the mangrove coasts of Southwest Florida. For the last few years, he has spent much of his time chronicling the adventures of Matt Narvik and Dexter Rubino.

Nash's first book, *The Vengeance of Ben-Bal*la, was published in 2011 and is available on Nash's website at www.cbnashnovels.com, as well as on Amazon.com and BarnesandNoble.com. The book may be purchased as a paperback or as an eBook formatted for Kindle and Nook.

For more information on *The Pursuit of Alba* or *The Vengeance of Ben Balla* and the locations mentioned therein, please visit our website.

www.cbnashnovels.com

Books by C. B. Nash

Narvik/Rubino Series
The Vengeance of Ben-Balla
The Pursuit of Alba

Dedication

As always, to my R.C.

Je t'aime

Thank You

Authoring "the Pursuit of Alba" is the result of much travel, research and revision. Much of this was made possible by friends and family who believed in the project and offered encouragement and hospitality to the author. The Werner and Chovanec families of Orlando, Florida, as well as many others, are recipients of our gratitude. May God bless you in all your endeavors.

Prologue

Alba Cologne, once a promising actress and model, became a reluctant participant in her father's plot to assassinate a former President of the United States. Her task in the scheme was to secure the services of a sailboat captain and his boat.

She quickly seduced an unsuspecting Matthew Narvik. While his faith and openness intrigued her, she never hesitated to ensnare him.

On December 24, 2009, the assassination scheme fell apart when Matt fired a flare into the sky giving away the position of the plotters. The flare signaled both the death knell of the scheme and seizure of Philippe Ben-Balla's heart.

Dexter Rubino and his team took the vessel as Alba's father died in her arms. As Matt's unconscious body was transported from the scene, Alba cared for his wounds.

In the aftermath, Alba calmly surrendered her custody to those who had betrayed her father. Promises of a renewed career caused her to hope for a brighter future, but she often wondered about the fate of the simple sailor, Matthew Narvik.

Her heart ached for the true love of one man, and a family. Things she had never truly known.

Chapter 1

While Anton Carmella rode past the campus of his alma mater, he noticed the young co-eds offering their pasty mounds of flesh to the sun god. There had been a time in his life when he would have spent hours leering at the young female bodies. In recent years, he had lost interest.

As his town car left the city and sped toward the village of his youth, he summoned the attention of his driver. "Rocco, stop at the cemetery on the way to the church."

Rocco Vecchiarelli looked into the mirror. "You sure, Chief? The ground will be all wet and the grass will stick to your shoes."

"I have to make sure those cemetery jerks dug the hole in the right place. They wanted to bury him on the other side of his wife. That's the plot where my baby brother is. My old man was too cheap to buy a stone for a dead baby. Joe and I should have done that when Mom died. My brother made sure his whore of a wife had a headstone."

"It's kind of funny what people think is important."

"What's funny about it?"

Rocco shook his head as he spoke, dislodging one of his black curls. "Well, maybe funny isn't the right word. I'm just sayin'. Joe spent a lot of money on his rotten wife but forgot about his baby brother."

"So just who are you to judge my brother, or me?"

Rocco used the rearview mirror to repair the damage to his coiffeur. "I'm sorry, Chief. I didn't mean any disrespect. I was just sayin'."

Rocco approached the entrance to the cemetery and stopped at the closed gate. "The place is still locked up, Chief. Guess they heard people are dying to get in." Rocco started to laugh but upon sighting the displeased look on Anton's face, he stifled the joviality. "Do you want me to take you to the church, or would you rather go get some coffee to kill the time?"

"No, pull over to the side of the road and wait here. I know how to get into this place. We used to play army here when we were kids."

"You want me to go with you?"

"No, you wait here. I want to be alone for a while."

Anton exited the vehicle and started walking down the road. His arthritic hips and knees caused him to have a slow, stiff gait. With the steel resolve of a younger man, he gritted his teeth and stoically refused to acknowledge his pain. He estimated the distance to the end of the fence line was one hundred yards. He recalled the days of his youth when he could easily run the hundred-yard dash in less than eleven seconds. *Fast for a big kid*. At the end of the fence, a stand of hemlock trees formed a boundary between the cemetery and the lawn of a suburban ranch house. "This used to be a cow pasture," he said, then grew conscious of talking to himself aloud.

Once Anton disappeared behind the hemlocks, Rocco pulled a cell phone from the glove compartment and made a call.

"I'm in the car at the cemetery gate . . . No, he got out and started walking down the road. He thinks he knows some other way in . . . I don't have a clue what he's doin'. He said he wanted to be alone. I think his brother's dyin' has pushed him over the edge. Youns guys are gonna have to make a move fast . . . I know the stash is somewhere on the old farm, but only he knows where . . . OK, if the dude shows up to unlock the gate, I'll drive in, but till then I'm stuck here . . . Yes, sir, I will."

Anton hobbled along the tree line for perhaps fifty feet and noticed an opening in the foliage. He ducked under some branches and entered the dark cover of the narrow forest. There was a profusion of daffodils and trilliums in bloom, their shaded environment having extended a long hibernation. Mud squeezed up around Anton's wingtips. He remembered picking blackberries here with an Irish girl from his high school. She had smooth, pale skin and dark hair. Her feigned resistance had only increased his ardor. He had gotten his way. *Anton Carmella always gets his way. Was that senior year? No, it must have been junior year, just before football season.*

A chipmunk scurried over a fallen branch and interrupted his reminiscence. Refocusing on his intent, he followed a faint path through the trees toward the Carmella family plot. He crossed the wet grass to where a grave lay open, awaiting the remains of his older brother, Joe, five years his senior. *How many more good years can I expect? Then what will happen to me?*

Anton Carmella stood quietly at the foot of his brother's gravesite.

"Mr. Carmella?"

Anton looked over his shoulder and saw a dark skinned man wearing a blue blazer and khaki pants approaching. "Who are you?"

"My name is Desmond Quest. I'm sorry to disturb you at such a sensitive time, but we have important business to discuss."

"Are you with the undertaker?"

"No, sir, I represent a business interest with whom you have had dealings in the past. Our new CEO is anxious to resume doing that business and regrets the delay in contacting you. With the rise in commodity prices, the delay will only serve to benefit you."

Anton turned to confront the man and carefully looked him over. He was a little shorter than Anton, muscular, with very dark skin. He always tended to be suspicious of blacks, and this one had an odd accent, almost British but not quite. "I'm standing here in the cemetery next to my brother's fresh-dug grave and you come to me about business? How do I know who you are? You could be the FBI for all I know."

The man chuckled. "I assure you, Mr. Carmella, I am not associated with law enforcement in any way."

"You expect me to take your word for that?"

"What evidence would be acceptable to you? Would you like a full accounting of your investment history with the Windswept Corporation? Perhaps a recounting of your initial dealings with our former CEO would be more appropriate. I believe her grave is there, next to your brother's."

"Shut up!" Sighting a concrete crucifix over the man's shoulder, Anton genuflected and stepped back. His right heel landed on the edge of the open grave, and he began to flail his arms in an attempt to regain his balance. Desmond Quest leaped forward and seized Anton by his black suit coat. Anton feebly tried to break his fall with his left hand, which slipped forward as he hit the ground and collided with a headstone. As he endeavored to push himself upright, he saw the inscription on the stone: "Cynthia Duckworth Carmella, 1962-1994."

Desmond helped him to his feet, then began brushing the grass clippings from the elder man's suit. "I've heard the expression of having one foot in the grave, Mr. Carmella, but never thought it could be taken so literally."

"What do you want from me?"

"I told you, I represent the Windswept Corporation."

"Is Philippe alive?"

"Unfortunately, no. He died in a boating accident. During the resulting restructuring of the corporation, there was a delay in contacting some of our investors. I thought we could find some privacy here."

"In a cemetery? This is holy ground. We can't talk about our business dealings here."

"I was not aware of your religious taboos, Mr. Carmella. I would think that since you are standing on the grave of a woman you had murdered, you were devoid of superstition."

Anton stepped away from the grave and straightened his tie. "Look, I had to get rid of her before she ruined everything."

"It's of no consequence to me, Mr. Carmella. We are a forward-looking company. We wish to concentrate on our future dealings, not the past."

"I had to shut down the smelter. Some of those EPA snoops were nosin' around."

"Do you have an inventory?"

"Yes, I had no way to dispose of it."

"We will be happy to take it off of your hands at the previously agreed rate of compensation."

"How soon will you be ready?"

"Unfortunately, it will be late summer or early autumn before we can accept delivery."

"What am I supposed to do in the meantime?"

"I'm sure you have adequate storage facilities available."

"That isn't the problem. I didn't pay some of my suppliers, now they are getting a little irate."

"So you need an advance."

"No, I need a place to hide. I started doing business with Philippe because he could set me up somewhere in the third world. You know, a little castle I could call my own."

"Your agreement with Windswept calls for you to continue investing until 2018. At that time we would reward you with a new identity in a safe haven."

"I don't have that long! I need to leave the US before the end of the year."

"You're shortening your time table significantly, Mr. Carmella. It will, of course, affect the projected returns."

"Waiting that long is not an option. I need an advance on my inventory."

"We can only issue an advance on your current investment, Mr. Carmella. That will also impose a penalty on your account."

"That isn't fair. Philippe never did business that way."

"I assure you, sir, Philippe always adhered to sound business practices. Now how much of an advance are you in need of?"

"I need one million US dollars."

"Due to the valuation of your currency, that amount would significantly reduce your investment, Mr. Carmella. I am unsure if my superiors will agree to such a transaction."

"Tell them I have two million more in inventory. If they don't advance me the money, I'll take my business elsewhere."

"I'll see what I can do. Either way you will be hearing from us in the next week. Isn't it time for you to go to the church?"

"How did you know to find me here?"

"Rest assured, Mr. Carmella, we can always find you."

Chapter 2

Matt Narvik stretched as he walked across the parking lot. The sub-tropical sun felt good on his pallid skin. After six months in a rehabilitation facility, his demands for release had finally come to fruition. His only visitor while in the home was Pete Walters, who described himself as "a fellow employee of the Windswept Corporation." Matt had never known Pete prior to that meeting, but since his new employer was paying the tab at the rehab facility, Matt accepted him as a friend. "Mr. Rubino said I was going to be a secret agent."

"You are, sort of. You are an employee of Windswept's security division, as am I. Right now you're in training."

"Right now I'm as weak as a kitten. All that time locked up in a nursing home has sapped my strength. I think my food was laced with sedatives."

"You were acting a little squirrely when you first got there so they gave you some happy pills. I'm sure everything they did was for your own good."

"They may have been well intentioned, but I began to feel like a prisoner in that place."

Pete slowed the car as they crossed the Tamiami trail, once the only road from Tampa to Miami. They entered a residential neighborhood in south Fort Myers known as the Villas. "Windswept spent a lot of money to keep you there, and don't forget they covered the cost of your hospital bills, the boat, and everything. Dex has been a good friend to you, and if you follow orders, he'll continue to be."

"I've been meaning to ask, just who is Mr. Rubino, and why has he gone out of his way to help me?"

"First of all, don't ever call him Mr. Rubino. He is Dex. Always call him Dex. He has gone the extra mile for you because he believes you have the potential to be a valuable agent someday. Here we are, Matt, your new home."

Pete pulled into the drive of a small house made of cement blocks painted white. It had a nearly flat roof, a one-car garage, and a frail-looking carport tacked on to the side. In the carport sat the one possession that Narvik had retained.

"Hey, my Jeep. I almost forgot about her."

"I had it at one of my other rentals while it was vacant. I brought it down here yesterday."

"Well, thanks, Pete. I can't wait to take her out for a spin."

"Hold on, sailor, you can't drive yet. You don't have a license. Your car insurance was dropped because you didn't make the payments."

"I hadn't thought about that."

"We'll take care of those details in the next few days. For now, come inside and I'll show you around."

In Narvik's eyes, the house and its furnishings looked like "a house of the future" from the 1950s. The chrome dinette set reminded him of one that his parents had when he was a child. There were two bedrooms, a single bath, a kitchen, and dining room separated by a bar, and a large living room with an enormous glass-block window at the front.

"This is fine, Pete. Looks like everything I need for now. How much is this going to cost me?"

"Windswept is paying all the bills. I'm supposed to take you clothes shopping soon. I picked up some jeans and shirts for you. They're in the bedroom closet."

"I'll be glad to get out of these sweat pants. It's all they gave me at rehab."

"You're not done with rehab yet. That's one of the reasons I put you in this place. You're only a block from Gold's Gym and less than a mile from a nice long bike path. You have a lot of conditioning to do, and I'm your trainer. We begin tomorrow morning at seven A.M. For this afternoon, we'll go to a late lunch. Do you like chili? There's a place just south of here that makes some of the best I've ever tasted. "

"Sure, I love chili. Let me get changed and then we can go."

Matt felt good slipping into actual men's clothing again. Wearing jeans and shoes instead of slippers and sweat pants restored his sense of self-worth. He didn't care for the golf shirts Pete had provided but wasn't about to complain. As they left the house, they went through the garage and parked there was a blue Crossfire roadster.

"This is Dex's baby. Your first assignment for Windswept is to protect it. The keys are hanging in the kitchen cupboard, but I advise you to leave it alone."

Matt exited through a side door to the carport, where he stopped to look over his Jeep. He opened the passenger's door and noticed his old navy blazer and tie lying on the rear seat. Alongside of them lay a black pillbox hat with veil and a pair of black lace gloves. He had forgotten Alba leaving them there, but he recalled his thoughts when she had. He picked up one of the gloves and sniffed it. Could he still catch the scent of her perfume? Or was it just his imagination? *Where is Alba Cologne now? Does she still care? Has she ever cared?*

"I don't know where she is," Pete said. "Dex hasn't said anything about her."

"Was she harmed that night?"

"No, she was OK. She was worried about you."

"Were you there?"

"Yeah, I was there, but I'm not supposed to talk about it. Officially it never happened."

At the restaurant, Narvik wolfed down the chili. "Sure beats that institutional food."

Pete nodded, and as they ate he laid out an ambitious plan for the restoration of Narvik's strength. Over the course of the next few months, the men bonded as Matt logged long miles on the treadmill and bike path. Pete insisted he take large doses of vitamins; one was unlabeled, and Matt forced the four large pills down four times each day. The use of the modern weight machines available at the gym restored his muscle tone. He went home every weekday aching, but it was a good ache. Pete had a small hot tub installed on the back porch and Narvik quickly grew addicted to it.

On June 1, Pete surprised Matt with a field trip. They went to a shooting range, and for the first time in his life Matt fired a handgun. After a few weeks of practice, he showed signs of improvement but not much promise.

On the weekends, Matt attended services at churches near his new home but never found one he felt at home in. He watched the Christian Worship Hour on television and began sending a contribution as his Windswept paychecks were deposited. He also read his Bible with the aid of a daily devotional and spent a lot of time in prayer. He believed his spiritual restoration was as important as his physical restoration.

Matt signed up for an adult-education class in computers. He had once said he would never use one, but after a few classes, he purchased a laptop and an air card for access to the Internet. One of his first online searches was for the company that employed him. It seemed Windswept was about to inaugurate a cruise line that would take passengers from Barcelona to a corporate-owned resort island named Sunset Cay. A video enticed viewers to lie back in the luxurious splendor of a world-class resort surrounded by azure water and acres of manicured forests. This was a continuation of the lavish opulence experienced while crossing the Atlantic aboard the stunning cruise ship *New Dawn*.

"Your hostess on the inaugural trans-Atlantic voyage and all subsequent voyages will be the famous entertainer and model, Alba Cologne," the voice said.

Chapter 3

Dexter Rubino stood at the window looking at the landscapers; the sweat on their black skin glistened in the tropical sun. "I guess Grand Cayman isn't paradise for everyone," he muttered.

"What's that, dear?" asked a voice in the kitchen.

"Oh, nothing, Cyn. Just talking to myself. How much do these guys get paid?"

Cyn entered the room with a frosty glass in each hand. "I don't know, more than they ever dreamed of in Haiti. The hotel pays for the service. Why? Are you thinking of starting a new career?" She handed Dex one of the glasses.

"Thanks, how did you know I was getting thirsty? If I wanted a job like that, I could have stayed in Florida. I doubt that I'd last more than a day."

She rubbed his arm and shot him a flirtatious flick of her eyebrows. "I think you have plenty of stamina. Not getting homesick are you?"

He touched her hand and smiled. "No, but I got an email from Windswept. They want me in Barcelona."

"Why?"

"They claim they need my input for the security of the new cruise line. Would you like to come along?"

"I'd love to, but I can't. I have meetings scheduled with the lawyers and insurance companies. The new owners will be taking over soon."

"How did a girl like you ever get stuck with that white elephant?"

"I told you, it was a parting gift from an old boyfriend."

"A hotel damaged beyond repair? Nice gift."

"It was a beautiful place when I met him, a real money-maker. He got sick and then the hurricane hit. He just didn't have the will to rebuild, so he signed it over to me."

"Where is he now?"

"He died. You don't have to worry about a rival. There aren't too many guys around looking for an over-the-hill floozy."

Dex set his drink on an end table and wrapped his arms around her. "You're no floozy. You're the best thing that's happened to me in a long time."

"You're sweet. Finish my drink for me. I have to run to the store. Need anything?"

"No, I'll make some phone calls while you're gone. Maybe I can stall the Dragon Lady for a while."

"OK. If you decide to fly to Florida, you're welcome to use the hotel's plane and pilot. I'm paying for its upkeep, and Julian is flying a barstool."

"Thanks, I may take you up on that. But is it safe to fly with Julian?"

"Sure. If he knows forty-eight hours in advance, he'll be as sober as a priest."

"Oh, yeah. That's comforting. Hurry home, pet."

"I'll be back in two hours," she said and kissed his cheek.

Dexter Rubino had spent the first six months of 2010 relaxing in the Cayman Islands. While there, he enjoyed playing the role of "rich American," which was made possible by living on Windswept's dime. He phoned the president of the company, Helene Adolphe, hoping to delay his departure.

"Helene, there must have been a clerical error in your main office. I just received an email directing me to report for orientation."

"Oh, I do not believe that was sent in error, Dexter. Mr. Quest is looking forward to meeting you."

"Just who is Mr. Quest?"

"Mr. Quest is the Chief Security Administrator for the cruise line. More succinctly, he is your new boss."

"You and I are partners, Helene. I am not just an employee."

"Dexter, I had to give you a job title to keep you on the books. If you recall, I offered to settle our accounts, but you wished to receive greater compensation for your services. If you prefer to resign rather than report for orientation, we can work that out."

"I refuse to resign until we have divided Philippe's treasure. You promised me a share, remember?"

"Yes, Dexter, but we have been unable to locate any such treasure thus far. It may be that the rumored treasure was just a figment of Philippe's imagination."

"Don't try to stiff me, Helene."

"Calm yourself, Mr. Rubino. I have always been more than generous to my employees."

"I remind you again, I am a partner, not an employee."

Helene let out a long sigh of exasperation. "I am aware that you wish to be a partner in Windswept's profits, but to do so you must partake in the labor that produces those returns."

"I have already contributed to Windswept's bottom line by stopping your predecessor's murderous plot."

"Watch your words, Mr. Rubino. Windswept is embarking on a new venture in a difficult economic climate. I value your expertise and appreciate your investment in the company. I thought you'd want to be here for the ship's dedication. Besides which, I have never thanked you personally for the service you rendered last December."

"All right, I'll report for orientation, but I want first class accommodations."

"Of course. When were you told to report?"

"The first of July."

"I'm sure Mr. Quest wouldn't mind if you waited until after the Fourth of July celebrations. I know how patriotic you are."

"I may go back to Florida for a few days and check in with my men."

"That would be wise, Dexter. We retained those gentlemen on your recommendation. I hope they prove profitable."

"I'm sure they're reliable."

"Then I'll be seeing you in July. I will have Mr. Quest's secretary contact you with the travel arrangements."

After Dex hung up, he went for a stroll and contemplated going to Barcelona. Was he walking into a trap? If he made contact with Alba, he might be able to use Narvik as leverage to find Philippe's treasure. It was time to leave vacation mode and get back to work.

Chapter 4

Dex accepted Cyn's offer and flew to Ft. Myers. Upon arrival, he called Pete.

"Dex, it's great to hear your voice again. I was afraid that you had gone island on us."

"It's good to be back home. I'm at Page Field. Can you pick me up or should I call for a cab?"

"I could, but I'm at the home visiting Ellie. It will take an hour to get there."

"Don't bother, I'll call a cab. How's she doing?"

After a long pause, Pete responded. "She smiled at me when I came in. Sometimes I'm sure she recognizes me. Other times she's lost in a fog. Hey, why don't I call Narvik? He could pick you up and take you to the Crossfire."

"Good idea. How's he been responding to your training?"

"Physically he's doing well. He does his best to keep up with me, but his marksmanship leaves a lot to be desired. I think he's half afraid of firearms."

"Perhaps he can overcome that with practice. I'm sorry about Ellie."

"Thanks, I haven't given up hope. They find new treatments every day."

"I'll say a prayer for her and you."

"I appreciate the thought, but you know she was the praying one in our house. If it was me, I could understand. I'm just an old sinner. She deserves better."

"Ellie is a good Christian woman. You were lucky to have her."

"Yeah, well, I'll call Narvik right now. He should be there in twenty minutes or so."

Matt Narvik sat at his computer studying the Windswept website—and the photos of Alba Cologne. He sighed. She had deceived him and nearly got him killed. Still he hoped that at some level she had feelings for him. He certainly still had feelings for her. The ring of his cell phone yanked him back to the present.

"What's up, Pete?" He listened for a moment, then said, "Sure, I can pick up Mr. Rubino . . . er . . . Dex."

"Don't fawn all over him," Pete said. "Just be sure to thank him for all he's done."

"Sure, I'll get there as quick as I can."

When Matt arrived minutes later, Dex pulled himself into the Jeep and Matt headed back toward the house.

"Your Crossfire is parked in my garage," Matt said. "I pulled it out last week and washed it. It wasn't very dirty, just a little dust."

"Thanks, Matt. How do you like the house?"

"Oh, it's just fine, really comfortable, and it's close to a lot of good restaurants. Do you like chili, Mr. Rubino? I mean Dex. There's a place just south of here."

"Sure, it's been awhile."

Over chili and barbecued chicken, Matt spoke of the training that Pete had been giving him and thanked Dex for all of his help. When Matt asked about the events that had landed him in rehab, Dex said, "What events? You fired a flare into some fireworks and burned your boat to the waterline. Other than that, all information regarding that night is classified, and I'm not at liberty to discuss it." Dex changed the subject with tales of his time in the Caymans and his new lady friend, then turned the conversation to Matt's future.

"I'll soon have an assignment for you. Is your passport in order?"

"Yes."

"In September our employer is launching a new cruise line."

"I know, I read about it online."

"Then you know who the hostess for the cruise is."

"Alba Cologne."

"You're going to be on that cruise, Matt."

"Per her request?"

"No, I haven't seen or spoken to her since I turned her over to our employer. You're going to be there to work for me, not Windswept."

"I don't understand."

"As far as Windswept is concerned, you are my assistant. You report only to me. Philippe Ben-Balla, Alba's father, founded the company. Now a woman who betrayed Philippe to gain control of the company heads it. Her name is Helene Adolphe. She made certain promises to me to retain my services; now she's trying to renege. I'm afraid that Alba may be a prisoner of Helene. I'd like to have all that Helene promised me, but I would also like to see Alba freed. I'll need your assistance in accomplishing these goals."

"You can count on me, Mr. . . . er . . . Dex."

"You'll be traveling under your own name and passport. I don't believe anyone at Windswept will recognize you. If they do, you're just on vacation. You will function as an extra set of eyes and ears. I'll be on the cruise, but if we cross paths aboard the ship, we won't acknowledge each other."

"I could book the cruise online to avoid any connection to you."

"That would be wise. Book your own flight, also."

"Should I take my gun along?"

"No. If I think you need one, I'll have it hidden in your cabin."

"What if I should come in contact with Alba?"

"Let's just see how that plays out. If you want to resume some kind of relationship with her, let her make the first move. She may be at liberty to do as she wishes, or Helene may keep her on a short leash. Either way you'll have a job to do while onboard."

"Is this cruise line just a front, or is it a legitimate business?"

"They spent a fortune purchasing and refurbishing the ship. That would indicate that they will try to operate at a profit, but all the investment money came from Philippe's dirty dealings. I'll learn more when I get to Barcelona."

"Spain?"

Dex nodded. "I'm going to supervise the security procedures of the ship."

"How soon do you leave?"

"I'm waiting for the call. Why don't we finish here and you can take me to my car, then I'll check into a hotel nearby."

"Why don't you just stay at my place? There's an extra room and it's fully furnished. No sense in you paying for a hotel while I'm living there all alone."

Dex hesitated before answering. "All right, if you're sure I won't be in the way."

"Not at all. It will be good to have someone to talk to."

Chapter 5

"No! No! No! Alba, you have to stay with the beat," Nancy Rivers shouted, her face flushed with frustration. "I have to deliver a Vegas-quality floorshow, and I'm stuck with a star that has the grace of a hippo in heat."

A deafening beep preceded the amplified "Enough!" A raspy voice boomed across the warehouse like the voice of a Norse god. "Clear the rehearsal area. I wish to speak to our star. Alone!"

The choreographer and dancers quickly retreated to the dressing rooms. The lighting and tech people exited the building into the heat of the Catalan sun.

A diminutive woman walked toward the temporary stage and motioned for Alba to come to her. With an audible groan, the woman sat down in a folding chair.

Alba stopped several paces from her and stamped her foot as she shouted, "I can't work like this! I need proper facilities for rehearsal. I've been working in this disgusting warehouse for months. When will my boat be ready?"

The target of her rage calmly folded her arms. "Stop acting like a petulant child, dear. It is not a boat, it is a ship, and it belongs to the corporation, not you. I have been assured that the theater will be ready for rehearsals next week."

"Then let the cast and me take a holiday until it is ready. We have all been working too hard for too long in this oversized garage."

"I'm sorry, Alba, but the choreographer insists that you keep practicing until the day we sail."

"That old crone doesn't have any idea what she is doing. She has only worked in strip clubs."

"She has choreographed some of the most successful stage performances in Las Vegas. If we are going to meet our competition in the gaming industry, our entertainment has to be on a par with them. Also, she is only three years your senior." Helene saw that the barb had found its mark.

"I am Alba Cologne, model and movie star, not some dancing prostitute from the United States. I am the one that is bringing the continent to our ship and our resort."

"Dear, you are a great attraction. Two or three times a month someone will mention booking passage on the *New Dawn* because of your old movies." She took a dramatic pause to let the full weight of her words fall on Alba's ego. "Do you remember when I came to live with you? You were just a frightened little girl, but I saw the potential behind those dark eyes. That is when I began to train you for a successful future. I taught you that exploiting the vices of the weak was the way to amass great power and wealth. Just look at all I have accomplished in my lifetime. My father sold me to my first husband as if I were a camel. Now I control all of Windswept Corporation. I have the finest resorts in some of the most beautiful places on earth. Soon we will launch our new venture in the cruise industry with an on-board casino, movie theater, and a modern stage theater featuring the finest of entertainers. All hosted by the beautiful Alba Cologne. I have sacrificed much to afford you this opportunity, my child. I have watched as the men of our family succumbed to their various vices, drugs, gambling, vengeance, and, saddest of all, religion. These weaknesses have decimated an entire generation and put our empire in peril. It would be heartbreaking for me if the first female groomed to lead our family destroyed this opportunity to resurrect her career, all because of pride."

Tears ran down Alba's face. She stepped forward and knelt, sobbing. "I'm sorry. I didn't mean to seem ungrateful. I'm just so tired, please forgive me." As a bony hand touched the top of her head, Alba reached for it and kissed it repeatedly. "Please forgive me. Please, Aunt Helene, forgive me."

Chapter 6

Dex grew weary of waiting for a phone call that never came. Finally, on July 16, he decided to act on his own and bought a coach ticket on the red-eye flight to Barcelona. He hoped a clandestine arrival would give him time to study the lay of the land. He sensed that Helene Adolphe was not above eliminating a partner.

He had a miserably crowded flight that, for some reason, had an undue number of screaming children. With every mile, his seat constricted just a little and the seat in front of him further encroached on his personal space. When the plane touched down in Barcelona, a blurry-eyed Dex bolted from the cabin and jogged to a serpentine line for customs and immigration. It was mid-morning before he retrieved his luggage and headed for the cabstand. That's when his eye caught sight of a blond giant in a chauffeur's uniform. When Dex had last seen the brute, he was lying unconscious in the hull of Pete's boat. While Dex had seen Arnan before, Arnan had never seen Dex. Arnan kept shifting his weight from one foot to the other as he awkwardly held a neatly printed sign that said "Mr. Rubino."

Dex boldly approached the man. "I am Dexter Rubino."

"Oh, ah . . . welcome to Barcelona, Mr. Rubino. I am Madame Adolphe's driver, Arnan. I am going to take you to her home in town. Let me take your luggage."

Dex was about to protest that he had already booked a hotel but thought better of it. If Helene were aware of his presence in town, she would also know where he planned to stay. "Thank you. What did you say your name was again?"

"My name is Arnan, sir. Madame Adolphe said that I'm to be your driver while you're here."

"That's very well, but I think I'd rather drive myself."

"Driving is very different here than in the states, sir."

"I'm sure I can adapt."

"Madame Adolphe was adamant about it, sir. You'll also be lodging at her penthouse."

"Very well. You are an American, aren't you, Arnan?"

"Yes, sir, I was born and raised near Detroit." He opened the rear door and stood at attention as Dex climbed in.

Dex had wanted to continue quizzing Arnan, but the man had raised the glass partition intended to separate the serfs from the elite. In thirty minutes, they were in the Port Vell neighborhood near the beaches. Dex had expected an ancient pile of bricks, but instead futuristic buildings constructed of glass and steel surrounded them. Arnan guided the vehicle to the front entrance of a sea-facing skyscraper. There Dex spotted another face he had encountered a few months previous.

"Welcome to Barcelona, Mr. Rubino," the man said. "I am Desmond Quest. It is so good to see you again. I hope you had a pleasant flight." Quest grasped Dex's hand as if they were old friends.

"So we finally meet, Mr. Quest. The last time we didn't exchange names."

"Much has changed since then. I am now the head of security for the cruise enterprise."

"This would mean you're my new boss."

"We find that type of terminology counter-productive, Mr. Rubino. We are a family whose well-being depends on one another. Please walk with me." Desmond turned to Arnan and said, "Take care of the luggage and I will see you upstairs."

Quest escorted Dex into the building and onto a glass-enclosed elevator. "As I was saying, everyone at the executive level is a Windswept investor, not just an employee. When I learned that we were going to have access to your experience and acumen, I was overjoyed."

As the express elevator launched toward the penthouse level, Dex braced himself and wondered if this personal welcome was just a prelude to being thrown from the roof. "I'm not well acquainted with the cruise industry, but I do have a lot of experience with security operations."

"Now, there is no reason to try and impress me, Mr. Rubino. I know how well you handled the Philippe affair. It was marvelous, a sheer stroke of genius, and not a peep about it in the press. Brilliant! Oh, by the way, Arnan does not know you were involved so let us keep it our little secret. He has been led to believe that Madame Adolphe bribed law enforcement to release him to into her custody. You and I are going to be working very closely, so just call me Desmond."

As the elevator came to an abrupt stop, Dex tightened his grip on the handrail to steady himself. "You can call me Dex."

"Very well, Dex. Madame Adolphe has been singing your praises since the new year. She credits you with saving the entire corporation from the behavior of her predecessor."

As the elevator doors opened on the posh foyer of the penthouse, Dex responded. "I can't take all the credit for that operation. I had a great team behind me."

"There you are being humble again. How American of you, Dexter," Madame Adolphe said as in greeting. The woman wore a chic, gray business suit as she stood under an imposing Dali painting that did not look to Dex like a print. Beside her stood a gentleman who Dex assessed as being middle-aged, medium height, balding, and a little overweight, but the man had hidden his midriff well behind an expensively tailored suit.

"Dexter, did you think you could sneak into Barcelona without me knowing of it?" Helene said, and then turned toward the man at her side. "Doctor Zhan, this is Dexter Rubino, our Deputy Chief Administrator of Cruise Line Security. Dexter, this is Doctor Zhan, a leading pharmacologist here in Catalonia. He is also one of Windswept's newest investors."

"I thought I would try to acquaint myself with the area before you needed my services," Dex said as he extended a hand. "It's a pleasure to meet you, Doctor Zhan."

They shook hands, but Zhan did not speak. Instead, he bowed his head and avoided any eye contact. Zhan's hands were sweaty, and Dex was tempted to wipe his hand dry on his houndstooth sports jacket.

Helene stepped forward and warmly embraced Dex, kissing him on each cheek. Turning to Quest she said, "Doctor Zhan was just leaving. Desmond, would you please escort him to his hotel. Arnan can drive you." She turned back to Dex and said, "Come Dexter, we have much to discuss." She took Dex's arm and led him through a well-furnished parlor to a rooftop garden overlooking the seaport.

Dex was just beginning to relax. If there were going to be any fisticuffs, he thought he could take the old woman on his own. "You don't seem surprised to see me, Helene."

"Dexter, this is my city. Few things happen here that I don't have advance knowledge of."

"I thought if I got here on my own, I could take a few days and explore. I've never been to this part of Spain."

"You're not in Spain, Dexter. This is Catalonia. We think of our homeland as a separate nation, a separate people."

"Are you originally from here, Helene?"

"No, but it has been my adopted home for many years. I was born far from here, across the Mediterranean, in a very different world. Look there in the distance. Do you see her?" She pointed to an area where five or six cruise ships lay berthed. "That, Dexter, is the *New Dawn*. I wish you would have been here for the shakedown cruise."

"Which one is it?"

"It is the furthest out, the one with the gold trim and white hull."

"It looks like a fine vessel, much larger than I expected. The pictures I saw on the Internet don't do it justice."

"Wait until you board her; a ship like that can give you a new hope, a new sense of well being." She turned to face Dex and embraced him, pressing her silver head into his chest. "Just think of it, Dexter, a new dawn, a chance to be young again."

Desmond and Doctor Zhan conversed in the back seat while Arnan drove the limo into a seedier part of town. Desmond handed the doctor a large envelope. "This is your new identity, Doctor. We went to great lengths to secure a clean passport for you. The accompanying driver's license and identity card all match. Please give me your passport and all other identification."

The doctor handed his passport and wallet to Desmond and began examining his new identity. "But this is not a Pakistani passport, this is from the US. I cannot live as an infidel! I specifically requested that I have a Pakistani identification packet. At the very least, I must have identification from a Muslim nation."

"But the United States is a Muslim nation, Doctor. Their president has said so."

"Who is Anton Carmella? I believe that is an Italian name. Do I look Italian to you? This man looks nothing like me. I must see Madame Adolphe again. She promised me a new identity. If my adversaries find me, they will kill me."

"You have a new identity, Doctor. You are Anton Carmella."

"People will think that I'm an infidel. This will not do, Mr. Quest."

"It will do until you get to Sunset Cay. From there we can arrange another identification. You will be aboard our ship, so you will not need to use your passport once we embark. Besides which, you may decide you like being an American."

"What a repulsive idea. I wish to evade my creditors and wife, not degrade myself to the level of an infidel. No offence meant to you, Mr. Quest."

Desmond glanced out of the door window. "Here we are, your new home for the next few weeks."

Arnan pulled to the curb in front of a shuttered building. He exited the vehicle, opened the passenger's side rear door, and held it while Desmond slid across the rear seat, gently pushing the doctor out on to the sidewalk. Broken glass crunched beneath the doctor's shoes.

"Where are we? I cannot stay in such an unstable building. What's going on?"

"We are trying not to attract attention, please lower your voice. My employer owns this building and it is perfectly safe." Desmond unlocked the door and the three men entered a clean and well-lit lobby. "I have your key. I'll go ahead and check the room. Arnan will stay here with you."

"Very well, but I don't think all this security is called for," the doctor said. "My wife and associates believe that I am in Madrid for a conference. They have no idea what my future plans are."

"We can't be too cautious," Desmond said. "Arnan, keep an eye on the door and give me five minutes to sweep the room."

As Desmond left, the doctor turned to Arnan. "How are you feeling? Have there been any side-effects to the nutritional supplements I prescribed?"

"No, sir, I really don't feel any different."

"Over time the chemicals will counteract the harmful effects of your steroid abuse. Please be aware that it may take several years."

Arnan whispered, "Will it restore my virility?"

The doctor chuckled. "Certainly, just don't increase the dosage. I originally intended to market my formula as an aphrodisiac, but there are so many other benefits that I needed help in marketing the product. That is when Madame Adolphe offered to buy the formula."

"Then why go into hiding?"

The doctor smiled. "I have some unsavory business associates that would try to cheat me. With a new identity, I can enjoy my wealth in a secret location."

"Will it be worth living with infidels?"

"The demise of the western world is at hand. Adherents of Islam are scattered throughout the third world. As the US and its friends retract, I will be in place to exploit the expansion of Islam."

A few moments later, the ancient elevator rattled to a stop at the lobby

Arnan nodded and said, "All right, Doctor, we can go up now."

They boarded the elevator, and Arnan pushed the button for the fifth floor.

"I hope my protest did not offend you," Zhan said. "I am sure America is a lovely country, but in my circle the American government is not well thought of."

"Relax. You will soon be headed for a new life in a new land, just as Madame Adolphe promised."

The elevator shuddered to a stop on the fifth floor. The gate screeched as Arnan forced it open, allowing the doctor to exit first, then followed him out.

"These old contraptions sure don't look like much, but they have been in operation for years. Some people think they add charm to the building." Arnan said and chuckled.

"I trust that elevators in the US are more modern."

"For the most part, they are," Arnan replied and closed the gate. The elevator rattled back to life and moved upward, "Wait. You're forgetting something."

The doctor, who had begun walking away, turned and shrugged. "Forgetting what, Arnan?"

Arnan shot an arm out, grabbed the doctor's coat, and dragged the shocked Zhan back to the elevator. With one motion, Arnan flung the gate open and propelled the screaming Zhan into the open shaft. Zhan's left hand brushed against the elevator cable. As he fell, he made a futile attempt to grasp it. Arnan smirked as he looked down at him. Zhan landed with a thud at the bottom.

Arnan closed the gate, then walked to the end of the hall and opened the door to the stairwell where Desmond Quest stood waiting. Desmond looked at him with a smile and said, "They keep telling people that the stairs are much healthier, but no one listens."

"I'm sure Anton Carmella would testify to that."

Chapter 7

Dex gently extricated himself from Madame Adolphe's embrace and backed away. "Actually, Helene, I'm happy acting my own age. I have lived a full and exciting life. Now I look forward to the quiet monotony of retirement. An attempt to regain my youth is not what I'm here for."

"Dexter, you are still a young man, much too young to sit in a rocking chair and watch as the world leaves you behind."

"You're wrong. I'm more than ready for that rocking chair. If we could just conclude our business, you will have seen the last of me."

"But I need you," she said and slinked closer. "I want you to be my partner in every way."

Dex looked at her and saw the scrawny old woman beneath the layers of makeup and expensive clothing. He searched for words to gently deter her advances but found none. As he tried to hide his revulsion, he could see it reflected in her glassy eyes.

Helene's countenance became as an asp about to strike. "Very well, Rubino; but if you wish to have a part in Windswept's good fortune, you'll have to pull your own weight."

"There is the matter of Philippe's treasure. I have certainly earned my share."

"I'm right here, Mr. Rubino."

Dex turned and saw Alba Cologne as she stepped out on to the rooftop. "My father's greatest treasure was within my heart. He often spoke of me in that way. I am truly sorry if Aunt Helene was not as clear as she should have been."

"Aunt Helene?"

"Why, yes, I assumed you were aware that Madame Adolphe was my father's aunt. Perhaps I should refer to her as Great Aunt Helene." She did little to hide her smirk.

Looking over his shoulder at Helene, Dex gasped as she glared at Alba. Recovering his demeanor, he turned his attention to the stunning actress. "Ms. Cologne, it's good to see you looking so well."

"It is good to see you also, Mr. Rubino. I can finally thank you for rescuing me on the night of my father's death."

"I'm glad you were unharmed, and I hear you'll be hosting the voyage of the new ship."

"Yes, the cruise line is a new dynamic of my career. It is a wonderful vessel, but my notoriety is what attracts the right clients. So you see, by assisting us in the security of the *New Dawn*, you will be adding to the treasure you wish to take part in."

"I was led to believe that your father had a great treasure hidden somewhere. That is what enticed me to interrupt his plans."

"Mr. Rubino, surely you realize that my father was very ill. Reversals of fortune, grief, and betrayal led him to act irrationally. I am so thankful that a strong man like you was able to stop him before he harmed anyone."

"I'm sure Mr. Rubino is tired and would like to freshen up," Helene said as she placed a hand on Dex's arm. "Why don't I show you to your suite? I believe Arnan has already delivered your luggage."

"Perhaps Mr. Rubino would be more comfortable staying aboard the boat."

"Actually, I already booked a room at a hotel on Las Rambles."

Alba threw her head back and chuckled, then said, "Please, Mr. Rubino, those hotels are for the tourists. The name of the street you mention is La Rambla. Here we prefer to speak Catalan, but nearly everyone speaks Spanish and English as well. You will be much more comfortable aboard my boat. I will have Arnan drive us there so I can help you choose a nice cabin."

"Arnan is not here, dear. I sent him on some errands with Desmond."

Alba's eyes flashed as she faced Helene. "Then I'll call the restaurant downstairs and have a luncheon delivered for the three of us. They are aware of your dietary restrictions, Aunt Helene."

"I was going to suggest that you abstain from lunch, dear. You know how snug those expensive costumes are."

Dex waved a hand at the two women. "Ladies, let's all calm down. Why don't we go down to the restaurant and have lunch together?"

Alba glared at Helene as the old woman cackled. "Alba is under restriction. She can only leave the penthouse to go to rehearsals, and then she must be accompanied by Arnan or Desmond."

"As Desmond's deputy, I will assure the safety of both you ladies. Let's go, I'm famished."

Chapter 8

Matt glanced at his watch as he ran. Eight o'clock on a late August morning. He could already see heat waves rising from the railroad tracks that ran parallel to the trail. Perspiration soaked his T-shirt and ran down his legs into his New Balance running shoes. His MP3 player blasted some old Beach Boys' tracks as he neared the end of the trail at Colonial Boulevard.

Matt slowed to a stop in the shade of a great live oak. He had expected Pete to overtake him in the stretch. He removed his ear buds and turned around with a victorious grin, then drained his water bottle. *I must be getting too fast for the old timer. Serves him right for training me so well.* Pete was at least a decade older than Matt but had stayed in terrific physical shape. Only in the past few weeks had Matt been out-running his trainer.

Three minutes passed and Matt grew concerned. Never before had Pete been so far behind. Matt started to jog toward the starting point, increasing his pace. He had retraced his steps nearly a mile when ahead he saw a group of people on bikes. Kids, he thought. When they saw him, a girl started waving her arms and a feeling of unease overtook him.

She shouted, "Do you know CPR? Some old dude just crapped out. We called 911; they said they were on the way."

"Pete!" Matt cried as he pushed his way into the circle of teenage boys that surrounded the fallen man. Pete lay pale and gasping for breath in the grass beside the trail.

One of the boys spoke into a cell phone. "There are no street addresses out here. Lady, we're in Zombie Land."

"Tell them you're a quarter mile north of Landing View Road, across the canal from the bus terminal," Matt said, then fell on his knees, panting. "Pete what happened? I thought you were right behind me."

Pete struggled to speak. "The way, tell the way."

Matt looked up at the boys. "Does anyone have an aspirin?"

They just looked at one another. Matt turned to the girls, who were on the other side of the path. "Do any of you have an aspirin?"

"No, but I have some Midol," said one.

Matt shook his head. "We need aspirin. Hang on, Pete, help is on the way."

Pete grabbed Matt's arm and nodded his head. "The way . . . the way to . . . Jesus."

Matt froze in place as he saw the pleading look in the man's eyes. The man was his friend and mentor, asking for the way to Jesus, and he had no words. "You're going to be all right. Just lie still. Help is on the way."

Pete pleaded. "The way, need the way."

One of the boys fell to his knees on Pete's left and glanced at Matt. "I know the way. They taught us in children's church." The boy then looked down at Pete's graying face. "It's as simple as ABC . . .

"A: Admit that you are a sinner.

"B: Believe that Jesus is the son of God.

"C: Confess him as your Lord and Savior."

Pete gave the boy a feeble smile. Matt looked on in stunned silence.

"Do you know John 3:16?" the boy said and fired off a recitation of the verse in such rapid fashion that Matt found it hard to distinguish what the boy was saying. "Well, you need to personalize that," the boy continued. "God so loved Pete that He gave His only Son. That if Pete would believe in Him, Pete would not perish but would have everlasting life. The next verse says that God didn't send His Son to condemn Pete, but that Pete through Him might be saved. God has been waiting all this time to give you a gift He paid for before you were born, the free gift of salvation. All you have to do is accept it."

The blast of a siren startled them all. Matt and the teens moved out of the way. EMTs went to work, stabilized Pete and loaded him into the ambulance.

"Please help him. He's my friend," Matt said.

A female deputy arrived and ordered the teens to form a line and produce identification. Matt tried to intervene on their behalf, but the deputy advised him to come up with a good reason for being in such a secluded spot with a bunch of kids. Just then, one of the EMTs told Matt that he had to get into the ambulance if he was going to ride along. Despite the protests of the deputy, Matt bounded into the ambulance and accompanied his unconscious friend to Gulf Coast Hospital.

Alba Cologne was finally fitting into the role of headliner aboard the *New Dawn*. The miscues and errors that had plagued her and the cast of younger entertainers on the inaugural cruise were beginning to disappear. Unfortunately, precision came too late for one of the young dancers. Meaghan Miller had collided with Alba during a performance and fell from the stage. Much to the shock of the select audience of investors and government officials, the poor girl broke her ankle and split her head open. Alba felt humiliated, but, in an uncharacteristic moment of humanity, took full responsibility for the accident. Further, as soon as the girl left the hospital, Alba moved her into a cabin adjoining her suite. Meaghan soon became Alba's greatest fan and confidant. She began singing the praises of the star to the rest of the cast. Consequently, they began treating Alba in a way befitting the main attraction.

When Meaghan saw Arnan making a late night call at Alba's door, she assumed they were having an affair. The next day she giggled when she asked Alba if she slept well.

"Very well, Meaghan. Yesterday's rehearsals left me exhausted."

"Are you sure it wasn't your boyfriend that left you exhausted?"

"I have no boyfriend. I have no life outside of rehearsals."

"You might as well give it up, Alba. I saw him come to your cabin late last night."

Alba turned to her with a quizzical look. "Do you mean Arnan? He is my aunt's driver, not a boyfriend. He was delivering a message from my aunt."

"Sure, a big blond guy like that is every girl's dream. Moreover, he's a servant. You could make him do anything you want. You could make him your love slave and totally dominate him."

Alba broke out in hysterical laughter. "You are a broken sack of eggs. If you only knew how silly an idea that is."

"Why? I think he's kind of cute."

"Do you have a crush on Arnan?"

"No, he never even looks at me. He's always doing your bidding. I guess that comes with being a star."

"You realize that he can't . . . I mean, he is three times your size."

"I can't help it. I think big guys are just so sexy, all those muscles and blond hair."

"I could put in a good word for you, if you want."

"Really? You mean he isn't yours?"

"How soon will you be off those crutches?"

"The doctors said I won't need them after the end of the month. The bad thing is, I won't be able to dance for a few months. I guess that means I'll miss the cruise."

"No, you won't. I have a job for you. How would you like to go back to the States for a few days?"

"Sure, I'd love to see my folks."

"Not a pleasure trip, Meaghan. I will have an important mission for you."

Chapter 9

Dexter Rubino had never imagined how much work was involved in securing an ocean liner. It carried all the responsibilities of a casino and hotel. The added dimension of terrorist activities in the area they would be cruising contributed to the impossible mission of his duties. Dex soon realized that Desmond was in over his head, which explained why he often deferred to Dex as they developed procedures.

The number of security personnel with Arabic names concerned Dex, but Desmond explained that they were holdovers from Philippe's era. "Many of them are second-generation employees who have an unflagging sense of devotion to Philippe and his Aunt Helene."

Those words offered little comfort to Dex. The one reassuring factor was that all the men were conversant in English.

After a long day, Dex retreated to his home on the water, the lower decks of the *New Dawn*. This tiny cabin would be his home for the duration of the cruise. He had requested better quarters of Helene, but she insisted that this was the best she could do for a crewmember. After all, the cabin was intended to house three passengers. Having rebuffed her advances, he consoled himself with the knowledge that he would somehow uncover the secret of Philippe's treasure. As his head hit the pillow, his cell phone rang. He sighed and answered. "Rubino."

"Dex, this is Matt Narvik. I have bad news."

"Oh, no, Matt. I asked you not to drive the Crossfire!"

"Your car is fine. It's Pete. He had some kind of stroke."

"Is he receiving medical care?"

"Yes, he's at Gulf Coast Hospital."

"Oh, well. Any port in a storm. I wish he'd been taken to Health Park. I have connections there."

"The EMT said it was the closest."

"What's the prognosis?"

"I don't know. They wanted the name of the next of kin. He never even mentioned any family."

"His wife is in a home in North Naples. She has Alzheimer's."

"I had no idea. Does he have any children or siblings?"

"His son died in an accident while in college. I know of no other living relatives."

"I feel terrible after all he has done for me, and I can't do anything to help him."

"Well, there isn't much either of us can actually do, but you're a praying man."

"I've been praying since I got into the ambulance. It's funny you should mention it. Some teenagers found him lying beside the trail before I got there. One of them gave him the plan of salvation. I think he was coherent enough to understand."

Dex sat up, growing uncomfortable with the conversation. "Look, Matt, just explain to the doctors that his wife is incapacitated and you are a co-worker. I think they will relent and at least let you see him."

"I'll try."

"Matt, I had planned on giving Pete some assignments for you. I thought if he walked you through them, you would do fine. Now you'll have to carry them out on your own."

"It's about time I started earning my paycheck."

"I'd prefer sending you an e-mail, look for it sometime tomorrow."

"OK."

"And I was serious about the prayer business. Pete needs somebody reliable in his corner."

"Sure, I'll do all I can."

As Matt closed his cell phone, he felt the warmth of another body invade his personal space. Perhaps it was a result of having spent so much time with Pete and Dex, but his first inclination was to prepare to defend himself. He sprang to his feet, fists raised.

A pallid, heavy-set man did likewise, raising his hands to a defensive posture. "Excuse me, sir, I was just wondering if you had been on the Ten Mile Canal bike path this morning?"

Matt noticed that the man—who appeared to be about forty-five, had salt-and-pepper hair and wore a soul patch dyed jet black—carried a black Bible in his left hand. "Yes, I was."

"Were you with the poor gentleman who fell ill?"

"Yes, I'm sorry. You surprised me." Matt lowered his fists and his eyes. "My name is Matt Narvik. The man you're talking about is my trainer, Pete Walters."

"I'm Pastor Jerry from the Great Light International Tabernacle. Some of our teens found your friend before you got there." He offered his hand and Matt shook it, noticing that it was as soft as a woman's.

"Yes, there was one young man there who I want to thank," Matt said. "He gave my friend the plan of salvation before the ambulance arrived."

"That was Tyrone. He told me all about it. I had to go to the Sherriff's office and vouch for them. It seems the deputy thought they had assaulted your friend."

"No, the doctors told me he had a stroke of some kind. They were reluctant to give me any details because I'm not a relative. The problem is, his only relative is his wife, and she's in a home with Alzheimer's disease. I don't even know which one."

"I know some of the folks on staff here. Perhaps I can grease the wheels a little and get some information for you. I want you to know that our prayer team is already praying for your friend."

Matt's shoulders dropped as he raised his eyes to the ceiling. "How does he do it?"

"How does who do what?"

"How does God answer my prayers before I know to pray them?"

Chapter 10

Matt awoke the next morning at 5:30 A.M., just as he usually would for a training day. He walked through the shower, then ate a light breakfast with coffee, the decaffeinated brand that Pete had prescribed. It helped wash away the sickening sweet taste of the tablets he swallowed. A case of the tablets had come via express delivery in June but had no label. It was a special formula made exclusively for Windswept security employees. Pete had abstained from taking it due to his age, but he insisted that Matt needed it.

Matt began his stretching regimen and listened for Pete's car pulling into the drive before reminding himself Pete would not be coming. At least not for awhile. After he finished his stretches, he started to leave the house, then he spotted his laptop on the kitchen bar and decided to check his email first. His air card took a long time to log on, but when it finally connected, he found a message from Dex.

Matt:

Hope Pete is doing well. I want you to focus on your training and the mission I have for you. Pack one bag with enough casual clothing for a week, also take an empty bag. You will also need your passport. On 9/3/10, you are to go to the Big Carlos Pass Bridge at the south end of Fort Myers Beach. Be there at 3:00 A.M. You will need fifty feet of ¾-

inch line and a bolt cutter to remove the lock on the ladder leading to the fender system. Tie the line to the top side, go down the ladder to the fender, and wait. A package will arrive before 5:00 A.M. If it fails to arrive, go home and call me. If it arrives, tie the line on to it and then pull the package up after you. Take the package to the intersection of I-75 and Daniels Road and call me from the rest stop there. I suggest you wear black and avoid any contact with the anglers who hang out there.

    Dex

    This doesn't sound right, Matt thought. *This is the kind of thing criminals do, drug dealers or smugglers. Dex would never put me in that kind of situation. I'll be a good soldier and follow orders.* He left the house, jogged to the bike path and continued wrestling with his conscience.

At her penthouse in Barcelona, Helene lay in her lovers arms. Her companion breathed heavily and quivered on the verge of exhaustion. He had been a reluctant suitor, but her persistent seduction and her pharmaceutical resources had eroded his timidity. "Are you sure you don't care for a cigarette, dear heart?" she asked.

    "No, what did you give me?" he said. "I feel like I'm on fire."

    "It is just the burning desire of restored youth, dear heart. My business dealings give me access to the miracles of advanced pharmacology. Just relax with me for a few more moments, then the sensation will pass. I think I'll have a smoke. You don't mind do you, dear heart?"

    "Stop calling me dear heart. My name is Anton. Dear heart makes me sound like a sissy."

"Oh, you're no sissy, dear heart. Sorry ... Anton. Perhaps I should call you by your new name, Rayhan Zhan."

"That's worse. Couldn't you get me an ID with an American name? I hate for people to think of me as one of those Arab pukes."

"I would think that the title of "doctor" would overcome your prejudices, dear . . . Anton."

"I got my pride, you know. I started out with nothing. Now I'm an international investor."

"I know, you have every right to celebrate your success. I hope you do not think that I celebrate with all my investors this way. I spent many years in celibacy to set an example for my niece. Not that she noticed. You and I have both struggled to achieve success. Now we can share the rewards of our sacrifice."

"Tell me more about Belize."

"You will love it there. It is much like the United States was fifty years ago. After the cruise you can spend a few weeks at the resort while we await the completion of your new villa."

"Ocean view, right?"

"Of course. With all the modern conveniences. You will enjoy a well-trained domestic staff to cater to your every whim and top notch security for peace of mind."

"That's important to me. I don't want any ghosts of my past hunting me down."

"There is nothing to worry about, Anton. I have arranged this type of relocation before. When you reach your new home, you can rest in peace."

Chapter 11

Matt Narvik decided that if he had to sneak around in the wee hours of the night, he would do so on his own terms. He purchased bolt cutters, rope, coveralls, and a hardhat from a discount tool house in Fort Myers. On the appointed night, he drove his Jeep to the north end of Big Carlos Bridge and parked in the spot reserved for the bridge tender. He placed a computer-generated sign on his dashboard indicating that he worked for Lee County maintenance, exited his vehicle, and marched up the narrow walkway of the bridge. His bright coveralls and yellow hardhat destroyed any element of stealth, but he thought it more important to camouflage his intent than to hide himself. When he reached the crest of the span, he located the cable and lock that secured the ladder. The bolt cutters severed the lock, and Matt pulled the cable through the expanded metal guard that prevented access to the fender system. Matt raised the guard and began climbing over the railing to the ladder when he sensed a presence behind him.

"What're ya doin', dude?"

Matt turned to see a disheveled homeless man leaning against the railing. The man reeked of alcohol and sweat.

"I'm the county electrician. I'm here to work on the fender lights."

"Oh, that's cool." He turned and shouted to his companion, "Hey, Skeeter, this dude's got bolt cutters. Come on over."

"If you'll excuse me, I have to get to work."

The man cocked his head as he spoke, "Don't the county give you keys?"

"Yes, but I forgot them. It will be easier to replace the lock than drive home and get them."

Skeeter ran to his companion's side, panting. "What's the deal, Pablo?"

"This dude says he's here to fix the lights, so he cut the lock on the ladder with bolt cutters."

Skeeter shrugged. "So?"

"So now you and me can go down and fish from the fenders. If we get a hit, we don't hav'ta pull it all the way up."

Skeeter nodded. "We won't lose so many and there are always fish around the structure. That's cool. I'll go get our stuff."

"Wait, you two are here to fish?"

"Why else would we be here?"

"Look, I can't allow anyone on the fender system, but when I'm done, I'll leave it unlocked. What you do after I leave is up to you."

"Cool, dude. Let's go get our stuff, Skeeter."

Matt tied off one end of the rope to the railing and dropped the other to the fender. When he reached the bottom of the ladder, he looked at his watch. 3:08. He stood in the darkness and listened to the water lap over the wooden beams. His thoughts turned to Pete. *Was he going to pull through? Had he accepted the Lord, or was he just looking for a fire escape?* He hoped that was enough.

A few minutes later, he heard a small engine straining against the tide. In the distance, he could see the starboard light of a small craft. As it drew near, his heart began to race. He knew he was to retrieve a package, but he had no idea what it contained, or what sort of characters would be delivering it. When the vessel passed the navigation lights, he could see it was a bow rider, probably an eighteen-footer. The vessel scraped along the fender and a male voice shouted from the helm.

"Ahoy, mate. Are you waitin' for me?"

Matt wasn't sure if he should laugh at the salutation or cry for the damage being done to the boat. "I don't see anyone else here, throw me a line."

"I ain't got a line. Just take the package so I can get this thing back."

Matt could see the brawny silhouette of the man at the helm but couldn't make out any facial features. The skipper tried to keep one hand on the wheel while handing the package up to Matt. It was a medium-sized, aluminum briefcase. As the boat bobbed in the water, chafing against the timbers, Matt gripped the handle of the briefcase.

"Tell Quest that's the last of it. I'll be in touch." The man opened the throttle and peeled a strip of rub rail off the side of the vessel as he motored away.

The package was a little heavy, so Matt summoned his sailing skills to fashion an elaborate hitch around the case and ascended the ladder. When he reached the top, Skeeter and Pablo were waiting.

Skeeter offered a hand as he climbed over the railing, "You done down there, dude?"

"Almost. I just have to pull my tools up."

"You didn't take any down with you," said Pablo.

As Matt pulled the rope hand-over-hand, he answered the inquisitive derelict. "I left them there this afternoon. I had an emergency repair in North Fort Myers and came here tonight to finish up."

"Without your keys," Pablo said as he pulled a survival knife from his beer-can shorts.

Ignoring the knife, Matt balanced the case on the railing. "Yeah, without my keys." Matt looked out at the darkness of Carlos Bay, a rage building inside him. Suddenly he swung the case at Pablo's head, making contact with the man's temple. Pablo fell onto the roadway as his knife skidded onto the bridge grating. Matt drove his heel into Pablo's crotch while Skeeter beat a hasty retreat. Pablo gave an anguished cry and curled into a fetal position. Matt set the case on the walkway and retrieved Pablo's knife. He grabbed the derelict's shirt with his left hand, then held the knife an inch from Pablo's right eye.

"Why did ya have to mess with me, jerk wad? You think you want what's in that case? You saw it and thought it should be yours? The Bible says that if your right eye offends thee, pluck it out. Ya want me to pluck your eye out for ya, jerk wad?"

"No, dude, be cool. I don't want any trouble."

"Well, you just found more trouble than you could ever imagine." Matt leaned forward and the blade's tip pierced Pablo's flesh just below his eye. Blood spurt over his face as he howled in agony and fear. "I'm goin' to let you live, but I want you out of Lee County before sun-up. Understand?"

"Yeah, dude. Please let me go. Be cool."

Matt raked the knife across Pablo's nose and forehead making a superficial furrow across the screaming man's face. He then lifted Pablo to his feet. "Get out of here, white trash."

The bleeding Pablo ran off in the same direction as Skeeter had.

Matt pitched the knife into the channel and grabbed the briefcase. He was tempted to send it to the depths as well but turned and marched back to his Jeep. He started the engine and sat there trembling with rage—a rage he could not explain to himself. Why was he involved in this? Loyalty to Dex wasn't a good enough reason. He would complete his mission, then he was through.

Chapter 12

In a show of appreciation for improvements by the performers, Nancy Rivers cancelled rehearsal and gave the entire troop the day off. Alba knew she would have to act quickly to enjoy a few hours of freedom. "Meaghan, come with me. I want to show you something."

The unlikely pair of beauties, one on crutches, slipped past the security guards in the corridor leading to their cabins and went to the Grand Lobby. There Alba called Arnan on her cell phone and told him to bring the limo to the dock to pick them up when they disembarked.

"I will need an authorization from Madame Adolphe," Arnan said.

"If you want my assistance in your quest to be a fitness instructor on the cruise, you will do as I ask. Besides, my aunt is entertaining a houseguest. She will not appreciate a disturbance by an incompetent servant. I only wish to visit my home for a few hours. Then I will return to the ship."

"Very well. Just don't let her find out."

"I did not call you seeking advice. Just bring the car around as I ordered." As she snapped her phone shut, she muttered, "Imbecile."

Meaghan winced at the word. "Weren't you a little hard on him, Alba? Will he be a fitness instructor on our cruise?"

"Perhaps. I have learned that I must always keep a servant in his place." Then she smiled at her friend and chuckled. "We must keep all men in their place."

"Can we go to the beach?" Meaghan asked. "It's been ages since I went to the beach."

"I want you to see my home."

"You're going back to your aunt's? When you moved onto the ship, you said you'd never go back."

"No, I have a home north of here in a small town named Saint Cugat del Valles. It has been nearly a year since I've been there. I wish to make sure it is being well cared for."

"Why do you need me?"

"I'm only allowed off of the ship in the company of Quest or Arnan. Quest is busy, so Arnan will have to drive us there. You and Arnan can become better acquainted while I visit the home I grew up in."

"Oh, Alba, that would be wonderful. Do I look all right?"

"You look marvelous. Remember to play coy with Arnan. He is a little shy around women. Just keep him occupied while I inspect the main house."

"OK," she said as she winked. "I'll keep the big guy busy."

"Not busy, occupied. You must win Arnan's heart before you can bed him."

Meaghan wrinkled her nose. "Isn't that sort of a role reversal? A stud like Arnan should be hungry for action."

"If you want to have a relationship with Arnan, you must be . . . demure. Trust me. I have known him for several years. He is an unusual man."

"Oh, yeah! He's a big hunk of unusual!"

As the limo pulled up to the gangway, Alba and Meaghan scampered across to the freedom of a day off.

In a dark security room, Dexter Rubino removed his headphones. He turned to a young trainee named Omar and said, "Call the gate and have them send a cab in for me. I have business to take care of. He raced down sparse corridors intended only for the eyes of the crew and emerged in the palatial lobby of the *New Dawn*. As he crossed the gangway, a taxi pulled in to pick him up. Dex climbed into the back and told the driver, "Follow that limo."

"OK, Joe."

"I'm with cruise-line security and we are following some of our employees. We want to make sure they aren't consorting with a bad element."

"OK, Joe."

"Hablas inglés?"

"OK, Joe."

Dex shook his head. He had managed to find the only driver in Barcelona that didn't speak English. As they traveled, Dex glanced at his watch. Ninety minutes later they entered the town of Saint Cugat. He nearly lost sight of the limo in a roundabout but urged the driver to speed up and caught sight of it again. Dex took notice of the imposing homes that sometimes looked as if they had escaped from a Dr. Seuss book. The limo pulled on to a quiet boulevard and signaled a right turn.

"Stop here," Dex said. "I don't want them to see us."

"OK, Joe."

The limo pulled into a drive and disappeared behind the tall hedges that lined the property. Dex pointed forward and motioned for the driver to proceed slowly.

"OK, Joe."

As they passed the driveway, Dex noticed a pair of stone knights in armor on either side of the gate, each bearing the head of a snarling lion. The iron gates were closing, but he could see Arnan exiting the vehicle. Then the hedge blocked his view. He motioned for the driver to turn around as he fumbled for his cell phone, which had a camera. He couldn't find it, then remembered leaving it on his desk. He pulled a notebook from his jacket pocket and wrote down the address as the driver turned around. He again motioned for the driver to go slowly.

As they passed the drive the second time, he saw Alba embracing a small man who wore a work uniform. Arnan stood at attention as Meaghan exited the vehicle.

Dex muttered to himself, "This will have to wait for another day. Could be the home of a boyfriend, a very wealthy boyfriend." He raised his voice to speak to the driver. "Back to the ship, please."

"OK, Joe."

Dex looked at his watch and thought he'd combine a little pleasure with business. "Driver, take me to the Cathedral de la Sacred Family."

"OK, Joe."

When they reached the imposing structure, Dex signaled the driver to go around the block, then told him to stop a block away. "I'm going to grab some lunch at the diner. Would you like to join me?" Dex pointed at the restaurant where they parked.

The driver looked confused, then held up his right hand "No, gràcies, Señor. No."

"Keep the meter running. I won't be long."

Dex left the cab and entered the KFC. He took a deep breath and savored the scent of home.

The cab driver watched Dex go into the restaurant, then pulled a cell phone from his glove box. He punched the requisite buttons and held the phone to his ear. After a moment, he said, "May I speak to Mr. Quest, please?"

Chapter 13

"*Eduardo*, it is so good to see you again!" Alba embraced the little man as if he were a family member. "Where is Juca?" she asked, speaking Catalan.

Eduardo bowed his head. "Juca was getting older, and it pained the poor beast to walk. Madame said it was for the best."

"No! Not Juca. When did this happen?"

"Three weeks ago. I thought Madame would have told you."

Alba's face contorted in pain.

Meaghan touched the woman's arm. "Alba, what's happened?"

"My dog has died. My aunt knew of it but said nothing," Alba said, reverting to English.

"I'm so sorry," Meaghan said. "She probably didn't want to upset you. With the show and all the pressure you're under, that's the last thing you needed to hear."

"I thought that dog would live forever," said Arnan.

Alba turned to him. "You mean you didn't know either?"

"No, I haven't been here since . . ." His eyes shifted to Meaghan. ". . . for quite a while."

Alba shook her head and raised her eyes skyward. Her voice trembled as she spoke. "Meaghan, I am sorry but things are in disarray here. The house has been closed for some time, and I want you to see it at its best." She flashed her dark eyes toward Eduardo and spoke in Catalan again. "I trust the gardens are in good condition."

Eduardo recognized the fury building and lowered his eyes to the ground. "Si, mi princesa. Si."

"Arnan, take Meaghan on a tour of the gardens," Alba said in English, then shifted back to Catalan and raised her voice, "Eduardo, open the house for me. I wish to see the shambles that was once my home."

The trembling servant began fumbling through his keys as his mistress followed him to a pair of huge doors at the base of a brightly tiled turret.

Meaghan watched the pair as they moved toward the house, a troubled expression on her face. She felt a touch at her elbow and turned to face Arnan, who said, "You should come with me."

As they strolled down a pathway, Meaghan, who struggled with her crutches, asked, "Will she be all right? What's wrong with the house?"

"She will be fine. Just give her some time to blow off steam. If you hadn't been here, she would have gone off on me."

"Is this all about the dog?"

"Yes and no. She's under a lot of pressure and has suffered a lot of setbacks."

Meaghan looked around at the manicured lawns and blooming shrubs. "I knew she came from a wealthy family, but I had no idea she lived in a mansion. Heck, this place is more like a palace."

"Her family is very wealthy . . . and powerful . . . but this place belongs to her and her alone."

"How long have you worked for the family?"

"Almost six years now. Her father gave me a job when no one else would. When he became ill, he came here to live with Alba. See that brick building?" He pointed and Meaghan nodded. "Those were once stables. Philippe had them converted to apartments for the servants. I used to live in the second one from the left."

"Is anyone living there now?"

"I was told that only Eduardo is here full-time."

The petite blonde wrapped her arms around his massive bicep and leaned into him. "Why don't you take me in and show me your old home."

Arnan looked down at the clinging beauty and wet his lips. "No, it will be locked up. If we are going to see all of the grounds, we'll have to keep moving."

"Arnan, with this bad ankle I'm not sure I can make it."

The giant smiled and swept her up in his arms. "We'll just leave those crutches here. We can pick them up on the way back."

"Oh, Arnan," she said and giggled.

Alba dismissed Eduardo as soon as he unlocked the door. She entered the foyer of the place she thought of as a refuge from the world. The afternoon sun shot streaks of light through the stained-glass dome ten meters overhead. A kaleidoscope of color reflected off the marble floor. Embedded in the center lay a heart-shaped stone of polished pink granite. Alba slowly walked to the center of the heart and sank to her knees. Her hands traced the edges of the stone. "The seal is unbroken," she whispered. She looked upward into the cascade of colored light. "The seal is unbroken, father." She raised her fists and shook with rage. "The seal is unbroken, father. You shall be avenged!"

Chapter 14

Dex returned to the ship carrying a bucket of chicken and a large bag of side dishes. Desmond Quest and Omar were waiting in the lobby.

"Dex, we need to talk."

"Sure, let's go up to the lido deck. You too Omar, there's enough for all of us."

Desmond looked warily at the bucket. "I'm really not hungry. I had a gourmet lunch with Madame Adolphe at the Sultan's Palace, but out on deck would be a better place for us to speak."

As they boarded an elevator, Dex said, "You mean that gilded steakhouse on top deck? I don't care for it. The steak is underdone. I asked for well-done and mine was still a little pink in the middle."

The scent of the fried chicken filled the elevator and Omar began licking his lips. Desmond felt a rumble in his stomach. "You should have sent your steak back to the kitchen," said Desmond. "The kitchen staff is still in training."

"No, once it's mine I never let it out of my sight."

As the trio stepped out on to the lido deck, Desmond turned to Omar. "Go to the bar and get us some beverages. What are you drinking, Dex?"

"A tall glass of lemonade would go well. Hey, let's sit at this table in the shade."

"Make it three, Omar."

As soon as Omar was out of earshot, Desmond's voice hardened. "Dex, where have you been?"

Dex gestured toward the bucket. "KFC."

"Prior to that."

"I went on a little tour of the countryside. You know all work and no play . . ."

"Where?"

"A little place named Saint Cugat. Ever hear of it?"

"That is where Alba's mansion is. You followed her there, didn't you?"

Dex shrugged. "Yes. I had no idea she owned a place like that."

"If you knew she was leaving the ship, you should have called me."

"Arnan was with her. One of the dancers was there, too, the one with the bum leg. I know Helene is overly protective of her, but she is an adult." Dex held up a drumstick. "Come on, dig in. Omar won't mind if we start without him."

"Dex, with all the separatists and terrorists lurking about, we have to be careful. Alba is a prime target for a kidnapping."

"Arnan is a pretty intimidating guard dog."

"Arnan is about to be reassigned. He wants to be a fitness instructor on the cruise."

Omar set a tray of lemonade on the table and Dex said, "Sit down, son. Grab a piece of this fine American delicacy."

Omar bowed slightly and said, "It is a great honor, Mr. Rubino."

"The honor is ours, Omar. I told you to call me Dex."

As Omar began devouring a large chicken breast, Desmond stood and looked down at Dex. "Let me know when you are leaving the ship."

"Am I a prisoner here?"

"Certainly not, but I've been trying to call you all morning and only got voice mail."

"Sorry, I forgot my cell on the desk."

"All right, but in the future . . ." He shot a look at Omar. "Keep me informed of any developments."

"Will do, boss."

Desmond walked away and Dex turned to Omar. "Did he make you tell him why I left?"

"No, sir, he was looking for you about an hour ago and received a phone call. Then he asked if I knew where you were. I have your cell phone in my pocket. I put the ringer on mute. You have received several calls."

"Hand it over, then grab some more chicken. I'll need your help finding the bottom of this bucket."

Dex looked at his incoming calls and saw that Narvik had called three times. "Oh, I forgot! I have to return one of these calls. Keep eating, kid." Dex stepped to the rail and dialed Narvik. When the man answered, Dex apologized and said, "Things are a little busy here. What time is it there?"

"It's eight-fifty A.M."

"Did you pick up the package?"

"Yes, I did, but I demand to know what's in the case. I want no part in illegal activity."

"OK, look inside and tell me what you see."

Dex heard Matt open the case and say, "It's just boxes of Easter candy."

"What kind of candy and from what company?"

"Marshmallow peeps. The box says Carmella Candy Co. I've heard of that company."

"That's what I expected. Now put that case in the empty suitcase you have with you."

"OK."

"Enter this address in your GPS—eight-ten Channelside Drive, Tampa."

"Done."

"When you get there, go to valet parking and ask for a man named Sean Harrison. He has your tickets and further instructions for you."

"Dex, I told you, I won't do anything illegal."

"Well, you've found us out Narvik. Windswept is an international candy smuggler, specializing in marshmallow peeps. Don't try and reason why the wealthy behave the way they do. Just do the job you're being overpaid to do."

"I'm sorry, Dex, this is just too bizarre."

"You better get moving, Matt. You have to be aboard by two. Have a nice cruise."

"OK, Sorry if I snapped at you."

"Good-bye, Matt." Dex closed his phone and returned to the table. "Any of that bird left for me, Omar?"

"Yes, I saved a few pieces for you." Omar's voice dropped to a whisper. "In the future, if you wish to visit Saint Cugat, take a taxi to the rail station and the subway from there. It will be a much shorter trip. If you need a guide, I would be happy to volunteer."

Dex gave his young friend a sidelong glance. "Yes, it would be beneficial to have someone to guide me. Good bird, isn't it, son?"

"Yes, sir, excellent bird."

Chapter 15

Arnan stopped the limo at the end of the gangplank and assisted his passengers as they exited the vehicle. He then popped the trunk and retrieved several large boxes. Two security guards lent their assistance to the perky blonde known to them as "Miss Meaghan." They nodded to Alba but did not speak. Arnan followed them carrying the boxes that contained several of Alba's favorite gowns.

Desmond Quest intercepted Arnan in the lobby.

"Just where have you been?"

"Alba wanted to get some things from her home."

"You know Miss Cologne isn't allowed to leave the ship. You deliberately disobeyed orders and shirked your duties."

Alba walked back from the elevator and intervened. "Arnan is my driver. He will drive me wherever I order him to!"

Desmond smiled at her. "Miss Cologne, my only concern is for your safety."

"I refuse to be a prisoner on my own boat, Mr. Quest. This entire enterprise is dependent on my hosting the cruise. I am the attraction to this cruise line, and you are nothing but an overpaid bodyguard. Arnan works for Windswept and I am the embodiment of Windswept. If I have to remind you of this again, I'll banish you to the banana grove my aunt found you in." Alba turned and stomped to the elevator, where Meaghan waited.

Arnan gave a sympathetic look to Quest who quivered with rage but was reluctant to speak. "Sorry, Desmond, welcome to my world."

Alba shouted to him, "Arnan, we are waiting!"

Three floors above them, two men had witnessed the scene from a balcony overlooking the lobby. "It appears your superior is about to be sacked," said Captain Auesnehmer.

"I don't think it's as bad as all that," Dex replied. "Alba's outbursts are legendary. Quest is a good man and is a favorite of Madame Adolphe."

"This could mean a promotion for you."

"I'm not seeking any advancement. After this cruise, Quest will have enough experience to handle things on his own."

"If Alba Cologne has turned against him, he is doomed. She is not so different from her father."

Dex gave the captain a sideward glance. "I didn't know the man."

"I only knew him by reputation, and yet I accepted employment with his company. We all compromise our principles for economic advancement. Am I right?"

"Emile, I told you this is just a one-time gig for me. After we reach Sunset Cay, I'm returning to the States."

"Do you really believe you can extricate yourself from Windswept so easily? When I signed on to this cruise, I knew I was selling my soul to the devil. But I got a good price."

"A beauty like Alba Cologne doesn't bring the devil to the minds of many men."

The captain chuckled. "No she brings out the devil in many men. I fear this will be an eventful voyage, my friend. We have to worry about adversaries without and within."

"Emile, you just keep us on course and let me worry about security. With any luck this cruise will be the most boring in your career."

The GPS guided Matt Narvik to the docks in Tampa. He spotted a kiosk with a sign that read "Valet Parking" and pulled in. He asked the girl at the kiosk for Sean Harrison. She rolled her eyes, then pointed toward a sandy-haired man in a white dress shirt and cargo pants. Matt approached the man, introduced himself, and showed his ID and passport.

"I'm all ready for you, Mr. Narvik," Harrison said. He pulled an envelope from one of his pants pockets and handed it to Matt. "Where is your luggage?"

"In my Jeep. I only have two bags."

Your ticket is in the envelope. I'll get you a claim check for the Jeep and you can be on your way."

"On my way where, Mr. Harrison?"

Harrison smiled and pointed across the street. "Just get on the ship and read the instructions in the envelope."

Matt fell in line with the throng of vacationers, presented his ID, and gave the appropriate answers to any questions. Before long, he was aboard and waiters offered him complimentary cocktails. He waved them off and found a comfortable chair in a lounge just outside of the casino. His eyes grew heavy and he started to nod. He knew he should not relax while on a mission, but in a few minutes, sleep overtook him.

Chapter 16

As the sun set on Barcelona, Arnan helped Helene Adolphe out of her limo. She looked at the giant sternly and said, "This may be my last opportunity to ask you in private. Do you wish to stay here as my driver or do you really wish to be a fitness instructor on the voyage?"

"While I enjoy being your driver, I feel that I could be of greater use to Windswept on the cruise. Not only could I be a fitness instructor, but I could provide an extra layer of security for Alba."

"I may need you to be a layer of protection for my interests as well. I do not fully trust our star. I fear she is as emotionally unstable as her father was. In addition, Dexter Rubino is becoming troublesome. There is no reason for him to stay with the ship all the way to Sunset Cay. After we leave Madeira, there will be several days at sea. The Atlantic is cold and deep. If there should be an accident, a recovery search would be futile. I'll agree to let you leave if you'll be as loyal to me as you were to Philippe."

"Of course, Madame, you are the embodiment of Windswept. It is my duty to look after your interests."

Helene chuckled. "Don't let Alba hear you speak those words. She thinks it is her ship. I will allow you to go if you assure me that you will be discreet with the pharmaceuticals you use."

"Certainly, Madame."

"Don't speak of this to anyone. Remember, your first loyalty is to me. I'm the one that kept you out of Guantanamo."

"Yes, Madame."

"In this evening's meeting I must protest your inclusion, but in the end I will acquiesce and allow you to go."

"Thank you, Madame."

"Sir . . . mister, are you OK?"

Matt opened his eyes to see a teenage ginger girl standing beside his chair. She looked at him as if he were a science experiment run amuck.

"Ah . . . yeah, I'm OK . . . I just dozed off."

"Daddy, will you please come over here? I think this man is ill or something."

A middle-aged man appeared on Matt's other side. "Candace, leave the gentleman alone. I'm sorry my daughter disturbed you, sir. She means well but doesn't use common sense sometimes."

"No problem. I didn't mean to fall asleep. I'm glad she woke me."

"I'm Todd Sterling; this is my daughter, Candace."

Matt realized he should stand and introduce himself as he shook Sterling's hand. "Nice to meet you, Mr. Sterling. My name is Matt Narvik."

Candace stepped closer and brushed against his right arm. "I'm sorry if I disturbed your nap, Mr. Narvik. I saw you twitching in the chair and thought you might be having a seizure or something." Her green eyes stared into his, causing an unsettling sense of fear to well up within him. The girl smiled broadly, revealing her silver orthodontics.

Sterling asked, "Are you traveling with your family, Mr. Narvik?'

"No, sir, I'm alone." He heard a small gasp come from Candace.

"Why don't we step out on deck and grab one of these free cocktails while they're still free?"

"I'm not a drinker."

Candace placed both of her hands on Matt's right arm as she tugged him toward the door. "You must come out on deck with us, Mr. Narvik. We'll soon pass under the bridge. You don't want to spend your whole vacation sleeping."

The trio joined the hoard of other passengers and watched as their ship passed under the Sunshine Parkway Bridge. A boisterous cheer swept the ship as they entered the Gulf of Mexico. Sterling drained his glass and grabbed another as a waiter passed by, while Candace focused her attention on Matt.

"You must have dinner with Daddy and me tonight," she said. "I don't know anyone else onboard and I refuse to be herded off with a bunch of adolescents. I would much prefer being escorted by two handsome gentlemen. I've been told that I'm very mature for a girl my age. Do you think so, Matthew?"

"Uh . . . sure . . . how old are you?"

"I'm eighteen."

Sterling grabbed the railing to steady himself and laughed. "She's fourteen going on twenty-one. What's a father to do? Her mother lets her run wild. I surely can't rein her in."

Candace placed her hand on the small of Matt's back and looked up at him, batting her green eyes. "I guess I'm just a problem child." She beamed another smile.

Matt felt the recurrence of fear. "If you'll excuse me, I want to make sure my luggage made it to my cabin all right."

"There's no need to worry about the luggage. These guys have it down to a science," Sterling said, slurring his words.

"Just the same, I'll feel better when I unpack."

As he walked away, Matt heard Candace say, "See you at dinner, Matthew."

Matthew? Why would she call me Matthew?

After wandering around the ship for twenty minutes, Matt found his cabin. His luggage was waiting for him and the marshmallow chicks were fine. He wondered if they should be refrigerated but then decided that there was little chance of them spoiling in an air-conditioned room.

He sat down and read his instructions. *Odd way to deliver candy.*

He unpacked his clothes and stashed the luggage in the closet. Stepping out on to the balcony, he thought of how different the ship was from his sailboat. On this voyage he'd have no worries. *Just relax and act like a tourist. Where is the adventure in that?*

Chapter 17

After a shower and change of clothes, Matt felt refreshed and headed to the ship's store and picked out a few T-shirts bearing the cruise-line logo. He requested a larger shopping bag than needed, one large enough to accommodate the briefcase. He returned to his room and rechecked his cargo of marshmallow chicks. They seemed fine and he wondered if they were really drugs or perhaps some plastic explosive.

Dex must really think I m naive to expect me to believe I'm smuggling candy. Whatever they are, I'm getting a free cruise, although not one I would have chosen.

According to the itinerary, they would spend a day at sea, then the ship would anchor off Georgetown. His ticket for a bus tour of Grand Cayman would get him ashore, then he had to find the red cab number seven. *Will customs check the bag I'm bringing ashore?*

A knock interrupted his thoughts. He opened his door to find Candace standing there. She wore a low-cut evening gown that looked as though she had outgrown it a year earlier. A strand of pearls drew Matt's eyes to her freckled cleavage, and it wasn't until he heard her sniffle that he noticed her glistening eyes.

"What's wrong?"

"Why didn't you come to dinner? I was stuck at a table with a bunch of old people. Daddy wasn't feeling well so I was all alone. I felt like a fool!"

"I'm sorry, but I didn't bring any formal wear. I was just going to order room service."

"You don't need a tux. A sport jacket would have been enough. Are you going to let me in or do I have to stand in the hall?"

Matt took a step back, then thought better of it. "Let's go out on deck. You shouldn't be in a man's room alone."

"What am I, some kind of mutant? It's this red hair, isn't it? I should shave it all off! Bald girls get more dates than I do. I wish I'd get cancer and it would fall out!"

"Don't say things like that. There's nothing wrong with red hair. Look at mine; it's turning white. Now that's something to cry about."

"Oh, Matthew, it just makes you look more distinguished."

"It makes me look old. Why don't you go back to your cabin, get out of those fancy clothes, and put on some jeans and a T-shirt. I'll meet you at the pizza place on deck six."

"Are you going to ditch me again?"

"No, I didn't ditch you. Now go change, and I'll meet you there in fifteen minutes."

The girl's face brightened with a smile. "All right, in fifteen minutes. I'll hurry."

Matt felt uneasy about meeting the girl, but sometimes little girls do desperate things. Sometimes they tell tall tales, too.

Candace returned to her cabin and began changing her clothes. A blurry-eyed Sterling watched in quiet amusement. "He didn't take the bait?"

"It's only my first turn at bat. I have all week to wear him down. I'm going to meet him at the pizza shop in a few minutes."

"Perhaps he would be more interested in me."

"Not all boy scouts are gay. I'll win him over eventually."

"You'll be paid the same either way."

"It's not about the money. This is an audition for an acting career. If I can't make this old fossil think I want him, how convincing of a performance can I deliver on screen?" She squeezed into a tight pair of short-shorts. "Besides, I have to prove my value to the rest of the family."

"Candace, you shouldn't regard those people as family. In my opinion, they are just a basket of rattlesnakes. To seduce this Narvik fellow, I suggest you try being a little less aggressive. As you said, you have all week."

She slipped a silk camisole over her bare torso. "The sooner it's done the better. Don't wait up, Todd."

"Try to be quiet when you come in. I'm anticipating an awful headache."

"With any luck I won't be back."

When Candace entered the pizza shop, all the male heads turned. She smiled sweetly at Matt, and as she sat beside him, she moved her chair closer to his. "Oh, Matthew, you didn't ditch me a second time. I'm so glad."

"How's your father?"

"Oh, he'll be OK. It's just a mild case of sea sickness."

"I thought we were going to wear jeans and T-shirts."

"Denim makes me look fat."

"I hope you like Hawaiian. Ours will be ready in a couple minutes."

"None for me. Way too many carbs."

"I hear there's a teen club onboard. You should check it out."

"I'd rather get to know Matthew Narvik."

"I'm almost old enough to be your grandfather, kid. And why are you calling me Matthew?"

"Well, it's your name isn't it? Hasn't anyone ever called you Matthew?"

"Yes, but I prefer Matt. It would do you good to spend time with some kids your own age."

"They're children. Tell me about Matthew Narvik. Where are you from? What do you do for a living? What's your status?"

"My status?"

"Yeah, are you married, divorced, single . . . gay?"

"I'm single. I'm a retired steelworker from Fort Myers, Florida, and I'm way too old for you."

"You're not old, just mature. A man like you knows how to please a woman."

"Cool it, Candace. I'm getting over a bad break-up. Besides, you're still a little girl to me . . . and your dad."

She snuggled closer to Matt. "I could help you get over her. I'd do anything to make you feel better."

"Our pizza is ready. Will you eat a slice for me? That would make me feel sooo much better. "Would you like a Coke?"

"No, it's all fizz and sugar. I would like some bottled water, though."

Matt left the table to retrieve the pizza and their drinks. When he returned, he set the pizza on the table and took a seat opposite Candace.

"Dig in kid, before it gets cold."

"Matthew, do you know how many calories are in that thing? I can't eat anything like that," she said and opened the water bottle instead.

"Someday, years from now, you're going to realize that you spent your youth trying to be old. You should enjoy being a girl and put off becoming a woman for as long as you can." Matt lifted a slice of pizza to his mouth and took a bite.

Candace stood and leaned over the table. In her eyes, he saw not passion, but anger and determination. "I have a woman's body and a woman's desires, Matthew Narvik. Before this cruise is over, you and I are going to be lovers. I won't have it any other way." She tipped the bottle over and water spilled onto the table and dripped into Matt's lap. She then stormed out of the pizza shop as Matt felt the stares of the other patrons.

That was a scene worthy of Alba. What is she doing now? Is she with someone else? Has Dex made contact with her?

He ignored his soaked jeans and calmly finished eating the pizza. He pledged to himself that the rest of his meals would come via room service.

Chapter 18

The next morning, Matt rose with the sun and stretched himself awake. He headed for the gym and went to work on the weight machines. After an hour, he stepped onto a treadmill and was surprised by how much the motion of the ship affected his stride. He switched to the stationary bike and logged twenty miles. When he got back to his cabin, he ordered breakfast, then took a hot shower. Only a few minutes after emerging from the steamy bath his meal arrived. As he ate, he perused the ship's newspaper, which had come with the food. It was just promo for the tourist traps on the island. Nothing that seemed of interest to him. *Perhaps Grand Cayman is just a spot for the mob to hide its money*. Feeling a little soreness in his shoulders, he headed for the hot tub, which sat next to the swimming pool.

The adult pool area was already crowded but only a young couple was using the spa. Matt politely asked if there was room for him and the couple cordially said there was plenty of space. They exchanged names and hometowns and talked about the weather and the economy. Then Matt felt two soft hands cover his eyes.

"Guess who, Matthew? Oh, that rhymes. I could do a rap."

Matt felt hands pull away, but he kept his eyes closed. However, he could not shut out her impromptu performance.

"Guess who, Matthew? . . . What ya do, Matthew? Do me, Matthew! Set me free, Matthew."

When Matt opened his eyes, he couldn't see what was going on behind him, but the shocked expression of the couple across from him suggested it was inappropriate. He turned his head as Candace, clad in a few skinny strands of black Lycra, sat on the edge of the hot tub. She deftly swung her feet over the side and splashed in, landing on Matt's lap.

"Morning, lover! How did you sneak out on me so early?"

"Candace, I told you last night to cool it. There is no romance, and there will never be any romance." He wanted to push her away but was hesitant to touch her.

Candace turned to the woman opposite them and giggled. "He is so shy in public, but in private . . ." she wiggled her bottom against his groin.

"Candace!" Matt shoved the girl off his lap. "Where's your father?"

"In his room, of course, still sleeping off his bad behavior. I'm all yours today."

The woman in the tub stood up. "It's time for us to get out, Jim."

Her opened-mouth husband didn't respond. His eyes were focused on Candace.

"Jim!"

"Yes, dear, I heard you. Time to get out," he said as he rose. "Nice meeting you, Mr. Narvik." As soon as his wife turned her back, the man winked at Matt and directed a lecherous smile at Candace.

Candace spoke to Matt in a baby-like voice. "Is little Matthew grumpy today? Does he need a nice piece of Candy?"

He pointed to a sign on the ship's bulkhead and said, "Minors are not allowed in the adult pool area without a parent or guardian,"

She stood in front of him, beads of water glistening on her freckled flesh. "I may be a minor, but I have a major crush on you, Matthew Narvik. Take me right now, here in front of everyone."

"I'd like to spank you right here, in front of everyone."

"If you want to hurt me, it's OK. Let's go back to your room."

"No, Candace! It is not going to happen."

She bent forward and wrapped her arms around his neck in a tight embrace. Matt couldn't help but notice that her hair smelled of coconut. She slid her legs on either side of his and whispered in his ear. "What did she do to you? Did she hurt you?" He felt her tongue touch his cheek and make a small arc to his ear. "Let Candace make it all better."

Matt put his hands on her shoulders and shoved her away. This time she landed on her back and struggled to get her head back above water.

"Good-bye, little girl," he said and stepped out of the spa. As he walked away, he heard people laugh. A pair of older women smiled at him as he passed by, then gasped as they stared toward the hot tub. Matt stopped and turned to look.

Candace stood in the tub, her auburn hair draped over her face. One of the Lycra bands had slipped, exposing a breast. She pulled her hair away from her eyes and called out. "Dinner's at eight, lover!"

Matt marched back to his cabin. His flesh reeked of chlorine, but the lingering scent of coconut filled his mind. He needed a shower—a cold shower. He had managed to rebuff the girl so far, but each of her passes had become increasingly aggressive. In the shower, he washed his hair and again caught the aroma of Candace. *Coconut shampoo! Why does everything have to be coconut?* He rinsed his hair and stepped out, toweled off and retrieved his Old Spice cologne from his travel bag. He splashed a liberal amount on his chest and wiped his hands on his face. *Demons be gone!* He dressed in jeans and a T-shirt and headed for the guest relations desk.

On his way back to his cabin, Matt took the wrong elevator and got lost aft of the casino. As he walked the corridors, he heard piano music coming from one of the show rooms. The music was familiar, an old hymn. He walked inside and his eyes adjusted to the dim light. At the end of the room, a man who appeared to be in his late thirties played the keyboard, his eyes shut and his head wagging to the beat.

"This bar isn't open yet, sir. There are drinks available on deck." The voice came from behind the bar. Somehow Matt had not detected the burly bartender who was busy counting his stock.

"Is it OK if I just sit and listen? I love these old hymns."

The piano player opened his eyes and stopped playing. "It's OK, Ronny. Would you like a cup of coffee, sir?"

"Sure, if you don't mind. Just cream, please."

"Ronny, please serve this gentleman from my private stock." Turning to Narvik he said, "Sit down and relax, brother. What would you like to hear?"

Matt made his way to the piano and said, "The hymn you were playing was nice." Matt offered his hand, "My name is Matt Narvik."

"Oh, sorry, I don't shake hands. These are how I make my living. I'm Dave Carpenter. Nice to meet you, Matt. Do you know the name of the song?"

Matt sat in one of the chairs, and Ronny set a cup of coffee next to him. "No, but I'm sure I've heard it before."

"It's called 'The Ninety and Nine.' A man named Ira Sankey wrote it long ago. He was from my hometown in Pennsylvania."

Matt leaned forward in his chair. "I'm from Pennsylvania. I use to live in a town called Sycamore Mills. Now it's a reservoir."

"You mean the Sycamore Reservoir? I use to go there when I was a kid."

They both chuckled. "Small world, isn't it," said Matt.

David returned to playing as he spoke, "Very small; my world is this room. I'm seldom free of it. Soon I'll be leaving for another small room on another big ship. I've been hired by a new cruise line."

"Which one?"

"Windswept. The name of the ship is *New Dawn*. I'm sure it will smell as bad, and the same drunks with different faces will be waiting. My contract here was up, and they offered me more money."

Matt sipped his coffee; it was lukewarm. "You're going on the transatlantic cruise?"

"Yes, how did you know about it?"

"I saw it online, so I booked passage."

"Funny, I was told it would be mostly Europeans. Well, I guess I'll have at least one fan onboard."

"You bet. Now I'm looking forward to the trip."

"Are you a 'true believer,' Matt?"

"Yes, I am."

"Bet you're wondering how I went from playing in church to playing in Satan's recruiting office."

"Well, it doesn't look all that bad to me."

"It is. You should see all that goes on here. I used to be on the straight and narrow, even married a preacher's daughter. She grew unhappy, we divorced, and I got my walking papers. All the beloved brethren said they were praying for me but didn't care to have me around."

"I've heard it said that only the army of God shoots it's wounded."

"Yes, I've heard that one, too. You should come back tonight. I'll be taking requests. The crowd here isn't all that bad. I just made some poor career decisions. My mother warned me to stay out of bars."

"Well, I don't drink or hang out in bars, but I'll be sure and see you on the *New Dawn*."

"Don't wait that long. Come back tonight. I'll be here all week."

"I will, but this is my last night onboard. I'm getting off at Grand Cayman."

"You'll be missing the best part of the trip."

"Yeah, well, I'm sort of here on business, and I'm trying to separate myself from a nuisance. I'll be sure and come see your show tonight."

"Do you have a request?"

"Do you know 'Crying in the Chapel' that Elvis used to sing?"

"Sure, I used to sneak it into the offertory now and then. See you tonight, Matt."

Chapter 19

A sharp knock on his cabin door awakened Dex Rubino. "What is it?"

"It is Hakim, sir. We need you in the Grand Lobby."

"I'll be there in a minute." Dex pulled himself out of his bunk, ducking his head to avoid the berth overhead. *Why can't these people handle the simple things?*

He slipped into a pair of dress pants and a golf shirt, and started for the Grand Lobby three levels above his cabin and, in terms of décor, a world away. As he opened the concealed bulkhead door that led to the opulent lobby, he heard heated voices barking commands.

"You get out of my way or I'll make you eat that taser!"

"Mr. Arnan, you know that you cannot bring your belongings aboard until they have been inspected by the port police."

"This is my personal property. As an American citizen, I'm entitled to privacy. I was working for Windswept when you guys were parking cars."

"Yesterday you were driving Madame Adolphe's car," Hakim said.

Arnan reached for the man, who instinctively thrust his taser toward the giant. Arnan grasped Hakim's wrist and raised it overhead while punching him in the chest. The taser, and Hakim, fell to the floor. Hakim's four compatriots stared in awe at the powerful giant as he reached for the taser.

Dex called out, "Don't do it, Arnan!" He strode across the room and glared at Hakim and his companions. "What's going on here?"

Arnan straightened up and turned toward Dex, visibly relaxing. "Mr. Rubino, I didn't see you there."

"I just got here. Now, why don't we all calm down, and someone tell me what's going on."

One of the foursome helped Hakim to his feet while another started to explain that Arnan was bringing his personal property aboard without the proper inspection.

"I'm not some silly Arab rent-a-cop," Arnan shouted. "I'm a trusted employee. I've been in service to Philippe's family for over six years. I refuse to let these goons go through my stuff."

"Cool off, Arnan," Dex said. "These men won't be going through your things. The port police have to check the crew's belongings before they can come aboard. It's not just you. Even I had to have my things inspected. Captain Auesnehmer was subject to a search also. It's nothing to get excited about."

"Can I speak to you in private, Mr. Rubino?"

"Sure. Your baggage will have to stay here, but we can go up to my office and talk."

They left the room and stepped into an elevator. Dex looked up at Arnan and said, "You have to be careful. You could have killed that little guy."

"He was trying to use a taser on me. Those things hurt. I don't have to take that from him or anyone else."

"I'm sorry things got out of hand. I'll speak to my men about using those tasers indiscriminately. Because they aren't lethal, we tend to reach for them too readily."

The two men exited the elevator. Dex used his security card to open the door of the monitoring room, and they entered his minuscule office. Arnan's bulk seemed exaggerated by the tight quarters.

"Just why are you so upset about having your things inspected?" Dex asked, and motioned to a chair.

Arnan sat down, bowed his head, and began rubbing the palms of his hands on his thighs. "It's personal."

"Arnan, Mr. Quest told me that Windswept is a family. If that applies to me, I'm sure it applies to someone who has given all the years of service to the company that you have. Whatever you share with me tonight is in confidence. Now, what's this all about?"

"I have a vitamin regimen that I must follow. Some of those vitamins are considered controlled substances." He began to shake his head, "They are not drugs. . . . I would never use drugs."

"Arnan, are you using steroids?"

Tears began to stream from his eyes. "You don't know about me, do you?"

I know more than you realize, thought Dex. "Just that you were Madame Adolphe's driver, and now you're going to be a fitness instructor on the cruise."

"I was a world-class bodybuilder. My career ended in disgrace. The work of my life was destroyed. That's when Philippe found me and took me in."

"What does all that have to do with steroids? Don't you understand what they can do to your health?"

Arnan looked across the desk at Dex. With quivering chin and tears dripping from his face, he answered. "You can't imagine how well I understand."

Chapter 20

Matt forsook the air-conditioned cabin and sat on his balcony watching the waves. He hadn't eaten since breakfast but wasn't feeling any pangs of hunger. Perhaps the tablets he was taking provided enough nutrition to curb his appetite.

He returned to the cabin where the phone flashed the number four, indicating he had messages waiting. Suspecting they were all from Candace, he had ignored them earlier. He sighed and listened to them, confirming his suspicion, then hit the delete button.

As he made his way to the piano bar, he kept a wary eye out for the ginger menace. Outside of the bar, hors d'oeuvres were offered and he filled a plate. Upon entering the dimly lit room, the piano player stopped playing a Bacharach tune and began playing "Crying in the Chapel."

A pretty server greeted Matt. "Welcome, Mr. Narvik. We've been expecting you." She escorted him to a table and comfortable chair at the front of the room. David Carpenter offered him a smile and a nod as he continued to play. Matt gave him a thumbs-up signal as the server set a mug of piping-hot coffee on the table. Matt leaned back in the chair and took in his surroundings.

Helene Adolphe glowered at Arnan. "You imbecile, how could you confide in Rubino! I have kept you supplied with all the supplements you could use for nearly a year. Did you think I would abandon you now?"

Arnan sheepishly sat in a straight chair as Helene paced the room. "I'm sorry, Madame, but I thought I would need to get a supply onboard before we left port."

Desmond Quest sat opposite Arnan in a stuffed leather chair and shook his head. "I have told you many times before, Arnan. You do not get paid to think, you get paid to do as you are instructed."

Helene stopped in front of Desmond and pointed a bony finger in his face. "You are not without blame in this matter. Why is your security team inspecting the luggage of a trusted employee?"

"They were not inspecting his luggage, only holding it for the port police."

"Do they work for Windswept or the port police?"

Desmond leaned forward in his chair, "Your partner, Rubino, has inspired my people to reach for a new level of diligence. They turned to him because he was on the ship. If I had been there, they would have come to me."

"Do you wish to live on the ship as well?"

"Really, there is no need for that. I have a home here, and I've spoken to my men. I think that perhaps it is time to rid ourselves of Rubino. I will handle all the security from now on."

Helene gave Arnan a sideward glance, "I have already made plans for Rubino's termination. You are to stay out of it. Act as if nothing has occurred."

Arnan dared to speak. "I'm not sure that killing Dex is a good idea. He was very sympathetic to me last night and said he would help me find medical treatment. He said we are all part of a family."

"We are a family!" Helene said, "Dexter Rubino is an interloper. I hired one of the finest pharmacologists in the world to help you. His formula works wonders on healthy subjects, such as Anton and me. You have ruined your body by self-medicating. Your only hope is that in time, with continued treatment, there will be some improvement."

Arnan began to weep, "Doctor Zhan is dead, and you made me kill him. Who will help me now?"

Desmond slipped his hand inside of his blazer, where his fingertips touched the grip of his handgun. Helene stood in front of Arnan, blocking the line of fire. Her voice shifted to a soothing tone as she spoke to the weeping giant. "Calm down. I have access to the doctor's formulas. If continuing your medication does not improve your health over time, we will try something else."

"I need help now . . . there is a woman. How can I tell her I can't be a man for her?"

Helene placed her bony hand on Arnan's head. "You poor boy, give me a few days. I will have a solution before the ship sails. Until then, confide only in Desmond or myself. Avoid Rubino as much as possible."

"Dexter has been a friend to me."

Helene looked into Arnan's eyes, "As soon as your meeting with Rubino ended, he called me. He advised me that you were unstable and that you should be dismissed. That is how I learned of the incident. Now return to the ship with Desmond. You can assist him in finding a cabin onboard."

As Desmond and Arnan waited for the elevator, Anton Carmella entered the foyer. The man had a spring in his step as he bounded to Helene and embraced her. "Honey, let's go down to the beach and take a nice long walk. I'm sick of being cooped up in this high-rise."

Helene tried to push him away. "Dear heart, you know you can't be seen in public. Go out to the garden and wait for me there. I will soon conclude my business with Desmond."

"Desmond can show himself out while you and me get busy. Desi and Arnan are men of the world. They can tell when a couple needs some alone time, especially Arnan. The chicks always go for us athletic types, right kid?"

When the elevator arrived, Desmond and Arnan boarded. Helene saw the smirk on Desmond's face and the tears in Arnan's eyes before the doors closed. She followed Anton to the garden, muttering to herself. "Americans are such a mongrel race. They behave as beasts. Their nation is a curse upon the earth. I can't wait to be rid of them!"

Chapter 21

Dex took a taxi to the Plaça de Catalunya and wandered around, acting like any other visitor. He spotted Omar's yellow Honda scooter parked near the Hard Rock Café. As he was about to enter, he heard his name whispered. There stood Omar, dressed in a charcoal hoodie and jeans. "Follow me to the train station. The next train leaves at seven-fifty."

"All right. Will you leave your bike here?"

"One of my cousins is taking it home. He'll have it waiting here in the morning."

"I didn't intend to spend the whole night there."

"The next train back won't be until eight A.M. We may need all night to search. I have two flashlights."

"Is there an alarm?"

"I saw none, and the caretaker leaves at six. I scaled the fence and walked through the gardens last night. I have a friend who lives a few meters away. If we set off an alarm, we can head there."

"How far is the mansion from the train station?"

"It is just a fifteen-minute walk. We can go to a coffeehouse nearby and wait for darkness."

"It's odd that Alba doesn't have an alarm. The wealthy usually fortify their homes against intruders."

"The locals believe that the place is haunted, or at least cursed, a belief that Philippe was happy to reinforce."

"Well, son, let's get going."

Matt Narvik rose before dawn and prepared his gear for a quick departure. He carried his two bags, one inside of a large, plastic bag with the cruise-line logo emblazoned on it. He reported to the auditorium to wait for the shuttle that would take him and others ashore. He was in the first group to leave, and the boat crew seemed to avert their eyes as he boldly carried his luggage off the ship. When they docked, the port officers were busy keeping tour guides and hucksters away from the dock and no one questioned Matt's purpose. He slipped through the crowd and out to the street, where he spotted a red Mini Cooper with the number seven on the door. The driver was leaning over the hood reading a newspaper.

"Excuse me," said Matt. "I'm trying to get to the turtle farm. Can you get me there?"

The tall black man straightened up and looked over his shoulder. "Yes, sir, I've been waiting for you." When the man spotted the plastic bag, he shook his head. "These folks are getting bolder all the time. No matter to me. Let's put your bags in the back seat and get goin'. Next stop, the turtle farm."

They rode in silence until the driver made a quick left into the parking lot of the turtle farm. "You know what to do from here?" he asked.

"There's been a change in plans," Matt said. "I want you to wait for me. I'm going to the airport from here."

"Oh, no, sir, I can't do that. My orders are to drop you here, and then you take the tour bus."

"As I said, there has been a change in plans. Quest ordered it." Matt saw the spark of recognition at the mention of the name.

"OK, OK, man, I'm just a driver. You want me to wait I'll wait, but somebody got to pay me for this extra."

"I'll make sure you're compensated." Matt got out of the vehicle and entered the building. Inside, a well-stocked gift shop retailed every imaginable thing related to sea turtles, even their meat. As he approached the checkout counter, the clerk looked away and stared out of the back windows to the pools where hundreds of turtles frolicked in reservoirs of seawater. Matt set his package down in front of the counter, then exited the building. He stood beside the door for about thirty seconds, then looked in through the glass and witnessed the pickup. A redhead in a white sundress grabbed the bag and headed for a door on the other side of the building. A floppy white hat hid her facial features, but she wore white sandals with laces that reached half way up her calves. As she exited the gift shop, she got into the driver's side of a classic Jaguar XKE roadster, light blue with a white boot. Matt scurried back to the Mini Cooper and got in. "Follow that Jag," he ordered.

As the Jaguar left the parking lot, Matt got a good look at the woman who had removed her hat. She wore wraparound sunglasses with a gold chain around her neck. She was an older woman but still quite attractive.

"You said the airport," the driver pleaded.

Matt stared into the man's eyes. "It will go easier for you if you cooperate."

"Yes, sir. Yes, sir. I'll do as you say."

Chapter 22

As Omar scurried over the iron fence, Dex huffed and bent forward, hands on his knees.

"I'll go to the front and open the gate. Are you all right?" There was genuine concern in the youngster's voice.

"Sure," said Dex as he forced himself upright. "Just give me a minute to catch my breath. Don't go to the gate. If there is any alarm in this place, that's where it will be."

"I told you, there are no alarms. I've been all over the property except for the main house. Go to the front gate and I'll open it for you."

"No, Omar, and that's an order. I can scale this fence." Dex struggled his way to the top of the fence, then stole a glance at the impatient teen shrouded by evergreens. "Go on over to the main house, son. I'll meet you there."

"Are you sure you'll be all right?"

"Yes, I'll be fine. Now go!" As Omar disappeared into the trees, Dex eased himself over the top of the fence. While hoping to make a gradual descent and land on his feet, he fell to the ground with a thud, landing on his right shoulder. *Never could get a grip with gloves on.* The bed of fallen needles provided a soft landing, but his ego sustained a severe bruise. Using the fence for advantage, he raised himself to his feet and plunged into the evergreens.

On the other side of the hedge, Dex saw the flicker of Omar's flashlight. He rejoined his young protégé, who was busy cutting the glass from a window at the rear of Alba's mansion. "Don't be in a hurry, son, just take it slow."

"I've done this before. We will have access in a few minutes, but then where do we go?"

"We'll just have to nose around. You look for a safe or treasure room on the second floor. I'll check out the basement and first floor."

"I think we should stay together. I need your experience to guide me."

"We have too much ground to cover. This place is huge."

Omar snapped the glass out of its frame and lowered it to the floor inside. He turned to his mentor with a pleading look in his eyes. "I wish you would stay with me. I might miss a valuable clue."

Dex realized that Omar was concerned for his well-being, not apprehensive about the mission. He smiled and nodded to the young man. "OK, amigo, we'll stick together."

Since Dex hoped that Philippe's treasure was a massive one, he began his search in the basement. Much to his amazement, the entire floor was a lab. There was nothing elaborate about it, and he saw no chemicals of any kind. A sickening sweet aroma lingered in every corner. It wasn't meth or marijuana, but Dex was sure he'd smelled it before. Perhaps Alba Cologne had been manufacturing her own line of cosmetics. Dex found some anchor bolts protruding from the floor. *Some type of machinery had once been anchored here.*

"Whatever was here is gone," Dex said. "I doubt if it was treasure. Let's look around upstairs."

The duo climbed the stairs to the main floor, where sheets of cloth covered the furniture and Dex noticed dark rectangles on the walls where artwork had hung. He paused to pull any piece of architectural detail that might release a hidden door or panel. They found their way to the front entrance and a flash of lightning illuminated the dual stairways. A low rumble of thunder followed the sudden burst of light, and the two intruders took a moment to reconnoiter.

"You take that one, I'll take the other," Dex whispered.

"I thought we were going to stick together," said Omar.

Dex had a tone of impatience in his voice. "They meet at the top. I can go that far alone. Just do as I told you." He turned on his flashlight and noticed a change in the color of the marble floor from white to a shade of pink. A closer inspection revealed a heart-shaped piece of pink granite in the center of the circular room. The heart was outlined by a shiny, metal border. *Is that silver? Or is it lead?*

Dex heard a creak from the stairs Omar was climbing. Not wanting to fall behind, he quickly ascended the other side. At the top, they entered an ornate ballroom. They crossed the floor and entered a long hall that had three private suites on each side. At the end of the hall, a narrow stairway led to a third floor.

"Probably goes to the servants quarters," said Omar.

Dex shined a light on his wristwatch. "We only have a few hours before dawn. Let's check out the ballroom again."

As they reentered the room, a flash of lightning revealed a spiral staircase near the entrance.

"There's something special at the top of those stairs, Dex. I can feel it." Omar raced across the room and took the stairs two at a time.

Dex was dubious but willing to indulge his young friend. As Dex reached the top of the stairs, the lightning increased in frequency and a mirrored wall that stretched the width of the room reflected the flashing light. A heart-shaped bed sat in the center of the room, and a crystal chandelier hung over it.

"Reminds me of my honeymoon in the Poconos," said Dex.

"What?"

"Nothing, kid, I was just reminiscing. There are no windows in this room. Where is the light coming from?"

Another bolt of lightning answered his query. Directly behind him, a pair of glass doors illuminated. He opened the doors and passed through onto a half-round balcony. A gilded railing marked its edge. As the storm increased in ferocity, a stained-glass dome overhead glowed like a multicolored fireball. Omar stood beside Dex, unsure if he was witnessing a natural light show or the supernatural wrath of Philippe Ben-Balla.

"Freak-o-rama," Dex said.

"What?"

"Nothing, just something my daughter used to say. I can see it: The princess would stand here and her adoring guests would be held in the entryway. She would greet them from above and allow them to ascend to the next level. Then she would condescend to meet them there. Alba Cologne would make a classic theatrical entrance."

"Dex, I'm not comfortable here. I think we should go."

Dex leaned over the railing and surveyed the foyer. The pink heart in the floor seemed to glow in response to each flash of lightning. "OK, Omar, I'll get back here later. Maybe we can make it to your friend's place before the rain hits."

Matt and his driver followed the Jag through the traffic-clogged streets of Georgetown. The driver kept whining about other fares that were waiting. Matt answered him with an icy stare. The Jag turned onto a side street, then into the parking lot of a KFC.

"Pull in behind her," Matt ordered.

The driver continued past the entrance and said, "No way, man. It's locals only."

Matt felt a rage building within him. He grabbed the driver's arm, causing the vehicle to swerve. "I told you to pull in behind her. That chicken joint doesn't care who drives in."

"She's not there for chicken, mister. She's there to buy spliff."

"How can you know that?"

"Folks park out front to get food, round back to get spliff. No tourists allowed!"

"I need to follow that Jag."

"She won't be there for long. I'll turn around and we can pick up her trail when she leaves."

The driver parked near the curb and turned toward Matt. "What kind of cop are you?"

Rage erupted within Matt's mind. "I'm the kind that will crush your skull if we lose that Jag."

"Stay cool, man. I've made a lot of deliveries like this. I never had no problems till you showed up." As he spoke, the Jag exited the parking area and made a right turn onto the main road. The driver didn't move.

Matt fist-bumped the driver's head. "Follow her! If you lose 'er, I'll tear you apart."

The driver slid as far toward the door as he could while he resumed his pursuit. "Stay cool, man. Stay cool."

They entered an area of tall concrete structures, manicured hedges, and tiny lawns that lined the street. The Jag made a quick right onto a narrow side street, where a line of small cottages stood on the far side of the street. Again, the driver passed the street the Jag had used.

Before Matt could react, the driver explained. "Dead end street. There are only four bungalows on one side, a shutdown hotel on the other. I'll pull in here and wait. You walk down that street and see where her car is parked, and then you can introduce yourself to her."

Matt couldn't understand why he felt the need to confront this woman. It had suddenly become an overwhelming passion. He left the Mini Cooper and trudged to the dead end street. As he turned the corner, he heard his taxi speed away. Again, rage overtook him. He couldn't catch the cab, but he was going to confront the woman. He jogged down the side street and spotted the Jag parked near the last of the cottages. Each of the frame buildings bore a pale shade of yellow paint with white trim. A metal hip roof topped each. Without any game plan, Matt charged to the door of the cottage and knocked. He waited for what seemed like several minutes and no one responded. He pounded the door again and a voice called from inside, "Who is it?"

Matt resumed pounding on the door. Again, the voice, now just beyond the door, asked, "Who is it?"

"You have the wrong bag. Let me in."

"The door opened and Matt pushed his way in. The woman, clad in a bathrobe, back-stepped and shrieked at him. "Get out now!"

"You took the wrong bag at the turtle farm. Where is it?"

"You idiot! You followed me here? Get out now while you still can."

Matt was sure this was the woman from the Jaguar. Her auburn hair was pulled back in a ponytail and he noticed a slight malformation in her face—it wasn't symmetrical. It looked like one of her cheek bones had caved in. He could tell she had once been a beauty. "Turn over the bag and I'll leave."

She put her hands on her hips and snarled at Matt. "I don't know what you're talking about. Get out of my home this minute, or I'll call the police."

"I don't think you want the police involved." Matt heard the floor creak behind him, then a flash of white light filled Matt's vision as he fell to the floor. He heard garbled voices, then plummeted into a dark abyss.

Chapter 23

Dex shivered with the cold; Omar burned with embarrassment. On the way to the home of Omar's friend, the two treasure hunters were caught in a downpour, then no one answered the friend's door. After a night in the coffee shop, they sat in silence on a commuter train headed back to Barcelona, water pooling around their feet. One of the commuters spoke to Omar in Catalan. Omar responded by shaking his head, no.

"What do they want?"

"They asked if we needed money."

Dex started to chuckle. "We must look like a couple of hobos."

Omar sighed in relief. "I'm sorry my friend wasn't at home. She assured me she would be there."

"I'm just wondering how we can get back onboard the ship like this with no one noticing."

"I have a friend that works at a small hotel on the Rambla de Catalunya. We can go to the back entrance, and she will give us a room to get cleaned up in."

"Is this girlfriend more reliable than the one in Saint Cugat?"

"I believe so. She will be able to get the mud cleaned from your clothes also."

"Good, I feel like a bum. Don't let last night get you down. We'll find our pot of gold eventually."

"I hope you are right."

Dex looked around him to see if any of the commuters were eavesdropping. "Do you know anything about the lab in the basement?"

"No, I was as surprised by that as you were."

The sting of ammonia returned Matt Narvik to consciousness. "Come on, bud, wake up."

Through blurry eyes, Matt saw a chubby man in a tan uniform and a bad hairpiece.

"Come on, bud, I want to make sure you're all right before we take off."

Matt's head throbbed, "Who are you?"

"My name is Julian. I'm the pilot."

Matt tried to lift his shackled hands.

"You have quite a knot up there. You'll be OK in a few days. I taped an ice pack to the back of your noggin."

"What happened?"

"I think you stepped out of line. Someone took it upon himself to set you straight. I'm supposed to take you home."

"I have to call my boss."

"I imagine he has already been contacted."

"Take these cuffs off of me."

"No way. With the juice you're on, you'll stay cuffed until we land. I just wanted you to come around before takeoff. Sit back and relax. Next stop, Fort Myers."

As Alba Cologne left rehearsal, she spotted Desmond whispering to Helene. Thinking the head of security was complaining about her recent actions, she interrupted them. "Aunt Helene, I must speak with you."

"Not now, child. We are discussing important business."

"What part of Windswept is more important than I am? Surely this banana picker is not more valuable to the company than I."

"Alba, hold your tongue. Mr. Quest has brought me some disturbing news. Someone has broken into your home in Saint Cugat."

"What! How can this happen? I demand that you hire security to guard my home."

"It has never been necessary before. All the important artwork is in storage." Helene scowled at her niece. "You have the resources to hire around-the-clock security. That hulking old palace belongs to you, not Windswept. We provided security in the past as a courtesy to your father."

Desmond forced a smile as he bowed to the beauty. "Ms. Cologne, Eduardo called me this morning to report the break-in. There was no damage done, just a few muddy footprints. If you wish, we could hire a private security firm to watch over your home."

"Where is Dexter Rubino? I want him to arrange for security."

Helene gave a sidelong glance to Desmond. "We have been asking the same question. No one has seen him since yesterday. Do you have any idea where he is?"

"No, I have been in rehearsal all day. When you find him, tell him I want to see him. My home must be secured."

Desmond responded with another bow. "Ms. Cologne, I have already sent a team of my best men to Saint Cugat. Your home will be secure by nightfall. Several of my men will stand guard overnight. If you wish, I'll put Dexter in charge."

"That is what I demand, Mr. Quest!" Alba stamped her foot and walked away.

Helene whispered, "Do you think Dexter had anything to do with the break-in?"

"No, he is not that foolish. He has probably found some female companionship."

"I thought he was past due for infidelity. He has made no effort to contact our friend in the Caymans."

"What are we to do about that situation?"

"The courier is to be dismissed. Erase all traces of any relationship with him."

"He is a protégé of Rubino's. I will let him take care of the details."

"Was any damage done to the lab?"

"No. Any equipment of value has been shipped to Belize. Our stockpiles are in secure locations."

"Make sure there is enough onboard to control Arnan."

Chapter 24

Clad in a bathrobe, Dex paced the floor of his room in the Hotel Murmuri. He'd taken a long, hot shower and sent his clothes out for cleaning. A brief nap had restored his vigor and he impatiently waited to get back to the ship. He looked out of the glass doors to the backstreets of Barcelona. Each building, even the most mundane, bore some architectural detail that displayed the artistic nature of the city. In stark contrast to his sleek hotel, these buildings were devoid of modernization. Electrical wiring ran on outside walls from room to room and building to building. In the alleyways, laundry hung from clotheslines stretched between balconies. Dex reached for his cell phone to check the time. He had three messages, all Desmond Quest. *It must be important.*

He punched the speed dial and Desmond answered immediately.

"Dex, we were getting concerned about you. Where are you? We have a problem that requires your immediate attention."

"I'm at a hotel in town. I needed a change of scenery. I'm sure you can handle anything as well as I."

"This concerns your courier; he has failed."

"It just isn't possible to screw that mission up."

"I would agree, but the fact remains."

"Did he make the drop?"

"Yes, and then he followed the contact and demanded the package back."

"Oh, no. Where is he now?"

"I have taken the liberty of putting him on a flight back to the US. He will be delivered to the home Windswept provided for him."

"Just how big a mess did he make?"

"Madame Adolphe is not pleased. Fortunately, we had professionals in place to take control of the situation. Madame insists that all traces between Windswept and this man are to be eradicated. His final disposition is up to you."

"I'll call him right away."

"Not yet. Madame wants a meeting with you at her residence. Let's say around seven o-clock."

"Am I in trouble?"

"Not really. There are some security issues she would like to discuss, as well as the Cayman Island problem."

"I'll be there."

"Will you need to return to the US to take care of this? Or do you have an operative that can do it for you? If you wish, I could make the arrangements."

"It won't be necessary. I can fire him over the phone."

"This individual might have compromised our entire organization. I think the consequences of his actions should be most severe."

Alba motioned for Meaghan to join her in her suite and said, "The time has come for your mission to begin."

"Do you think Arnan is finally ready?"

"This has nothing to do with Arnan."

"Oh, pooh! Alba, I'm a healthy young woman. All this wooing is getting old."

"Completing your mission in a satisfactory manner may arouse Arnan to jealousy."

"How?"

The plane touched down at Page Field and sat on the tarmac for half an hour. Matt stared out of a window wondering what would happen to him. Finally, Julian, the pilot, returned and released the bonds.

"Your vehicle will be brought to your home tonight," he said. "I am to put you in a cab and they will take you home. I've been instructed to tell you to stay there and wait for further instructions."

"Should I call Dex and tell him what happened?"

"I have no idea who Dex is. I don't know who you are. You're just a package I'm delivering." Julian gave him a sympathetic look. "Look, bud, my only advice for you is to find a place to hide, soon."

"What I need to find soon is a restroom."

After using the facilities, a cab returned Matt to his home. Somehow the suitcase he had left in the Mini-Cooper had found its way back also. Matt paid the driver and staggered to his front door. His head throbbed, he felt dog-tired, and he still had no idea what had happened. His answering machine had three calls waiting. One was from the local Jeep dealer. The second was from an exterminator that wanted to save him a fortune on pest control. The third was from Reverend Jerry. Pete had died.

Reverend Jerry said he had found a distant cousin of Pete's in Tampa who was making the funeral arrangements. The reverend had gone to see Pete's wife in the nursing home, but she gave no reaction to the news. He closed his message by saying, "If you want to talk, you can call me day or night. I'm praying for you, Matt."

Matt stripped off his clothes and got into the shower. It was easier there: no one could see him cry, no one could judge him. He wasn't sure if his tears were for Pete's death or because of the throbbing pain in his head. *Or are they in response to my most recent failure?* He had moved to Florida seeking a life of adventure. Why was it that each time adventure was at hand it slipped away, leaving him to deal with the disastrous consequences? *Is this all part of God's plan for my life?*

"Maybe I should return to PA," he muttered. "I'll go back to my shack in the woods. There I'll touch no one and no one can touch me."

Chapter 25

"Would you like a drink, Dex?" Desmond asked.

"No, thanks, I like to keep a clear head when discussing security."

"It is not anything that important. Someone burgled Alba's home last night. Nothing is missing, but Madame Adolphe has hired a security firm to guard her majesty's palace. It is more for peace of mind than anything else. All the valuable artwork was removed some time ago."

"I could take care of security for her place," Dex said. "Just let me pick out a few of our own people." An elderly man running laps in the rooftop garden distracted Dex. "Who is that?"

"That is Anton Car . . . I mean, that is Doctor Zhan. He is Madame Adolphe's houseguest."

"Didn't I meet him when I first got here?"

"No, no, that was someone else. Dr Zhan is Madame's companion. Just ignore him. The less you know about him the better."

"That's an odd attitude for a security professional."

"You Americans have an expression about minding your own business. Considering the near fiasco in Georgetown, I would think that you had enough to keep you busy."

"Yes, Dexter, what kind of buffoon do you have working for you?" Helene Adolphe had entered the room wearing a black business suit and a shocking-pink blouse, its ruffled collar designed to hide her sagging skin.

"I haven't spoken to the man yet, but if you're displeased by his performance, he's gone."

"Displeased isn't the word, Rubino. He assaulted one of my best associates and endangered a very lucrative business transaction."

"I'm sorry, Helene. It won't happen again. I'll give him to the end of the month to clear out of the home Windswept provided for him."

Quest cleared his throat. "Dex, I don't think you realize how important these transactions are to our corporate income. Our investors need a reliable way to make discreet deposits to their retirement accounts. Those investments are what enable us to build resorts, cruise ships, and casinos to cater to consumers. Anyone who attempts to interfere with our operation must be eliminated."

"Rubino, this man is a threat to your investment as well," said Madame Adolphe. "If some of our other investors knew of this man's actions, your life would be in danger. It would be advantageous for you to take care of this problem before word gets out."

"I'll take care of it. Don't give it another thought. I could also solve the security problems for Alba's mansion. As I was telling Desmond, with a few of our security personnel, I could turn that place into a fortress."

"Do not trouble yourself, Rubino. I've already contacted a security firm. Their guards are going to be there by midnight."

"Can you really trust outsiders to handle this? This is the home of Alba Cologne. The average security guard would be awestruck. Why not have my team take care of it for you?"

Quest shook his head. "Dex, the cruise embarks in two weeks. I need you onboard to finalize the security details."

"You're capable of handling those meager details, Desmond."

Helene Adolphe hissed at Dex. "Rubino, I have the final say in this. The *New Dawn* is your priority. One of our associates can deal with the imbecile in the States. Alba's home is of little consequence to the corporation."

"If Alba is worried about her home, it may affect her performance."

"I will worry about my niece, you worry about the ship."

A perspiring Anton Carmella burst into the room. "This guy givin' you a hard time, honey?"

"No, Anton, everything is all right. You should go, Rubino."

"Yeah, you'd better go, Rubio. Little squirt like you could get hurt around here." Anton charged Dex and swung at him. Dex ducked the punch and stepped aside, taking a boxer's stance, fists poised for action.

"The name is Rubino, Doctor Zhan. I have no quarrel with you. What's your problem?"

"Rubino? I thought she said Rubio. You a Piazon? Me, too. I'm Anton Carmella." The big man offered his hand and as Dex took it, Anton pulled him close and wrapped his arms around him in a great bear hug. "You take care of this Dago, honey. He's all right. Where are your people from, pal?"

"My great-grandfather was from Naples. Now I live near Naples, Florida."

"Ha ha, that is so cool! My people are all from Calabria; thick heads and weak ankles. Not this guy, though. I work out. The meds I'm on have me sailin' like I was nineteen. No more arthritis for me. Desi, get my pal a drink of that vino!"

Helene approached Anton cautiously. "Dear heart, Mr. Rubino is on duty. He is in charge of security on the ship. He really must go now."

"OK, but when the cruise begins, you and me are going to knock a few back, right Rubino?"

"Yes, sir. I really must be going."

Turning to Quest, Anton pointed toward the elevator. "Why don't you walk my friend out, Desi? It's time for me and Madame to play a little game of cowboy and squaw."

"Madame and I have important business to discuss."

Helene waved Quest toward the elevator door. "We will take care of business tomorrow, Mr. Quest."

"Are you sure, Madame?"

"Yes, I can handle him. Walk Rubino down to his car and call me in the morning."

In the elevator, Dex began grilling Desmond Quest. "I met Doctor Zhan when I first got here. That is not the same man."

"Indeed not. You heard him say that his nutritional supplements made him feel like a youth again."

"That's not the same person, Quest. He said his name was Anton Carmella."

"Senility is a cruel disease."

"He didn't seem senile to me."

"Doctor Zhan is a long-time investor in the Windswept Corporation. Madame takes pity on him and allows him to stay in her penthouse. Frankly, he is none of your concern."

"What about Alba's home? Who was in charge of security there?"

As the elevator reached the lobby, Quest ushered Dex to the front door. "Alba's home is not a Windswept property. At one time, we provided security services as a favor for

Philippe when he lived there. Where is your vehicle, Dexter?"

"I came here in a cab. Shouldn't you provide the same services to Alba as you did her father?"

"Alba has her own resources. Before you retire for the night, please take care of that courier's elimination. We have associates in Miami that could handle it for you."

"Just leave it to me."

Chapter 26

As had become custom, Dex met Captain Auesnehmer for breakfast. "What are you reading, Emile?"

"The damage reports from Sunset Cay. Some of the docks for small craft were damaged by a fishing vessel."

"Will that affect our trip?"

"No, we don't dock at Sunset Cay. We will pick up a mooring a mile offshore. The guests will be shuttled to the island by tender boats. The only damage to the island was a little beach erosion and the docks in the old marina."

"The 'old marina'?"

"It is no longer in operation. At one time Windswept was glad to welcome small vessels to dock there, but Madame decided to make the island a nearly exclusive resort for our cruise ship passengers. What money they do not gamble away on the ship, they can lose in the hotel casino." The captain shook his head. "Madame will not be pleased." The captain set the papers down on the table as a server set his breakfast before him.

"Do you mean that the hotel facilities are only used when the ship is there?" Dex asked.

"No, the resort guests that are there now flew in. My understanding is that some of our passengers will remain on the island and fly out at a later date. A few may remain there until our return."

"I know there's an old landing strip on the island. Is there regular air service?"

"No, only charter flights from Nassau."

"Does it look like we will encounter any more hurricanes?"

"Possibly." The captain paused to sip his coffee, then resumed. "We may need to reschedule our departures from some ports-of–call, but nothing serious. With our modern technology, we can avoid most problems. Tell me friend, where were you yesterday?"

"I needed a change of scenery."

"What, you are tired of looking at the grizzled face of this old seafarer?"

"Not at all, Captain. I just decided to stay in town last night."

"You met a young lady?"

Dex tried to force a blush. "Let's just say a lady mature beyond her years."

As the captain and Dex chuckled, Omar appeared at their table. "May I see you for a moment, Mr. Rubino?"

"Sure, son, but remember the name is Dex. Always call me Dex." He stood and accompanied his young friend to the rail, then noticed Omar's trembling hands.

"Mr. Quest was waiting for me this morning. He wanted to know why I was absent yesterday."

"Did you tell him your scooter broke down in the rain?"

"Yes, but I do not think he believed me. He asked if I had been to Saint Cugat lately."

"What did you tell him?"

"I told him that I had friends that went to school there and that I had visited them a few times."

"Did he say anything about Alba's place?"

"No."

"Good, just play it cool for now. If he says anything else to you, let me know. Now go about your duties as if nothing happened."

"Yes, sir."

Suddenly, the beauty of Alba Cologne arrested Dex's vision. She was dressed in a form-fitting rehearsal costume that left little to the man's imagination. "Good morning, Ms. Cologne."

"Good morning, Dexter. Must I remind you to call me Alba?"

Dex smiled. "Alba, the Arabic word for dawn, isn't it?"

"Yes, a tribute to my father's heritage."

"I don't believe I've ever seen a prettier sunrise, Alba."

She released a slight giggle. "Surely you jest, Dexter. I hardly slept last night. I must look like a haggard old woman. Who is your young friend?"

Omar smiled at the beauty. "Can it be you do not recognize me, my princess?"

"Omar! I never would have known you. What are you doing here?"

Dex watched sheepishly as the entertainer embraced the young man that he thought of as his sidekick.

"I am working for the security department of Windswept. Mr. Rubino is acting as my mentor."

"Is he treating you well?"

Turning to Rubino, she wrapped one arm around the shoulders of the grinning young man. "Omar's family has worked for my family for generations. His father was my protector when I was a little girl. How is your father, Omar?"

"Not too well. The years since his injury have been difficult."

"I am so sorry to hear that. What about your brother?"

Omar gave a sidelong glance to Dex. "He is doing well. He often asks about you. If you will excuse me, I must return to my duties."

"I understand, but we must meet soon. We have a lot to catch up on."

As Omar walked away, Alba moved closer to Dexter. Her voice took on a sadder tone. "Seeing Omar brings so many memories to mind. When he was a little boy, he helped care for the horses I kept at my home. Now, he is a young man. Suddenly I feel very old and very vulnerable."

"Don't let these things trouble you."

"Someone has broken into my home. The caretaker called Mr. Quest yesterday morning to report the damage. Nothing was taken, but I find the idea of someone invading my private home quite unnerving."

"Mr. Quest and Madame Adolphe informed me of the break-in. I offered to set up a security detail to protect your interests, but Madame wants me to concentrate on my shipboard duties. She has already contacted a security firm to look after your place."

"I find no comfort in having more strangers prowling around my home. It may seem silly, but I grew up there. I hate the thought of some strange men handling my possessions. I would feel much better if you and I could go there and assess the security needs."

"I'm afraid it's impossible. Helene was adamant about it. I'm sure the security firm she has chosen will protect your property. Don't let a little thing like this make you anxious. You need to concentrate on your performance."

Alba gripped his bicep as she slinked even closer. "I have heard that Desmond Quest is living on the boat now. Surely you could slip away this afternoon and accompany me to my home. I need the advice of a man I can trust."

"The captain and I are going over some security details this afternoon. I won't be able to get away." Dex patted her shoulder as she sunk her head into his chest. "Alba, is there something at the house you're worried about in particular?"

As she sobbed, she explained. "My father purchased that home for me shortly after my mother's death. Aunt Helene raised me there. It has always been a sanctuary for me. Now even it has been violated." She wrapped her arms around him. "I'm so alone, Dexter."

Dex saw the captain steal a glance in his direction. "Alba, you are not alone. Everyone on this ship is on your side." He gradually pushed her away and raised his voice in a fatherly tone. "All of Windswept is depending on you. Some of the finest people in Europe have booked passage on this voyage just to see you perform. Unless there is something irreplaceable at the house, put it out of your mind. Is there anything there that you treasure?"

"No, Dexter, there is nothing irreplaceable, just a lifetime of memories."

"On this cruise you'll be making the memories of a lifetime for thousands of your fans. Isn't that the ultimate dream of every entertainer? Aren't you late for rehearsal?"

She smiled at Dex as she wiped away nonexistent tears. "You are right, Dexter; I owe it to my fans." Alba turned and walked away, pausing to look over her shoulder at Dex and give him a shy smile before she climbed the stairs. Dex returned to the table where the captain was finishing his meal.

"Are you not ordering breakfast today, Dex?"

"Yes, Emile, I apologize for the interruptions. I am actually quite hungry this morning."

"I thought that you might be full after having scorpion for breakfast." The captain stood and bowed to his friend.

"Please excuse me; I have things to tend to. I'll see you on the bridge this afternoon."

"Very well." When his friend was out of earshot, Dex opened his phone and dialed Matt Narvik's number. The call went to voice mail. "Matt, I suppose you knew this call was coming. You really blew your assignment. The Windswept team and I are very disappointed in you. You are hereby terminated. I have arranged for you to be able to stay in the house until the end of the month. Please be gone before that. I'll have your severance pay sent to your PO Box. I suggest you leave the area as soon as possible. Remember, everything you know about Windswept or me is confidential. If you violate that confidentiality, the authorities would be interested in the true nature of your boating accident. There is no need for you to contact me. Just clear out of the house by the end of the month. Also, be sure to cancel your passage on the *New Dawn*. I have everything under control here. Goodbye, Matt. Good luck in your future endeavors."

After his meeting with Captain Auesnehmer, Dex went on the hunt for Omar. He spotted the youngster leaving a break room below decks. Dex called to him, his voice echoing down the steel-walled corridor. "Omar!"

Omar slowly turned. "Yes, Dex?"

Dex jogged to where his sidekick stood. "Why didn't you tell me you knew Alba Cologne?"

"You never asked me."

"Don't try to get cute, kid. You knew any relationship with the management of Windswept would be of interest to me. The whole time we wandered around that old castle you never mentioned having been there before."

"I was there when I was a little boy but never in the main house. My father was a servant. We were not invited guests."

"Why didn't you tell me?"

"It didn't seem important. Most of the security personnel have been with Alba's family for generations. We have known Alba for many years. You are the stranger."

"Is there anything else you haven't told me?"

"You heard Alba ask about my brother. They were involved romantically when they were young."

"How involved were they?"

"I do not know. I was a child. Alba was still making cinema films at the time. Her Aunt Helene did not approve of her seeing a servant. I believe it was she who sent my brother away."

"Where is your brother now?"

Omar smiled. "He is a very successful importer living in the UK."

"So why are you working for Windswept? Wouldn't you be better off working for your brother?"

"I felt a sense of loyalty to Alba. Besides, London is cold and damp."

Chapter 27

Following a belated workout, Matt Narvik walked toward his home. He was disappointed in the day's performance. Each time he exerted himself, his head began throbbing. He felt a little dizzy as his thoughts raced. *How was he going to explain his actions to Dex?* As he continued down the street, he spotted his Jeep parked in the drive. "How did you get here?" he muttered. He considered the fact that some unsavory character had returned his vehicle and might want to deliver a message from his adversaries.

Using his neighbor's hedges as cover, he slipped to the rear of his home and peered into the windows. All seemed as he had left it. He decided to enter through the side door in the garage and grabbed a hammer as he passed by the Crossfire. He opened the door into the kitchen and scanned his surroundings. Nothing appeared to be out of place. The kitchen clock ticked loudly, amplifying the pounding in his head. He crept to his bedroom and opened the top drawer of his dresser. He set the hammer down and silently removed the lid of the cedar-wood box that contained his LCP 380. As he rammed the loaded magazine into the pistol, he heard a noise in the living room. He gripped the tiny pistol with his right hand and cocked it with his left, then spun around ready to fire. Pete's voice echoed in his mind: *palm over palm, thumb over thumb, breath normally, keep your arms rigid, knees bent slightly.* Matt advanced to the living room, pivoted in the doorway, and swept the room with the gun site. Nothing seemed amiss.

Matt trembled as he sat down in his rocking chair. "I have to call Dex. I have to tell him what happened," he whispered. He pulled his phone from his waistband and discovered the battery was dead. "Guess I'll have to charge it up first." He plugged his phone into the charger and slipped the pistol into the pocket of his workout shorts. He walked out of his front door to the Jeep. The driver's seat had been adjusted for a shorter driver and the key was in the ignition. He retrieved the key and reentered the house. "I'll get a shower while the phone is charging. Time for some more power potion, too." Matt marched to the kitchen cupboard, opened the unlabeled white plastic bottle, and shook out four tablets. Power potion was the name Pete had given it. Four tablets four times daily, one hundred tablets to a bottle and Matt was starting his fourth bottle. Eight more waited in storage.

After his shower, Matt caught a glimpse of himself in the bathroom mirror. His pectoral muscles had developed dramatically, his shoulders were broader, and his biceps and triceps were beyond anything he had ever experienced. Still the ravages of time had left its mark on his face. His hair looked more white than blonde. He was an old man with a younger man's body, but a lonely man still. He dressed and decided the time difference might mean Dex had retired for the night. *I'll call him tomorrow.* Matt squeezed his holstered pistol inside his waistband, then headed to the eatery he enjoyed most. A bowl of chili always improved his outlook.

On his way home, he passed the Cineplex in the Bell Tower Shops. The marquee had the name of the latest George Clooney film emblazoned on it. He decided he deserved some light-hearted entertainment and went to see the film. As the story line unfolded, he became aware that it centered on an assassination plot. This film wasn't the exciting spy movie Hollywood usually provided. It was much more realistic, at least much more like his reality.

Returning home, he drove past his house. It was dark, as he had left it. He proceeded to a convenience store and turned around. As he approached his drive, he jerked the wheel to the left and drove through the lawn. Brushing past some hedges, he pulled in behind the house. His headlights illuminated the rear of his dwelling, and he was satisfied no one was around. He killed the engine and the lights, and crept to his back door, pistol in hand. He heard the neighbor's hound barking wildly, which was as unusual. He entered the house and checked each of the darkened rooms before noticing the illumination of his cell phone on the kitchen bar. Confident he was alone, he picked the phone up checked for messages.

After listening to the message Dex had left, Matt felt like crumpling to the floor. Then a blinding rage swept over him, and he pitched the phone into the living room. It hit the back of his couch and bounced onto the floor. He let out an angry howl that rebooted the neighborhood dogs. He tried to reason with himself.

"Calm down, Narvik," he said aloud. "It doesn't matter. You don't need to be chained to some job anyway."

Think about the money you have in the bank. The insurance settlement from the boat, your pension payments, plus most of what Windswept has paid you. You're not hurting for money. Who needs Dexter Rubino and his stupid job? But what about the cruise? I was hoping to see Alba again. If I could see her, we could start fresh.

"Rubino can't stop me from going," he muttered. "What can he do now that he's fired me?" Matt was so keyed up he knew he had to relax. He stripped off his clothes and put on the new swimsuit he had purchased for the next cruise. He grabbed his MP3 player and set it to his Beach Boy playlist. Walking through his darkened house, he went to the back porch and removed the cover from his hot tub.

Matt boosted the volume to drown out the baying hounds of the Villas and tried to let the bubbling streams of heated water lure him to relaxation. He imagined his mind as a black board. As each thought appeared he would quickly erase it.

Alba has forgotten you—erase.

You're a failure—erase.

You should be meditating on God's word—erase.

It was beginning to work; the mellow harmonies of his favorite group were helping him relax. *When I leave here, I will have to take the hot tub with me*—erase.

A weight suddenly bore down on him, forcing his head under water. Two strong hands throttled his neck. The force of the attack propelled Matt into the deeper center of the tub. He felt the attacker's hands tighten their grip as Matt began to slip away. Instinctively, Matt reached over his head and gripped the hair of his assailant, then spun his body and pulled the attacker halfway into the tub. Gulping for air, he savagely kidney punched the assassin. He kept punching as the body of his attacker flailed helplessly beneath him. The neighborhood dogs barked in a panic as Matt locked his legs around the assailant's head and continued to pummel the body below him. When his fist struck the grip of a revolver holstered in the small of the man's back, he winced with pain and stopped. The body no longer moved, and Matt raised its head above the water line and tried to see if he recognized him. *Too dark, but I can't turn on the porch light.* Matt wrestled the body out of the tub and dragged it into his kitchen.

What if he wasn't alone? Matt looked out of the window to the empty street. *He had to have driven here. Check his pockets.* Matt found a large roll of cash, a set of keys, and a wallet. The only auto key bore a Lincoln emblem. Matt opened the wallet. The assailant's Ohio driver's license indicated his name was Rocco Vecchiarelli, if it could be believed.

Matt dressed and carefully pocketed his .380. He slipped out his front door and walked down the street, reigniting the furor of the hound next door. When he got to the convenience store, he saw a powder-blue Lincoln parked in the shadows. He approached the vehicle cautiously and saw no one inside. The driver's door was unlocked so Matt got in. He started the car and drove back to his home. He backed up to the garage door. *Rocco Vecchiarelli's fancy ride is about to become his casket.* Matt exited the car and opened the trunk. Two aluminum briefcases were there, similar to the one he had carried to Grand Cayman.

If this is more candy, I'll use it to choke Dexter Rubino.

Matt removed the cases and carried them inside. He turned on the lights and on the floor of his kitchen lay the body of the only man he had ever killed. The man's pale face and blue lips caused Matt's stomach to churn. He ran to the sink and vomited. He ran the cold water to rinse out the sink, then cupped his hand under the faucet. He brought the cool liquid to his lips and gulped as he rinsed the taste of vomited chili from his mouth. Looking down at the dead man, he whispered, "God please forgive me. It was kill or be killed. What else could I do? Oh, please, Lord, I don't want to be responsible for this man going to hell."

Focus Narvik, you have to get rid of this guy and leave here for good.

Matt checked the man's pockets again, removed the revolver and holster, then dragged the body to the garage and opened the door. He paused to look in each direction. The neighborhood dogs continued to bark as he stuffed the lifeless form of Rocco into the trunk. Returning to the house, he locked all the doors and turned out the lights, then he drove the Lincoln north to Colonial Boulevard and turned east to the railroad crossing where the bike path ended. Turning north again, he left the roadway and, with his lights out, followed the grassy path that ran parallel to the railroad tracks. He bounced along for about a half a mile, then nosed the big car into a thicket of small trees. The impact wasn't sufficient to trigger the airbags. Matt left the car and crept from shadow to shadow until he reached the road. He sprinted across the boulevard and followed the bike path back to his own neighborhood.

By the time he returned home, Matt was soaked with sweat and the full impact of what had transpired had begun to hit him. He turned on his kitchen light and saw the puddle where Rocco had lain. The two briefcases stood next to the bar. *Shower first, then I'll dissect some chicks.*

Chapter 28

Alba Cologne sat alone at a table in the Sultan's Palace restaurant. She hoped that by meeting her dinner guest there, she could assess the ability of the servers and the quality of the food. Like Helene, she wanted supreme quality to be associated with the Windswept name. *Helene is an old woman, eventually this will all be mine.*

"Ms. Cologne."

Alba looked up into the smiling face of her young guest. He held a yellow rose in an outstretched hand. "Omar, thank you for joining me. What a beautiful rose. Thank you. Please be seated, and stop calling me Ms. Cologne. You must always call me Alba."

"Are you certain? I don't wish to overstep my bounds. I am just a humble intern in the ship's security staff. Mashal told me you always preferred yellow roses."

"You are family, Omar. I will see to it that you have a promotion in rank before we sail."

"It is not important what rank I hold, only that I am of service to you. I do not seek any special treatment because of our family's shared histories. Mr. Rubino has taken me under his wing and is teaching me valuable lessons. May I ask why we are speaking English?"

"Most of the crew speaks English and most of the guests will as well. I have attained the rights to my old films and are having them dubbed in English. I hope to have them rereleased in the US. It is an important part of renewing my career. Dexter Rubino is a valuable man. Does he know of our history?"

"No, he was quite surprised that we knew each other."

"Your English is excellent. Have you spent time in the US?"

"A short time, but I attended university in London. Mashal lives there."

"Yes, you mentioned that. How is your brother doing these days?"

"He is prospering. I hope you harbor no ill feelings because of the way he left your father's employ."

"He left my father to work for al-Qaeda. They took control of some of my father's business ventures and he fell in line. It is nothing to be upset about. It is just business."

"Every time I speak to him, he asks about you. I doubt that he could ever marry anyone else."

Alba genuinely blushed. "Omar, your brother and I were just children when we became lovers. I am sure he has forgotten about me."

"I am certain he has not. If you ever needed his help, he would be anxious to provide it."

Alba smiled, "That is good to know."

Dexter Rubino let the Labor Day holiday pass without celebration. There was just too much work to do. The plethora of video cameras in the casino had to be switched to a separate circuit from the other security cameras. The monitors for these were hastily installed in what had been Dexter's tiny office.

Helene hired a separate staff to monitor the casino gaming tables. She had lured them away from a competitor. Dex resented not having any input into the decision, but Helene dismissed him by saying, "Just take care of the external security needs, Rubino. Leave internal matters to me."

As Matt dissected the marshmallow chicks, he realized what he had actually transported to Grand Cayman: tiny gold bars, each stamped with the figure "2 oz.," sixty bars in each case. *No wonder that case felt so heavy.* Then he exclaimed aloud. "Holy cow!" *Gold is over a thousand dollars per troy ounce. That's one hundred twenty thousand dollars a case!*

Matt wrapped the gold bars in a black garbage bag and placed it in one of the aluminum cases. He then went to his back porch and opened the access door of the hot tub. There was just enough room to get the case inside, and he slid it to the farthest corner.

Back inside the house, Matt quickly packed his belongings and stowed them in his Jeep. He placed Rocco's revolver, ID, and credit cards in the remaining case and placed it under his passenger's seat. Then he counted the roll of bills and whistled quietly.

Twelve hundred dollars. Thank you, Rocco. This will help pay for my escape.

After a stop at the ATM machine to ensure he had enough cash, Matt headed north on I-75. His eyes grew heavy as he drove, so he pulled into a rest stop near Venice. There he stretched out on the bench of a picnic table, but as he dreamed, the face of Rocco Vecchiarelli appeared. Matt woke with a start, and for a moment felt disoriented. Once his mind cleared, he resumed driving northward until he reached the exit for I-275.

He headed toward Tampa and pulled off before he crossed the Sunshine Parkway Bridge. The remnants of the original bridge had been repurposed as a fishing pier. Matt found a lonely area, parked, and pulled the aluminum case from beneath the passenger's seat. He took a large screwdriver from his tool kit and punched ten holes in the metal case. He scanned the area to make sure he wasn't under observation. No security cameras in sight. He left the Jeep with the case, walked to the railing, and dropped the case into the water. "Saltwater corrodes everything," he whispered. He patiently watched as the case sank and the trail of air bubbles disappeared.

Matt reversed course and returned to I-75 north, where he transitioned to I-4 east and headed to Orlando. *It's always easier to hide in a crowd.*

Matt used his GPS to find a hotel near the interstate. He saw the name Buena Vista Palace and associated that with Disney. When he reached the hotel, he backed his vehicle up against a large bush so the license plate wasn't visible. He checked in, hung a "do not disturb" tag on his door, and collapsed into a comfortable bed. Matt awoke in his darkened room unsure of how long he had slept. The noise of a vacuum cleaner echoed down the hall. He located the clock on his nightstand: 7:28. "Must be morning," he whispered.

He pushed himself out of bed and into the shower. As he became more alert, he considered what his game plan should be. *My flight to Barcelona is on the fifteenth. I can lay low here until then. I left my fingerprints all over that Lincoln. When I got my concealed carry license, the state obtained a copy of my fingerprints. If I can just elude them until I leave the country, I'll be OK.* After exiting the shower and toweling off, he hooked up his laptop and checked Yahoo news. In the Fort Myers local news there was no mention of a body being found. No mention of Rocco's demise. *It doesn't matter Narvik, you killed a man and sent his soul to hell. How can you ever atone for that?*

Dexter Rubino spent the balance of the week preparing his staff for every possible scenario. He saw very little of his sidekick, Omar. Alba Cologne had requested Omar's reassignment to her personal security detachment. Dex knew better than to protest. A shadow of distrust had fallen on Dex's young friend, but Dex was too busy to dwell on it. *If Omar mentions our gambit to Saint Cugat, he will only be incriminating himself.*

On Saturday evening, the crew of the *New Dawn* went ashore to enjoy their last weekend before embarkation. Dex spotted Arnan helping Meaghan Miller load her suitcase into a cab. Dex approached the couple and greeted Arnan. "What are you doing, friend? We can't let Meaghan leave us now that her ankle is healed."

"She will be back before we sail, Mr. Rubino."

The perky blonde smiled at Dex with the innocent look of a schoolgirl. "I'm going back to the States for a few days. Just a little visit to my family."

"Have a nice time, Meaghan, but don't forget to come back. Alba has come to depend on you."

"I'm afraid you have it backwards. I've learned so much working with Alba and the rest of the Windswept entertainers, and I just can't wait to be back aboard ship. This is the most exciting thing that's ever happened to me."

"Glad to hear it, kid. Is the fitness center all set to go, Arnan?"

"Yes, sir, Madame Adolphe has allowed me to have a free hand in the operation. It is good to be a part of the Windswept family."

As they pulled away, Dex saw Helene Adolphe leaving the ship, escorted by Desmond Quest. When they reached the pier, he approached them. "Are you leaving for the weekend, Helene?"

"No, I will return tomorrow. There is simply too much to be done. The housekeeping staff is going to be a problem. Few of them speak English and the Philippine dialect of Spanish is incomprehensible to the rest of the crew."

"It truly is an international crew. I'm sure with time these little wrinkles will iron out."

"We cannot afford little wrinkles, Rubino. Are there any wrinkles in your security department? Are you having any problems?"

"Smooth sailing, but I'm sure Desmond has kept you well informed."

"Yes, I just wanted to hear it from you. A wrinkle in your department can become a matter of life and death!"

Chapter 29

Matt availed himself of the family-themed entertainment in the area and enjoyed each park and attraction he visited. The sight of young families and couples enjoying the same environs was heartwarming to him, but he ended each day going back to the hotel alone. He comforted himself with the knowledge that he would soon be seeing Alba.

Sunday morning he skipped the parks and worshiped at a local mega-church. The building dwarfed any church he had seen, and the pipe organ caused the floor to vibrate. He listened to a casually delivered sermon in which the preacher held the attention of thousands without raising his voice. When the pastor issued an invitation at the end of the service, Matt bowed his head and without leaving his seat asked God to direct his path. A vision of Rocco writhing in hell's flames caused him to shutter.

As Matt walked to his Jeep, his phone vibrated. "Hello."

A female voice said, "Hello, I'm trying to reach Matthew Narvik."

"Speaking." then it dawned on him that this might be someone pursuing him.

"Mr. Narvik, my name is Meaghan Miller. I'm calling to congratulate you on being chosen for the Grand Upgrade program for the *New Dawn*, Transatlantic Adventure."

"Pardon me, are you with Windswept?"

"The Windswept Corporation is our parent company. The upgrade program is to reward select passengers for booking early. Your name was picked at random from all early North American entrants."

"I don't remember entering any contest."

"You were entered automatically. Since so few of our guests are from North America, your odds were quite favorable. Actually, this is a little embarrassing for us. We had contacted your hometown newspaper and television news to record the rewarding of your prize. We had hoped the attention would help publicize the cruise line. When we arrived at your home, you were gone."

"I decided to take a little pre-vacation trip." *Lord, please direct my path!*

"Well, it doesn't matter where you are now. The free upgrades are yours and, of course, your traveling companions."

"I plan on traveling alone."

"Are you available to travel earlier than you had planned?"

"I could."

"That's wonderful, Mr. Narvik. What is your current location?"

"I'm in Orlando."

"That was where your original flight was to depart, correct?"

"Yes."

"If it suits your schedule, I could have you on a first-class flight from Orlando to Barcelona via Atlanta on Tuesday morning. I will arrange for a luxury hotel room until our embarkation date. A personally guided tour of Barcelona will be included, of course."

"Why would Windswept do all this for me?"

"Because you're the grand prize winner, Mr. Narvik. I'll meet you at the Air France ticket counter. You can cash in your old ticket and the new one will be complements of Windswept."

That's on this side of security. I'll have to sneak around the airport and make sure it isn't a trap. "All right, I'll meet you at the Air France desk. What time?"

"It is an early flight, seven AM sharp, Mr. Narvik. Please dress appropriately. The press will be there to take a few pictures."

"How will I know you?"

"I'll be the blonde with the reporters. Try to wear a smile, Mr. Narvik. It's your lucky day!"

Omar, supposedly to visit his ailing father, arranged to borrow a company car to enhance his last day off before embarkation. He headed out of Barcelona on C-32 to AP-7. After nearly an hour of driving, he took exit 35, the exit for the Salou Amusement Park. He headed straight to a tiny coffee bar located within the park. There a man was waiting for him.

"Why are you so late?" the man whispered.

"Alba Cologne delayed me. I am on her personal security staff now."

"Very good. Keep your voice down. How well is she guarded?"

"Two men are nearby at all times. I think her great aunt is more interested in controlling her than protecting her. I have searched her old home and found nothing to indicate the device is there, but I have information Mashal will be interested in."

"Please, I do not wish to hear stories about an old love affair."

"No, it is not that. There is a laboratory in the basement of Alba's home. I thought it odd at first, but then I heard Alba mention Doctor Zhan."

"Are you certain?"

"Yes, Alba was joking about her aunt's lover, Doctor Zhan. He will be aboard the ship when it sails. If he is involved with Helene Adolphe, we can be sure the gold he stole has gone to Windswept."

"When does the ship sail?"

"Saturday evening. I know where Helene Adolphe lives. Let me see if Zhan is there."

The man slowly stroked his beard as he thought. "No, you are not to act without specific orders. If Zhan is trying to disappear by sailing away, we can turn his escape into a trap. There is a handsome price on his head."

"Let me find him now. I can kill the thief without any help from Mashal."

"No, Zhan is more valuable alive. He has knowledge worth more than the gold he stole. Mashal will make the decision." The man reached into his backpack and retrieved a satellite phone. "You are only to make emergency calls on this phone; the ringer has been disabled. Mashal or I will leave you a message when we have instructions for you. What are your ports of call?"

"We sail from Barcelona on Saturday but don't arrive in Gibraltar until Monday. Then we sail to Madeira, arriving on Wednesday. From there we cross the Atlantic to St. Maarten, then on to Sunset Cay."

The man chuckled. "Madeira, I've always liked Madeira. You have done well, Omar. Do not let your success cause you to act on your own. When we strike is up to Mashal. Keep that phone hidden and check for our messages frequently."

"How is my brother?"

"He is well and enjoying the desert. Any news of your father?"

"I plan on stopping to see him on my way back to the ship."

As the man stood to leave he said, "Give my regards to the old Haddad."

"What about Alba?"

"That is a decision for Mashal. "

Chapter 30

Matt spent Monday morning renting a storage facility for the few things he had brought with him. After lunching at Planet Hollywood, he caught the same movie he had just seen in Fort Myers at a nearby theater. As the sun set, he wandered around the Disney Marketplace. He noticed the little girls dressed as Disney princesses. He had a full-grown princess of his own waiting in Barcelona, he hoped.

He parked his Jeep at the airport, in the long-term lot, then stowed his .380 in the glove box, *I wish I could take you along,* then cautiously made his way to level three of the terminal and located the Air France ticket counter which was deserted. He casually wandered around looking for any possible assailants or reporters. Matt was still convinced that Windswept was responsible for his attacker.

"Mr. Narvik?"

Matt turned to see an attractive blonde, whom he judged to be in her early twenties. She held a cluster of helium balloons in her hand, two unshaven young men stood behind her. He braced for an attack, "Yes, I'm Matt Narvik."

"Congratulations, Mr. Narvik!" she said as she thrust the balloons toward him. The men behind her raised expensive looking cameras and began taking his picture.

"I take it you're Meaghan Miller."

"Yes, but please just call me Meaghan. I'm so excited for you, Mr. Narvik. Is this the first time you've won anything?"

"Yes, it is."

One of the men spoke. "OK, Meaghan, we have all we need."

"Oh, no. Wait! Get one of us together. Smile, Mr. Narvik." She took Matt's arm and put her cheek to his bicep. She gave his arm a squeeze and said, "Wow, big guns, Mr. Narvik." Turning toward the cameras, she smiled while a flurry of electronic flashes blinded them. "That's enough. Email those to the address I gave you, OK, guys?" She looked up at Matt and smiled. "I want a copy of that one."

"Will do, Meaghan. You'll have to sign this release, Mr. Narvik."

After Matt signed the paperwork, Meaghan escorted him to the ticket counter while an Air France representative appeared from a back room. They quickly finalized the travel arrangements and headed toward the train that connects to the gate area.

"Is this all the luggage you have?" Meaghan asked.

"Yes, I believe in traveling light. Can I get rid of these balloons now?"

"Sure, just tie them off to the railing there. Somebody will enjoy them. If a woman would have won, we would have brought flowers, but you don't seem to be a bouquet kind of guy to me. The balloons were to give the photos a festive feel. I hope you don't mind."

"Why would I mind? First class has to be better than coach."

"Oh, this is just for starters. You'll get luxury accommodations before and during your cruise, a shopping spree in Barcelona and guided tours to all the points of interest on the voyage."

"Wow that will be nice."

"Best of all, you'll get to meet the captain and ship's officers. You even get to see Alba Cologne perform. You may not have heard of her, but she is a great entertainer. She's been a movie star in Europe and is the main attraction for the cruise. She is such a lovely person. I just adore her."

When they reached the security gate, Matt finally found the words to respond. "Thank you for being so helpful, Meaghan, but I'll get through security on my own."

"Oh, you don't understand, Mr. Narvik. I'm going with you. I'm to be your escort for the entire trip. From here on, Matthew . . . your wish is my command!"

Dex patted Omar on the shoulder. "Thank you for attending our little meeting, Omar."

"If you'll excuse me, I'll return to my duties."

"Just a minute, Omar." Desmond smiled slyly at the young man as he placed his open hand on Omar's chest. "How is your father?"

Omar swallowed hard. "He is doing as well as can be expected for a man his age."

"Did he enjoy the amusement park?"

"I went to the amusement park alone. I stopped at his home on my way back."

"Oh, I see. You can return to your duties, Omar."

As Omar left the room, Desmond approached Rubino. "Your protégé deserves watching. His family has a long history of disservice to Madame Adolphe. If she had known who he was, she would never have hired him."

"Alba was glad to see him aboard. If you believe he's a security risk, we should get rid of him before we sail. How did you know where he went?"

"The vehicle he borrowed was equipped with a GPS tracking device. Madame Adolphe has decided that he may prove useful. Just keep a close watch on the little viper."

Anton Carmella reclined on a chaise as he tried to lasso the Catalonian sun with the smoke rings from his cigar. "Sit down and relax, honey. You're going to wear a rut in the roof."

Helene Adolphe continued pacing across her rooftop garden. "How can I relax? I have a fully staffed ship sitting at dock waiting for fifteen hundred people to wander into town. My reputation is at risk as well as the financial future of Windswept."

"Que, sera sera—whatever will be, will be."

"I can't afford your cavalier attitude. I've spent my entire career trying to succeed where the men of my family have failed."

Anton patted her buttocks as she walked by. "Calm down. It ain't no big thing. The ship is sold out, you got a good crew, and everything will go off without a hitch."

"I wish I shared your confidence."

"Come on, baby, curl up here with me and tell me more about Belize."

"Why does your driver not call? How are we to know if he has completed his mission?"

"Don't worry about Rocco. He's been with me for years. I've trusted him with the delivery of my life's savings. Even Quest says he's a good guy. I'm sure he could knock off some Florida bagman."

"Perhaps he has contacted Desmond. I'll call and find out."

Anton gripped her wrist and pulled her toward him. She tried to resist but Anton's strength and the feebleness of her heels caused her to fall atop him. "Stop fretting about business. You're my woman. That means you come when I call."

Helene struggled against his embrace. "Stop it, Anton! I'm the president of the Windswept Corporation, not some call girl."

Anton flipped her on her back and using one hand pinned her wrists above her head. "Call girl? Listen you old hag, I ain't never paid for it, and I ain't about to start now!" He used his free hand to slap Helene's face repeatedly. "You oughta get on your knees and thank me for even looking in your direction."

"Anton, stop this at once!"

"I'll stop when I'm done and not before."

Chapter 31

On the first leg of their flight, Meaghan quizzed Matt about his background. She took notes on a steno pad as he answered each inquiry. While Matt found some of the questions invasive, he enjoyed the attention of an attractive woman as much as any man.

"So you're an orphan? That must have been a hard way to grow up."

"Yes, but I had some positive role models in my life."

"How long were you a steelworker?"

Matt hesitated before answering. "Longer than you've been alive. How long have you been a reporter?"

"Oh, I'm not with the press. I work for Windswept. Until a few months ago, I was a dancer. I had a little accident and broke my ankle. Instead of getting rid of me, Windswept kept me on as a personal assistant to Alba Cologne. It was she that decided I should come to the States and be your escort."

Matt grinned. "Really? Alba knows I'm coming?"

"Yes, the names of the winners were announced in a staff meeting. She, like, asked me to be your escort for the entire cruise."

"Did she say anything else about me?"

"No, she was concerned that an American might feel out of place aboard ship. Like, since I'm an American, they sent me to award your prize."

"Why would I feel out of place? Millions of Americans take cruises every year."

"This cruise is geared to a European mindset. There will be few US citizens aboard."

"I'm sure I can adjust."

"I'm willing to help with your adjustment any way I can, Matthew."

Alba Cologne leaned over a computer in the ship's business center. She shook her head in frustration and slammed her tiny fist into the keyboard.

"Can I be of assistance, Ms. Cologne?"

"Oh, Omar, I did not see you come in. These machines must be defective. I can't get this picture to print out."

"Let me try it for you. Here now, what size do you wish?"

"As big as I can get."

"Very well, we will do a full page. Now I'll click on print." The printer grunted and groaned as it printed out a portrait of Meaghan and Matt Narvik.

"Thank you, Omar. I'm afraid that I'm hopelessly techno-challenged."

"I recognize Miss Meaghan, but who is the gentleman?"

"It is some relative of hers, a brother I believe."

"He looks too old to be her brother. Perhaps it is her father. Do you wish to print out the rest of the pictures in this album?"

"Yes, print them all out, and then you can return to your duties."

"Fulfilling your wishes is my utmost duty, Alba." He stared into the notorious dark eyes of Alba Cologne. "I stopped to see my father a few days ago, and he asked about you. He prays that Allah will smile upon you and your latest venture."

"That is very sweet of him. Please thank him for me the next time you speak with him."

"I'm afraid that I'll not see him until our return."

"Won't you phone him before we sail?"

"There is no point; he is quite deaf. He has been since the explosion. Fortunately, Mashal has provided him with full-time care."

"Oh, the poor man. It is good of your brother to care for him."

"Yes, Mashal is a very good man."

Desmond Quest exited his vehicle and made his way to the express elevator of Helene's building. *At least when we are all onboard the ship I won't have to travel across town every time I'm summoned.* When he reached the penthouse level, all the curtains were drawn and the lights were out. He poked around the foyer looking for a switch and noticed the door to Madame's office was ajar. He knocked softly as he eased the door open. The only light in the room came from the computer screen on her desk. The desk chair was turned facing a blank wall. Desmond thought he saw it move a little. "Madame?"

The chair spun around. It was Madame Helene Adolphe but not as Desmond had ever seen her. Her bruised face and swollen lips caused Quest to step back.

"Hello, Desmond," she said, her voice sounding tried and dry.

"Madame, what has happened?"

"Nothing. I called you here to escort Anton to the ship."

"I thought you planned on keeping him here until the day we sailed."

"I have changed my plans. Remember, you are to refer to him as Doctor Zhan. Have you heard from his driver yet?"

"No, I've tried calling him several times and left messages."

"Could he have embezzled any of Anton's investment?"

"No, I believe he has been a trusted employee for a number of years."

"Have you heard from the Caymans?"

"Yes, Madame, they will arrive the day before we sail. They have gone to New York to do some shopping."

"Good, now about Anton. According to our records, he was advanced half a million dollars on the strength of his inventory. His subsequent deposits were only three hundred thousand in gold. We expected a deposit of two million before sailing."

"Remember, we do hold the deed to his farm and house. This could be a simple accounting error. I'll have Vecchiarelli tracked down by some of my contacts in Florida."

"The real estate market in the US is depressed. That farm you refer to is an overgrown wasteland. I want you to escort Anton to the ship and get him into his cabin." She reached into a desk drawer and withdrew a white plastic bottle. "While you are getting him settled, switch this bottle with his supplements."

"What is it?"

"A sedative. He will be easier to handle after taking this."

"Our plan was to wait until he got to Belize."

"The time table has changed. We will wait until we leave Madeira. I have tasked Arnan with Rubino's demise at that point."

"Isn't that going to attract a lot of attention?"

"No. Before sunrise the next day Anton will fall overboard and Dexter will try to rescue him. No one will notice that they are gone until morning. Rubino's passion for heroics will be his undoing."

"I cannot say that I'll miss him."

"Rubino is searching for Philippe's treasure. He may resort to violence in an effort to find it."

"Madame, do you mean to say that there really is a treasure?"

"Philippe thought of it that way. He refused to believe that it had degraded to the point of worthlessness."

Chapter 32

Matt had taken a nap in-flight and awoke to find Meaghan's head resting on his shoulder. Her hair smelled of strawberries. When he shifted in his seat, she seized his arm and snuggled her head against him. After landing, they sailed through customs and caught a cab into town. The cab dropped them a few doors down from the Hotel Murmuri. Matt felt awkward as Meaghan paid the fair and thought he should say something when she gave the driver a two-euro tip. "Meaghan that isn't much of a tip. Give him a couple more."

"No, here you don't tip as much as in the States. People would be insulted if you gave them more than that."

"Let me carry that suitcase for you."

"Thanks, but I can manage it all right."

"Meaghan, I'd be insulted if you didn't let me carry your suitcase."

"All right, Mr. Narvik, I wouldn't want you to be insulted. The hotel is right down here."

They entered and found themselves in a warm and inviting lobby. The desk clerk spoke excellent English and showed them to their rooms. Matt shed his coat and tie and was about to strip down for a shower when he heard a knock at the door. He answered and Meaghan greeted him. "This fruit basket is for you. They put it in my room by mistake."

Matt took the basket. "Thank you, would you like some?"

"No, thanks. Is your room all right?"

Matt stepped back from the door and set the basket on a table.

"Yes, the room is great. I was going to take a shower and then go see the ship."

Meaghan followed him and closed the door behind her. "No way, hombre. Like, security won't let you near until the day we sail. You know there's a water shortage here in Spain. They encourage people to shower together."

Matt was stunned at first but caught a glimpse of a smile on Meaghan's face. "It's not nice to make fun of the old guy."

"I wasn't making fun. We could have fun, if you want. Remember, I said your wish is my command." She placed a hand on his waist.

"I was hoping to see Alba tonight."

Meaghan pulled away. "Afraid not. She is way too busy to see you. You act like you have met her before."

"I did. Didn't she tell you?"

"No, she told me you won the contest and that I was to be your escort and guide."

Can it be that Alba has forgotten me? Matt offered a faint smile. "It's kind of a long story, but I really am anxious to see her again."

"You'll see her onboard. For the rest of the day we could take a bus tour of the city or just, like, stay in and take a nap."

"I'm not that old. Let me get a shower, then we can take that bus tour. I'll meet you in the lobby in an hour."

Meaghan left his room shaking her head.

While en route to the docks, Anton Carmella boasted of how he had worn the old girl out. Desmond held his tongue. He found the descriptive details of Anton's latest conquest disgusting. *Perhaps his brutality will deter Madame from leaving Barcelona.*

"What do you have for me on the ship?"

"A luxury cabin."

"No, I don't mean that. I'll need some female companionship while we travel. Just because I'm stuck on that boat don't mean I'm gonna become some kind of monk. Helene was OK for a few days of fun, but I need someone younger, someone more physically fit. Her niece, Alba, is a cute little thing. She might welcome the attention of a seasoned lover."

Desmond chuckled. "There will be many opportunities for social interaction on the cruise. I am sure you will find a plethora of females vulnerable to your charms."

"Yeah, women are hungry for real men like me."

As Dexter Rubino leaned over the railing on deck eight, he observed Desmond Quest escorting Doctor Zhan aboard. *How am I going to avoid that jerk for the entire cruise?* As the pair disappeared from his sight, Dex returned to making phone calls. Over the last three days, he had called his friend in the Cayman Islands five or six times only to receive an invitation to leave voice mail.

A voice interrupted him. "What troubles you now, my friend?"

Dex turned to see Captain Auesnehmer dressed in his finest white uniform. "No problems, Emile, just trying to call a friend on the other side of the globe. Why are you so well dressed?"

"Management wanted photos of me on the bridge. Madame believes they will give our guests a sense of security. The more secure the guests feel, the more likely they are to gamble."

"I suppose you're right."

"I know I am. I have spent many years in this industry. Now I have my own command, and I wish to deliver a secure and penniless group of tourists to Sunset Cay."

"How will they make it back here?"

"On credit, of course. They have learned that much from the Americans."

Chapter 33

Meaghan answered her cell phone and heard Alba's voice.

"Where are you?" Alba asked.

"I'm so glad you called. We've checked into the hotel. I'm going to meet Matt in the lobby in a few minutes. I'll take him on a bus tour just like we planned."

"No, it is too late in the day for the bus tour. Take a cab to Sagrada Familia. That will keep him busy for the rest of the day."

"Like, do you think he'll be that interested in a big church?"

"Matthew is a very religious man. I am certain he will be interested in Europe's newest cathedral. Speaking of interest, has he shown any in you?"

"He has been a perfect gentleman, painfully dull until I mention your name."

"That is good news. I have to know he can be trusted."

"I've dropped every hint I can. He's just not into me."

"You have three more days. Keep testing him. I must be certain that he will be a faithful consort. Also be sure to take him shopping. He will need some formal wear for the cruise."

"He's wearing an ugly sport jacket and only brought a carry-on bag."

"That is what I feared. You have my card. Buy him anything he might need, including decent luggage."

"How is Arnan?"

"He is very busy with the fitness center, but I'm sure he feels your absence. Do not contact him until you have Matthew onboard the ship. No one from Windswept can know you have returned to Barcelona."

"Alba, Matthew is a nice guy and all, but he is a little past his prime. Like, are you sure he's worth all this trouble?"

"He is a very unusual man and we share a unique history. If I decide to take him as a lover, I will share the whole story with you. Keep him occupied with shopping and sightseeing for the rest of the week. Once we embark I will make my decision."

"All right, Alba. I've got to run. He's probably waiting."

Meaghan made her way to the lobby and there, as she suspected, Matt Narvik was waiting.

"I picked up a brochure for the bus tour, but it's all in Spanish."

"No, it's probably in Catalan. It may be a little late to start a bus tour. Let's take a taxi to the cathedral. We can take one of the bus tours tomorrow."

"Whatever you think is best."

She turned to the desk clerk. "Please call for a cab to take us to Sagrada Familia."

The young man nodded and picked up the phone.

Matt frowned. "How far is this cathedral?"

"Don't worry, Windswept is picking up the tab for everything."

"Winning that contest was a huge blessing. I was going to have to count my pennies to pay for the entire trip."

"It's my good fortune, too. I got to meet you. Is there anything in Barcelona you're looking forward to seeing?"

"I'm really anxious to see Alba."

Meaghan sighed. "You'll see her in a few days. Until then, let's enjoy this beautiful city."

"Lead the way, Meaghan."

Desmond Quest summoned several of the security staff to help move Doctor Zhan's belongings into his cabin.

"This cabin sucks, Desi. I have a closet at home bigger than this room. How can I entertain a chick in here?"

Desmond smiled. "This is a standard inside cabin, sir."

Anton clenched his fists and roared. "I'm not a standard passenger. I invested big bucks in this outfit and I want a better room!"

"Speaking of investment, several expected shipments of your inventory never arrived. Are you sure your man was trustworthy?"

"I'd trust Rocco with my life. You guys have the deeds to my home and farm as well as my gold. I expect to be treated as a valued investor, not a standard passenger." Anton grabbed Desmond by the shoulders and began to shake him. "Tell that old woman I want a better room. Now!"

Desmond slipped from Anton's grasp and one of his men touched the back of Anton's neck with a taser. Anton cried out and fell to the floor. His attacker hit him with another jolt from the device.

Desmond smirked at his fallen adversary. "This ape must be restrained and sedated. He will spend the remainder of his life here. See to it now. I have important things to do."

Desmond Quest made his way to the eighth level and stepped out on to the deck. He retrieved his cell phone and scanned the area around him; no one in sight. "Madame, Doctor Zhan is secured in an interior cabin. On our way to the ship, he confessed that he had deceived you. We have already received his entire inventory."

He paused and listened to her reply, then responded. "He simply lied, Madame. The scoundrel should have his tongue cut out. The shortage will nearly consume the balance of his investment. I made it clear that his life depended on his investment. My men have charge of him. He is restrained and sedated, and I suggest that we dispose of him as previously planned."

Desmond smiled and nodded as he listened to Helene's comment, then said, "I appreciate your confidence in me, Madame. I have the situation under control. Anton Carmella will not trouble you again."

Chapter 34

Matt and Meaghan arrived at the cathedral and joined the queue waiting for a tour. An elderly woman dressed in a long, black dress and wearing a tattered scarf approached each person in the line and held out a small can. She blessed each one that gave her a coin. When she reached Matt, she paused, but he was inspecting the statuary. Meaghan reached around him and deposited several Euros in the can. The old woman pressed her fingers together and bowed as she pronounced a blessing on the couple, then continued down the line.

"You shouldn't give money to beggars. It encourages idleness. What did she say?"

"My Spanish isn't as good as it should be, but I think she said our children would be bright and beautiful."

"You said they speak Catalan here."

"Like, I think they all speak Spanish but prefer to speak Catalan. People from the other parts of Spain come here and retain their native tongue. If you ask me, it's just a political thing."

"This is some structure. How long have they been building it?"

"I forget, maybe a hundred years or so. They'll tell us on the tour. There's a big push to get things cleaned up before the Pope gets here."

"Have you been here before?"

"Several times. The last time they told us it isn't a church until the Pope says so. I'm not religious, but I admire the architecture and the sculpture. The entire building is like a sculpture. See how the pillars are like the roots of a tree supporting the porch roof?"

"Frankly, I think the statues are kind of ugly."

"This side is expressionist. You'll probably enjoy the other side more. Gaudi did that side. He designed the entire cathedral. Unfortunately, he died before this work was completed."

"A hundred years ago?"

"No. After he died, there were delays because of a civil war and political upheaval. Now they plan on having it done by 2050."

"How much is the tour?"

"Don't worry, Windswept is paying. It's all part of your prize." Meaghan pointed at a stone square with numbers carved in it. "That is called the magic square. No matter which way you add the numbers the sum is thirty-three. That's the number of years Jesus lived before he died."

"He is still living, Meaghan."

Meaghan chuckled. "Is he in witness protection or something?" Matt didn't laugh. "I'm sorry, I don't mean to offend you. Alba told me you're very religious."

"Then she does remember me."

Meaghan bowed her head. "Yes, Matt, she does remember you. Please don't let her know that I told you. I'm supposed to be testing you. She wants to be sure you can be trusted."

"Have I passed the test?"

"Narvik, you pass with flying colors, but she planned on it taking all week. I've thrown my best pitches and you won't swing. Is there something about me that turns you off, or am I just not your type?"

"I don't have a type. God brought Alba to me under extremely unusual circumstances. I can't go into the details, but I'm sure this is all part of His plan for my life."

After Meaghan paid for the tour, they were each handed a listening device so they could hear the guide over the din of construction noise. The guide gave detailed explanations of the statuary and the carvings that covered the building.

Inside, the soaring arches that resembled trees in a forest left Matt speechless. Stained-glass windows in the ceiling gave the impression of light filtering through the leaves of the trees. The tour continued on to the other side of the building, known as the nativity side. Matt appreciated the sculpture there much more.

As they turned in their listening devices, Meaghan tugged at his arm. "Follow me. There's a park near here that offers the best view."

The park encircled a small pond, and they sat beside it on a bench taking in the majestic view. "Do you see the green at the top of the gable, Matt?

"It looks like a Christmas tree."

"It's supposed to be a cypress tree. See how the doves are descending to the manger at the base of the tree? Someday when I have a home of my own I'll design a Christmas tree just like that."

"That would be really cool and fairly easy."

"Sure, you just cut off some of the lower branches and put a crèche at the bottom of the tree, then decorate the tree with white doves."

"Don't forget the lights."

"Of course, all white lights. Maybe twinkle lights."

"No, you need to use colored lights."

"But, like, that's so middle class. White lights are classy. They look like stars."

"All right, but you need a star at the top."

"No, an angel. We always had an angel on our tree."

"Did your family celebrate Christmas?"

Meaghan shrugged. "Doesn't everybody?"

"No. I guess what I'm really asking is did you celebrate Santa Claus or Jesus?"

"Both, I guess. We were never very religious."

"Despite what Alba told you, I'm not religious either. I have a relationship with the Lord not just a religion. It's the most important thing in my life."

"Hold on, Matt, you're getting too deep for me. Let's take a walk up the street. There's one landmark I'll know you'll like."

A short distance from the park, Matt caught a familiar scent, then he saw the Colonel's equally familiar portrait. "Yeah, I'm ready for a taste of home."

Chapter 35

Dex looked at his watch and understood why his stomach was rumbling. The professional crew was dining in a restaurant on aft six. Unwilling to encounter Desmond Quest, he went to the piano bar on aft-four, where he'd find a supply of cold sandwiches and a soda fountain kept there for the enjoyment of anyone entrusted with a key. He welcomed the promise of solitude and an opportunity to think.

As he passed down the long, porthole corridor that bordered the starboard side of the casino, he heard music coming from the piano bar. Instinctively, he reached for his Ruger and hugged the inside wall as he approached the red-leather padded doors. An overstuffed chair held open the door on the right side; at the far end of the room, a man played the white baby grand. Seeing no one else in the room, Dex holstered his weapon and approached the man.

"Say there, who are you and why are you here?" The man continued playing and Dex noticed he was wearing ear buds. Dex moved to the piano and thumped his fist on the top of the instrument.

The musician was startled but smiling as he looked Dex in the eye and shouted, "Hola!"

Dex made a pointing motion to his ears. The man removed the ear buds and offered his salutation anew. "Hola. Parla anglès?"

"Si, I mean yes, I do speak English, and I'm an American. My name is Dexter Rubino. I'm the Deputy Director of Security for the cruise line. Who are you?"

"I'm Dave Carpenter." He played a fanfare on the piano and bowed slightly as he added, "I'm the Piano Man."

"I thought you were coming in tomorrow. I like to welcome the entertainers as they board. I want you to know that the security personnel are interested in the safety and welfare of the passengers and crew. If you cooperate with us and follow a few simple rules, there won't be any problems."

"That's pretty much what Mr. Quest told us."

"You've met Desmond Quest?"

"He picked us up at the airport and read us the rule book on the way to the ship."

"Who was traveling with you?"

"Marcel Jeanblanc, the mime. We weren't traveling together until Quest picked us up."

"Where is he?"

"I have no idea. I haven't seen him since we boarded."

"A French mime. Does he speak English?"

"He thought he was speaking English. I got the impression he was African, not French, but I can't say for sure."

"I was just about to have a snack. Would you care to join me?"

"Sure, they told me dinner was being served on deck six but I wanted to check out my new girlfriend here." He gently patted the piano. "We'll be spending a lot of time together for the next few months."

"If you don't mind me asking, Dave, how did you get in here? We keep it locked so the maintenance crew can't rip off the sandwiches and beer."

"I came in the back way. I propped the door open so any of the crew passing by could hear me playing and come in. You're the first one I've snared so far. I hope to see you here."

Dex furrowed his brow in puzzlement. "See me where?"

"On Sunday morning I'm holding a worship service here. All the passengers and any of the crew who have free time are welcome to come. We'll sing a few songs and I'll share a brief message. Mr. Quest said it was OK."

"It's news to me. Tell me about this back way you used to get in."

Dave pointed to a curtain behind the bar. "There's a pantry behind that curtain. At the back of the pantry is a ladder that leads to the lower decks. You know, where the crew quarters are."

"Who told you about it?"

"The maintenance crew showed me how to get in. Nice guys. They promised to be here Sunday morning."

Matt and Meaghan relaxed as they enjoyed the view of the cathedral from the comfort of a booth in the KFC. Meaghan used a drumstick as a pointer as she indicted Christianity. "How can the church spend millions of dollars to build a place like that and let people starve all over the world?"

"That building is the work of a church, not the church. The Bible tells us that the true church is made up of all those who believe in Christ and accept Him as their Savior, not some formal, manmade organization. I've been in many churches that have humble buildings and do a lot of good work for the poor."

"Don't you think that God deserves the best house they can build him?"

"All over the world there are temples built by various religions. In time, they decay or are abandoned. The Bible says that God does not live in temples built by hands."

"So where does He live, like, in heaven?"

"Sort of. The Bible also says He lives in the hearts of believers."

"The Bible says, the Bible says . . . What do you say, Matt Narvik?"

"If you're asking for my opinion, it doesn't matter much. Everyone has an opinion. The Bible is the Word of God and I read it every day. I know of no higher authority, do you? Do you ever read the Bible, Meaghan?"

"My chicken's getting cold."

Omar carried a frosty bottle of beer and a brown paper bag down the corridor to where Hakim stood watch at a door. He greeted the man with a cheerful, "Break time."

"Bless you, Omar, I'm starving."

"Take it out on deck and enjoy the evening air. I'll take your post."

"Thank you, son. I've been standing here for hours."

As Hakim walked out of sight, Omar tried the door; it was unlocked. He entered the darkened room and closed it behind him. He flipped the light switch and there lay the unconscious Doctor Zhan. The elderly man's wrists were cuffed to screw eyes in the headboard. He lay clad in an adult diaper, breathing heavily through his open mouth.

"I could slit your throat right now, you thieving jackal. Fortunately for you, I am required to wait for orders. When my brother gets here, you will wish I had killed you." He spat in the face of the restrained old man, turned out the light, and left the room.

Chapter 36

After a sandwich and pleasant conversation with Dave Carpenter, Dex wandered the corridors of the ship. When he encountered Hakim standing outside of a cabin door, he asked him why he was there.

"I am following the orders of Mr. Quest. No one is to go in or out."

"I'm the Deputy Director of Security, Hakim. I demand to know what's going on here."

"You will have to speak to Mr. Quest. I cannot answer your questions."

"I will, and I won't forget your insubordination."

"Please, Mr. Dex, I have to follow orders. If you disturb Mr. Quest tonight, it will go badly for me. Please wait and speak to him in the morning."

"All right, Hakim, but I won't forget this."

Dex stomped away but with a faint smile on his face. *At least I know where Doctor Zhan is. Now I need to find out why.*

Omar hid himself in the shadows of the top deck as he spoke into his satellite phone. "I saw him. He is shackled to a bed in a cabin on this ship. He has been drugged, I am sure of it."

Omar stamped his foot in frustration, "You do not understand. I was in his room, alone with him. I could have slit his throat and let him bleed out without anyone seeing me."

He was near tears as he pleaded, "What if he should escape? Very well, I shall wait for orders"

Matt and Meaghan took a cab to the Plaça de Catalonia and walked back to their hotel.

"Matt, I think we should go shopping tomorrow morning and take the bus tour after lunch."

"Shopping for what?"

"You need more clothes for the cruise."

"I have plenty."

"You'll need more if you're going to be seen with a star like Alba. Like, you need a tuxedo and dress shoes, a couple nice suits and some casual clothes. You can't be seen in jeans and T-shirts anymore. Those sneakers have to go. They are completely unacceptable in Europe."

"I'm comfortable in these clothes. I can't afford to buy all this stuff."

"It's all part of the prize, Matt. Windswept is picking up the tab."

Chapter 37

"Omar, come with me!" Alba said.

"Of course. Where are we going so early?"

"To my aunt's home. The old crone has gone too far this time."

"We should contact Mr. Quest or Dex before you leave the ship."

"I am a grown woman, and I will come and go as I see fit. I do not need a professional babysitter's permission."

"Alba, I only have my scooter. To get access to a company vehicle we will have to fill out a form in the security office. Why not go to rehearsal while I arrange for a vehicle?"

"Are you afraid of the old crone also? I will call a cab and go alone."

"I would gladly lay down my life in your service, Alba. I fear no one. However, you must calm down before you leave the ship. Words spoken in anger can live long after our spirit cools."

"Omar, you are too young to understand. My future depends greatly on the success of this voyage. Now this old woman has hired another entertainer to usurp me. I must confront her or my career is over."

Desmond Quest heard the commotion and approached the couple, unhappy to intervene in another of Alba's tantrums. "Good morning, Ms Cologne. You are looking particularly lovely this morning."

"Quest, I want to see my aunt immediately. Get us a company vehicle so that Omar can drive me there."

"I can't recommend that course of action. I spoke to Madame Adolphe last evening. She isn't feeling well. I took the liberty to call for a private nurse to attend to her needs. It is nothing for you to worry about. You can return to rehearsal and put your mind at ease."

"She will be feeling much worse when I see her, Quest. The old witch has hired another singer in an attempt to undermine the rejuvenation of my career. I will not be disrespected like this!"

Desmond wagged his head in the negative. "Who has told you such a fantastic story?"

"Captain Auesnehmer told me last night after dinner. I was awake all night trying to understand why she would undermine me this way."

"The captain is misinformed. We have hired another singer to entertain the children and young people on the cruise. Madame Adolphe hired her on the recommendation of Nancy Rivers. Ms. Richards has trained the young lady in the art of dance as well as singing. She is in no way a threat to you or your audience. Madame never mentioned it because it is unimportant."

"Who is this girl and why is she not aboard already?"

Desmond rolled his eyes upward. "I am sorry, Ms. Cologne, but I am not sure of her name. She is an unknown, of no consequence to you. She will be entertaining on deck, at the stage near the pool."

"You see, Alba, you lost a night's sleep over nothing."

Alba bit her lower lip before speaking. "Are you certain of these things, Quest?"

"As certain as I can be. As I mentioned, it is not a matter of importance. I suggest you go on to rehearsal and not trouble Madame Adolphe until she is felling well."

"Will you tell my aunt I wish to speak with her as soon as possible?"

"Certainly, Ms. Cologne, I will tell her later today."

Dex finished his usual breakfast with Captain Auesnehmer and returned to the corridor where he had seen Hakim the night before. Hakim was gone; another man stood in his place.

Dex smiled and asked. "Had breakfast yet friend?"

"No, Mr. Dex."

"Go on and get some grub, son. I'll take over here until you get back."

"Thank you, Mr. Dex."

As the man walked away, Dex turned his back to the door and surreptitiously tried the door handle. It was unlocked. He eased the door open and immediately the stench of urine filled his nostrils. It brought back the memories of the nursing home where his mother died. He stepped inside and placed his handkerchief over his nose while he fumbled for the light switch. The light revealed the hulk of Doctor Zhan, shackled, unshaven, and lying in his own filth. There was no need to see if he was alive. Dex could hear the mucus rattle as he breathed.

This man smothered me in a bear hug a few days ago. He must have displeased Helene Adolphe.

Dex turned to leave and found Desmond Quest standing in the doorway. "What are you doing here, Dex?"

"Oh, good morning, Desmond. I was just passing by and allowed the guard to go to breakfast. You can imagine my surprise when I saw the occupant."

"Sad, is it not? If you recall, I said he was struggling with dementia. He finally had a complete breakdown. Madame called me, and it was all I could manage to get him here. We will, of course, be bringing a nurse in to care for him during the cruise."

"I think he needs some immediate attention. Has the ship's doctor arrived yet? Why is he shackled?"

"Doctor Zhan has cognitive moments, then he tries to leave. You can testify to the man's strength. We have no choice but to keep him restrained."

"When is the doctor getting here?"

"Tomorrow. Our men can tend to him until then."

"He needs tending now, Desmond. Let me out of here. I can't stand this stench."

Desmond stepped aside and Dex exited the room. "I'm not kidding, Desmond. You have to do something about the smell or the entire deck will reek."

"I'll call housekeeping straight away. The next time you think one of my men needs relief, check with me."

Chapter 38

Matt rose early and went for a run. Unfamiliar with the area, he stuck to the main streets and took note of landmarks to find his way back. He wheeled around the massive statue of Columbus at the lower end of La Rambla and returned to the hotel, where he showered and dressed. Afterward he met Meaghan for breakfast at the buffet adjacent to the lobby. They enjoyed simple fresh food and fruit. Matt drank coffee while Meaghan sipped bottled water. Matt opened his wallet to pay the tab with cash but balked when he saw the total of thirty-two Euros.

"That's reasonable, Matt. Windswept is picking up the bills anyway."

Matt shook his head. "This is entirely too much, Meaghan. I have a responsibility to protect the interests of Windswept."

"Matt, you're a winner of a contest, not an accountant. Like, prices here are different than they are in the States. This is a tourist location. Prices are going to be a little steep. While we're shopping today, let me worry about the cost. Alba can't be seen on the arm of some sloppy old goat, so don't give me any arguments."

The words stung but Matt realized that she probably was right. "OK, Meaghan, I don't mean to seem ungrateful."

"Like, I don't want to be mean, but Alba is a friend of mine, and she is a celebrity. You have to understand that if you're along side of Alba, you're in the spotlight also."

"OK, whatever you say."

"Good, I have arranged for a car to take us shopping. It should be here in about five minutes. Do you need to go back to your room?"

"No."

"Great. If you'll just relax, you might enjoy a day of shopping. We may even have time to get you a haircut."

Arnan spent two hours a day on his own resistance training and an hour and half reviewing the performance of the massage therapists. This day his massage was the task of the newest member of the staff. She was a Haitian girl who stood five foot one and weighed about one hundred pounds. Arnan chuckled when she entered the room. "What's your name? Tiny?"

"My name is Chantal, Mr. Arnan. It is an honor to be chosen for your massage."

Arnan found her accent pleasing but doubted she would have the physical strength to give a man of his build a deep-tissue massage. "This is not an honor, Chantal, it's a test. If you don't cut the mustard, you may be spending a lot of time cleaning toilets."

"I will give you a very pleasing massage, Mr. Arnan. Please remove your robe and lie face down on the table."

While Arnan complied, she moved gracefully around the room with her back to him. Arnan placed a towel over his buttocks and said, "I'm waiting."

The girl covered his back with a hot towel, then placed three black candles in a triangle on the floor below his face and lit them. The music shifted to a steady drumbeat.

"This is a very special massage, Mr. Arnan. I will be using secret oil found only on my island. Just relax and let the scent of the candles fill your mind."

She applied the oil to his feet and began the massage, gently stroking each toe, putting pressure in specific areas to spark an involuntary twitch from Arnan. She then squeezed his Achilles' tendons. The strength in the little girl's hands surprised Arnan. As she worked her way up to his calves, he thought he should make a confession.

"Careful there, I have implants."

The girl continued, probing the giant's massive leg muscles. She then removed the towel from his back and began massaging his shoulders. The scent of the candles, the increasing beat of the drums, the fragrant oil, and the sheer power of the diminutive girl caused a sensation in Arnan he vaguely remembered experiencing years before. She used her forearms to massage the small of his back, digging her elbows into his spine. She deftly slid her hands under his towel and massaged the gluteus maximus. She panted as she gripped one side of the towel and spoke.

"You can roll over now, Mr. Arnan."

Arnan complied and as he did, he ripped the towel from the girl's hands and threw it against the wall. He grasped her around the waist with his powerful arm, then swept her atop of him.

Chantal's face beamed as she asked, "Are my efforts satisfactory to you, Mr. Arnan?"

Desmond Quest winced as he held his phone away from his ear. "I meant no disrespect, Madame. In your current state, I thought a nurse would be useful to you."

"No, Madame, I am not implying that you are an invalid. You are the heart and soul of the Windswept

Corporation. Without your guidance and wisdom we would be rudderless."

"Of course, Madame, first thing in the morning I'll have four men and a suitable vehicle to transport your belongings."

"I will welcome your presence onboard, Madame.

Yes, Madame. Good day, Madame."

As he ended the call, Desmond spotted one of his most trusted men. "Hakim, come here."

"What is it, sir?"

"The suite next to Ms. Cologne's is reserved for Madame Adolphe. I want you to contact housekeeping and have them scour the room. Tell them I will be giving it the white-glove test tonight. Madame will be moving in tomorrow morning."

"Yes, sir."

"I want you to relay to the rest of the security staff that Madame Adolphe is coming aboard to stay. Going forward, we must all stay on our toes."

"I will, sir. Does Ms. Cologne know this is happening?"

"She will tomorrow. Keep a safe distance."

Chapter 39

Matt's shopping adventure began at Diagonal Mar and continued throughout the city. As he and Meaghan returned to the hotel, Matt felt exhausted but Meaghan's enthusiasm seemed boundless.

"Change into some of your new clothes and we'll go to a tapas bar."

"No, Meaghan, I'm beat. I saw a restaurant on my run this morning. I want to go there. You don't have to escort me. Go do whatever you want."

"You went on a run this morning? Matt you shouldn't have done that. Like, you might have been lost or wandered into a bad part of town. Most of Barcelona is great, but it is a city."

"I'm a big boy. I let you drag me all over town today and pick out all my new clothes, but I don't need you to hold my hand while I walk to Planet Hollywood."

"Matt, you're in a beautiful European city. Why do you want to go to Planet Hollywood? It's, like, so American. Aren't you anxious to experience new things?"

"I want to see if it is as good as the one in Orlando. I appreciate your help with the shopping, but I didn't come here to try on clothes."

"Tomorrow we'll just do sightseeing. I'm sorry if I wore you out. Friday we have to pick up the suits that were sent for alteration, but other than that you can choose what we do with the rest of the week."

"All right, I'll walk down to the Plaça de Catalunya on my own. You're officially off duty."

"What? Matt are you seriously ditching me? I thought, like, we were getting along really well."

"It's OK. I'll be fine."

"I don't want to go to dinner alone. Will you allow me to accompany you? Maybe if I were a celebrity like Alba, you wouldn't be ashamed to be seen with me."

"I just don't want to hold you down."

"You're not holding me down, Matt. I enjoy your company."

"Then let's get started."

"Do we have to walk?"

"The fresh air will do you good."

As Desmond Quest enjoyed the sunset, he sipped his coffee and contemplated the ramifications of Madame Adolphe moving aboard. His phone rang, and when he identified the caller, he hit the end switch, preferring to sacrifice his comfortable spot for some privacy. He wandered through the Grand Lobby and across the gangway to a vast paved area that teemed with trucks and dry goods waiting to be loaded. He ducked between two large shipping containers and returned the call.

"Where are you, Rocco?"

"Did you complete your mission?"

"Where is the target now?"

"He's a retired factory worker. I could have purchased his demise with a bottle of rum. Where are you at this minute?"

"I will be glad to help you, Rocco. I can have someone there to assist you by morning. Tell me where this mission house is."

"Very well, stay where you are I will send someone to assist you."

Quest ended the call and searched for the number of two contacts in the Fort Myers area. He dialed the number and greeted his compatriot. "Hola, Pablo, I have another opportunity for you and Skeeter. Carmella's lackey has failed to eliminate the currier, now he must be terminated. Your reward will be the gold he has skimmed for himself."

After dinner, the piano bar became the center of activity aboard the *New Dawn*. David Carpenter served as master of ceremonies as a sing-along and karaoke competition began. The performers ranged from the dancers to kitchen staff, and even a few of the housekeeping personnel took part. While some of the kitchen staff struggled to sing an old disco song in English, several of the dancers jumped up and gyrated to the beat. Dex signaled David to step aside.

"Did Quest OK this party?"

"Yes, I sold it as a team-building experience. Quest and I have been trading a few horses."

"Like what?"

"He needs a keyboardist for some young singer. I asked for a free hand in the utilization of the piano bar, including a worship service every Sunday."

"Be careful, Quest is a shrewd negotiator."

"I will, now come on and enjoy the sing-along."

Dex joined in the singing; but when he recognized one oldie that his daughter had sung, he slipped out. He meandered through the ship, casually approaching the cabin of Doctor Zhan.

Chapter 40

On Thursday morning, Matt heard the anticipated knock at his hotel-room door, followed by Meaghan's voice. "Are you ready, Narvik?"

He opened the door and said, "Ready and waiting. I really didn't think you'd show up."

"Just don't think that I'll, like, take it easy on you. I warn you, I ran track in high school."

As they took the elevator to the lobby, Matt asked, "Do I get a head start?"

"No way, hombre, I want a fair race."

"It's not a race. I just run to stay in shape."

"Making excuses already? Did you ever run track?"

As they left the elevator, Matt smiled and said, "We used to race the dinosaurs. Losers got eaten."

She giggled and began stretching. "Since we're sans dinosaurs, loser buys brunch."

"You're on, Miller."

Meaghan pointed toward Mountjuic, "Look at that, Matt."

He looked, then turned back toward Meaghan. "What . . ."

She had taken off at a full run, heading south on Ramblas de Catalunya, and looked over her shoulder, "Ready, set, go!"

Matt laughed and took off in hot pursuit. At the next intersection, she had to wait for traffic. Matt closed to within a few strides behind her as traffic cleared and she took off again. "Cheaters never prosper, Miller," he shouted.

She laughed. "You snooze, you lose, Narvik!"

Matt's long strides put him along side of her in a minute. He slowed his pace to match hers. "You're faster than you look, kid."

"Dancers are athletes, too." Meaghan looked up at him and tried to smile but her breathing had already become labored. "You do this every day?"

"Just about. I usually lift for an hour, too. Are you OK?"

"Sure. How far is this statue?"

"Just a couple miles. We can stop any time you want."

Meaghan was panting, but suddenly a gleam appeared in her eye. "Ow, oh, my ankle!"

Matt stopped and took her by the arm. "Now I know you're not OK."

"My ankle isn't ready for this. You go ahead and I'll walk this off."

"I'm sorry, Meaghan. I'll walk you back to the hotel."

Meaghan winced in pain. "Go ahead. I'm a big girl."

Desmond Quest escorted Madame Adolphe from her penthouse to the *New Dawn*. The matriarch of Windswept wore a hat and veil with a long beige dress. As Quest had ordered, a large segment of the staff and crew assembled to welcome her. Rubino was the first to greet her. "Welcome to your new home, Helene."

"Thank you, Rubino. Desmond and I are going to the Sultan's Palace for lunch. I would ask you to join us, but I'm sure you are busy securing things."

"Always, Madame. If there is anything I can do to help make you comfortable, just let me know."

"Desmond will see to my comfort, Rubino. I would like a detailed summary of what you have been doing since you came aboard. The shareholders are sure to ask me."

"I'll get right on it."

As Desmond helped her into the elevator, she whispered, "Keep that American pig away from me."

"Of course, Madame. After lunch we can go and see the other American pig. Pity they can't share the same sty."

"I wish to see him now, Desmond."

"Our lunch is already ordered. Anton isn't going anywhere."

"We will leave the elevator on level eight, then we will take the stairs down to his cabin. I don't want any of the crew to see me near him."

"Doctor Stuart came aboard this morning, and I asked him to look in on our honored guest. I'll explain our treatment plans for him over lunch."

"You should have spoken to him first. Doctor Stuart is a Windswept investor, but he is a little naive."

Desmond helped Madame Adolphe down the four flights of stairs to the deck where he had imprisoned Anton Carmella. As they walked down the narrow corridor, the stench of urine permeated the air. Quest was taken aback when he saw the doctor supervising Anton's removal.

"Doctor, what are you doing?"

"Mr. Quest, are you responsible for the conditions here?"

Helene answered for him. "Doctor, I told you when you invested in Windswept that there would be times you would be required to follow orders without question."

"Madame, these living conditions are atrocious. The condition of this cabin is a health hazard for all aboard."

"Desmond, have housekeeping disinfect this cabin and those adjacent to it." She reached into her purse and pulled out a surgical mask. She placed it between her veil and her face and entered the malodorous room. She looked down at the unconscious Anton, who had been strapped to a gurney. She began to chuckle, then broke into an insidious laugh. "Sleep well, dear heart, sleep well."

Chapter 41

Alba left rehearsal and headed for the Sultan's Palace when she heard that the president of the cruise line had come aboard. She assumed that would be her aunt's first stop. She ascended the glass staircase and knocked a serving tray from the hands of a harem girl to announce her arrival.

Helene looked up, seemingly unfazed by Alba's dramatic entrance.

"You and I are going to have a talk, you old witch!" Alba said.

Helene raised a wine glass in a mock salute. "Hello, dear, please join us for some refreshment."

"I know of your treachery. You seek to usurp me by bringing another entertainer aboard. I will not tolerate this type of disrespect."

"Alba, sit down and be still. If you are ever to lead Windswept, you must practice decorum."

Desmond Quest rose and held a chair out for the enraged beauty. Alba pulled out the chair furthest from Quest and sat down. "I will not continue to tolerate this disrespect, Aunt Helene. Who is this singer and why was I not told about her?

"She is a complete unknown, Alba. She is no threat to you or your career. Nancy Rivers discovered her and suggested we employ her to entertain the children during the cruise. You may be the featured entertainer on this ship, but you cannot bear the entire load. At the very least, you will need to sleep in after your late performances."

Alba then noticed the bruising in Helene's face. "What happened to you?"

"Nothing, dear, I am fine."

"What is the name of this singer?"

Helene smiled. "I really don't recall. Do you, Desmond?"

"No, Madame, it is of little consequence."

"I will ask Nancy Rivers. I do not desire any more American trash on my boat."

"Alba, you have made too much of this already. Do not infuriate Nancy Rivers. Concentrate on your own performance."

Desmond Quest set a glass of wine in front of Alba. "Please join us for lunch. You will feel much better after a gourmet meal."

"No, I am abstaining from wine and intoxicating beverages for the balance of the cruise."

Helene nodded. "A laudable sacrifice, my dear. I am happy to see your level of commitment."

"I should return to rehearsal."

"If you must. Please do not question Nancy Rivers about this singer. She is tired and worn from the ceaseless rehearsals, just as you are. We should be appreciative of her efforts in finding this youngster to help."

"Whatever you think is best, Aunt Helene."

Matt and Meaghan enjoyed lunch at a street café, then walked to Plaça de Catalunya to buy tickets for the bus tour.

"Like, which do you want, Narvik, Red or Blue?"

"Red or Blue what?"

"The bus routes; there is a Red Line and a Blue Line. There's a Green Line, too, but that goes out to Port Olimpic. Most of the tourist's areas are on the red or blue lines."

"Then let's take the blue line, blue like your eyes."

Meaghan blushed. "I'm surprised you noticed. Blue Line it is."

They boarded a double-decker bus, and Matt headed for the front seat on the second tier. Meaghan took his arm and pulled him back to a seat near the rear.

"Why can't we sit in the front?"

"This isn't a rollercoaster. That windshield is splattered with bugs and bird droppings. Do you want to see that in your pictures?"

"I didn't bring a camera. I take lousy pictures."

As the bus left the curb, Meaghan shook her head. "I don't know about you, Matt. You win a contest for a great vacation and, like, don't even spring for a camera to record your good fortune."

"I don't need pictures. I'll remember every moment of this trip as long as I live."

"Here, put your earphones on and I'll find the English station. The radio will describe the sights as we drive past them. If we ride the entire route, you'll get an idea of what you'd like to see close up. We'll pick up a disposable camera somewhere."

"Whatever you say, Miss Miller."

Chapter 42

Dex joined the rest of the professionals on level six for the evening meal. Quest made a formal welcome speech for Helene, and the two engaged in hushed conversation throughout the meal. David Carpenter, having won the admiration of the crew at the piano bar the previous night, garnered all of the attention anyway.

Dex kept a sharp eye on Alba, who had seemed to drift away as she picked at her meal. With Narvik out of the picture, he would have to charm her himself. His time spent with Cyn having renewed his confidence, he thought he had enough sex appeal to seduce her. *She's the key to the treasure. I can feel it in my bones.* "Any plans for the rest of the evening, Alba?"

"No, rehearsal has left me exhausted. I will retire to my suite as soon as I finish my coffee."

"You won't be going to the piano bar then?"

"No, I need my sleep."

"Why don't we take our coffee out on the deck? Then I'll see you to your cabin."

"Yes, that would be nice. I am sorry that I am such poor company. I just have much on my mind."

As they exited the dining room, Dex looked longingly at the beauty. *She is so much younger than I am. Would any advance repulse her?*

Clutching the coffee cup with both hands, Alba moved to the rail and stared beyond the lights of the port facility.

"Are the rehearsals going well?" Dex asked.

"Yes, quite well. The show is sure to be a success."

Her uncertain smile devalued her words. "You said you have a lot on your mind. Can I do anything to lessen your stress?"

"Much of my future depends on this cruise. Stress is to be expected."

Dex swallowed hard and moved closer. He placed his left hand on her side. "If you ever need to talk, I'm a good listener."

Alba turned to face him, and he wasn't sure if she smiled or smirked at him. His focus shifted to the dark eyes and fluttering lashes that had lured so many men before him. She spoke just above a whisper. "That is so good to know. At times such as this, I am thankful for a good and trusted friend like you. Can you see me to my cabin now?"

They climbed the stairs to the seventh deck in silence. While walking down the ornate corridor that led to the luxury suites, Dex grew mindful of how far he was from his lowly berth near the water line. When they reached her door, Alba swiped her keycard and the door unlocked. Dex reached in, turned the handle, and gave the door a shove. Alba stepped into the room and turned to face him. "Thank you for seeing me to my room, Dexter." She stood on her tiptoes and kissed his cheek. "Pleasant dreams." She slowly closed the door and Dex stood there frozen. He hadn't felt that way since he walked Laura Stanko home from the homecoming dance.

He turned and walked away. *Helene Adolphe is on this ship, Alba is on this ship and Philippe's treasure is not. I need to redeem the time I have left here.* He went to the elevator and descended to the Grand Lobby. Two members of his security team snapped to attention when they saw him approach. "I need one of you to drive me into town, now."

"We will have to inform Mr. Quest."

"No, you do not need to inform anyone. I'm giving you a direct order to get a vehicle and drive me into town."

"Yes, sir."

In a matter of a few moments, Dex was on his way into town. "Do you know a club called Bikini?" he asked the driver.

"I'll find it."

When they reached the club, a line of people less than half Dex's age waited to enter. Dex stepped out of the car and thought he could feel the sidewalk vibrate with the beat coming from inside. He looked back at his driver and said, "I'll find my own way home. You can go now."

As his driver sped into the night, Dex passed the queue of young hipsters and knocked on the side window of a cab. The driver unlocked the doors and Dex got in. "Take me to Port Vell."

"Are you satisfied Mr. Quest?"

"Yes, Doctor, the restraints seem to be adequate."

"The sedatives Madame Adolphe demanded make the restraints redundant. What has this man done that makes her hate him so much?"

"It is of no consequence to you. Just follow orders and we will get along splendidly."

"I'm a medical professional, Mr. Quest, not a servant. I have a responsibility to my patient."

"You also have a warrant for your arrest in California. You work for Windswept now that is where your responsibilities lie."

The doctor's chin dropped. "You may own me, Quest, but I will not be a partner to murder."

"I believe the correct word is accomplice, Doctor. I am going to my cabin for the night. You can leave the patient alone. His nurse will be coming aboard tomorrow morning."

Chapter 43

In Port Vell, a cab stopped a hundred yards from a sea-facing skyscraper. A solitary figure exited the cab and paid the driver, then slipped from shadow to shadow. He crept into the garage area beneath Madame Adolphe's building. The elevator to the penthouse required a key. Having none, Dex searched for and found the stairway. He sighed in relief when he found it unlocked. As he ascended the stairs, he scanned the walls and ceiling, looking for security cameras. None were visible but that didn't mean they weren't there. After reaching the sixth floor, he stopped to catch his breath. "Twelve more flights to go," he gasped. *Would I have been up to Alba tonight?* He shook his head and resumed the climb.

When he reached the top floor, soaked in perspiration, he sat on the top step. His heart beat wildly and he felt dizzy. *If there is any trace of Philippe's treasure here, it is owed to me. You can't play with sharks and play by the rules.*

Dex struggled to stand, and with an assist from the wall, he made it. He reached for his wallet and retrieved his lock-picking tools. He knelt in front of the door and inserted the pick, finding that the door was already unlocked. *This isn't right.* As he opened the door, the light from the stairwell cut a path through the expansive kitchen.

He entered cautiously. Spotting a light switch near the door, he flipped it on. The room filled with light. It was immaculately clean, with the scent of lemons in the air. Dex proceeded to the adjacent rooms and noticed nothing amiss. When he entered the foyer, he found the body of an elderly man dressed in a guard's uniform sprawled on the marble floor. A puddle of blood surrounded him. Dex spotted bullet holes in the man's chest and forehead.

Dex edged his way along the wall to avoid stepping in the blood. An open door led to an office. On the far side of the room, a wall safe stood open. *Somebody beat me here.*

As Dex left, he noticed the Dali painting that had hung in the foyer was gone. *Picked clean and a dead guard to seal the deal!*

Dex made his way to the stairwell and tried to run down, but his legs were wobbly and his head was spinning. He collapsed on the eighth floor and lay there for several minutes before pulling himself up and staggering to the ground floor. His chest felt tight as he walked out of the garage.

The lights of a vehicle going by startled him. He dove behind some shrubs and hit the ground. His head felt like he'd been smacked with a shovel, his chest ached. He rolled on to his back. *I'll rest here for a while. I'm OK, I just need to rest.*

Matt stopped at the door to his room and said to Meaghan, "Thank you for a fun day. This city is steeped in a history unlike anything back home." Then he grinned and added, "Want to challenge me to another run in the morning?"

Meaghan pushed past him and stepped into the room. "We're not done with today yet, Matthew Narvik."

He stared at her for a moment. "What? It's getting . . ."

She put a finger to his lips. "Tomorrow night we'll go to a dance club called La Paloma. It will be good practice for the cruise, and you'll get to wear some of your new clothes."

"I can't dance."

She grabbed his hands, pulled him into the room, and closed the door. "Who told you that you can't dance?"

"Nobody told me, I just never learned."

"I can teach you. My mother taught dance lessons for twenty years, and I've been dancing all my life."

"Is that how she met your father?"

"Yes, now put your arm around my waist." Matt reluctantly complied. "In most lessons you're told to put your hand on my shoulder blade but we don't want you to look like an amateur."

Matt pulled her close. The strawberry scent of her hair unnerved him as she nestled her head against his chest.

Meaghan stared up in to his sky-blue eyes and her voice trembled as she spoke. "We'll start with the waltz."

Matt let go of her hand and wrapped his arms around her. She leaned into his strong embrace. Without thinking, he kissed her, then gently pushed her away. "You should leave."

"What about your lesson?"

"I guess I failed. You should leave. Now."

"No, Matt."

"Yes. I still have feelings for Alba. I think its love, but I can't be sure."

Meaghan opened the door, then turned to him, tears in her eyes. "Don't worry, Matt, I won't say anything. Nothing happened."

Matt stared at the door as the lock clicked into place. *What's happening to me?*

Desmond Quest escorted Madame Adolphe to her suite and she invited him in for a nightcap.

"Is the artwork secure?"

"Yes, Madame, it is being transported to a climate-controlled facility near Madrid."

"How did you stage the scene?"

"An elderly gentleman who was terminally ill. His family will benefit from their share of the insurance. The police will receive an anonymous tip Sunday morning."

"Where in my home is the body?"

"He was positioned just outside of the lift. The police will theorize that he surprised the thieves."

"Was there blood?"

"I suppose there was."

"Will it stain the marble?"

"I am not sure, Madame. If it does, we will have the flooring replaced."

"Very well then, drink up. I'm going to bed. Have my breakfast brought here at nine. Also, please contact Captain Auesnehmer and tell him that he will join us for lunch in the Sultan's Palace."

"Yes, Madame."

Chapter 44

As a flock of gulls heralded the dawn, Dexter Rubino lifted himself from the cover of the shrubbery. He wasn't sure if he had slept or passed out, but was sure he had to distance himself from Helene's building. *I can't call a cab. There will be a record of having been here.* The sound of a diesel engine caught his attention. In a nearby parking lot, a double-decker bus rumbled to life. He'd seen them around town, usually full of tourists, but this one appeared, with the exception of a driver, to be empty. Dex mustered his strength and set a course to intercept the bus as it pulled out. His spirit felt strong, but his flesh refused to cooperate. When the bus stopped before entering the roadway, Dex was still forty yards away. In desperation, he frantically waved his arms overhead.

The driver hesitated, then exited the vehicle and came around the front as Dex approached, gasping for air.

"Parla anglès?"

"Si. You OK, Señor?"

"Yes, but I have to get back to my hotel, the Hotel Murmuri. Do you know it?"

"No, I am mechanic. This bus broke down. I make repair."

"Take me to Rambles de Catalonia. I'll show you the way to the hotel."

"No."

Dex reached into his back pocket and pulled out his wallet. He removed a wad of Euros. He didn't care how many there were as he waved them in the face of the man, "Hotel Murmuri, Rambles de Catalonia."

The man grabbed the cash and quickly counted it. "Si," he said and motioned for Dex to get in the front seat. Dex complied, happy to put distance between himself and the body in Helene's foyer. In a few minutes, Dex knew the man driving was a mechanic and not a regular driver. The rolling red behemoth lurched to a stop at every light, then shuddered each time the man resumed driving. As they turned north at Plaça de Catalonia, steam poured from under the hood of the bus. The driver began to jabber in a language unknown to Dex. Dex assumed he was hoping for more money. Not having any cash left, he peered out of the side window. Through the steam and dirty glass he saw a tall muscular man jogging. "Narvik!"

Dex slid down in the seat. *What is he doing here?*

The driver backhanded Dex's shoulder. "No l'entenc."

"Hotel Murmuri, there it is. Let me out of this jalopy."

The bus screeched to a stop and Dex exited the bus. Inside the hotel, he pulled out a charge card and looked boldly into the eyes of the clerk. "I need a room, and I need to get these clothes cleaned."

"Señor, the checkout time is . . ."

"I don't care. You have a room and I have a valid credit card. Get it done, son."

"Si, Señor."

After his run and shower, Matt met Meaghan for breakfast, but their eyes seldom met. The friendly banter they had shared since meeting had gone. After a long silence, Matt decided he had to say something.

"Will we take the Red Line today?"

Meaghan answered without looking up. "If you want. We can do that after picking up your suits."

"That will take all morning."

Meaghan lifted her head and he could see tears brimming in her eyes. "Like, I'm sorry, Matt. You came here with a wardrobe befitting a homeless person and I tried to help make you presentable. I should have known better. We'll pick up your clothes as quickly as possible and bring them back here. Then we can get back on the bus and go wherever you want. It's your vacation and my job is to see to it that you have a good time." A single tear escaped from the woman's right eye and she stood. "I'm going to the powder room. You pay the check."

As she walked away, Matt chuckled. He knew she intended for him to pay with his keycard. If he did, the bill would go to Windswept. He pulled out his wallet and counted out forty Euros, enough to cover the tab and an American-size tip.

Chapter 45

As Matt had predicted, the pickup of his altered clothing took all morning. Then the hair styling Meaghan insisted on took over an hour.

Matt glanced at his watch. "I thought I was going to see more of the city today. Time's a wastin'."

Meaghan pouted for a moment, then her face brightened. "I have an idea. Let's send your clothes back to the hotel with our car, and we can take the bus tour from here."

"Why don't we just have the driver follow the bus?"

"That's silly. We don't have a radio to tell us what we're looking at."

"The driver could tell us."

"He pushes the limo around town. He's not a tour guide. Come on, you've complained all day about not seeing the sights. Now is our chance. It will be fun."

"OK, we need to buy tickets."

"We should have gotten the multiday pass, but there's a booth not far from here."

As they boarded the Red Line bus, the animosity of the morning disappeared. The quick smile returned to Meaghan's face as the bus headed up the inclines of Mountjuic. Matt found himself exclaiming enthusiastically over the many facilities that had been built for the 1992 Olympics. He was tempted to leave the bus tour to explore but didn't want to miss whatever came next. Using a disposable camera, he snapped pictures of many points of interest. When the bus drove past the Columbus monument, Matt said, "Hey, this is on my run."

"Our hotel is right up the street, do you want to go there?"

"No, I want to see more of this beautiful city."

Meaghan briefly touched his arm. "Good, I'm glad you're enjoying it."

By the time they reached Barri Gothic, Matt had exhausted the film in his cheap camera and Meaghan suggested they leave the bus and buy another.

"Can we make it a quick stop?" Matt asked.

"There's something I want to show you," she said.

"Is it right here?"

"No, just up the street a little. You're probably ready for a walk anyway."

The pair left the bus and found a shop where Matt purchased another camera. Meaghan smiled as he took several shots of her in front of a cathedral. Then they walked northward.

"Here it is Matt, Palau de la Musica. Come on, we'll take the tour."

"What about the bus?"

"They keep coming, like, all day. Don't worry we'll get back OK."

Matt grinned like a child as he stared in awe at the sculpture and massive stained-glass dome that lit the interior. "Have you been here before?"

"Only once, and I didn't want to leave. I dream of dancing on this stage."

They rejoined the bus tour, then disembarked at Plaça de Catalunya. While visiting some small shops, Matt surprised Meaghan by buying her an ornate hand fan. It was pink with black lace on the edge. Meaghan practiced flipping the fan as they walked back to the hotel. "I'm sorry you don't have more time here."

"Yeah, this is a great city."

"We still have tomorrow morning. Matt, would you mind doing me one little favor?"

"After all you've done for me, sure."

"The whole time I've been here I've wanted to go to the beach, but I never got there."

"There's a beach near here?"

"Yeah, like, we can go there in the morning and then go directly to the ship in the afternoon. I can arrange to have all our luggage taken to the port after we check out, OK?"

"Sure, I'll skip my run for a walk on the beach. Is it within walking distance of our hotel?"

"I'm not sure; we could ask at the front desk. Do you want to get something to eat?"

"I noticed a Burger King down the street."

"Are you serious?"

"Just kidding. You can pick where we eat tonight."

"Let's change clothes before dinner."

As they entered the lobby, a clerk motioned to Matt, who went to the reception desk. The clerk leaned toward Matt and whispered, "Mr. Narvik, I must speak to you."

Matt frowned. "Is something wrong?"

"I hope not. An unsavory American checked in here this morning. He was only here until three, but when he checked out, he asked if you were staying here. I refused to answer, citing corporate policy, then he showed me a gun. I had no choice but to comply."

"What was the man's name?"

"Mr. Dexter Rubino."

Matt sensed his head jerk in response to hearing the name. *How did he know?*

"He is clearly a man of low degree," the clerk continued. "I hope you and Miss Miller are in no danger. If you wish, I could notify the police."

"No, it will be all right."

Meaghan joined them. "Is something wrong, Matt?"

"Nothing. I was asking Pere the best nearby beach."

The clerk smiled at Meaghan. "The nearest beach is Nova Icaria, but I would suggest that you go to Bogatell. It is much quieter. There are three restaurants along the walkway."

"Is it within walking distance?" Matt asked.

"Too far to walk, but I could arrange for a cab."

"Please do that, Pere. What time, Meaghan?"

"Like, nineish."

"We will also need to send our luggage to the ship in the morning."

"No, I'll call Windswept and have them take care of our luggage," Meaghan said. "Pere, please send a bellman to bring it down before eight thirty,"

"Si, Miss Miller."

In the elevator, Meaghan looked up at Matt. "That beach quip didn't fool me. Is everything OK?"

"Sure, I'm anxious to swim in the Mediterranean."

Meaghan frowned. "Would you tell me if anything was wrong?"

"Probably not, but we have nothing to worry about. Tomorrow we go to the beach, and then we take a nice long transatlantic cruise. What could possibly go wrong?"

Chapter 46

Dex tried to slip aboard the ship unnoticed, but Hakim hailed him as he crossed the Grand Lobby. "What is it, Hakim?"

"Madame wishes to see you as soon as possible, Mr. Dex."

"Notify Mr. Quest that he will have to deal with her. I'll be in my cabin. I'm a little under the weather."

"Mr. Quest has gone to the airport to welcome some VIPs. Madame wishes to see you."

Dex sighed. "More investors I suppose."

"Perhaps. Madame was quite upset that you left the ship last night."

"Where is she?"

"I believe she is in her suite. Would you like me to check for you?"

"No, I'll go see if she's in." Dex walked to the elevator and pushed the button for the seventh level. He walked down the corridor and stopped at Alba's cabin. He thought about knocking but assumed she was in rehearsal. He moved on to Helene's cabin and rapped on the door. When he heard her acknowledgement, he opened the door and stepped in. Madame Helene Adolphe was reclined on an ornate chaise with a bottle of champagne nestled in her arm. "Welcome back, Rubino. If this were the military, you could be shot for deserting your post."

"I'm glad I didn't enlist. Quest has been here the whole time. He's the head of security."

"Desmond is dependent on your expertise. When you didn't return to the ship, he worried some ill fate had befallen you." Madame Adolphe filled a glass to overflowing.

"I had some business to take care of in town."

"I hope she was worth all the worry you caused. Take a glass from the tray, Dexter. I will pour for you. I am in a celebratory mood."

Dex considered refusing but thought it might lessen the pounding in his head. He held the glass while Helene poured. "Thank you, Madame. May I ask what we're celebrating?"

Helene raised her glass. "Doctor Zhan's formula has finally cured Arnan. Since I own the rights to this wonder drug, I will make a fortune."

Dex responded, "Speaking of fortunes, there is the matter of my compensation."

Helene's countenance hardened. "You are the most overcompensated employee in the history of Windswept. I deposited over two million dollars in your Cayman account."

"I remind you that I am a partner not an employee. I split the money you paid me with my men. If it weren't for our actions, Windswept would have been ruined. I was promised a share of Philippe's treasure. Now you say it doesn't exist."

"My nephew was delusional."

"Here is the reality, Helene. I came over here to lead your former bodyguard by the hand while I secured this ship. All I've received since arriving is a meager paycheck. I demand my share of the treasure."

"I wish I could give it to you, Rubino, but it doesn't exist." An evil smile creased her face. "I could offer you another form of compensation for your services."

"Consisting of what?"

"Doctor Zhan was building a beachfront mansion in Belize. He will have no need of it now. Since Windswept holds title to the property, I could sign it over to you, providing this cruise is completed without incident."

"How do I know this isn't just a tree house on the beach?"

"I know if I cheated you, I would never be rid of you, and I sincerely wish to be rid of you, Rubino."

"The feeling is mutual."

"We have an agreement, then?"

"Yes, providing that the property is all you say it is."

"When we reach Sunset Cay, if we have had no security breaches, I will sign the property over to you. I will even allow you to use the corporate jet to get there."

"Let's shake on it."

"Candace! There you are. I was worried."

"Is he gone?"

"Yes, he wanted to see you before he left, but he was summoned to the ship."

"I don't like that guy. He's a creeper."

"That is not a nice thing to say. He is our business partner. Until you ascend to your rightful place, we will have to be nice to him."

"You're nice enough for both of us. Don't these people realize how important I am?"

"Dear, it's nice to be important. It's more important to be nice."

The girl placed three fingers of her right hand into her mouth and pretended to gag.

"Stop that! You could damage your vocal cords."

"I could sing like a frog."

"Stop behaving like a child. This is a great opportunity for you. I will not allow you to squander your talent. Your father abandoned us and fled to his other family when he got sick. Now you will usurp Alba and we will have the lifestyle we deserve."

The girl squinted at her mother. "What does usurp mean?"

"Overcome, seize, and grab what should have been yours by birthright. You'll be the princess you were born to be."

"What if I don't want to be a princess?"

"You're too young to know what you want. I want you to be a princess, so a princess you shall be!"

"I still don't like the idea of changing my name."

"Would you like to go back to Candace Duckworth? Cologne isn't her real name either, but it is commercially viable."

"What about Todd?"

"He's fine with it. He has been a good surrogate father for you, but it's time to claim your birthright."

Chapter 47

Dex rose before dawn and began making his rounds. This was the big day, beginning with a meeting with the port officials at eight. The dive team would inspect the underside of the hull before noon, a necessary chore in this age of terrorism. At noon the passengers would start boarding. At six o'clock in the evening, they would cast off.

He stopped to look in on Doctor Zhan. The cabin smelled fresh, but Zhan still lay unconscious. At least a nurse was looking after him. Dex tried to exchange pleasantries with her, but she spoke no English.

After breakfast, he went to the Grand Lobby to greet the port officials as Captain Auesnehmer escorted them aboard. *Smile, Rubino, you're on!*

A Windswept van whisked away Meaghan and Matt's luggage while they enjoyed their last breakfast at Murmuri. A cab took them to the beach, and Matt rented a double chaise with a clamshell cover. It wasn't as warm as Matt would have liked, but Meaghan thought it was perfect.

Remembering what Alba had told him, Matt expected to see topless women lying in the sand. But judging by the sun worshipers he saw, he concluded the beach was family oriented.

Meaghan wore a black one-piece suit with strategically placed cutouts. The canopy provided shade for their upper bodies while the Catalan sun warmed their legs. Meaghan responded by throwing a towel over her legs. She handed Matt some sun block and asked him to put a little on her back.

"Why? You're in the shade."

"Like, I burn really easy. Even the reflection off the sand can turn me into Lobster Girl. It's the curse of being fair-haired. You should understand."

"I never worried about it."

"You probably didn't get that much sun in Pennsylvania."

As Matt massaged the sun block into her shoulders, he said, "Oh, I had my share of sun burns. When I was a teenager, we used to skinny-dip in an abandoned quarry. I got some very painful sunburns that way."

She laughed. "You skinny dipped in Pennsylvania? Just guys or did you lure some poor Amish girl into the pond?"

"They weren't Amish. And they lured me there."

"Oh, I'm sure. Debauchery in the heartland. Who knew?"

"Where did you grow up?"

"I'm an Air Force brat. I lived in California the most."

"Did you ever live overseas?"

"No. Daddy was stationed in Germany for a while, but Mom wouldn't leave the States."

"Where are they now?"

"When Daddy retired, they split up. He went to Alaska; she lives in Oregon."

"I'm sorry, it must have been hard on you."

"I'm OK with it. See, Matt, we're both sort of orphans."

Matt winced at the comparison, then laughed it off. "I guess you're right."

Meaghan began to speak, then hesitated before saying, "Alba's an orphan, too."

"She told me her mother and brothers died in the war. Her father died recently."

Meaghan looked him in the eye. "I didn't know she ever had brothers. At least she has her aunt, but I don't think they get along."

"I don't know anything about the rest of her family."

"How did you meet her?"

Matt smiled. "It's classified."

Chapter 48

Matt waded up to his knees and thought the waters of the Mediterranean were a little cool, but he concluded that could be because of his familiarity with the warm waters of the Florida Gulf Coast. Meaghan seemed to revert to childhood as she frolicked with abandon, as if she were a hundred miles from civilization. All the while, a thriving European city lay just steps away.

They toweled off and lunched at a beachside restaurant. Matt noticed a wistful look on Meaghan's face as they waited for their food, and she blushed when she grew conscious of his gaze. "So, Matt, what are your plans for the cruise?"

He shrugged. "Just to enjoy the cruise, I guess."

"Are you planning to sweep Alba off of her feet?"

"Alba and I have a lot to talk about. I'm not sure of her feelings for me, or mine for her."

"She wouldn't go to all this trouble for just any guy."

"I'm nothing special, but the way we met was. I think my meeting Alba was ordained by God."

"Why do you bring God into everything? Life is complicated enough without some higher power interfering."

"You've got it backwards. I have a relationship with the God of the universe. Being in the center of His will is the most important thing in my life. He only wants what's best for me and His way is always best. My faith actually makes life much simpler."

Meaghan shook her head. "It's all too deep for me. With all the problems in the world, who would want to have a relationship with God? I mean, like, if He really loved the world, wouldn't He stop all the hate and war?"

"Hate and war are the result of sin. He loved the world so much that he sent Jesus to free us from sin and the penalty of it."

"The world doesn't seem very free to me."

"No, freedom is a choice. You can choose to be free."

"How?"

"It's as simple as ABC."

For Dexter Rubino, the morning of embarkation became a whirlwind of activity. Several times, he felt a tightening in his chest and he had to sit down.

"Are you OK, Mr. Dex?"

"Yes Hakim, I'm just a little worried about the final preparations. Where is Mr. Quest?"

"He is with Madame Adolphe. He is to be her escort at the reception."

When the first group boarded, Dex was busy getting last minute details done with the port officials. Helene delivered a slurred speech, which ended with her wishing the passengers a Happy New Year in French. The captain took control of the situation and ordered the security team to let the guests board at will.

The change in plans resulted in a smooth boarding process. Dex watched with a smile until he caught sight of a tall, red-haired woman in the throng of passengers. "It can't be her," he whispered. The pain in his chest increased, so he sat on a bench. *I must be hallucinating. First Narvik, now her.*

"You need the doctor, Mr. Dex?"
"No, Hakim, I'm just a little tired."

Chapter 49

Matt and Meaghan left the cab at four o'clock and made their way through customs. As they approached the ship, Meaghan stopped and turned to Matt. "What will I do now? I know I'm different. Like you said, I'm a new creature."

"Just take it one step at a time. Let the Lord lead you and learn to wait for His leading."

Meaghan spotted Omar standing near the gangway. "Here goes nothing."

"Omar, it's so good to see you again."

"Welcome back, Miss Meaghan. Is this your father?"

"Ahh, no, Omar, this is Mr. Narvik. He's the grand prizewinner of the cruise upgrade contest. Matt, this is Omar. He's an old friend of Alba's."

"Nice to meet you, Omar. Can you tell me how I can get in touch with Alba?"

Omar shot a glance at Meaghan. "Alba will greet all of the guests at the bon voyage party."

"I'd like to see her beforehand, if you don't mind."

"I am afraid that is impossible, Mr. Narvik. Alba is resting at the present time."

When Matt started to speak again, Meaghan placed a hand on his chest, silencing him, and said to Omar, "Do you know if my cabin adjacent to Alba's is being held for me?"

"Yes, Miss Meaghan, your room is waiting for you."

"Thank you, Omar," she said and turned to Matt. "Let's find your cabin. We want to make sure your luggage arrived."

"Oh, OK. We'll see you on the ship, Omar."

The couple proceeded to check-in, where Matt received the key card to his suite on level seven. Meaghan giggled, "You're across the hall from Alba and me."

"We should have known she'd take care of me."

"I can't wait to give her the news."

"Meaghan, you'd better wait until I talk to her. She was a little confused about my beliefs the last time I saw her. Alba is a good person but not a believer. She may not share your enthusiasm."

Desmond Quest gently patted Helene's cheek. "Madame, can you hear me?"

She answered without opening her eyes. "What is it?"

"Your enemies have been delivered into your hands, Madame. Rubino is in the infirmary; he has had a cardiac episode."

"What?"

"Dexter Rubino has fallen ill. Doctor Stuart is taking care of him. He will offer no resistance when we dispose of him."

Through a champagne-colored fog, Helene Adolphe grasped the significance of this news. She smiled broadly.

"Mr. Rubino, I'm Doctor Stuart. Do you remember me?"

Dex blinked and his eyes wandered around the room. "Where am I?"

"You're in the infirmary. You've suffered a mild cardiac event. With a few weeks rest and preventative care, you'll be fine."

"I have work to do."

"No, this cruise is strictly rest and relaxation for you."

"You don't understand, Doc, I'm the deputy director of security on this ship. I can't be laid up for weeks."

"Doctor's orders, Mr. Rubino."

"Are you sure I wasn't drugged?"

"There's no evidence of that. You do have high blood pressure. A man your age should monitor his vitals. Mr. Quest asked that I keep you sedated. While I see no valid medical reason for this, it might be wise to let him think you're sedated."

"I can't fake a coma for the entire cruise."

"If you had signs of a communicable disease, I could put you in isolation. Perhaps you could share a cabin with Doctor Zhan."

"Doc, I can't go into all the details, but I believe Quest plans on murdering Doctor Zhan. That's part of the reason I think I've been drugged. Windswept management would like to get rid of me as discreetly as possible. You may not realize it yet, but these people are not entirely on the up and up."

"I told Quest you should be hospitalized. He wouldn't hear of it. I'm aware of some ethical lapses, Mr. Rubino, but I don't think they would stoop to murder."

"You're wrong Doc. Helene Adolphe could order anyone's death without blinking."

"Meaghan, welcome home." Alba rushed to embrace her friend. "Where is Matthew?"

"He's in his suite. I told him to wait while I checked to see if you where up to company."

"I want to see him but not like this. I want him to see me tonight when I take the stage in my new gown."

"I don't think he cares what you're wearing, Alba."

"Please, Meaghan, make some excuse for me. It is only a few hours more. Has he recovered from his wounds?"

"He seems fine to me. He has a little scar on his leg. He told me it was from a boating accident. How is Arnan?"

Alba took her hand. "Meaghan, I have sad news."

Chapter 50

Matt wandered around his suite. *This is bigger than my whole boat. It's nearly as big as my house. Whom am I kidding? I no longer have that house. It went with my job at Windswept. I hope the package I hid there is OK.*

He stepped on to his balcony and watched the drug dogs sniffing what appeared to be a pallet of ice cream containers. The forklift driver was having an animated discussion with the port police, while two ebony German Shepherds shopped for their favorite flavor.

That package is the only connection I have to draw me back there. I could go anywhere in the world, with anyone I want. Will Alba want to share the future with me or will I continue wandering alone? Lord, I ask you to direct my path so that I might be of some service to you.

A knock at his door interrupted his thoughts. He crossed the spacious living room and opened the door to find Meaghan smiling at him, but her eyes were red and her mascara a little smudged.

"Alba is resting up for tonight," Meaghan said. "She asked me to show you around the ship until after the bon voyage party."

"Is she really resting, or is she reluctant to see me again?"

"Matt, she's anxious to see you, but she has a lot of pressure on her. This cruise is the rebirth of her career. This could be a springboard to more movies. At the very least, it will affect the future of the cruise line."

"I just wanted to see her for a minute."

"Let her make a grand entrance at tonight's party. She wants you to see her at her best."

"Should I wear the tux?"

"I don't think so. Let me familiarize you with the ship. It's nearly time for the emergency drill; we'll have to go to deck four. When we get back, I'll help you pick out your clothes."

"There's a piano player onboard I'd like you to meet. His name is Dave Carpenter."

"I don't know him. He might have come aboard while I was away. The piano bar is on deck four also. How do you know this man?"

"I met him on another cruise. He told me to look him up when I boarded. Do you know most of the crew?"

"I know most of the professional crew and entertainers. While I was laid up, I was Alba's girl Friday. I got a good look at how the other half lives."

"Do you know a man named Dexter Rubino?"

"Sure, he's, like, in charge of security or something. He and Alba are pretty tight."

"Is that so?"

"Mother, I am not a child. I like having my own cabin."

"Don't think for a minute that you have a license to entertain boys in this cabin."

The girl grinned, revealing her orthodontics. "I don't like boys, Mother. I much prefer men."

"Listen to me, you little tramp, you are here to launch your career, not to ruin your reputation."

"What was it Father used to say? "The fruit doesn't fall far from the tree?""

"I've made enormous mistakes in my life. I won't sit by while you repeat them. You are the only good thing to come of my relationship with your father, a father you barely remember."

"By good thing, you mean free ride. It's OK, I've known it for a long time. When I make it big I'll see to it you're taken care of." She began to giggle. "I'll choose a nice retirement home for you."

"I hate it when you behave this way. Can't you at least feign appreciation for the sacrifices I made on your behalf?"

"Cool down, Mommy Dearest, I'm just yanking your chain. Is your boyfriend Hector on this cruise, or will it just be Quest?"

"His name is Dexter. Yes, he is, but I have to see Helene before I see him. She will tell me what my relationship with him will be. As for Desmond Quest, I only tease him to have an ally in Helene's good graces."

"How soon will she want to see me?"

"She will send for us before the bon voyage party. We have to be ready to see her at any time. Right now, I want you to change into your blue mini-dress. We have to meet the piano player on deck four. Flirt with him, but don't give anything away. Put on your sweet little girl act. Hurry, it's almost time for the emergency drill."

"OK, Mommy. I hope he's cute."

"Please, Madame, you need to recover your bearings before the bon voyage party." Desmond Quest valiantly tried to pour a tomato-based concoction into Helene Adolphe's mouth.

"Enough, Desmond, I can't stand anymore or I shall vomit."

"That would be a good thing, Madame."

"Then you drink it, you buffoon. This is a terrible turn of events. Someone laced a drug with my champagne. You must find the perpetrator, Quest. It was that scoundrel Rubino, I'm sure of it."

"Madame, Rubino is in the infirmary. He is totally incapacitated. I've given the ship's doctor orders to keep him sedated."

"Where is Anton?"

"Anton Carmella is not here. You remember he is now Doctor Zhan. He is securely restrained in an inside cabin. If you want, we could put both American pigs in the same sty, just as you wished."

"Keep them both under sedation until we leave Madeira, then arouse them before we toss them overboard. I want to be there, Desmond. I want to see them flailing in the wake of the ship."

"They will pay for their impertinence, Madame. While the crew conducts the emergency drill, we could give an audience to the child and her mother."

"Does Alba know of her yet?"

"No, it will be a complete surprise."

"This will be wonderful, Quest. Both enslaved to me for the rest of my life. I will control Windswept and both of my nephews' surviving offspring."

"Yes, Madame, you are the heart and soul of Windswept."

Chapter 51

When Matt and Meaghan arrived at the piano bar, they found Dave Carpenter surrounded by a cadre of other entertainers. They all welcomed Meaghan back aboard, and she introduced them to Matt. Dave began playing "In the Garden."

Matt ushered Meaghan to the man's side. "Dave, this is Meaghan Miller. She was an entertainer on this ship until she was sidelined by an injury."

"Hello, Dave."

"Nice to meet you, Meaghan. Are you and Matt a couple?"

Meaghan giggled politely and blushed. "Matt and I are friends. I've also had the honor of being his tour guide for the past few days."

"Lucky, Matt. Do you sing, Meaghan?"

"I'm primarily a dancer, but I can sing a little. If we have time to practice, I'll be singing backup for Alba on a couple old standards."

"Dave is a believer, Meaghan. Meaghan just accepted the Lord today."

Dave, who had continued to play during the conversation, stopped. He rose, embraced her, and whispered in her ear. "Welcome to the family."

Dave turned to the others and said, "Hey, everybody, I want you to meet my new sister in Christ."

The other entertainers fell into a hush. Meaghan blushed as she looked into the astonished faces of her friends. Meaghan was not ashamed of her decision, but the sudden exposure surprised her. In their eyes, she could see the judgments falling on her. She had changed and they could see it in her face. One of the other dancers broke the silence, saying, "That's sweet . . . Now, it's about time for us to get up on deck for the welcome aboard routine."

A voice came over the loud speaker asking all passengers to report to the appropriate deck for the emergency drill. The party ended as the entertainers filed out of the room.

Dave shouted as they left. "See you all later tonight. Don't forget about the worship service tomorrow, nine A.M. sharp."

Matt leaned toward Dave and said, "Don't you think Meaghan should have been the one tell her friends about her conversion?"

"Why? They know now. You don't mind do you, Meaghan?"

"No, I don't mind. I'm sure it was a surprise to some of them."

"Let me hear you sing, Meaghan. We have a new singer coming aboard. She is very young, and I'll be in charge of some of her performances. Nancy Rivers showed me some of her videos, and I think your voices may be compatible."

"Matt has to report for the emergency drill."

"It's OK, Meaghan," Matt said. "I'll find my own way around. You and Dave need to practice."

"Look, Mr. Rubino, I can give you a sedative that will put you to sleep for a few hours, at least until we are at sea. Then I'll diagnose you with the noro virus and order you quarantined. Just the mention of the scourge will scare them into compliance with my orders."

"Then I can be moved back to my cabin."

"Right. When we put in at Gibraltar, you can sneak off of the ship."

"I can't thank you enough for helping me like this, Doc."

"Quest is holding some legal problems over my head. If you make it back to the States, perhaps you can help me out, too."

"I'll help any way I can, if I make it."

As the doctor filled a syringe, he asked, "How did you get involved with this bunch of hoodlums?"

"It's a long story. When I wake up I'll tell you all about it."

"This is going to pinch."

"Ouch!"

During the emergency drill, Meaghan and David practiced a solo that Meaghan agreed to sing at the worship service. They were getting along fine until a middle-aged woman entered the room.

"Excuse me, are you Mr. Carpenter?" the woman said.

"Yes, I am."

"Mr. Carpenter, I'd like you to meet the next sensation of the music industry and the new headliner of the Windswept cruise line, Candace Cologne!"

As Matt wandered around the ship, he had to keep shaking his head 'no' to the servers distributing free drinks. When he encountered a movie poster touting a much younger Alba, he stopped. He stared into those dark eyes that had captured his heart so many months ago.

The ship was much more ornate than the other cruise ship he had been on, but about the same size. Everything looked new, or at least freshly painted. On the pool deck, a rock band played while some of the dancers he had just met stepped and wiggled to the beat. Several lured members of the crowd to join them on stage.

Matt was more interested in watching the release of the lines that were the last tie of the ship to terra firma. The maneuvering of the mighty tugs helped the ship move away from the dock and the crowd shouted gaily as a long blast of the ship's horn signaled that they were underway.

It was early evening. Matt leaned on the railing as Barcelona, the most exotic and beautiful city he had ever seen slipped away from him.

Meaghan rushed to Alba's door and knocked frantically.

"Omar, I must see Alba at once!"

"I am sorry, Miss Meaghan, I have strict orders that she is not to be disturbed."

"You know that Alba and I are friends. What I have to tell her is, like, really important."

"Then it will be just as important after the performance. My orders are explicit— no one is to disturb Alba Cologne. Not even you, Miss Meaghan."

Chapter 52

"Where is the child, Quest?"

"I am not sure, Madame. Perhaps she is on the pool deck at the embarkation party."

"She was to board with the passengers, not celebrate with them."

"Let me call her cabin, or perhaps she is with her mother."

"You have to keep better tabs on the girl. Leave her mother to her own devices and she will soon fade from the picture. She has long had a proclivity for drink and narcotics. The girl can be a valuable asset. We must protect her from evil influences."

"There's no answer, Madame. I'll try the mother."

"Encourage the girl to spend her free time with Nancy Rivers. If it were not for Ms. Rivers, I never would have known the girl had genuine talent. Did you see to it that the gift shops have a quantity of her recordings?"

"Yes, Madame, there is a prominent display of her video also. I just hope Alba stays out of the shops until we introduce Candace. There is no answer at the mother's cabin either. Do you wish for me to search the ship?"

"Not you personally. Send your security team to look for her. It might be wise to assign one of your best men to guard her."

"I would think that Hakim was the most trustworthy."

"Yes, he will do. What is the casino security team doing until the casino opens?

"They are busy testing the machines and security apparatus. I have been assured that everything will be ready before we leave Gibraltar."

"I hope they realize the casino is our most lucrative enterprise."

"I have informed them thusly."

Is there any news of Rubino?"

"No, I ordered the doctor to inform me of any developments. I will stop at the infirmary after we locate the girl. I trust Dexter will remain alive until we leave Madeira."

"You mentioned putting the two swine in the same pen. That may have been a stroke of genius. I would enjoy seeing my two nemeses caged together."

"We could keep them in Rubino's cabin."

"No, his cabin is on the same level with the crew. I don't want to involve any more of them than need be. We have Anton in an inside cabin. Put Dexter there also. The nurse can take charge of both of them."

"She will request greater remuneration."

Helene released an evil laugh. "Promise her anything, except a life vest!"

Matt wandered to the seventh level. He paused at Alba's door. He wanted to knock but thought better of it. *I'll meet her on her terms, this time.* He entered his own suite and checked the itinerary card. He was scheduled to dine on the next level up at a place called the Sultan's Palace at 7:00 P.M. He glanced at his watch. "It's six-thirty now," he whispered. "I thought Meaghan would be here to tell me what to wear." He found his new luggage in the large closet next to the shower room and his new clothing neatly hung for him. *Let's see . . . I can't go wrong with basic black.*

After a quick shower, he donned the black suit and a black dress shirt. He had several ties to choose from but decided to skip the choker. "Not bad, Narvik," he said as he looked in the mirrors on the closet doors. "You look like the cover of *Gangster Quarterly*."

He left his room with seven minutes to spare. He headed forward to the end of the corridor and found himself on a small balcony that overlooked the Grand Lobby. *Impressive view.* A winding glass staircase led upward. He shrugged and proceeded up the stairs. At the top, a scantily clad harem girl met him.

"Mr. Narvik, we are so glad to be serving you this evening." Her eyes locked on to Matt's unfettered neckline. "Mr. Narvik, when dining in the Sultan's Palace, neckties are required. I have several here that you may choose from."

"If it's all the same to you, miss, I'd rather dine alone."

Meaghan Miller emerged from the elevator wearing a beautiful gown that highlighted her slim figure. "I'm sorry to be late. I stopped by your cabin and you had already left." She, too, noticed his unfettered neckline. "Why aren't you wearing a tie?"

"I hate ties."

"You're eating at the Sultan's Palace; you must wear a tie." She grabbed one from the harem girl. Here, take this pink one and use the men's room over by the elevator. And hurry, the captain is on his way."

"Can't you and I get a table, just for us?"

"It's a great honor to be asked to the captain's table. You'll get to meet some of Alba's family as well as the captain."

"Meaghan, I don't know if I can do this."

"You can't tie a tie?"

"I can tie my own tie. I just don't know how to behave around important people."

"You told me to pray about it and let the Lord lead one step at a time. Maybe you should take your own advice. Now go put that tie on."

"Yes, ma'am!" he replied and delivered a mock salute, then reluctantly headed for the men's room.

Meaghan turned to the hostess. "Miss, my name is Meaghan Miller. I work for Windswept."

"Yes, Miss Miller, you are on the guest list for the captain's table."

"I'd like you to please not serve any wine or strong drink to Mr. Narvik or myself."

"Certainly, is this just tonight or for the entire cruise?"

"For the entire cruise, please."

The captain stepped off the elevator and Meaghan greeted him.

"Good to have you back, Meaghan," he said. "How is your ankle?"

"Good as new, Captain. I'm here in a professional role tonight. I'm escorting the American who won the upgrade sweepstakes."

"I was not aware of such a thing. I will be glad to have you at my table. Madame Adolphe and Quest have cancelled, so you can answer any questions about the company."

"I'll try." she said as Matt exited the men's room. "Oh, Matt, come over here. Captain Auesnehmer, this is our grand-prize winner, Matt Narvik. Matt, this is Captain Auesnehmer."

"Congratulations, Mr. Narvik, on both the contest and having such a lovely dinner partner."

"Thank you, Captain. It's an honor to meet you."

As they walked to the table, Meaghan whispered, "See? You can do this."

"I don't know if I can keep breathing with this tie on."

Chapter 53

"Candace, Hakim will escort you to your dressing room. Ms. Rivers and the makeup people will help you get ready for your grand entrance. Mr. Quest and I have business to discuss with your mother."

"Thank you for this opportunity, Auntie Helene."

As Candace left Madame Adolphe's suite, her mother spoke. "I must go with her, Helene. If they don't use the right makeup, her freckles will stand out."

"Nonsense, Cynthia, our people are competent professionals. They are familiar with the lighting and the theater. Nancy Rivers will see that the child's best interests are served."

"I know you hate me, Helene, but I won't let you harm my daughter."

"Hate you? Why, dear Cynthia, I have no animosity towards you. You are family and family is the most important thing in the world to me. Is that not true, Mr. Quest?"

"Oh, yes indeed, Madame. Mrs. Sterling, I assure you that, having no children herself, Madame places great affection on the daughters of her late nephew."

"Speaking of his daughters, where's Alba?"

Quest answered before Helene could. "She is preparing for her performance."

"Does she know that Candace will be performing also?"

"I know Alba better than anyone," said Helene. "If she were to learn that another entertainer was going on with her as an equal, she would react violently."

Cynthia smirked. "How are you going to control her after the fact?"

"Our fitness director will be backstage. He has been with the family for a long time. He will know how to subdue her until I can reason with her."

"She hasn't seen Candace since she was a baby."

"I imagine she still thinks of her that way. Alba is a child emotionally, but physically she is maturing too quickly to salvage her career. The rehearsal schedule has been a struggle for her. Several times Nancy Rivers advised me to forget her and concentrate on Candace. After Candace usurps her tonight, Alba will realize that Windswept needs the appeal of a younger star."

"Just so you don't expect Candace to stay locked up on this boat."

"No, Cynthia, that is the plan for Alba. She can continue here for several years until she is in retirement. We are proceeding with our plans for a movie and television expansion all centered on Candace Cologne. The money you received is just a down payment for your concessions."

"What about my nonmonetary demands?"

"It is taken care of, my dear. Desmond, please escort Cynthia to Doctor Zhan's cabin so she can see for herself."

"Wait a minute, who is Doctor Zhan?"

Quest beamed and said, "Doctor Zhan is the man previously known to you as Anton Carmella."

Matt struggled to swallow his food as his necktie seemed to grow ever tighter. He joined the conversation only when forced to.

Meaghan touched his arm. "I know you're feeling anxious, but this is an honor. "

Matt nodded and glanced at the faces around the table. *At least Alba's family isn't here.*

At a table intended for twelve, there were but ten. Besides he, Meaghan and the captain, there were seven passengers who spoke either German or French. Captain Auesnehmer conversed in both, seemed to enjoy sharing the stories of his maritime career, until a messenger interrupted him, and whispered into his ear.

The captain nodded and rose to his feet. "Excuse me, ladies and gentlemen. An iceberg has been spotted just ahead. I must go to the bridge." He gave a hearty laugh as even the most naive realized he was joking.

Dessert was served and the guests ate in relative silence until the sound of applause echoed through the atrium.

Matt whispered to Meaghan, "Can we go now?"

"We should stay for coffee."

"I can't drink coffee this late. It will keep me awake all night. Besides that, it's nearly time for the show."

"We have forty minutes before the show starts. What's your hurry?"

"I want a good seat."

"Matt, you're on level seven. There are reserved seats for everyone in the luxury suites."

"I didn't know that. Can we take a walk on deck before the show?"

Meaghan smiled and rolled her eyes. "OK, you've earned that much."

Omar dutifully offered his arm to Alba, and she lightly planted her hand on his forearm. A security detail rushed ahead of them as they slowly walked down the corridor to the balcony. Alba was dressed in an ornate gown with a plunging neckline that accentuated her curvaceous figure. A diamond-studded choker graced her delicate neck.

A dozen members of her fan club were assembled in the Grand Lobby. Quest had ordered several of the crew members to encourage passengers to gather and greet the returning star. A crowd of about thirty stood looking adoringly up at the lofty perch.

Alba walked to the railing and waved to the passengers and crew. She threw them a kiss, just as she had done in several of her films. The crowd politely applauded.

Alba and Omar then boarded the glass elevator and began the descent to the level below the Grand Lobby. Omar whispered, "I wish Mashal was here to see this."

"Mashal has forgotten me."

"No, Alba, how could he forget the only woman he has ever loved?"

"I must concentrate on the task at hand. We will speak of this later, after my performance."

"Si, Princesa"

The elevator stopped in spartan surroundings that seemed even more austere in the glory of Alba's gown. "Where is Quest?" she said. "He was supposed to meet me here."

"Quest is busy with Madame Adolphe. He will be here in time to start the show."

"Quest is incompetent. You may be the head of security soon, Omar."

"I am happy to serve you anyway I can."

They walked half the length of the ship, where they were stopped by the dancers, who gushed over Alba's gown and her beauty. Alba saw an unfamiliar shock of red hair move beyond the gaggle of dancers. "Who is that?"

The group fell silent until one said, "That's the children's entertainer."

"Why is she here?"

The dancers looked at one another without responding. Finally, one of them stammered a reply. "She is . . . Mr. Quest is going to introduce her . . . after the grand finale."

Alba stamped her foot. "Where is Nancy Rivers? This is totally unacceptable."

Chapter 54

Desmond Quest escorted Cynthia down the narrow corridor to the cabin of Doctor Zhan. He knocked twice, then kicked the bottom of the door. The door opened a crack, a pair of brown eyes peered out at him, then opened fully, and a smiling woman in scrubs nodded a welcome.

Speaking Spanish, Desmond instructed the woman to go for a walk. He and Cynthia entered, and he closed the door behind her.

"Here he is, Cynthia, old, helpless, and alone."

"Serves him right. I'd like to choke him to death right now."

"Madame has other plans for him. What is it about this man that excites such fury from females?"

"I don't know about anyone else, but he tried to murder me."

"Madame told me that he contracted with Philippe for your demise. How did you escape?"

"The hit man Philippe employed knew Anton. He took pity on me when he saw how I'd been abused by Anton and my husband. He stole a body from a nursing home and substituted it for mine, and then he caused a gas explosion to destroy my house. The resulting fire consumed the body. In that county, coroner's reports were negotiable. The hit man promised he would take me to Miami. When Philippe found out what he'd done, he had the guy killed and took me for his own."

"Is the child really Philippe's?"

"Yes, surely you saw the DNA reports. Helene insisted they be repeated three times."

Quest shrugged. "That red hair is what causes the question."

"I admit, she doesn't look much like a desert princess."

"No, but it doesn't matter now. Helene has accepted her, and Nancy Rivers has trained her. She will live like a princess as long as she behaves. Oh, my . . . Look at the time. I must get backstage."

"Do you want me to wait here for the nurse?"

"No, you should come with me. Anton Carmella isn't going anywhere."

"I have one remaining question. Dexter Rubino is on this ship. How am I supposed to act when I see him again?"

"That is no longer an issue, love. Nature has begun what we intended to cause. Dexter Rubino is as good as dead."

Matt and Meaghan entered the theater as the rock band played some forgettable tunes from the '80s. An usher escorted them to their seats in a separate part of the balcony.

"These are great seats, Meaghan. Any closer and we'd be on stage."

"This is all part of the prize."

"There really wasn't a contest, was there?"

"Oh, so you're finally catching on? Alba planned all this for you. Don't you think I deserve to know the extent of your relationship with her?"

"I haven't hidden anything from you. I'm not sure what will happen when I see her again."

Meaghan sighed. "I know that she will need some true friends after tonight."

"The best thing a friend can do is pray for you. Will you join me in praying for Alba?"

"Sure, Matt."

Matt uttered a short prayer, and as he whispered "Amen," the rock band stopped playing and the house lights dimmed.

Desmond Quest took the stage, introduced himself, and greeted the packed house in the name of "the Windswept Cruise Line and the Cologne family."

"My friends, we have gathered onboard the *New Dawn* from many places across the globe. Let me introduce you to the most important man in our lives for the next fortnight, Captain Emile Auesnehmer!"

The captain entered from the right and saluted the crowd. He then gave a hearty wave, shook hands with Quest, and exited.

"Another gentleman who may play an important role in our lives is a former Mr. Galaxy, now our fitness instructor, Arnan!"

Matt sat up at the mention of the name. *It can't be the same Arnan.* As the giant of a man took the stage, dwarfing Quest, he knew it was.

Quest continued introducing the heads of various departments, but Matt tuned him out as he spoke to Meaghan. "Do you know anything about Arnan?"

"Yeah, like I know a lot about him. Why?"

"I met him before and it didn't end well."

Meaghan chuckled. "It didn't end well for me, either, and I had a crush on the big jerk. Until a few weeks ago, he was the chauffer for Alba's great aunt. Now he's the fitness instructor and has a girlfriend a third his size."

"I'm sorry if he hurt you."

"I'm a big girl. Besides, I trust in the Lord now, not some muscle-bound moron."

A spotlight sweeping past startled them and fixed its light on the booth next to theirs. The roll of a snare drum filled the air and Quest's voice took on an even more bombastic tone. "Ladies and gentlemen, let me present the woman whose foresight and ingenuity are responsible for the Windswept Cruise Line, former diplomat and current president of the Windswept Corporation, Madame Helene Adolphe!"

A prerecorded blast of trumpets vibrated through the theater and a shriveled old woman stepped into the light. She walked to the railing and gave a royal wave to the applauding audience. The applause lessened as the wave continued. Finally, the lights swung back to Quest, who was still looking lovingly toward Helene. "Thank you for your leadership, Madame. Thank you." He turned back to the audience. "Now for the moment you have all been waiting for, the Windswept Dancers, featuring the Cologne sisters!"

Meaghan gasped and left her seat to lean over the railing that separated the old woman from their booth. With the increasing volume of the music, Matt could not hear what they said, but he did recognize Alba's name. Then the harsh voice of the old woman said, "You are an employee, Miss Miller. This is family business."

Meaghan returned to her seat and Matt heard her sniffle. "Is there anything I can do?"

"We've already prayed for her, I don't know what else to do. It's all so cruel."

The swirling dancers, with their elaborate costumes, the blasting disco music, and spinning lights held Matt's attention for a few moments. Then a great artificial rose in the center of the stage opened as an elevated platform at its center lifted the most beautiful woman he had ever seen above the flurry of activity. All the dancers faced her and knelt, lifting a hand in salute. The crowd cheered loudly.

Matt whispered, "Alba".

Chapter 55

"I'm sorry, Mr. Jeanblanc, I don't speak French."

"Oh," the man said and doubled over, grasping his abdomen.

"You don't have a fever or elevated blood pressure. How long have you been feeling ill?"

The man held up one finger and gave another groan.

"Do you have a private cabin?"

"Oui."

"For the safety of the passengers and crew, I will have to quarantine you to your cabin. I'm sorry, but this will preclude your performance, at least until you're feeling better."

"Merci, Doctor Stuart."

"This type of virus usually runs its course in three or four days. I'm afraid you're the third person who has had similar symptoms. All I can do is restrict your contact with the rest of the ship. Can you make it to your cabin unassisted?"

"Oui, Doctor."

"Take the medicine I gave you, drink plenty of fluids, and order a bowl of chicken noodle soup from room service. I'll be in to check on you in the morning."

As the man left the infirmary, two of Windswept's security men entered. "Doctor, we have been ordered to move Mr. Dex to the same cabin as Doctor Zhan."

"There must be some miscommunication, gentlemen. Dex is showing signs of a virus as well as his heart ailment. He should be placed in his own cabin."

"Mr. Quest wishes him to be kept away from the other crew members. He also ordered us to secure his firearm."

"His weapon is in my safe. I'll get it for you. I insist that Dex be taken to his own cabin."

"We must do as ordered, Doctor. You can discuss it with Mr. Quest."

Matt Narvik gazed in wonder as the blaring music and dizzying lights accompanying the voice of Alba as she sang in French. At least what he thought was French. The stage filled with dancers in various states of dress, but Matt's vision locked on to the dark eyes of Alba Cologne. The spell broke when Meaghan whispered into his ear.

"What? . . . What is it, Meaghan?"

"I said this is a disaster."

"What's a disaster?"

"Alba is out of sync with the recording. She is starting to get flustered, can't you tell? This is like watching an old Japanese movie."

For the first time Matt noticed that Alba's mouth and the voice of the singer were not in sync. Alba seemed to stumble as she left the raised platform. One of the male dancers caught her arm as she regained her balance. She took two steps toward the audience and collided with another of the dancers, then fell to the floor, face first. A collective gasp rose from the audience. Several of the dancers helped Alba to her feet while the recording continued.

The dancers rushed back to their correct positions and two of the female dancers tried to occupy the same space at the same time. This led to a collision with one of the male dancers. A hint of laughter rolled through the audience.

"What's going on, Meaghan?"

"Oh, Matt, it's like, horrible! Poor Alba."

Matt noticed the old woman in the next booth had covered her eyes and was shaking her head. Mercifully, the computer-controlled spotlight was off Alba as she again stumbled and fell to her knees. This led to a less kind response from the crowd. Alba dutifully rose and entered the piercing brightness of the light and continued mouthing the words to the song as tears ran down her face.

"Oh, Alba!" Meaghan said. "I have to go back stage, Matt."

"I'll go with you."

"No, she won't want to see you tonight. Maybe tomorrow but not tonight."

As Meaghan scampered away, Matt turned his attention back to the fiasco on stage. Some of the dancers looked to the left and began to leave the stage as Alba continued valiantly. Matt saw a tall woman take one step from behind the curtain and motion to the remaining dancers. They also left the stage, leaving the solitary figure of Alba Cologne in the spotlight.

Tears ran down her face and Matt's heart broke for her. The song ended and the spotlight disappeared, leaving the entire house in darkness. Matt heard a polite attempt at applause, but it soon died. He could perceive dark figures moving on stage, surrounding Alba. Then the entire mass moved left, behind the curtain.

The murmur of the crowd became louder. Matt heard some laughter and several derisive remarks, and clenched his hands into fists. Then he heard the motors on the lights as they repositioned themselves. *Someone is changing the program.* A single spotlight erupted as Desmond Quest walked to center stage.

"Ladies and gentlemen, due to technical difficulties, our feature entertainer will not be able to continue her performance."

A discontented rumble and a few whistles came in response. The rock band hastily assembled on stage and began to play in subdued tones as Quest continued.

"Do not be dismayed, my friends. The *New Dawn* is always eager to welcome new talent to the international stage. Here tonight, in her first Windswept appearance, is the glorious new entertainer that you have been hearing about. This young woman is a future legend of popular music, soon to be staring in her own syndicated television series." Desmond swept an arm wide. "Ladies and gentlemen, Candace Cologne!"

The back curtain suddenly became a projection screen for a lava lamp display. The same stage that had lifted a gilded Alba to the applause of the crowd now elevated a fiery-haired teen. The old woman in the next booth leapt to her feet in mad applause. Several members of the audience, particularly those in the front row, did the same. The girl wore a yellow peasant dress reminiscent of the hippies from the '60s. A leather headband and multicolored plastic bracelets were her only adornments.

The girl writhed seductively to the beat of the music. Matt recognized her immediately. "Candace," he whispered. "Candace Sterling is Candace Cologne. Candace and Alba are sisters!"

Chapter 56

Disregarding Meaghan's command, Matt left his seat and approached a uniformed man he thought was an usher. "How can I get backstage?"

"You cannot, sir. The backstage area is only for employees."

"You don't understand. I'm a friend of Alba Cologne. I must see her."

"If you like, sir, you can give me a note for her and I will give it to Madame Adolphe."

"My name is Matt Narvik. I'm the grand-prize winner. I just want to see Alba for a few minutes."

"It is quite impossible, sir. Please return to your seat or leave the theater."

Matt could feel the rage rising inside of him. He looked toward the stage as Candace broke into song. He wasn't going to get anywhere arguing with an usher. "All right, I'll leave." He proceeded to the exit and boarded an elevator. He pushed the button for the lowest level but the light remained dark. That's when he noticed a lock next to the button for the second level. A key was required to go to those levels.

"This stinks," he muttered and pushed the button for the third level. The button lit up in response and the elevator began to move. He exited in a tiny lobby connecting narrow corridors and wondered how to proceed. A door opened, revealing a stairway. A steward stepped out and brushed past him. The steward tried to stop Matt as he took the stairs. Matt ignored the shouts in Spanish that followed him. He continued down the stairs, then headed aft. Astonished stares greeted him as he pushed past crewmembers who were unaccustomed to seeing passengers at that level. Finally, he saw a sign on a door reading, *Stage Entrance: Authorized Personnel Only.* He beat on the door twice; no response. He hammered his fist into the center of the door again. It opened, and a small woman with a tape measure around her neck held a finger to her lips in a plea for silence.

"I need to see Alba."

"Alba, not here, Señor. She go back to her cabin."

"Are you certain?"

"Si, Miss Candace on stage. Alba leave."

Matt retraced his steps to the elevator and pushed the button for the seventh level. Once more in the plush surroundings that epitomized the *New Dawn*, he headed for Alba's cabin. He paused before knocking and tried to get a hold of his emotions. *Calm down, Narvik, this isn't about you. It's about Alba. She doesn't need to see anger; she needs empathy.* He took a deep breath and gently knocked on her door. In seconds, the door swung open; Omar stared up at him.

"What is it?"

"Hello, Omar. I want to see Alba."

"That is impossible, sir. Miss Cologne is ill."

"I only want to see her for a moment."

"The answer is no. Please return to your cabin, sir." Omar swung the door nearly closed but Matt kicked it back open.

Matt took one step into the room as Omar pulled a pistol from his jacket. Matt heard the safety release, then a woman's scream.

"No! Omar put that gun away," Meaghan said. "Matt, what are you doing here?"

"I want to see Alba."

"I told you she would not want to see you tonight."

"I must see her!"

"Tell this ignorant American to leave or I will blow his head off," Omar said.

Meaghan walked between them and placed both of her hands on Matt's chest. Using all her strength, she shoved him back into the hall and stepped out with him. "Shut the door, Omar."

When the door closed, she looked up at Matt. "What is wrong with you? You could have been shot. Omar is Alba's bodyguard."

"I just want to see her. I can make that dwarf eat his gun."

"She doesn't want to see you, not tonight. She's had a terrible experience, like, the last thing she needs is to have you shot to death in her suite. Wake up, Narvik!"

"I just want to comfort her. I know she's very emotional and needs a strong man to rely on, not that little pup."

"Omar is a professional bodyguard. Alba has known him since he was a little boy. Your little fit of jealousy could have gotten you killed."

"All right, I'll go wait in my cabin."

"No, you go straight to the piano bar and tell David what's going on, and then you explain your behavior to him."

"What?"

"I may be a new Christian, Matt, but I know you're not acting like one."

Dexter Rubino regained consciousness in strange surroundings. He kept his eyes shut in an act of self-preservation. *What is that smell? It smells like Doctor Cushman's office, disinfectant, and cigars.*

He could hear Spanish being spoken. *Sounds like a TV, not a radio.* Then came the voice of a woman. *She's nearby.* Dex peeked through his right eyelid and saw a woman in scrubs sitting in a straight chair; she held a plastic cup in her hand.

A gruff voice spoke in English. "Wake up, Rubino. You gotta get us outa here."

Chapter 57

Matt Narvik returned to his cabin, where he changed into his more familiar wardrobe of shorts, T-shirt, and sneakers. He held the pink tie loaned to him by the Sultan's Palace in his right hand. As he left his cabin, he paused to count the number of doors from Alba's suite to the end of the hall. He scaled the glass stairway and presented the tie to the receptionist.

The mouth of the hostess gaped when she saw Matt in such casual dress. "Oh, Mr. Narvik."

"I just thought I should return this."

"Thank you, but there was no need. We have a good supply on hand."

"I didn't want you to think I was a tie thief. Say, I noticed that little walkway just beyond the windows. Is there any way I could get out there in the morning to take some pictures of the sunrise?"

"No, sir, that is a maintenance walkway. It is off limits to passengers. I suggest that you go to the deck directly above us. I believe that is the highest point on the ship accessible to passengers."

"How do I get there?"

"You can go back to the seventh floor and take the elevator, or you can use the stairs just outside of the rear door of the dining room."

"Thank you, you've been very helpful," Matt replied and began walking the length of the Sultan's Palace.

The hostess chased him and grasped his arm. "You cannot be here in that state of dress.

Matt never slowed as he made his way to the target door. "I understand, miss, but I don't think that tie would match what I'm wearing."

When he exited the door, he saw the stairs to the next level on his left. He also spotted a group of passengers climbing the stairs from deck seven. Much to the consternation of the hostess, Matt dutifully held the door for them as they filed in. He couldn't understand the conversation of his fellow voyagers, but twice he heard the name of Candace Cologne mentioned. Judging from the jovial attitude of the late-night diners, Candace had been a smash. *This will only add to Alba's woes.*

On the top deck, some vacationers sat in a large hot tub, and Matt nodded as he passed by. A glass wall surrounded the deck, and on the starboard side a door provided access to a ladder, which led to the narrow catwalk just below the windows of the Sultan's Palace. Matt muttered under his breath when the door was locked. After a moment's consideration, Matt used the door handle as a foothold and scaled the wall, hoisting himself over the top and lowering himself until his foot rested on the outside door handle. The safety railing of the ladder provided his next foothold. No one on the top deck seemed to have noticed his acrobatics. He scurried down the ladder to reach the level of the Sultan's Palace.

The moonlight illuminated the catwalk, a metal grating about twelve inches wide and mounted to standoffs that projected about eighteen inches from the hull. Matt had walked narrower surfaces before, but he found the apparent wind striking his face and the movement of the water below a little disconcerting.

With his left hand on the ship's surface, Matt proceeded with caution, counting the balconies as he went. A male patron of the restaurant stared in awe as he passed by. He then saw someone leaning over the rail of a balcony below him. He sank to his knees and called to her, "Alba?"

Dex recognized the voice of Doctor Zhan. He had considered playing opossum a bit longer, but apparently Zhan had found him out. He reluctantly opened his eyes and looked around his new accommodations.

Anton chuckled. "Welcome back to the land of the living. Thought you were goin' to sleep all night."

Dex raised himself on his left elbow and looked square into the face of his cabin mate. "It's nice to see you again, Doctor Zhan."

"Don't call me that, Rubino. My name is Anton Carmella. You and I are in the same jam and we need to help each other out."

Dex nodded toward the nurse, who sat between their beds, "Is this lady our compatriot?"

"This is Isabella. She's OK." Anton winked at his nurse. "We have an understanding."

Dex nodded to the nurse and she smiled back. "How did I get here," he asked, "and how do I figure into this understanding?"

"I don't play well with others, Rubino. Besides that, Doc said your ticker skipped a beat or something. So, Isabella is off limits to you. That weasel Desi and his goons jumped me and then kept me doped up until the Doc came aboard. Doc has some legal problems stateside. I told him if he helped me escape, I'd make those problems disappear."

"What's our plan of escape?"

"I was kind of counting on you for that."

"Where are we?"

Anton touched the hand of the nurse and signaled her toward the door. After the woman left, he said, "Fourth floor of the *New Dawn*."

"But where is the ship?" Anton started to answer, but Dex interrupted him. "Can you turn down that TV? I can't hear you."

"Sorry, but it keeps anyone outside the door from listening in." Anton pointed a remote control device at the TV, which had been blasting a news program in Spanish. The noise stopped as the screen switched to a map showing a superimposed model of the *New Dawn* just a few miles into the Mediterranean Sea. The current speed, longitude, and latitude, as well as the day and time, scrolled across the bottom of the screen.

"We have a full day at sea before we make Gibraltar," Dex said. "That's where we'll have to jump ship."

Anton nodded. "That's what I figured, but how do we do that without getting killed?"

Dex rubbed his chin as he contemplated their predicament. "Is the room being guarded?"

"Not since we left port, but that might change when we put into Gibraltar."

"Do you have a gun or any kind of weapon?"

"No, I was lucky they didn't find the five grand I had sewed into my jacket. I used that to win Isabella over."

"Why do I smell cigars?"

"I was smoking a stogie earlier. Isabella got it for me."

"You can't do that anymore. Quest or his men will smell it and know you've been coherent. That would place Isabella and us in jeopardy."

"You don't understand. Helene got me hooked on nicotine again. Without it, I get a little anxious."

"In   this   situation,   we   should   both   be   anxious."

Chapter 58

"Matthew, come down from there!"

"That's what I plan to do. Can you please move that chair out of my way."

As Alba dragged a chair toward the door, he had a sudden remembrance of failing Phys Ed in junior high, all because he couldn't do a pull up to the satisfaction of his teacher. He looked down at the swirling torrent of water. If he fell from this height, it would be like hitting concrete. Even if he survived the fall, the force of the water would sweep him under the ship and into the propellers. He placed his hand on the edge of the grating. It was wet with the slippery mist of the Mediterranean.

"Matthew, come down from there. You are frightening me!"

Matt visualized himself swinging in, ape like, on one arm. Perhaps like a swashbuckler sweeping in to rescue his princess. *Quit stalling, Narvik!*

He swung over the side and a merciful listing of the ship helped propel him into the shelter of the balcony. He'd hoped to make a graceful landing but fell awkwardly on his side, striking his head on the sliding door. His bad shoulder took the brunt of the impact.

Alba fell to her knees beside him. "Matthew, are you all right?"

Matt looked up into the face of the woman he'd dreamed of for nine long months. Her dark eyes, still wet with tears, mesmerized him. Ignoring the pain in his shoulder, he wrapped his left arm around her and pulled her down to him. They kissed as she embraced him. A light suddenly enveloped them as the sliding door opened. Startled, Alba looked up at Omar, who stood over them, his pistol pointed at Matt's head.

"Omar, put that away!"

"Move back, Alba, so that the blood of this cur will not soil your gown."

"I order you to put that gun away. Now!"

Omar hesitated a moment before holstering his weapon. "Who is this infidel and why is he breaking into your cabin?"

Matt groaned as he raised himself to a sitting position. *I think I undid some of my therapy.*

"Alba, tell junior to leave us alone."

"Matthew is a friend of mine," she said. "He is no threat to me. Leave us alone so that we may speak of matters of great importance."

"I cannot do that. When I heard the noise, I pushed the panic alarm. More security personnel are on their way. Besides, you cannot entertain a man alone in your suite. Think of your honor, think of what Mashal would say." Before he finished speaking, several more guards pushed into the room.

Alba stood and addressed the men who had just entered. "Everything is fine here. Return to your posts. You, too, Omar."

"But Alba, I cannot leave you alone with this infidel."

"You will do as I say, Omar." Turning to Matt she asked, "Are you injured, Matthew?"

Feeling duty-bound to prove he wasn't, he gripped the railing with his left hand and pulled himself to his feet. "The rocking of the ship threw my balance off as I landed. I'm fine now."

"Come inside, Matthew, we have much to speak about. Goodnight, Omar!"

Omar scowled at Matt before he turned and left the room, but the door did not completely close. Matt noticed the splintered door jam and trim.

"Sit down, Matthew. Would you like something to drink?"

Matt didn't speak. His shoulder ached, but not nearly as much as his heart. He pulled Alba to him and again kissed her. She melted into his arms and sighed.

"Oh, Matthew, I have dreamt of being in your arms like this, but this has been a terrible night."

"Let me make it better."

"You do not understand. My career is ruined. Someone sabotaged my performance. I was made to look like a fool."

"I was there. You're the most beautiful woman in the world."

"No, Matthew, I am a stumbling old crone."

"Don't talk like that. You had one bad night; it's not the end of the world."

"To further humiliate me, they have brought my illegitimate half sister onboard to steal the stage away from me. She has even stolen my name."

"Is Candace Cologne your half sister?"

"Yes, my father was old and lonely. He took pity on an American whore and fathered her cursed whelp. I never thought my aunt would stoop to these tactics."

"Are you sure your family doesn't live in a trailer park?"

"Matthew, this is not a time for joking."

"I'm sorry. You're making too much of this. You had one bad night. Tomorrow you'll be back on top. Now let's concentrate on us. We have a lot of catching up to do."

"Matthew, you do not understand. My professional career is the most important thing in the world to me. My entire life revolves around becoming the leader of my family. Now my Aunt and her minions have cast me aside in favor of this bastard child."

"You've built your life on sand, Alba. You can rebuild on the solid rock of Jesus Christ."

"Matthew, I know you are a man of faith, but I do not share this."

"You can, Alba. No one is born a Christian. To become a Christian you must be born again."

"Matthew, kiss me."

Matt took her in his arms and kissed her deeply.

"Excuse me!"

Matt looked toward the door and saw Meaghan.

"I've been waiting in the piano bar for you, Matt. Dave said you never made it down there."

"Oh, I got sidetracked."

"I see."

"Meaghan, thank you so much for taking care of Matthew for me. I feel much better now that he is beside me."

"Hurray for Matt and Alba. I just stopped by to invite you both to the worship service tomorrow morning. I'll be singing a solo while Dave plays. Dave is a wonderful musician and a great guy. Thanks for introducing us, Matt."

"We will be there. Nine o'clock, right?"

Alba had a troubled look on her face. "Matthew, I wish to sleep late. As you said, tomorrow's performance is a new beginning."

"Alba, you need to come to this service with me."

"All right, Matthew, I will go for you."

Chapter 59

Matt rose with the sun and stretched. His shoulder ached and his head had a knot where he had collided with Alba's sliding door. He had planned to use the gym, but since Arnan was the fitness director, he decided to avoid it. Deck five was the recommended track for joggers and walkers. It would have to do.

After an hour of jogging, he returned to his cabin, showered and shaved, and donned one of his new suits. He then crossed the hall and knocked on Alba's door. A security man answered and gave him a single questioning nod.

"Good morning, sir. I'm here to escort Miss Alba and Miss Meaghan to the worship service."

A voice beckoned from the next room. "Come in, Matthew. I will soon be ready."

The security guard opened the door fully and motioned for Matt to sit down. The man kept his right hand on his sidearm. His glare was reminiscent of a father greeting his daughter's first date.

Matt offered the man his hand and said, "I'm Matt Narvik."

The man snorted in derision and pointed to the chair.

"I think you want me to sit down. OK, I can do that."

After a three-minute wait, Alba pulled the broken door to her room open. "Good morning, Matthew."

Her beauty once more overwhelmed him and a moment passed before he replied, "Good morning, Honey. Is Meaghan ready yet?"

"Meaghan left hours ago. It seems she is scheduled to sing a solo. I had promised her that she could sing back-up for me if we had time to practice."

"She's a very nice girl. She gave her heart to the Lord yesterday."

"She said something about that to me last night. I did not know she was superstitious. At least it will provide her a stage to display her talent."

"It's not superstition. It's a relationship with the Creator of the universe."

Alba smiled at him. "Of course it is, Matthew. Where is the service being held?"

"In the piano bar, and if we don't hurry, we'll be late."

As the couple made their way to the service, they passed several crew members and passengers. There were polite nods and a few good mornings, but no one asked for autographs. Matt thought he heard a few snickers from behind them.

In the corridor that skirted the casino, they nearly collided with Omar.

"Omar, what are you doing here?" Alba asked.

"I am acting as a liaison between the ship's security and the casino security. Since Dexter Rubino is ill and Mr. Quest has taken on the role of cruise director, the coordination of security efforts has become a priority."

Alba feigned concern. "Dexter is ill? I knew nothing of this."

"He is restricted to a cabin forward of the lobby. Another passenger, Doctor Zhan, has been stricken by the same virus, as well as Mr. Jeanblanc."

Alba had a knowing look in her eye. "Does my aunt know of this virus?"

"I would assume so."

Matt grew tired of being a spectator. "We will pray for Dex's healing at the worship service. Would you like to come along with us, Omar?"

Omar shot a sidelong glance at Alba. "No, I have things to do. I will contact you later, Alba."

As Omar continued on his way, Matt whispered to Alba, "I'm surprised to hear that Dex is ill. We'll have to take extra precautions to avoid contracting the virus."

"Yes, we must assume it is contagious."

When they reached the piano bar, Dave was already playing a hymn on the keyboard. A member of the kitchen staff escorted them to a pair of overstuffed chairs near the piano.

Alba whispered into Matt's ear, "Most of these people are employees of Windswept."

"Yes, they are, but they are here on their own time. Some are passengers."

"I cannot socialize with employees. They will see themselves as my equal."

"I heard an old adage that says when the chess pieces are put away, they all go into the same box."

"What does this mean?"

"Queen or pawn, God sees us all as equals. We are all sinners; the only difference is that a few of us have accepted His free gift of salvation."

"Good morning, brothers and sisters." Dave Carpenter stood behind the piano as he addressed the crowd of about three dozen people. "Welcome to the first worship service aboard the *New Dawn*. My name is Dave Carpenter. As you might have guessed, I'm the piano player." He pointed to a dark-skinned man who rose and waved to the audience.

"This is Brother Jeffers. He is an ordained pastor as well as a sous-chef. He will be our speaker today. Our soloist is a beauty many of you already know, Meaghan Miller."

Meaghan stood and approached the piano, an anxious smile on her face. The crowd applauded politely. "Good morning, everyone. I feel a little unqualified being up in front of you all. You see I just accepted the Lord as my Savior yesterday. A Christian friend showed me the plan of salvation and I will forever be in his debt. Dave informed me that this is one of that man's favorite hymns, and I'm going to share it with you now. The title is 'In the Garden.'"

As Meaghan began to sing, Matt flushed with embarrassment. He was unaccustomed to the attention and felt he didn't deserve any credit for Meaghan's conversion.

Alba shifted in her seat and gave Matt an icy stare.

Chapter 60

Desmond Quest stood in the doorway of the piano bar and smiled at Meaghan as she sang. He counted heads, then quietly reached for the door and pulled it shut. He chuckled to himself as he walked away. *Alba Cologne in a church service; she may burst into flames.*

He went to level seven, where he tapped lightly on the door of Madame Adolphe's suite.

"Come in Desmond, I've been waiting for you."

"Good morning, Madame, I trust you had a pleasant night. How did you know it was I that knocked so early?"

"I recognized your knock, like a little bird tapping at the window begging for a few crumbs of bread. I missed some of the promised entertainment last night."

"I thought that the plan was to cut Alba's appearance short."

"Not that, you imbecile, the two American pigs in the same sty. You promised I would get to see them."

"We can go see them now, if you like."

"Yes, Desmond, to think of my old foe Rubino as helpless as a kitten gives me great joy.

I am also anxious to see Anton in a comatose state. What did Cynthia say when she saw him?"

"I believe she said something about strangling him."

"I can understand that but we must keep them alive until we leave Madeira."

"Why? They are of no use to us now."

"I want to wait until there is no chance of a witness. You see, it is very important that they be alert when we throw them into the sea. I want their last thoughts to be of how I defeated them both. I want them to be filled with despair as they see the ship leaving them in the dark and cold Atlantic."

"Will you dispose of the nurse also?"

"Yes, but she can be sedated first. If we allowed her to live, she would be a potential witness. Does she have a family?"

"I do not know for certain."

"Find out if you can and we will see to it that they are compensated for their loss. Now, take me to the Americans."

"Do you wish to have breakfast first, Madame?"

"No, we will share a champagne breakfast afterwards."

"We dock in Gibraltar before dawn," Doctor Stewart said. "Get a good night's sleep, but for heaven's sake, keep quiet. As we approach the port, slip into these coveralls. Make your way to the Grand Lobby and get ashore. Run toward town and don't look back."

Dexter Rubino looked pleadingly at the doctor. "We will need our passports."

"I secured your passport for you. It's in the bag with your coveralls. I also put fifty Euros in each bag."

"Anton scratched his head as he spoke, "Why three bags?"

"Isabella must go with you. There is no telling what Madame Adolphe or her flying monkeys might do after your escape."

Dex asked, "What will she do to you?"

Two knocks sounded on the door, then a kick at the bottom.

In hushed tones, Doctor Stuart said, "Hide those bags and keep perfectly still."

Anton and Dexter slipped their bags under their beds and Isabella placed hers in a drawer of the dresser she was leaning on.

"Who's there?"

"It is Quest and Madame Adolphe. Open this door, Doctor."

The doctor swallowed hard as he turned the door handle and swung the door open. "Good morning, Madame. Good morning, Mr. Quest."

"Stand aside, Doctor, we wish to see your patients."

"I'm sorry, Mr. Quest, they are quarantined."

"They are only quarantined from the other passengers. We know it is all a ruse."

"I'm afraid there is a viral infection aboard, Mr. Quest. Mr. Jeanblanc has all the symptoms of the noro virus. Dex is showing the same signs."

Helene Adolphe pushed Quest aside and entered the room. She held a surgical mask over her face as she inspected Anton, then Rubino. "Why are these men clean shaven?"

"Isabella, the nurse must have shaved them."

"Why are they not shackled?"

Quest spoke before the doctor could. "They are already heavily sedated, Madame. There is no need for shackles."

"Nonsense, Quest, these men are not to be given any comfort. No shaving and they must be shackled, like the beasts they are."

The doctor spoke calmly, even though he trembled with fear of what Helene might do. "Madame, if we shackle these men, there will be resultant scaring. You see, Doctor Zhan still has marks from the handcuffs that bound him. If someone should discover their bodies, it might lead to unnecessary questions."

"He is correct, Madame," said Quest. "There is no reason to take unneeded risks."

"Then I demand that a guard be placed on the door of this cabin at all times."

The doctor looked at Quest. "Won't that lead to a lot of questions?"

"Not if the guard is in the room."

"This cabin isn't big enough for the three people that are in here now."

Madame Adolphe stamped her foot as she barked. "Put the guard in the hallway and let everyone know that these men are contagious. It will serve as a reminder to the rest of the ship to wash their hands."

Quest bowed in deference. "A wise decision, Madame. I will see to it at once."

"First you will escort me to the Sultan's Palace. I must get out of here. The stench of death is in this room."

After they left, the doctor closed the door and turned to Dex. "How trustworthy are the guards?"

Dex opened his eyes, then shrugged. "It depends on the guard."

Chapter 61

As the doctor left their cabin, Anton and Dex faced each other.

"What's our next move, Rubino?"

"For the time being, we're stuck here. There is video surveillance in every corridor. If we wait until we make Gibraltar, we may make it off of the ship."

"You heard the old witch; she wants a guard on our door. How will we make it past him?"

"I had a good relationship with most of the guards, but they have a strong sense of loyalty to Helene. If I had a gun, I would be more confident."

Anton groaned as he raised himself from his bed. "I'm as stiff as a board. Ever since Quest and his goons jumped me, I haven't taken my medication. If you can get us out of here in one piece, I'll give you an even share of my stash. I've got a farm in Ohio. I stashed gold all over the place."

"I don't need any financial inducements, Anton. I want to save my own skin."

"Locked up like this, waiting for the old witch to kill me, gold doesn't seem as valuable as it once did."

"I was under the impression you two were lovers."

"I'm done with women, Rubino, except for Isabella here. I've been investing in Windswept for years and that old woman has swindled me. She promised me a mansion in

Belize, servants, and a new name. All she did was hang this Arab name on me and take all of my investment."

"A mansion in Belize has a familiar ring to it. Did the doctor say when he was coming back?"

"No, but he won't abandon us now."

"Cheer up, Anton. I just might have an ace up my sleeve."

Alba Cologne fidgeted in her seat as the service continued; Matt was on the edge of his. The sous-chef shared his testimony and invited the congregants to accept the gift of salvation. When the homely ended, Dave Carpenter called on Matt to close in prayer.

"Please remember our friend Dexter Rubino in prayer," he said. "For those of you that don't know, Dexter is the Deputy Chief of Security for the Windswept Cruise Line. He was suddenly stricken by a heart ailment yesterday."

Matt was uncomfortable offering a prayer for the man who had fired him but did the best he could. As the closing hymn began, Alba turned and headed for the door. The close quarters impeded her exit and Matt came after her.

"Alba, wait for me."

She glowered at him and left the room. Matt caught up to her in the corridor. "Alba, what's wrong?"

"I do not discuss my personal business in public, Matthew. Please see me to my room. We can speak there."

"All right, but why don't we get some brunch first."

"I am not hungry, I am tired. I have a performance to prepare for and need to rest."

"OK, I'll see you to your room. Are you upset with me?"

"We will speak when we get to my room, Matthew."

Chapter 62

Matt held the door as Alba passed into her luxury suite. She ordered the guard from the room, but he did not close the door as he left.

Matt stared at Alba, his face softening. *Even with anger consuming her, she is the most beautiful woman I have ever seen.*

She stamped her foot and said, "Matthew, how could you humiliate me like that?"

"I don't know what you mean."

"You once told me that you retired and bought a sailboat seeking adventure. Am I not the greatest adventure you have ever known?"

"Yes, but . . ."

"I even considered taking you as my consort, but you have chosen to humiliate me with your peasant religion and your peasant friends. I am not some helpless urchin that is dependent on your attention. Millions of people all over the world worship me. You must choose now. Will you submit to me, or do you insist on practicing this feeble religion?"

"Alba, you don't understand. Christianity is as simple as ABC. Admit that you are a sinner and . . ."

"Silence! I am not a sinner. I am a princess. I am Alba Cologne, the daughter of Philippe Ben-Balla. I am the heart and soul of Windswept Corporation. I was born to rule, not subject myself to the foolish religion of an infidel. Leave my suite now and think of what I have said. If you choose to practice this insane religion, I do not wish to see you again. If you come to your senses, you must tell me before we leave Gibraltar tomorrow. You can finish the cruise and stay in the suite I provided for you, but do not contact me again."

"Alba, I don't understand."

A voice from the hall caught their attention. "Ms. Cologne has asked you to leave, infidel. I suggest you leave before I am forced to remove you." Omar stood in the doorway, smirking at him.

"If that's the way you want it, Alba."

"Adieu, Matthew."

He turned to leave and the thought of sending a right cross into the jaw of Omar entered his mind, but the little coward had already pulled his pistol and held it waist high. Matt crossed the corridor and entered his suite, closed the door and sank to his knees.

A moment later, he heard a knock at the door. Expecting it to be Alba coming to apologize, he jumped to his feet and swung open the door. His smile vanished when caught sight of a young woman dressed in medical scrubs, with a stethoscope draped around her neck.

"Señor, Narvik?" the woman said.

Matt looked up and down the hallway, then back at the woman. "Yes, I'm Matt Narvik."

The woman thrust a folded bit of paper toward him and Matt took it. Then she turned and hurried away. Matt closed the door and unfolded the paper to find a handwritten note.

Matt:

I need your help. Another American and I are being held on level four, cabin fifty. We dock in Gibraltar tomorrow before dawn. I will need you to distract the guard at our door so that we can escape. Use your training to create the distraction but do not endanger yourself or any passengers. I'm appealing to your Christian sense of honor to help me.

Thank you,
Dex

"Why should I help you, Rubino?" he muttered, then thought about it for moment. *Dex did help me financially, and gave me a place to live. If it wasn't for Dex I might have died the night my boat burned. Besides all that, it is the right thing to do. Why is he a prisoner? Does it matter?*

Matt crossed the cabin and stepped out onto the balcony. The deep blue of the Mediterranean reflected the late summer sun. Far below him, a pod of dolphins frolicked in the wake of the ship. Matt bowed his head in prayer.

Chapter 63

Matt wandered down the corridors of level four. He saw the guard pacing the hall and ducked into a restroom. It only took a few minutes to compose a plan of distraction.

He stopped by the gift shop, then proceeded to the upper decks and studied the rocky Spanish coastline festooned with wind generators and tiny villages. As he leaned on the railing, he contemplated the type of people living there. *How much power do those windmills really produce?* A poke in his side interrupted his thoughts.

"Hi, Matthew. How are you doing, lover?"

"Candace!"

The girl was scantily clad in an orange bikini and a black sash tied around her waist. She threw her arms around him and pulled him close. "You came to see my poolside show, didn't you? That's so sweet. Did you hear the big news? I'm going to do the evening shows in the theater, too. Old sister Alba really blew her big chance for a comeback."

Hakim stood a few feet from them. Matt could see the distrust in his eyes. "I was there. Alba had one bad night, but I doubt that it was career-ending."

"Makes you wish you'd taken me when you had the chance doesn't it. Why waste your time with that dried up old woman? Well, I don't hold a grudge. Meet me at the

Sultan's Palace after tonight's show. Maybe we can have some fun."

"Candace, I told you, you're too young for me."

"Forget about meeting me, I'll come to your room. What's the number?"

"No, Candace, it's not going to happen."

"I've got to change for the show now, but I'll see you tonight, Matthew."

A small crowd had gathered around them. Teenagers pleaded for Candace's autograph. She smiled and waved them off saying that she would sign them after her next show. Hakim gave Matt an evil stare as he followed his charge.

Matt shook his head as the admiring crowd trooped after Candace. *She's just a little girl. Why is she in such a hurry to grow up?*

Matt continued to explore the ship and found the movie theater as one of Alba's old films was beginning. Only a few dozen people attended. The dialogue was in Spanish with French and English subtitles. He had a hard time following the plot. She had been much younger when it was filmed, about the same age as Candace. Her lack of clothing in some of the scenes shocked him and he finally understood her lack of inhibition. *She's been on display all of her life.*

Matt watched mindlessly as the credits rolled, then a more recent music video began. It was Candace Cologne singing a rockabilly standard in Spanish. The young teen gyrated shamelessly to the beat as she sang. Matt stood and left the theater, and decided to dine at the restaurant on level six. He had no desire to rub elbows with the wealthy in the Sultan's Palace. He requested a private table and enjoyed a good meal and fine service. After supper, he headed for the piano bar. Dave was playing a Bacharach tune while Meaghan did her best Dionne Warwick impression. Matt ordered coffee and enjoyed the music. Dave and Meaghan didn't notice him. Their eyes locked on one another during every song.

Matt meandered through the corridors of the ship until he found himself on the seventh level. He stared at Alba's door and wondered if she had done the show that night, or had Candace eclipsed her. He wanted to console her, to show her that none of these things mattered. She had practically rejected him earlier in the day. Perhaps if he gave it some time she would soften.

He opened the door to his own suite and caught the scent of perfume. There were rose petals on the floor. They formed a trail to his bedroom door, and on the handle of the door hung a pair of black lace panties. "Alba," he whispered.

Could she have such a drastic change of heart in just a few hours? Will she understand that I want her love not just her body?

He turned the handle and opened the door. A pair of candles flickered, their dim light illuminating a bottle of champagne chilling on his nightstand. A plate of pâté and cheese sat to its right, two glasses to the left. The trail of rose petals led to his bed where beneath the white sheets lay Candace. He could hear the soft breathing of sleep. She looked angelic, lying with a halo of amber hair surrounding her child-like face.

Matt turned and gently closed the door behind him. He went to the balcony and stretched out on a chaise, where he enjoyed the beauty of the moon glow on the Mediterranean. *I'd better get a little rest. In a few hours, I have to create a diversion for Rubino.*

Chapter 64

Matt's internal clock told him it was time to rise. In the predawn light, he could make out a mountainous landform. "That's not Gibraltar, that's Morocco," he mumbled. "The Atlas Mountains are just fifteen miles away. Gibraltar will be on the starboard side."

He entered his suite and opened the door to his bedroom; Candace was still asleep. He closed that door, then flicked on the TV. He found the station that gave the ship's position and noticed that he had forty-five minutes before the ship docked. Grabbing the bag from the gift store, he crept out of his cabin and eased the door shut. The corridor was deserted, but the motion-activated video camera hummed as it focused on him. Ignoring the camera, he walked forward to the balcony overlooking the Grand Lobby. A lone workman was polishing the floor below. Matt continued forward to a staircase and descended to the fourth level.

He peeked around the corner and spotted a guard leaning against the wall. The guard's head bobbed as he tried to fight off sleep. Matt slipped into the men's room and located the trash container. He opened the access door and pulled it out. From his shopping bag, he pulled out two T-shirts and six small cigarette lighters. He smashed two of the lighters, sopping up the fluid with the T-shirts. He pulled the paper towels from the dispensers and stuffed them into the can, then the T-shirts atop them. Three of the remaining lighters went into the can, and he wedged it back into its cabinet.

From his many hours studying the refurbishment of the ship, Matt knew it was equipped with a state-of-the-art alarm and sprinkler system. By placing the trash can askew in its cabinet, no water would reach the flames. It would continue to smolder until some brave soul pulled it out and used an extinguisher. There would be no damage to the ship, but the resulting confusion would allow Dex to initiate his escape.

Matt pulled a roll of toilet paper from a holder and balled it up on top of the opening of the can. He used his remaining lighter to ignite the homemade smoke bomb and paused to make sure it caught. He left the cabinet door open to provide oxygen for the flame. Assured that the flame would continue to build, he threw the last lighter into the trash opening and left the room. He crossed the corridor to the elevator and returned to the seventh level.

As Matt stepped out of the elevator, the flash of a strobe light nearly blinded him, and the shriek of a siren filled the corridor. He tried to keep from smiling as shouting passengers pushed their way past him, their faces contorted with fear.

Above the din, a maddeningly calm female voice advised the passengers to report to their respective emergency evacuation stations and don their life vests. "Please avoid the elevators and use the stairwells. Please remain calm and orderly." The message then repeated in French and Spanish.

Matt grinned as he opened the door to his suite. Candace collided with him as the door opened. She wore a lacy, black, baby doll nightgown that at first demanded the attention of the man in Narvik, then he saw the panic in her eyes.

"Matthew, where have you been? Help me, the boat is sinking!"

"Calm down, Candace, everything is going to be all right."

"Can't you hear that alarm? We're all going to die!"

"I don't think we're going to die, just follow the directions. Let's go back into the room and get a life vest for you, and maybe a robe."

Candace threw her arms around him and pleaded. "Please help me, Matthew. I'm so afraid!"

"You're a real piece of work, Matt!" Matt turned to see Meaghan standing in the hall behind him. "You're nothing but a child molester!"

Alba exited her suite and saw the assembly outside of her door. "Matthew, how could you do this? You have chosen this bastard child over me."

Candace forgot her fear and wrapped her fury into two tiny fists as she went after her half sister. "Who are you calling a bastard, you dried up Arab whore?"

Matt caught Candace by the wrist before she could deliver a blow. "Candace, behave!"

Alba took advantage of the situation and slapped the teen's face hard, then she and Meaghan stomped away. Candace fell back into Matt's arms and sobbed. "She hurt me. She hurt me."

Helene Adolphe staggered from her suite still wearing her evening gown. "What is happening?"

"Oh, Auntie Helene, Alba hit me." Candace touched her face and looked at the blood on her fingers. "See? My nose is bleeding."

"Oh, no, we must get you to the infirmary. You need the immediate attention of a surgeon."

"I don't think it's as bad as all that, Madame. Alba just slapped her."

"And who are you?"

"This is Matt Narvik, Auntie Helene," Candace said. "He was about to rescue me when Alba attacked me."

"Is that what set off the alarm?"

"No, Madame," Matt said. "Alba and Candace both were leaving for their evacuation stations when they ran into each other here in the hall."

"Candace, you heard the alarm and came to help me. Bless you, child. No one else cared to inquire as to my well being."

Candace shot a sideward glance at Matt. "I thought you might need my help, Auntie Helene. I mean, you're old and infirm, and I'm young and strong."

"Thank you, dear heart, but you should have dressed before running up here."

"I was just about to get her a robe from my suite," said Matt.

"Yes, please do that, sir. What did you say your name was?"

"He's Matthew Narvik. Isn't he the sexiest man you've ever seen?"

"Why does that name sound familiar?"

"Candace, help your aunt with her life vest, and I'll get you a robe and a life vest from my room. We have to get to our emergency station."

Chapter 65

"What's that noise, Rubino?"

"I hope it's our diversion. Isabella, peek out the door and see if our guard is still there."

Isabella shrugged at the command.

"Never mind, I'll chance it," Dex said. As he placed his hand on the door handle, he heard the cries of panic from other passengers. He opened the door, saw the guard had vanished and the corridor was crowded with anxious people headed for their evacuation station.

Dex turned to Anton and Isabella. "Let's roll!"

Anton struggled to walk as his arthritic knees and hips reminded him of his malady and the weeklong absence of Doctor Zhan's formula. Dex considered abandoning his roommate but felt it would be a cowardly act. Isabella took Anton's arm and led him toward the stairway. Dex stood at the top of the stairs and surveyed the Grand Lobby. That's when he realized the ship had not yet docked. "We have to hide."

"Let's hide on shore," Anton said.

"The ship hasn't docked yet. We have to hide onboard."

"What kind of jerk do you have working for you, Rubino?"

"The kind I fired. If we get to the Grand Lobby, I know of a place to hide on the lower decks."

It took the efforts of both Dex and Isabella to help Anton down the stairs. Once on the marble floor of the lobby, Dex opened a concealed passageway allowing access to the bare-bones décor of the portion of the ship designed only for the eyes of the crew.

The alarm woke Desmond Quest out of a deep sleep. "What is it? What has happened?"

As Cynthia sprang from the bed, she shouted, "Candace! She will be frightened to death. I must go to her, Desmond."

Desmond pulled on his trousers and searched for his shoes. Finally locating them, he slipped them on and headed for the security office. As he opened the door to the office, he spotted Omar turning the alarm off.

"What has happened?"

"There was a small fire on the forward section of level four. A trash bin in the men's room was set afire. We had a security guard nearby. He extinguished the flames and notified me everything was all right."

Captain Auesnehmer burst into the room. "What is the problem?"

Desmond stepped in front of Omar as he explained. "A small fire on the fourth level set off the alarm. Everything is under control. Shouldn't you be on the bridge while we are docking?"

"The pilot is in charge of the docking procedure. He already contacted the port officials and reported the alarm. How did the fire begin?"

Omar answered. "The guard said that the fire was purposefully set, perhaps an act of vandalism."

"Is Rubino aware of this?"

The cause of the fire suddenly became plain to Quest. "Dex's health problems prevent him from being of any assistance at this time. I will take the lead on this investigation and find whoever is responsible. Now if you will Captain, please use the public address system to reassure the passengers that there is no danger and that they may return to their cabins."

"I will return to the bridge and make the call."

"No need, Captain, you can use the microphone here. I will go to the fourth level and begin my investigation. Come along with me, Omar."

As the captain began to reassure the passengers, Desmond and Omar left the office and went to the site of the fire, where a guard stood watch. "Who reported the fire?" Desmond asked.

"I did, sir."

"Were you guarding the quarantined passengers?"

"Yes, sir."

"Where are they now?"

The guard had a sick look on his face as he shrugged.

Desmond raced to the cabin and found it empty. "We must search the ship. The prisoners have escaped."

Matt helped Madame Adolphe to the evacuation station as Candace clung to his side.

"Thank you for your assistance, Mr. Narvik."

"It's no big deal, ma'am."

Candace interjected. "He is so brave, Auntie Helene, and he rescued me when Alba assaulted me. You have to do something about her, Auntie. I think she may be mentally ill."

"We will speak of it later, child."

The alarm ceased and the reassuring message of the captain put everyone at ease. Several of the crewmembers came to Madame Adolphe's aid and informed her that she was on the wrong deck.

Matt took the blame for the mix-up. "I was told to report to deck four. I thought everyone else would be here, too."

"It's not important, Matthew. You're my hero," Candace said.

Helene winced at the girl's words, then her expression softened. "Will you be going ashore in Gibraltar, Mr. Narvik?"

"Yes, ma'am, I am. I've looked forward to exploring this big rock."

"Candace is scheduled to take a guided tour today. I would be less worried if you accompanied her."

Candace squealed with delight, and Matt saw no polite way to decline. "It would be an honor, ma'am."

Chapter 66

"If we climb this ladder, we'll be in the pantry of the piano bar."

"I don't think I can do it, Rubino," Anton said. "I'm so tired and sore."

"Yes, you can. Isabella did it with ease. She's up there waiting for you."

"OK, I'll try."

Dex helped him to stand and placed the man's hands on the rungs of the metal ladder. Anton seemed to be aging before his eyes. Ever so slowly, Anton scaled the ladder; Dex pushed him from behind and Isabella reached down to assist from the pantry.

Crewmembers, whose routines were disrupted by the alarm, scampered about, preparing for a day of service. When Anton finally reached the pantry, Dex followed. He peeked through the curtain and saw that the room was deserted.

"There's a small couch out here, Anton. Why don't you lie down."

"Yeah, I need to rest for a while, and then I'll be as good as new."

Matt returned to his suite, showered and shaved, then called room service to have his breakfast delivered. He swallowed four of his power pills, then grabbed his Bible and devotional and went to the balcony. He turned to the scripture recommended for the date and read 1 Samuel 7:2-12. In the devotional, the writer told how when Israel turned from its sin, God gave them victory. In response, "Samuel took a stone and set it up between two cities and called its name Ebenezer, saying, 'Thus far the Lord has helped us.' "

The writer then recommended placing a small stone on a desk or shelf as the devotee's own Ebenezer, a powerful, visible reminder that by God's help, he has come thus far and He will see him through to the end.

Today I'm going to be crawling on one of the most historic rocks on Earth. I'll take a piece of the rock of Gibraltar to be my Ebenezer. With God's help, I will serve Him as best I know how, no matter what the cost.

A knock on his door interrupted his thoughts. He paused to read the last line of the devotional. "Because God is beside us, we need not fear what is ahead of us."

Concern etched Desmond's face. "We must search the entire ship. No one can disembark until Rubino is found. Start at the bow and search every cabin."

"Why not go back to the office and check the security cameras?" Omar suggested.

"You idiot! Rubino will evade the security cameras. We must do an exhaustive search."

Omar tried to calm him. "No one can leave the ship until the gangways are secure. I will check the cameras for our escapees. If nothing else, it will tell us where they aren't."

"All right, but we must hurry."

The two rushed to the security office and began scanning the entire ship. Omar pointed to the screen, "There, in the piano bar. See the orange coveralls?"

"Those are maintenance workers."

"Look closely. That is Dexter Rubino."

"Yes, you are correct. Is there another way into the room?"

"There is a ladder from the floor below into the pantry. We can send several men there and bring a few in from the main door."

"We must not delay. If Madame hears of this escape, she will extract vengeance on all of us."

In a matter of minutes, Quest had three security guards at the foot of the ladder and four waiting in the hall outside of the piano bar. Quest and Omar approached the door and addressed the troops.

"Go in guns drawn, but do not fire unless necessary. The culprits are unarmed," said Desmond.

"Remember these men are elderly and weak, but do not underestimate them," Omar added.

The four guards burst into the room, guns drawn. Anton lay on a couch moaning about gold as Dex raised his hands and Isabella wept in fear.

Desmond sauntered into the room and smiled. "Good morning, Dexter. You seem to have recovered from your illness."

"What gives you the right? Can't you see that Anton is in need of medical care? We need a doctor right away."

"Is that why you defied the quarantine order? You have enjoyed the medical expertise of Doctor Stuart for several days. Now you repay Windswept's generosity by endangering everyone on this ship with your contagious disease. I will see to it that you do not escape again."

"We are in port, Quest. Let us get medical attention on shore."

"Why would we endanger the good people of Gibraltar? You are all members of the Windswept family. We will provide for your care ourselves." Turning to Omar, he said,

"Take these two down the ladder and lock them in a storage room. I will have a gurney brought in for Doctor Zhan."

Chapter 67

"I can't explain it, Mr. Quest. If Dex and Doctor Zhan were given the sedative I ordered, in the dosage I ordered, there is no way they could have overpowered the nurse and tried to escape."

"I never said they overpowered the nurse, Doctor. I believe she was a co-conspirator in their escape."

"I find that hard to believe. Isabella seems to be a competent professional. I see no reason for her to betray your trust and assist two men she had never seen before. Look at Doctor Zhan here. He's dehydrated and delusional. I'll have to get him on an IV right away."

"Doctor, Doctor!" a woman's voice cried from the reception room.

"You tend to your patient, Doctor Stuart. I'll see who it is."

As Quest left the examination room, Stuart looked at his pitiful patient. The man was withering away before his eyes. *Am I doing the man a disservice by keeping him alive?*

"Doctor, this is Cynthia Sterling. Her daughter has had a slight accident and needs your attention."

"Accident? This was no accident, Desmond," Cynthia said. "Alba Cologne savagely attacked my little girl. She may be disfigured for life."

Doctor Stuart surveyed the mother and daughter who had stepped into the crowded examination room. The mother bore her own disfigurement. *Was it an auto accident or a beating?*

"Please go down the hall to the next examination room. I'll be right there."

Hakim walked through the doorway and delivered Quest a summons from Madame Adolphe.

"Doctor, please excuse me, but duty calls. Please confine yourself to the infirmary while I am gone. I wish to speak with you in more detail later. Cynthia, please cooperate with the doctor and follow his orders."

As Quest exited the infirmary, Omar intercepted him.

"Mr. Quest, I would like to go ashore to see one of my cousins. He works at a glass shop not far from the docks."

"If I remember correctly, you are scheduled to check the passengers' ID as they disembark."

"I am, but I silenced the alarms and located the escapees on my own time. Surely I have earned a few hours of free time in port."

"Very well, but don't be late in returning. We will not wait for you."

As Omar walked away, he thanked Quest profusely.

Quest turned to Hakim, who had stepped up beside him. "Follow that little snake. I want to know where he goes and who he sees."

"Sir, I am assigned to guard Miss Candace."

"I will find someone to take your place. Do not let him elude you."

"Yes, sir!"

"You can wait in the lobby, Mother. I'm too old to have my Mommy follow me into the doctor's office."

Cynthia huffed and turned toward the reception area. From the hallway, she could hear her daughter's conversation in the examination room.

"You won't have to disrobe, Candace. Your only injury is to your nose, correct?"

"Don't you want to give me a thorough examination?"

"It isn't necessary. Please button your blouse."

Cynthia crept back into the other room where Anton Carmella lay on a gurney. He was moaning about lost gold and paying for his sins. Cynthia looked down at him and an evil smile appeared on her marred face.

"Hello, Anton. Do you remember me?"

Anton turned his face toward the voice. His milky eyes tried to identify the speaker. "Who are you?"

"I'm hurt, Anton. I came all this way to see you and you don't remember me. Do you forget all your victims so easily?"

A spark of recognition came to Anton's eyes. "No, it can't be you. You're dead!"

"That's right, Anton. You had me killed years ago. Now I've come back from the grave to drag you to hell!"

"No, no, please don't. I'm a different person now. I'm sorry about what happened to you, but it wasn't my fault. It was Joe. He wanted you dead. Please, leave me alone!"

"Wasn't your fault? You lying old gangster. I'm going to make you pay for what you did to me and all of your other victims."

"Mother, what are you doing?"

Cynthia Sterling turned to see her daughter standing in the doorway.

"The doctor said I can go. If we hurry, I can still meet the limo for my private tour of Gibraltar. Let's get out of here."

Cynthia forced a pleasant smile. "All right, baby. I'm glad you're OK. Let's go back to your cabin and get you ready for the media."

"Media? I thought I'd get some alone time with Matthew."

"Just go back to your room, Candace. I'll be right behind you."

Candace left the room and Cynthia returned her attention to Anton. "Not yet, Anton, not yet; but soon, very soon, the jaws of hell will have to open a little wider to swallow you."

Anton Carmella shivered in fear and tears streamed down his face as he whimpered, "Our Father, Who art in heaven . . ."

Chapter 68

"Arnan, why do we have to escort that singing skank into town? I thought we could stay onboard and play."

"Quest asked me to do it as a favor to him. I told you I used to be a bodyguard."

"Bodyguard and body builder are things you were. Now you are mine."

"Yes, Chantal, I am yours, but I still have to please our employer. I did insist that you come along. Try to be nice to the girl and her boyfriend. Their goodwill could prove to be important."

"For the time being, love, I will play the game; but soon we will be free."

"Yes, Chantal, soon we will be free."

Matt paced the dock waiting for Candace. He was uncomfortable going into town with the girl, but at least there would be a tour guide and perhaps a bodyguard along.

"Excuse me, chap, I'm supposed to meet a celebrity here for a tour. Her name is Candace Cologne. Have you heard of her?"

Matt turned to see a portly gentleman in khakis and a pith helmet. "Yes, I have. In fact, I'm waiting to go on the tour with her. My name is Matt Narvik."

"It's a pleasure to meet you, Mr. Narvik. I'm Gerald Wood. I'll be your tour guide. I'm a lifelong resident of Gibraltar, except for the war years."

"Where did you go during the war? Were you in the Army?"

The man chuckled. "No, sir, I was just a lad then. Went to Scotland with my mum. Dad was stationed here for the duration."

"You should certainly know your way around. Here comes Candace now."

Candace scowled as she approached the two men. "I'm sorry, but we can't go until my bodyguard gets here. Mother is watching from the ship. If we try to ditch the guard, she'll go ballistic. Worse than that, he's bringing his girlfriend along."

"Grand, the more the merrier. Name's Gerald Wood, miss, at your service. If we don't get started soon, we won't see it all." Gerald threw an elbow into Matt's side. "Egad, mate, look at the size of that bloke!"

Matt watched as Arnan and his petite escort crossed the gangway and approached the group.

Arnan smirked as he said, "Hello, Captain. Didn't think that I'd ever see you again!"

Candace took Matt's arm and said, "I didn't know you'd been in the military, Matthew, but I'm not surprised."

Matt swallowed hard and kept his eyes fixed on the big man. "Hello, Arnan. You're looking well."

Arnan chuckled. "Like to keep things in the family, Captain? How's the shoulder?"

"I recovered nicely, thank you."

Gerald stepped forward. "No time for introductions now, friends. Let's jump into the van and start our adventure."

"Van?" protested Candace, "I want a limo."

"Sorry, miss, but the streets in Gibraltar are too narrow for limos. If we squeeze in, we will all fit fine. Now let's get started."

Dex sat on the floor of the darkened room while Isabella rocked and sobbed beside him. He tried to comfort her, but the woman was inconsolable. *How am I going to escape this time? Will Narvik help me again? Will he even know that I'm still on the ship?*

He felt around the room searching for some type of exit. All he found were several valves on the pipes that ran overhead. If he closed or opened each valve, it may disturb the usual operation of the ship's systems. If he did it while the ship was in port, it might alert the maintenance crew, and they might help him. *Might is a big word, Rubino.*

"What was the cause of the alarm, Quest?"

"A small fire, Madame. It appears to have been an act of vandalism. Because of the sensitivity of the alarm system, we are susceptible to such callus acts."

"Did you find the vandals?"

"I am about to review the footage from the security camera nearby. This should give us enough information to apprehend the culprits."

"I trust you will, Desmond. Will you be going ashore?"

"No, Madame, my duties will keep me here for the entire day."

"How are our prisoners fairing?"

Quest swallowed hard. "Anton has taken a turn for the worse. I have moved Dexter to a room below the water line where he will not have an opportunity to interact with the crew in any way."

"Please inform the doctor that Doctor Zhan is to be kept alive at any cost."

"Yes, Madame. If you will excuse me, I need to get back to work."

"One more thing, Desmond, the animosity between Alba and Candace has resulted in physical violence. When the alarm sounded, Candace ran to my suite to assure my safety. Before she reached me, Alba attacked her and caused her harm. This cannot happen again."

Chapter 69

Hakim watched as Omar entered a glass shop just inside the walls of the old city. Rather than follow him inside, he took a seat at a chips shop opposite the entrance. Assuming Omar would be a while, he placed an order. Before it arrived, Omar exited the glass shop and headed down Cooperage Street.

Hakim followed on the opposite side of the street until Omar turned into a fenced area. The sign above the gate read "Methodist Seaman's Mission." From across the street, Hakim observed Omar as he walked to a table where a bearded man stood and embraced him. *Perhaps this is the cousin.*

The bearded man returned to his seat as he handed something to Omar. Omar appeared to suddenly be filled with joy as he left the confines of the mission and jumped onto a scooter that was parked at the curb.

Unable to follow, Hakim watched as Omar headed down the street. *I must return to the ship and tell Quest.*

Gerald Wood chatted nonstop as the driver piloted the van into Gibraltar. Matt found his tales of life on the rock entertaining, but the others were soon bored. They arrived at the queue for the cable car, then, with a herd of other tourists, they squeezed into the metal box that transported them to the top of the rock. Candace closed her eyes and wrapped her arms around Matt's waist.

"I'm afraid of heights, Matthew. Please hold me."

"There's nothing to be afraid of. Look, the view is terrific."

Latter, as they approached the entrance of the siege tunnels, Chantal refused to enter. "My religious beliefs do not allow me to go beneath the Earth. I will wait while the rest of you go in."

 Arnan opted to wait at the entrance with her. Matt and Candace followed Gerald into the vast network of tunnels that had, for the past few centuries, served the British Empire so well. After a half hour of walking, Candace complained that her feet hurt.

Matt shook his head, "You should have worn more comfortable shoes."

"I can't wear ugly hiking boots. I'm an entertainer, and how I look is important."

"If you're unhappy, miss, we could go to the gift shop."

"Yes, I've seen enough caves for one day. Matt, will you carry me?"

"I can't carry you all the way back to the entrance."

"You're strong. Give me a piggy back ride."

"All right, let's go."

When they returned to the entrance, they found Arnan and Chantal in a warm embrace.

Candace stared in disgust. "We're going to the gift shop now, if the servants are ready."

At the gift shop, Candace spotted a shelf full of stuffed monkeys that resembled the Barbary apes that posed for admiring tourists outside.

"Oh, Matthew, buy me one, please!"

"OK, but they are a little expensive." He pulled out his wallet and counted out the Euros.

"Oh, thank you. That's the nicest gift anyone has ever bought me."

Candace walked out of the shop with the toy in her arms. Immediately one of the apes swooped down from a wall and ripped it from her grasp. As she cried out in fear, Arnan ran after the monkey and another ape leapt onto his back. The giant screamed in terror as the animal clung to his shirt.

Gerald cried out, "Hold fast, mate! Don't hurt the ape!"

While some of the tourists laughed, others screamed. Arnan collided with a wall as he tried to free himself of the primate's grip. He fell to the ground and the ape scampered away. The apes passed the stuffed animal from one to another until it disappeared into the brush.

Candace shoved Arnan as he picked himself up from the ground. "Why didn't you shoot that stupid monkey?"

"This isn't the US. You can't just carry a gun anywhere."

"Matthew, get me out of here. I want to go back to the ship."

Gerald waved his hands frantically. "Miss, there is so much more to see. The apes aren't just monkeys, they are a symbol of the British rule over Gibraltar. If anything were to happen to the Barbary apes, it would mean the end of British rule."

"Who cares? I lost a perfectly good monkey. Your barber ape stole my monkey!"

"I'm sorry. I'll see if I can get you another."

"No! I don't want another one. I want to go back to the ship!"

Matt placed his hands on the girl's shoulders, and she buried her head into his abdomen. "Calm down, Candace, it was just a toy. You may not be enjoying yourself, but I would like to see more of Gibraltar."

"All right, I'll do it for you."

"Thank you. Gerald, let's get out of here."

"Right, mate, we'll press on to Point Europa."

The van raced to the southern edge of Gibraltar. There were piles of earth near the parking lot, a result of recent construction. Gerald led his party to a plaque that declared the historical importance of the spot.

While Arnan, Candace, and Matt stared southward toward the coast of Morocco, Chantal slipped away from the group. She stood alongside of a dark skinned man who was looking at a nearby mosque through his binoculars. She whispered to him, "It is good to see you again, Jeanblanc."

"Careful, they cannot see us together."

"Are you making any progress?"

"Yes, look there at the mosque. Do you see the man near the entrance?"

"Yes."

"That is Mashal."

"Are you certain?"

"Yes, I have been pursuing him for months. After we secure Zhan, I will return here to apprehend Mashal. The man on the scooter must be a contact."

"Let me see." She took the glasses from him and smiled when she saw the two men in the distance embrace. "That is Omar, from the ship's security team."

"The price on Marshal's head is nearly as high as Zhan's. Return to your friends before they become suspicious."

"Yes, sir."

Chapter 70

As they boarded the van to return to town, Matt picked up a small stone from a mound of dirt.

Candace locked her arm in his as she asked, "Are you a rock collector?"

"No, it's sort of a souvenir. This will be my Ebenezer."

"You mean that Scrooge guy?"

"No, this is to serve as a marker, or reminder, that when I was in Gibraltar I promised God I would live for him to the best of my ability."

Arnan chuckled as he piled into the van. "You still Jesus freakin', Captain? I would have thought you'd given up on all that religious stuff after what happened."

"I lost my boat, not my faith."

Arnan's voice took on a bitter tone. "I was talking about the way I dislocated your shoulder and Alba dumped you. Where was your Jesus when you needed him?"

Gerald intervened. "We'll be at a gift shop in a few minutes. While you're there, be sure and purchase some of the fine Gibraltar glass."

Ignoring the guide, Narvik answered Arnan. "Jesus was right where he's always been, in my heart."

"Maybe I ought to punch a hole in your chest and let him out."

Chantal snapped her fingers in front of Arnan's face. "Silence!"

Arnan sat back in his seat and stared at the floor. Matt and Candace looked at each other and shrugged.

Gerald continued with his sales pitch. "Jewelry made of Gibraltar glass is prized the world over."

"Doctor, I know that Dexter is ill, but in light of the recent vandalism, I would like to consult with him."

"Captain Auesnehmer, Dex is quarantined. I'm afraid that only Madame Adolphe or Mr. Quest can allow you to see him."

"But you are the attending physician."

"Yes, but I just work here. Please contact the company's representatives if you wish to see Dexter."

"I am the ship's captain. I do not have to consult with management. I asked you about Dexter in deference to your role as the ship's doctor."

"I gave you my answer, Captain." Stuart walked back to the infirmary in a cold sweat. If he jumped ship there, Quest would notify the authorities and he would risk extradition.

He entered the exam room where Zhan clung to life. He looked down on the man who he knew only by reputation. "Big time gangster, look at you now. You're a career criminal and you get to live to old age. All I did was divorce a vindictive woman, and it has cost me my practice, my reputation, and maybe my life. If I hadn't helped you and Rubino, I wouldn't be so worried. Now I've got Isabella in a jam, too."

Anton continued to mumble something unintelligible. The doctor bent over him and listened carefully. All he could decipher was, "Our Father . . ."

Desmond glowered at Hakim. "You could have hailed a cab, you imbecile. Now we have no idea where he is."

"There were no cabs there," Hakim said. "He just jumped on a scooter and left."

"Did you recognize the man at the mission?"

"No, sir."

"Go to the gangway and wait for his return, then bring him to me. Let me know when Miss Candace returns, also."

"Did you assign a guard for her?"

"Arnan is guarding her, but her mother is concerned about her spending the entire day with a young man."

"This man Narvik is not so young."

"Who is Narvik?"

"The man she has been seeing. She spent last night in his suite."

"It is an odd name, but it couldn't be the same man." Desmond Quest began typing on his keyboard. He turned the screen toward Hakim. "Is this the man?"

"Yes, that is him."

"He is old enough to be her father." Desmond flipped the screen back and resumed typing. After a few seconds he again turned the screen toward Hakim. "It is the same man, correct?"

"Yes, I think so."

"Ah-hah, this man is an operative of Dexter Rubino. I think we have found our vandal, Hakim. As soon as he returns to the ship, notify me. I want him held until we decide how to dispose of him. Get down to the gangway and do as I have instructed."

Chapter 71

Gerald's cell phone rang as they approached the city. He nodded as he listened, then said, "Yes, sir, I understand." He then addressed his tour group. "That was the ship. Because of a storm system in the North Atlantic, they have decided to leave port a few hours early."

Matt leaned forward to whisper to Gerald, "How soon will we be leaving?"

"In two hours, whether or not all the passengers return."

"They can't just abandon people here."

Candace spoke up. "Are we all right? I have to rehearse for tonight's show. This is the opening night for the casino."

"In the name of safety, they can and will, but not to worry. We will have you safe onboard in less than an hour."

"Are you certain it is the same man, Desmond?"

"Yes, Madame. I have checked his employment records and our copy of his passport. There is no mistake. This man is staying in a suite down the hall from you, a suite reserved by Alba Cologne. Now he is in Gibraltar with Candace, and Hakim told me that she spent the night with him."

"What evil plot has my grandniece contrived?"

"I am unsure of the full scope of her treachery, but I am worried about Candace. After all, this ruffian did violently assault Cynthia in Grand Cayman."

"Send all of your men into town and retrieve the girl at once."

"We are contacting all of the registered tour groups. The captain has advised me that we should leave port in a few hours to avoid a storm. We will intercept Candace's party as they board."

"If any harm comes to Candace, I will make Alba answer for it. Is Cynthia aware of who he is?"

"She hasn't said anything, but I doubt that she would have entrusted her daughter's welfare to a man that botched a simple bag drop."

"Tell Cynthia to come to my cabin, and as soon as Candace boards, bring her here."

"What of Alba?"

"Is she still sulking in her suite?"

"I believe so."

"I will speak with her."

Captain Auesnehmer entered the infirmary and shouted for the doctor.

"Is something wrong, Captain?"

"Yes. As you are probably aware, we are leaving port early. I need to know the status of my friend, Dexter Rubino. Does he need to go ashore for hospitalization, or is he recovering?"

"As I told you earlier, Dexter is quarantined because he displayed symptoms of the noro virus. Madame Adolphe has taken charge of his care so that I can concentrate on Doctor Zhan's welfare."

"I would rather he was in the care of competent medical professionals."

"He is with the nurse, Isabella."

"What about Mr. Jeanblanc?"

"Between you and me, I don't think Jeanblanc is really ill. Perhaps he is a paid stowaway."

The captain shook his head. "I know he has gone ashore in defiance of your quarantine. He was retained as an entertainer and master of ceremonies, but he has yet to take the stage. I think we should confront Quest with our suspicions."

"You're the captain. Why don't you confront Jeanblanc yourself?"

"I would feel better if Dexter was with me."

The doctor sighed. "You'll have to take that up with Madame Adolphe, or Quest."

Dexter sat in the dark storage room and contemplated the path that had led him there. He had no idea what the valves he had opened or closed controlled. Perhaps they were remnants of the old systems that existed before refurbishing. Isabella's chanting didn't do anything to lighten his mood. *Why do people keep praying the same thing repeatedly? What do I know about religion? I know I wish I had read the Bible more. I wish I had spoken to Narvik about what he believed. Why am I thinking of myself as if my life is over. I will get out of here…somehow!*

Chapter 72

Helene shook her finger at Alba. "What is your relationship with this American?"

"It is yet to be determined. I told him if he wanted to be with me, he must renounce his foolish religion, or at least keep it to himself."

"You and I have had to deal with a zealot before. It ended badly."

"My father was desperate because of illness and your betrayal."

"I did what was best for Windswept and you. If I had not stopped Philippe, our empire would have fallen apart. Perhaps the entire world would have fallen apart."

"Are you saying that you betrayed my father to save the world? Your actions are always geared to serve your own greed, which is how you came to control Windswept."

"I have saved Windswept for you. How did you ever meet this American?"

"He was the captain of the boat Papa chartered. It was my role to seduce him into co-operation. He was a gentleman and I hoped that I could groom him to be my consort."

"Ha! You are as much of a dreamer as your father. This man is an operative of Dexter Rubino. Soon he will share his fate."

"No! You cannot harm him."

"Did you know your sister spent the night in his suite? The suite you paid for."

"Matthew is gullible; she must have seduced him. She is the daughter of an American whore!"

"She is the daughter of your stepmother, and she is taking your place on stage. Are you going to continue to shirk your responsibilities or are you going to fulfill your obligation to Windswept?"

"I am not prepared to perform tonight. I will resume tomorrow."

Quest stood in the Grand Lobby greeting passengers as they came aboard. Captain Auesnehmer tapped him on the shoulder and whispered, "Where is Dexter?"

"He is quarantined, Captain. You know that."

"Can I see him?"

"Of course not! We cannot risk exposing you to a contagion."

"We have a problem that needs his attention. Mr. Jeanblanc has gone ashore, and he was also in quarantine."

"I was not aware of this. I will speak to him when he returns."

"Do you realize that he is supposed to be an entertainer and has yet to take the stage?"

"Yes, but he has been ill. I will meet with Doctor Stuart to determine if the man is truly ill or if he is misleading Windswept."

"Very well, Mr. Quest, I will leave the matter in your hands. I must go to the bridge now."

"Thank you for calling it to my attention." As the captain walked away, Quest muttered, "Pompous fool."

Matt and Candace then entered the Grand Lobby and Quest greeted them but ignored Arnan and Chantel.

"Miss Candace, your mother is waiting for you in Madame Adolphe's suite. Mr. Narvik, please follow me."

Candace protested. "I have to go to rehearsal. I have to perform at the pool as we pull out of port, and then again in the casino."

"We are utilizing the piano player and Miss Meaghan at the pool. You will have time to meet with Madame before the casino opens. Hakim will escort you there."

As Candace stomped away, Desmond turned to Matt. "Please follow me, Mr. Narvik. You too, Arnan."

Chantal nodded her approval.

Matt asked, "Is something wrong?"

"We apprehended a burglar in your suite. We want you to identify the property we believe he stole. It is in a secure room on a lower deck."

"I don't think I have anything to steal."

Quest gave Arnan a knowing look. "We will see. Arnan is coming along to identify some items taken from the fitness center."

Arnan smiled as he followed the pair through a passage way and down a flight of stairs. They walked down a narrow corridor to a dimly lighted door at the end of the passage.

"Do you have anything in your pockets, Mr. Narvik?"

"Just my money clip and some change."

"Give them to me, please."

"Why?"

Arnan glowered at the man. "Just do it, Captain."

Matt complied with the request but was growing increasingly uneasy. Quest swiped his security card and turned the handle on the door. Arnan grabbed Matt's arm and twisted it behind his back. As the door opened, a woman screamed and Arnan launched Matt into the tiny space at the feet of Isabella and Dex. The door slammed shut and in the inky blackness, Matt heard Dex ask, "Are you the cavalry?"

Chapter 73

The ship sailed to the south as far as permitted to give the more studious passengers a good look at the Moroccan shore. Others snapped pictures of the famous rock of Gibraltar.

The party on the pool deck had already begun. Meaghan Miller and David Carpenter had a festive crowd dancing and singing along to old standards. Some members of the dance troupe recruited spectators to join a conga line and soon the line wound around the pool and up the stairs to the next deck. Most of the dancers carefully balanced plastic cups in one hand while the ship pulled out of the port. In Madame Adolphe's suite, three women sat on a silk-covered couch. Candace was in the middle, her mother to her left, and her great aunt to her right. Each balanced a delicate teacup as the ship pulled away from the dock.

"I know this is hard to understand, but the man you slept with last night is the same man that attacked your mother in her own home."

"Matthew would never do that. Besides, we didn't sleep together. I bribed the purser to get into his suite. I got into his bed, but I fell asleep before he came in. I don't remember anything until the fire alarm went off."

Cynthia patted her daughter's hand. "Candace, this man is an enemy of our family. He will stop at nothing to harm you. He and Dexter Rubino are responsible for your father's death."

"You mean your lover, Dexter Rubino? If Matthew is so dangerous, why did you have me flirt with him on the other ship? "

"Shut up, both of you," Madame Adolphe said. "This man tried to imprison me many years ago when I was a diplomat for an impoverished island nation. I avoided going to prison, and he swore to get revenge on me. Your mother sacrificed a great deal to win Dexter's confidence and inform me of his plans. You see, dear heart, last year he interfered with a project your father was conducting and caused his death. Your friend Narvik was also involved in that. Now they have returned to steal Windswept away from you and your sister."

"You mean Windswept belongs to me?"

"It is my hope that you and Alba will share the company after I pass on."

"Cool! I'm, like, really rich. I thought Daddy only left us with a ruined hotel."

"You must continue to concentrate on your career as an entertainer. My people and I will do all we can to promote you to stardom, just as we did for Alba."

"I'm going to be a bigger star than Alba ever was, and after I'm famous, I won't let myself go like she has."

Helene and Cynthia chuckled as they embraced the young girl.

Quest rushed to Madame Adolphe's suite and spotted Hakim at her door. "Have you seen Jeanblanc?"

"No, sir, you ordered me to escort Miss Candace to Madame's suite."

"I didn't mean for you to pitch camp here. Where is Omar?"

"I believe he is in the security office preparing for the opening of the casino."

"He has nothing to do with casino security."

"He has said that he is a liaison between Windswept and casino security."

"What rot! Come to the security office with me immediately. It is time this pup was slapped down."

"No, Dex, I'm not the cavalry. I thought you made it off of the ship."

"Matt, your diversion was too early. We tried to hide onboard, but the security cameras caught us."

"Sorry, who else is in here?"

"This is Isabella."

The woman continued sobbing.

"Any plan for getting out of here?"

"I felt around and found some valves in the overhead pipes. I have no idea what they're for, but if we turned the right thing off or on, someone will be by to investigate."

Chapter 74

"Omar, I trust Gibraltar was pleasant."

"Yes, Mr. Quest. It was good to see my cousin after so many years."

"What does your cousin do for a living?"

"He works in a glass shop. Didn't Hakim tell you that I went there?"

Quest gave Hakim a disgusted look. Hakim bowed his head in embarrassment. "He did mention seeing you in town."

"My cousin had left the shop to meet a friend at the seaman's mission. They often go there for coffee. When I got to the mission, I saw the friend and he told me that my cousin had gone to the mosque to pray. He was kind enough to lend me his scooter to go to the mosque."

"I'm glad you were able to reunite with a member of your family, but what is this I hear about you working with casino security?"

"Since Dexter is ill and you are busy substituting for Mr. Jeanblanc, Alba and I thought I should take on more responsibility."

"Oh, you and Alba made this decision, without consulting Madame Adolphe or me?"

"She is anxious to prove to Madame Adolphe that she is sincere about playing a greater role in Windswept's management."

"Omar, we need you to tend to the duties you have been assigned. I am the chief security officer aboard. Dexter's illness has put even more responsibility on my shoulders. The casino security team is to operate independently from Windswept's security. This is Madame Adolphe's order, and we are all obliged to abide by it. I believe you were scheduled to assist in securing the bon voyage party on the pool deck. You should go there now."

"But I am equipped to do so much more."

"Go now, Omar!"

Omar, quivering with rage, struggled to maintain a civil tone. "Yes, Mr. Quest."

As Omar stomped away, Quest gave Hakim a withering look. "Tell me 'master of the shadows,' how did you let this pup detect you? You are getting old and sloppy, Hakim. Keep an eye on him while you guard Candace."

"Yes, sir."

Alba Cologne stepped out to her balcony and breathed in the evening air. In the distance, she could see the two worlds of her family's history. To the south lay Africa, where her ancestors had sojourned for centuries before their empire spread around the world. To the north, Europe, the Iberian Peninsula, the place she thought of as home. A scant fifteen miles of water separated these two worlds, but they were as far apart as the Earth is from its moon. She was leaving Gibraltar with no reconciliation between her and Matthew. *Why will he not renounce his silly religion and rule beside me? I can give him wealth and adventure beyond anything he has imagined, yet he chooses the religion of slaves over me.*

"Alba, forgive my intrusion, but I must see you."

"What is it, Omar?"

"I only have a few minutes. Mr. Quest has ordered me to stand guard at the bon voyage party. It seems that his ego forbids my acting as a liaison between Windswept and the casino security."

"He is a silly man. A young man of your talents should not be guarding drunken tourists."

"Thank you, Alba. I also have good news. I have a message from Mashal."

"He wrote to you?"

"No, Alba, I saw him in Gibraltar, and he has given me a letter for you."

"I'm hungry."

"Shut up, Matt. Isabella and I have been in here a lot longer than you."

"I'm sorry, I was looking forward to the big spread they were having at the bon voyage party."

"Stop thinking about it."

"Sorry, but I'm a big man and require a lot of nourishment. Pete told me not to skip meals. Between the exercise I was getting and the supplements you supplied, I was building muscle without gaining much weight."

"I was sorry to hear about Pete's death. About those supplements, there may be side effects."

"I feel fine. The good news about Pete is that he accepted the Lord before he died."

"Pete wasn't always the man you knew. In his younger years, he got into a lot of mischief."

"What he did, or what he was, doesn't matter. Jesus said, 'If any man hear my voice and will open the door, I will come in.' When Pete was lying beside that bike path asking for 'the way to Jesus,' he was a soul in search of a savior. I'm glad there was someone there to show him the way."

"You mean you showed him your way?"

"No, there was a teenage boy there. He knew the right thing to say."

"Was he able to give him words of comfort?"

"No, Dex, the Word of Truth."

Chapter 75

Alba sat on the floor of her bedroom; her hands were shaking and tears streamed down her face. "I should have known. I should have known. He still loves me," she whispered. "How could she do this to me? How could she let me suffer all these years?"

Alba gathered her courage and stood. She half stumbled to the vanity and stared into the mirror. *When he last saw me, I was young and beautiful. Now I am old and withered. I will not continue to decline alone and end up like Helene. She has taken much of my happiness, but I will not allow her to take my future.*

"I will meet you again, my love. In two day's time we shall be reunited, at the place where we said adieu!"

A large contingent of Windswept's security force held back the crowd at the casino entrances. At the prescribed time, an image of Alba Cologne appeared on the video screens near the doors.

"Ladies and gentlemen, welcome to the grand opening of the *New Dawn*'s casino. We hope you enjoy the games of skill and chance as well as our entertainment. This evening all beverages will be complimentary and all registered adult passengers are granted a one hundred euro credit." At this, a cheer erupted from the crowd. "Please enjoy yourselves in this, the newest of Windswept's gaming palaces. Bon chance, good luck, buena suerte, buona fortuna, bona sort!

As the guests entered, they saw Madame Adolphe and Desmond Quest seated in throne-like chairs on the stage at the far end of the room. Few paid them any heed as most of them queued up in front of the cashiers' cages to buy chips.

Madame Helene Adolphe rose and greeted her guests. "Welcome, welcome children!" She opened her purse and reached inside, withdrawing a fistful of twenty-euro chips, then she scattered them on the casino floor. A stampede of impatient gamblers ensued, and Helene fell back into her chair laughing.

"Candace, Candace, come out here."

Candace, clad in a risqué schoolgirl outfit, peeked from behind a curtain, "Yes, Auntie?"

"Here child, feed the pigeons."

Candace looked down at the people crawling on the floor grasping and wrenching the chips from each other's hands. "All right, Auntie." She plunged her hand into the old woman's purse and grasped the plastic disks, then flung a handful as far as she could. The crowd went wild and Candace and Helene shared the same evil laugh.

Desmond Quest stared in disbelief as another handful of chips flew from the stage. He rose and slowly walked behind the curtain. Cynthia looked at him with despair in her eyes. "What is she doing to my little girl?"

"I would say she is baptizing her into the family." Turning to a stagehand, he ordered the curtain opened and the band assembled there began to play. Candace began her usual writhing to the music. She took Helene's hand and helped her from her chair. The two women of Windswept began dancing to the beat and the cheers from the crowd.

"Come with me, Cynthia."

"But I can't leave her here alone."

"She is in good hands." The couple slipped into the corridor and entered the piano bar.

"This place looks deserted."

"It is. The piano player won't be here until ten. Even then the crowds will be in the casino for the next day and a half."

"You mean they will gamble around the clock?"

"Of course, and it is a good thing for us that they do. The gaming parlor is our most lucrative endeavor. We must make as much as we can before we enter Madeira waters."

"What happens then?"

"In deference to their casinos, we shut down."

"And this casino will reopen as soon as we leave Madeira?"

"That is correct. Would you like to join me in a glass of port?"

"Shouldn't we be drinking Madeira?"

Desmond rolled his eyes as he went behind the bar. "It is a ghastly wine."

"I should probably pass on any wine tonight. Candace may need me."

"There is no need to worry. Madame has led little girls down the road to debauchery before."

On the top deck, near the hot tub, Omar whispered into his satellite phone. "Yes, the letter has been delivered . . . No, I have never been there . . . A white Renault Mégane Cabriolet. What color is the top? . . . All right, I will find it . . . Yes, Mashal, I will not fail you."

Chapter 76

"Dex, someone is coming."

"Quiet, Narvik. This could be our chance."

"Or our doom."

"I'm going down fighting.

As the door of their makeshift cell opened, Isabella bolted toward the light. She collided with the small man that was cautiously liberating them, knocking him to the floor. Her legs entangled with his and she fell atop of him.

"Mr. Dex, Mr. Dex," he shouted as he gripped the woman's urine soaked coveralls.

"Hakim, man, am I glad to see you!" Dex stepped into the corridor and helped Isabella to her feet. Hakim stood and used his hands to smooth his blackened hair.

Matt Narvik followed Dex out of the room ready to do battle with his captors, but Hakim was alone.

"I have disabled the cameras on this level, but we must hurry."

"Hurry where?"

"To your old cabin. If Quest finds that I have released you, he will kill us all."

"Who else knows you came to rescue us?"

"No one. I am afraid to trust anyone with Windswept."

"All right, my cabin will do as a hideout while we develop a plan."

Meaghan rested her head on Dave's shoulder as they strolled to the piano bar.

"I wish I didn't have to do a show tonight. But my contract calls for me to perform each night of the cruise."

"But you're doing so much more than you contracted to do. All the work you've done with Candace and me could not have been included in your contract."

"Quest told me that I'd be working with new talent. He promised me a bonus if things worked out well."

"That's not a good way to do business. I think Alba's aunt and her lackeys would cheat you if they could."

"Well, I already got more in bonus than I bargained for, I got you."

Meaghan giggled. "I was thinking of you as my bonus."

At the door of the piano bar, he turned to her and kissed her deeply. "I think I have someone higher up the chain of command to thank for bringing you into my life."

Meaghan wrapped her arms around his neck and yielded to his embrace. "My life has changed so much in the past few days."

"Well, it is good to see you two getting along so well."

Meaghan drew back from David and stammered, "Oh . . . good . . . good evening, Mr. Quest."

Withdrawing his hands from Meaghan's waist, Dave tried to change the subject. "The pool side bon voyage party was a huge success. The crowd fell in love with Meaghan."

"It seems everyone loves Meaghan."

Meaghan blushed. "Dave's music is what the crowd fell in love with. We were just going into the piano bar to rehearse for his performance tonight. I mean for tonight's show."

Quest chuckled as Cynthia stumbled through the door and leaned affectionately on his shoulder.

Dave saw an opportunity to divert attention from himself; "Hello, Mrs. Sterling. I thought you would be at the casino for Candace's show."

"We were just headed back there to catch the second show. What are you two up to?"

"We were just discussing tonight's show."

"I can't thank you enough for working with Candace. She's going to be a big star and she won't forget all the little people who helped her on her way. I promise you that."

"Your daughter is a delight to work with."

"Oh, Desi and I left a little mess in there. Not to worry though, he called somebody to clean the bar up."

Quest blushed. "Cynthia, please restrain yourself."

Alba Cologne crossed the hall and placed her hand on the door of Matt's suite. *I will be gentle with him. He will understand that I am reuniting with my first love.* She gently knocked on the door. When there was no response, she pounded on the door with her delicate fists. "Matthew, open this door. I demand it!" *Perhaps he has gone to the casino show. I cannot envision Matthew in a casino, but if he went to see Candace . . . I shall kill them both!*

Chapter 77

Sequestered in Dex's cabin, Matt paced the length of the tiny room while Dex searched for clothes to fit Isabella, who had commandeered the shower as soon as they entered the room.

"These sweatpants are the only thing that will come close to fitting her."

"Not very fashionable, but I doubt that she'll care. What's our next move?"

"I'm not sure, but this will make it a lot easier." Dex held his trusted Ruger revolver in his right hand.

"I'm sure they have greater firepower than that."

"I know and I know how to get to it. I am the Deputy Director of Security."

"I think it's safe to assume you've been sacked. I can sympathize."

"Matt, I had no choice. I gave you a simple assignment and you blew it. Your failure put me in a precarious position."

"I told you in the beginning that I wouldn't do anything illegal."

"Illegal is a matter of perspective. Windswept needs to move some of its assets undetected. You have benefited from their business plan, so don't go Holy Joe on me now."

Matt's face reddened. "I did what I did out of respect for you. I never wanted to be involved in criminal activity."

"Well, you're involved now. Your life and the lives of others depend on your ability to take orders. Can I trust you to help us get out of this, or are you going to let me down again?"

"I'll help you Dex, but remember, my life is in God's hands not yours."

Desmond Quest awoke to Cynthia's snoring. His head ached and he had a terrible taste in his mouth. He slipped out of the bed and entered the bathroom. He splashed water on his face and swallowed a mouthful. *I have to get back to my own cabin without waking her.* The reflection of his bloodshot eyes and haggard look repulsed him. He left the room and headed down the corridor.

"Mr. Quest, Mr. Quest!"

Desmond turned to see Omar pursuing him. "What is it now?"

"The captain has invited you to join him for breakfast. He left a message on your phone and sent me to find you. He says that several of the passengers are concerned about the security of the ship."

"Tell the captain that my duties prevent me from joining him today, perhaps later in the voyage."

"I believe that reassuring our passengers is one of your duties."

Quest attempted to slap the much younger and agile man. Omar evaded the blow and used a karate move to slam Quest to the floor.

Looking up at the smirking youngster, Quest bellowed, "I will have you killed, you impertinent pup!"

"You impotent old man, you cannot prevail against me."

Quest pointed a finger at Omar. "Alba cannot save you this time. Madame Adolphe has been suspicious of you since you were hired. You come from a family of vipers, and we know how to deal with your ilk."

"Be cautious of your language, Quest. Your fate may lie in my hands."

"Morning, sweetheart."

Dave Carpenter sat at the piano arranging some music to suit Candace's range. "Good morning, Meaghan. I trust you slept well."

"Not really. I kept thinking about our discussion last night."

"I'm not trying to pressure you into doing something you're not ready for, but it is the next step."

"I understand that. It's just, like, contrary to my upbringing, but I do want to be obedient. I wish I could find Matt Narvik and talk to him about it."

"Is he with Alba, or Candace?"

"I don't know. Alba has been locked in her room since her show tanked. Has Candace said anything?"

"No. Will Alba recover, or is she done for good?"

Meaghan shook her head. "I can't imagine her throwing her career away because of one bad show."

"It's not like she needs the money. I hear she's loaded."

"You should see her house. It's like a palace."

"I don't envy her. I would rather know that someone loves me than have all the money in the world."

"You have your wish. Now what?"

"I thank God for the blessing and try to win your hand."

"You have my heart. It's a package deal."

Chapter 78

Alba Cologne burst from her suite with her head held high. She walked to rehearsal with dignity while avoiding the stares of her supporting cast and ignoring their whispers.

Nancy Rivers smiled as she approached. "Ms. Cologne, I'm so happy you could join us."

"I am feeling much better. Shall we start rehearsal from my entrance?"

"Actually, we have arranged the show to focus on Candace's talents. You could use a few days of rest I'm sure."

"Talents such as Candace's are for sale on the streets of any city. This is my stage, my show, and my ship. If you wish to continue your employment with Windswept, you will bear this in mind."

"Alba, the time has come to step aside and allow Candace to take her place. It isn't fair to the other entertainers to disrupt the flow of the performance."

"That is enough, Miss Rivers. I know that you and my detractors have plotted against me from the beginning. All of you have conspired to sabotage my performance. I am Alba Cologne. I will not be undermined by peasants."

"Perhaps we should meet with Madame Adolphe and see what her opinion is."

"The opinion of that old witch is of no consequence. I am Alba Cologne!"

Alba saw Nancy's eyes look past her as she nodded toward the door. The sound of shuffling feet filled Alba with fear as a cold hand gripped her upper arm. "What is this?" she said. "What do you think you are doing?"

Nancy Rivers chuckled and said, "You're beside yourself, Alba. These men will return you to your suite so you can rest."

"You cannot do this. I am Alba Cologne!"

Following his confrontation with Quest, Omar headed for Alba's suite. He felt sure that she would support him and further erode Quest's authority. When he arrived at her door, he was aghast to find it unguarded. "Alba, it is Omar. Are you in your room?" He entered the suite and knocked on the door of her bedroom but got no response. He opened the door and stepped in. A quick search found that she was gone. *It is unlike her to leave so early in the morning.* The sound of someone entering the outer room caught his attention.

"Miss Cologne? Are you here?"

"She is not here, Doctor Stuart."

"Oh, I got a call that she was ill. I hurried here as fast as I could."

"Perhaps they have taken her to the infirmary."

"No, Miss Rivers said that she was returning to her suite."

Two men then wrestled Alba into the room. The shattered look on her face made Omar's heart drop.

"Let me go. I am Alba Cologne."

Omar shoved one of the guards away. "Take your hands off of her. Alba, are you all right?"

Doctor Stuart stepped between the guard and Omar. "Let's all calm down. What seems to be the problem, Miss Cologne?"

"I am fine. I went to rehearsal and was abducted by these infidels."

"Miss Cologne has had a breakdown, Doctor." They all turned to see Desmond Quest standing in the doorway. "Miss Rivers informed me that Alba became hysterical at rehearsal and was asked to leave. Finally, it was necessary to restrain her. I think a sedative is in order."

"Call me old fashioned, but I like to make my own diagnosis, Mr. Quest. I'd thank you all to leave me alone with my patient."

Quest entered the room and pointed at Omar. "Take this man into custody. Relieve him of his sidearm." The two guards turned on Omar as he pulled his weapon. After a brief struggle, Omar's gun hit the floor.

Alba screamed, "Leave him alone. He is just a boy."

"Quest, get these men out of here," ordered Doctor Stuart.

The guards quickly had Omar handcuffed and dragged him into the corridor.

"Let Omar go or I will have you eliminated, Quest," Alba said.

Quest grunted as he bent down and retrieved Omar's gun. "Doctor, you can see that Miss Cologne is beside herself. If you don't have a sedative with you, I can have one brought from the security office."

"You are not going to sedate me, Quest," Alba said. "I am not about to allow you to usurp me as you did your superiors."

"I only seek to protect you from yourself, Alba. Your aunt has been afraid that your emotional strength was lacking."

"Mr. Quest, please leave me alone with my patient."

"Very well. I have posted two guards at the door. I'll be nearby if you need me."

When Quest left the room, Doctor Stuart sat beside Alba. "Why don't you tell me what happened?"

As Alba told the doctor her tale of prolonged persecution, the doctor tried to assess his best course of action. "Do you have a history of emotional problems, Miss Cologne?"

"No! Can you not see that this man is attempting to steal my birthright from me?"

"Please remain calm. When you lash out like that, it only gives credence to his claims."

"What am I to do? Just stand by and watch while what is rightfully mine is stolen from me?"

"I'm in a difficult situation, Miss Cologne. You insist that you are fine and my superiors say that you may harm yourself. Is there anyone on the ship that you trust?"

Alba almost said Matthew but then remembered her last conversation with him. "Meaghan Miller is a friend that I can trust. Her cabin is adjacent to mine."

"Where is she now?"

"I'm not sure, perhaps in the piano bar."

"Let's call security and have them find her. She can stay with you while I explore other options."

"I do not need a babysitter, Doctor."

"I know, but I will feel better if you're not alone."

Chapter 79

Hakim's jaw dropped as he entered the security office. "What has happened here?"

A burly man with scarred knuckles answered. "This man has committed insubordination. He drew a gun on Mr. Quest."

Blood spilled from Omar's mouth as he whimpered. "It is not true, Hakim. I was trying to protect Alba from these men."

"Where is Alba now?"

"Ms Cologne is in her stateroom. With the ship's doctor."

"Is she ill?"

The big man averted his eyes as he spoke. "She became hysterical at a rehearsal. We escorted her to her suite for her own protection. This pup interfered and Mr. Quest ordered us to take him into custody."

"Did he order you to beat him also?"

"It was necessary to subdue him."

"We cannot keep him where a passenger might see him. We have a room on a lower level that will serve as a cell. Follow me."

As discreetly as possible, the guards took Omar to the same room where Quest's other foes had been imprisoned. As they approached the room, a team of maintenance workers exited.

"What is the problem here?"

A maintenance man shrugged. "Someone closed a valve that controls the flow of fresh water to the laundry. I think there is also a sewage leak in that room. The stench is terrible."

"Did you repair the valve?"

"We took care of the problem. We will return after lunch to find the sewage leak."

"No, this room is quarantined. Do not report that you entered this room to make any repairs. If you do, you will also be quarantined. Understand?"

The workers looked at the bruised and bleeding man the guards were holding upright. "Yes sir, we understand."

Speaking in Catalan, Hakim whispered in Omar's ear. "Keep quiet. I will return and release you later." Hakim then used his security card to open the door and forced Omar inside of the room. He turned to the other guards and bellowed, "Return to your regular duties!"

Quest entered Madame Adolphe's suite expecting her to be asleep. Instead, she was at a desk staring at the screen of her laptop. "Good morning, Madame."

"Something is wrong, Quest."

"You have heard already?"

"Of course. We are down nearly six hundred thousand Euros. We are the victims of card counters."

"Nonsense. Casino security would have detected such activity."

"I have seen it in the past. There is no way we could lose money if the games are run correctly."

"When we find the perpetrators, we will deal with them severely."

"No, you will eliminate them."

Quest swallowed hard. "Madame, there is another difficulty that has arisen."

"Is it Rubino?"

"No, he and his cohorts are safely locked in a storage room. It is Alba."

"Has she returned to work?"

"She became hysterical at a rehearsal this morning. Then the boy, Omar, tried to interfere with my staff. I had him taken into custody also."

"Deal with the boy as you deem appropriate. My niece is my concern. Did the doctor sedate her?"

"I'm not certain. I thought it more important to notify you of the situation."

"A day of rest would be good for her."

"Very well, Madame. If you will excuse me, I will be going to my office now."

"No, Quest, you are going to escort me to the security office. I must confront the casino security team and correct this situation."

Chapter 80

"Alba, are you OK?"

"I am fine, Meaghan. Once again my enemies are attacking me, but they will not prevail."

"When the security guards found me, they said you'd had a breakdown."

"I refused to allow that harlot, Nancy Rivers, to bully me."

"So are you back in the show?"

Alba hesitated. "That is no longer the issue. I have an exciting new opportunity, one that will allow me to take over all of Windswept."

"Is that what you really want?"

"It is my destiny. Allah has provided me with this opportunity so that I can do his will."

"You should talk to Matt about this, or Dave."

"I have not seen Matthew in several days. He has chosen to adhere to his silly religion rather than live a life of consequence with me."

"I share his faith, Alba. I was never very religious, but Matt explained that it isn't a religion, it's a relationship. It is all so simple. For the first time in my life, I truly understand that God loves me and sent His Son to die for me. Tomorrow when we put in at Madeira, some of the other believers and I are going . . ."

"Meaghan, do not fall victim to the religion of slaves. Christianity is nothing but cleverly devised stories and superstition. It is the reason that I have given Matthew up. Now I will be reunited with my true love, Mashal."

Helene Adolphe paced the width of the piano bar as she lectured the security team. "I will not tolerate any further breakdowns in security. I insisted on hiring your firm to provide security for the casino. Now I have to assign the ship's security team to detect who is evading your safeguards. Mr. Quest is now in charge of all security operations. If you wish to return to your homes and families, you will stop these card counters today!" She then turned and stomped out of the room.

Quest stood before the guards and cleared his throat. "You all heard Madame Adolphe. She does not make idle threats. These card counters must be brought to justice before we enter the waters of Madeira. I will be spending my time studying the videos of last night's disaster."

Quest's eyes searched the room, "Hakim, where are you?"

Hakim stood and moved through the room. "I am here, sir."

"Hakim, I entrust you with my regular duties. This problem with the casino will be rectified today. You can handle things for that long."

"I will do my best, sir."

In a more hushed tone, Quest said. "Check on the prisoners. Madame wants them to be available for questioning."

"We don't want a fire-fight," Dex said. "That's why we need to take over the armory. If we control the weapons, they will have to allow the Madeira police to board. At the very least, we will get off of this ship."

"What about the other people onboard? What about Alba?" Matt asked.

"When are you going to wake up? Alba is up to her eyeballs in this business. You have to concentrate on saving your life, not your love life."

Matt slipped his hand into his pocket and rubbed the stone he had taken from Gibraltar. "I told you, my life is in God's hands. I'm concerned about the lives of the passengers and crew."

"This is the best way to protect them," Dex said. "All the time and training you've been given is useless if I can't depend on you. You either cooperate with me or stay out of the way."

"There has to be a better way."

A knock on the door interrupted the conversation. Dex leaned against the door and said, "Who is it?"

"It is Hakim. I have brought food and supplies."

Dex opened the door and Hakim shoved a room-service cart into the tiny room.

Dex pulled the sheet from the cart and nodded approvingly when he saw the semi-automatic pistols. On a lower shelf sat three plates of gourmet food. Dex's mouth watered as he caught the scent. "Time out, gentlemen."

Chapter 81

The raging storms in the North Atlantic caused the seas to build around the *New Dawn*. The face of Captain Auesnehmer showed concern as he stared at a computer screen. He left the bridge and went to Madame Adolphe's suite.

"What is it, Captain? I have a breach of security in the casino to deal with. Card counters are robbing us of millions."

"If we don't evade this coming storm, none of that will matter."

"I have noticed the rocking of the ship but do not believe it to be excessive."

"Nor do I, but as we go further west, the sea will be rougher. This might cause a problem for the entertainers at tonight's show, particularly for the dancers."

A gleam appeared in Helene's eye. "This may also hamper activities in the casino."

"I doubt that it will have any effect on the gaming tables."

"Yes, yes it will, Captain. We must close the casino immediately, for the safety of the passengers. How soon will we be in Madeira's waters?"

"In about eight hours. Closing the casino now would cause a loss of revenue."

"The safety of the passengers and crew is paramount. We will close the casino and cancel tonight's show."

"If you think it is best, Madame."

A knock on the door interrupted them. At Helene's nod, Captain Auesnehmer opened the door and Alba, with a guard on each side, stepped in.

"Alba, it is good to see you up and around so soon," Helene said. "Did the doctor give you something to calm down?"

"I have no need of sedatives, Aunt Helene. I am here to demand that you release Omar to my custody immediately."

"I was told that he assaulted Quest. We have the safety of the passengers to think of. In fact the captain and I have decided to close the casino and cancel tonight's show to ensure their safety."

"Cancel my show? But—"

"Because of these rough seas, dear heart. We cannot imperil you or the passengers for our profit."

"What about Omar? Release him to me and I will take responsibility for him."

"Frankly, Alba, you are not responsible for yourself. Omar is in custody and will be dealt with when we reach Sunset Cay."

"I demand that he be released. I am the heart and soul of Windswept. Without me Windswept will fail!"

"You have already been replaced, dear heart. Now, these men will accompany you back to your room and I want you to concentrate on getting better."

Alba lurched forward and the guards restrained her. "This is not over, old woman." She turned and left the room.

Madame Adolphe turned to the captain with tears in her eyes. "It is so sad. She is as mad as her father."

Chapter 82

Hakim's report of Omar's beating and imprisonment saddened Dex. "It was just a few weeks ago that I thought of him as my right hand."

"Hurts when someone you trust turns on you, doesn't it?" Matt said.

"Let's not get into that again."

"Are we going to break him out?"

Hakim shook his head. "There is no need. He is safer in that room than he would be if Quest saw him walking freely about the ship."

"I still can't figure out why Quest had me thrown in there with Dex," Matt said.

Hakim shrugged. "I am afraid it is my fault. I identified you as Miss Candace's boyfriend. Quest found your picture on the computer and then connected you to Mr. Dex."

"Thanks, Dex."

Dex looked bewildered. "Who is Miss Candace?"

Hakim explained. "She is Alba's younger sister. She is now the feature performer for Windswept. Philippe fathered her by an American woman. When he was sick, he left her and the mother in the Caymans and went to live with Alba."

"An American woman in the Caymans? What is her name?" Dex asked.

"Miss Cynthia. I believe she remarried and her name is now Sterling. She has been sleeping with Quest on this cruise."

"Quest? Are you sure Hakim? Is she a tall redhead with a slight disfigurement?"

"Yes, Dex. Do you know her?"

"I thought I did."

"That sounds like the woman I made the drop for in Grand Cayman," Matt said. "She drove a blue Jaguar."

Dex shook his head. "What a couple of suckers we are."

"Hey, I just remembered, Dex. When I picked up that package at the bridge, the guy at the helm said to tell Quest that was the last of it."

"I imagine that Quest has been supervising these transfers for some time. Now he is the head of security."

"Why did he take us prisoner?"

"He knew you were connected to me. He knew I was a threat. When I was ill, he took advantage of the situation."

"Mr. Quest is trying to isolate Madame Adolphe from everyone else," Hakim said. "He is involved with Miss Cynthia and promoting her daughter to replace Alba."

Dex sighed. "The power struggle in Windswept is of little concern to us if we don't get off this ship."

Meaghan detected a bad vibe when she entered the piano bar. With the casino closed, the place was packed and noisy. Choking smoke filled the air. Dave kept playing in spite of the din. He smiled and nodded for her to come up to the piano. She squeezed through the crowd and joined Dave. "Sorry I'm late, but Alba needed me."

"No point in singing tonight. Everyone here is concentrating on getting drunk. We have a big day tomorrow. Perhaps you should get some sleep."

"Have you spoken to Brother Jeffers?"

"Yes. He said he would be happy to officiate. How is Alba?"

"Not well. She didn't show any interest in attending. Are we going to rent a car?"

"No, I checked the rates online and think we will be better off hiring a driver and a small van. That way we won't get lost and can all ride together."

"Is it far?"

"About an hour from the port. There is a restaurant nearby where we can have a nice lunch afterward."

"I'm really starting to get excited."

"Me, too. It's a big step."

Candace drifted from the piano bar to the teen club, where she scored a joint. She then entered the theater just in time to watch her video on a big screen. Everywhere she went she received praise and kind comments. Several of the male passengers invited her to dance, but she turned them all down. When she wandered past the infirmary, she noticed a light was on. Suddenly she remembered her mother saying that certain doctors knew the proper techniques to drive a woman to a state of sustained ecstasy.

She opened the door and entered the lobby. Seeing the light in the first exam room, she placed her left hand on the door jam and pivoted into the doorway, striking a sultry pose. "What's up, Doc?"

The scene inside the exam room caused her to emit an ear-splitting scream and she turned to run for the door but a small, dark man collided with Candace and sent her sprawling onto the lobby floor. He escaped from the room before anyone else arrived.

A security guard stepped in and asked, "Why are you here, Miss Candace?"

"I had a headache. I thought I could get some aspirin from the doctor. There was a man in there. He was doing something weird to that body. I think I'm going to be sick!"

Chapter 83

"Look at the television screen, Candace," Helene said. "That camera is mounted on the bow of the ship. Do you see those lights on the horizon? That is Madeira. We will be docking there before dawn. You can get off of the ship and visit the shops or take a tour if you like."

"No, Auntie, I want to go home. Is there an airport on the island?"

Cynthia pointed a finger at the girl. "Stop it, Candace. You have an obligation to perform. Besides which, the hotel has been sold. You have no home to go to."

"Well, then, where is Todd? He will take me in. He cares about me."

Helene Adolphe placed her hand on the girl's shoulder. "Calm down, dear heart. You always have a home with Windswept." She wrapped her arms around Candace and pulled her close. "You, like I, are the heart and soul of Windswept. You are a princess and have no need to go to strangers. I spent a lifetime preparing Alba to lead Windswept, but she has chosen to forsake her birthright. In just the past few days, you have usurped her and have taken her place as the next leader of our corporation. "

Cynthia's eyes welled with tears. "Oh, Candace, isn't it wonderful?"

Quest cleared his throat to announce his presence. "Madame, my investigation of the incident is nearly complete. Unfortunately, the perpetrator was shielded by the darkness and we could not identify him. Doctor Zhan is resting comfortably and the doctor says he seems to be unharmed."

Helene sighed. "Candace, please return to your cabin and get some rest. If you wish, I can have Quest assign a guard to your door."

"No. If it's all right, I'd like to stay with Mommy tonight."

Quest shot a troubled look at Cynthia, as Helene smiled at her. "I am sure that your mother would cherish some time alone with you."

Cynthia stammered a bit as she cast a soulful look at Quest, then said, "Of course, Candace, you can stay with me, just for tonight."

As mother and daughter left the room, Helene turned on Quest.

"Do you know what they were doing?"

"We found hair clippings on the floor and ink on Anton's finger tips."

"The intruder was trying to identify him?"

Quest nodded. "It would appear to be so."

"Anton is a worthless thug. Why would anyone want to identify him? Perhaps Zhan's body has been found and identified. Now law enforcement is trying to follow his documents."

"No, if the body was discovered, I would have been informed by now. I have a theory. It may be that someone is trying to make certain that he is Doctor Zhan."

Helene began pacing the room. "Zhan was worried about al-Qaeda pursuing him. He had embezzled funds from them to make his investment with Windswept."

"I thought that the formulas he gave you were his investment."

"Zhan didn't realize the value of his formulas, and I neither did I until I used Anton and Arnan as test subjects."

"I did see a change in Anton."

"Yes, it turned a crippled old man in to an aggressive pervert. If we could successfully market the formula, it would be worth billions."

"Did you experiment with anyone else?"

"My first choice was Dexter Rubino. He reneged but requested that I send some to one of his operatives. I don't know who took it or what the results were."

Matt Narvik paced from one end of the room to the other. "What if the authorities in Madeira don't cooperate? Windswept may have them on the payroll."

Dex rolled his eyes at the question. "Madeira is a Portuguese Island. I doubt that Madame Adolphe could buy off law enforcement there. We'll wait right here until we've been in port for several hours. Security will be relaxed. Most of the passengers and crew will be ashore, then we can head straight to the armory."

"Then you want to charge off of the ship, guns blazing?"

"No, it would be too dangerous. First, we take over the armory and secure the ship. We then contact the port authorities to help us get off of the ship."

"What about Alba? Are we going to rescue her?"

Dex sighed. "Alba is part of Windswept. She doesn't need rescued."

Matt grabbed him by the shoulders. "I don't agree. Hakim told us that she was under guard. I won't participate in any plan that leaves her behind."

"All right, if you feel so strongly, you can take my Ruger and go to Alba's suite. You take care of her guards. Then Hakim and I will take the armory. I'll call her suite when it's clear to bring her there. We contact the authorities and shut Windswept down. Now take your hands off of me."

Matt regained his composure and said, "What about that kid, Omar? He's locked in the same room we were."

Dex thought for a moment. "Hakim can release Omar before you rescue Alba. After all he's been through, he will be inclined to help us."

"Where is the armory?"

"Adjacent to the security office. Now get some sleep. We should be docking in Madeira in a few hours."

Chapter 84

Unable to sleep, Meaghan Miller paced the top deck. As the ship approached Madeira, she starred in awe. The lights of the island put her in mind of a village set under a Christmas tree. She had never heard of the island, save the wine that bears the same name. Here she was going to make a significant step into her new and unfamiliar life. She felt no fear, just a peaceful, reassuring calm. She was on the right road for the first time in her life; she was certain of it. If thinks didn't work out for her and Dave, she would still be thankful for his friendship in these early days of her new life. Where had Matt Narvik gone? He was the first person that had shown any concern for her soul and had pointed her in the Lord's direction. Now it seems he had disappeared.

"I would like to offer a penny for your thoughts, Miss Miller."

Startled, she turned to see Captain Auesnehmer. "Oh, Captain, aren't those lights just beautiful? Shouldn't you be on the bridge?"

"My officers are quite able to operate the ship until the pilot comes aboard. I just like to watch from a distance. Why are you here at such an early hour?"

"I couldn't sleep, just too anxious."

"About what?"

"Dave and I are going to the north side of the island. There are some volcanic pools there."

"Oh, you mean Porto Moniz. It is a very nice place, but today it may be dangerous. The storms to the north are causing rough seas. It is possible that the sea will overflow the pools."

"Oh, no, that just can't happen. It is important that the pools be open."

"The pools are lovely, but why are they so important to you?"

"Captain, promise me that you won't laugh."

Chantal awoke as the flame of an enchanted candle drowned in a pool of wax. She pushed Arnan's arm off of her, and he snorted and groaned as he rolled over. As her feet hit the floor, a soft knock came. She wrapped a sheet around her and opened the door a crack.

"Jeanblanc, why are you here?" she whispered.

He showed her an envelope. "Take this ashore and send it express post to my office in Lisbon."

"Quiet, Arnan is sleeping."

"Do you not control the giant?"

"Yes, but it is best to let him think he is in control. What is in the envelope?"

"Evidence. I am afraid that we have been pursuing a ghost."

"Zhan is dead?"

"No, the man we have pursued is probably not Zhan."

"Then our mission is a failure."

"No. Even if this man is not Zhan, we know that the gold Zhan stole went to Windswept. We only need authorization to adjust to a new target. Be sure to post that envelope. When the final determination is made, they will send me encrypted email."

"Must I continue to service this oaf?"

"Do what you must to control him. When the time comes, he may prove useful."

"Yes, sir," she said and sighed as she closed the door. As she returned to the bed, Arnan stirred and she whispered, "Soar, Arnan. Soar great eagle. Carry me to your nest in the sun."

Dex sat in a corner of the cabin, unable to sleep. The wheezing and snoring of Isabella and Matt made the hours go by slowly. When he heard a knock at the door and the hushed voice of Hakim, Dex welcomed the interruption. He opened the door, greeted his friend, and asked, "Has the power to the security cameras been turned back on?"

Hakim smiled. "Quest is too busy trying to find card counters to look at the security screens."

"Good, let's take a walk. I need to get out of here."

"Mr. Dex, most of the crew is beginning to stir. It would not be wise to let them see you."

Dex answered in a hushed tone. "We will have to take that chance. I need to speak with you in private." As they moved through the corridor, Dex continued. "I have no choice but to revise my plans. We will wait three hours after docking. Then you will release Omar. Bring him to my cabin and the three of us will launch our attack from there."

"What about Mr. Narvik?"

"Matt will wait for you to bring Omar to my cabin. Then he will go to Alba's suite to release her."

"Is he capable of taking on two guards?"

"Probably not, but I'd rather have him causing a diversion in another part of the ship than have him getting in our way."

"What time do you wish me to release the boy?"

"We're scheduled to dock at seven," Dex said. "Release him at ten."

"We are docking earlier than scheduled, in an hour." Hakim glanced at his watch. "It is four fifteen."

"We want the passengers off the ship before we begin. Wait until ten."

Chapter 85

As the *New Dawn* threaded its way behind the massive seawalls of Madeira, the first light of dawn tinted the sky over the Atlantic. A few passengers lined the railings to see the unique terrain of the island. Hand-painted signs of triumph left by the crews of smaller craft bedecked the docks of Funchal.

The first person to leave the ship was a diminutive woman who clutched a manila envelope in her left hand.

Meaghan and Dave played host to a group of friends at the breakfast buffet onboard and Brother Jeffers blessed their meals.

Dave advised the group. "We will have to wait a little while before we leave the ship. We have a special guest joining us today."

One of the women gasped. "Do you mean Meaghan got Alba Cologne to join us?"

"No, Alba's duties will keep her aboard while we're in Madeira. Our special guest will be Captain Auesnehmer. He has paper work to do before he can leave the ship."

As if on cue, the captain joined the little group. "Good morning, my friends. Let us be going. There is much of this island worth seeing, even before we reach Port Moniz."

"Meaghan said that you've been to Madeira several times before," said Dave.

"Oh, yes. Once I spent a month here. Please allow me to act as your guide."

Meaghan smiled at the kindly old seafarer. "We are honored to have you with us, Captain."

"The honor is all mine dear. I have traveled many places and seen many things but never witnessed such a ceremony as this."

The noise associated with docking woke Alba from a restless sleep. She was to meet Mashal, but Omar was to go with her. *How can I evade the guards at my door? Should I again appeal to my aunt or try to leave the ship undetected?*

She thought on these things as she showered and dressed. Reluctantly, she retrieved a small pistol from its hiding place and shoved it to the bottom of her purse. She swallowed hard and opened the door of her bedroom. No one was in the sitting room. She crossed the room and opened the outer door, startling the two guards.

"Tell Quest I want to see him, now!"

The guards looked at each other. Then one turned and left. "You must return to your room, Alba."

"I have not left my room. I'm standing in the doorway."

"Quest will be displeased if he sees you there."

"Quest is nothing. I am the heart and soul of Windswept."

"Please do not put me in this awkward position. I served your family for many years and wish to continue my employ."

"Do you think that my father would want you to turn against me to do the will of this infidel Quest?"

"It is not for me to say. I only take orders."

"Very well, I will wait for Quest inside."

"Wake up, sweetheart."

Candace groaned. "Oh, Mother, it's too early."

"Nonsense. I thought we could get some breakfast and then go ashore. We could take a tour, maybe do some shopping."

"It's just another island. Who cares?"

"You should. People here buy DVDs, too."

"Do they speak English?"

"I don't think so, but it doesn't matter."

"Oh, I get it. Your stash is running low and you want to replenish it."

"Candace, stop being so disrespectful. I've cut down on my usage since we came to Europe."

"Does your boyfriend approve?"

"If you mean Mr. Quest, I told you he is a leader in Windswept. He is as concerned about your career as I am."

"And I told you he's a creeper. When he looks at me, my skin starts to crawl. You could do a lot better. I think Todd is a lot cuter."

"Todd thinks so, too. Get up and get dressed. You have a public to be seen by."

Candace shot up in bed and smiled. "Can I take Matthew with us? I think you'd like him if you got to know him."

"Are you serious? Helene told you that he was involved with your father's death."

"Isn't that an occupational hazard in the crime business?"

Cynthia shook her head. "That man is old enough to be your grandfather. Forget about him."

"No, I like him. At least he's honest with me. I haven't seen him since Gibraltar. I don't want him to think I forgot about him."

"If you haven't seen him since Gibraltar, he's forgotten about you."

Chapter 86

Quest slammed his fist on the desktop. "We must uncover these card counters."

Hakim nervously glanced at his watch. "Surely you can identify who the winners were. They have to give their names when they cash in their chips."

"There are more than a few winners. They have a system involving several people at a time. They have not all cashed out yet. This is an evil plot to cheat Windswept."

"How will we proceed?"

"When we leave port, we will keep the casino closed due to sea conditions."

"That will anger the passengers."

"Let them be angry. We cannot continue to lose money. Have you checked on the prisoners?"

"They are secured."

"Have they been fed?"

"I have given them a minimal amount of food and water. Omar is still handcuffed. The others are taking care of him."

"Early tomorrow morning, before dawn, we will dispatch the lot of them."

"Even the woman?"

"Unfortunately, yes. We can't afford to leave witnesses behind." Quest stretched his arms over his head and yawned.

"I need some rest. You can continue to handle my duties while I take a nap."

"Yes, sir. Will you be in Miss Cynthia's cabin?"

Quest's countenance hardened. "No, I will retire to my own cabin." A smile appeared on his face. He opened a desk drawer and pulled out the key card to Narvik's room. "Since this suite isn't being used, I think I'll utilize it for myself. It is time for you to meet with the port officials, isn't it?"

"Yes, sir, I will be going now."

As Hakim spoke, one of Alba's guards came into the security office. "Mr. Quest, Alba Cologne has requested that you come to her suite."

Quest laughed. "Let the trollope rot. Her era is done. That reminds me, has Madame Adolphe left her suite yet?"

"Not yet, sir. I believe she is sleeping."

"Hakim, you are going to be late for the meeting."

"I am on my way, sir."

Hakim left the office and proceeded to the storage room where Omar was imprisoned. He unlocked the door and slowly opened it. Omar remained motionless on the floor.

"Omar, it is I, Hakim. We need your help."

Omar turned his head and blinked at the light streaming in the door. "You need my help?"

"Yes. Dex and I need your help to take control of the ship. Once we take the armory, we will notify the port authorities to rescue us."

"Then unshackle me."

As Hakim unlocked the cuffs, he whispered, "I have brought you some water. When we get to Dex's cabin, you can have a little food. Then we will take the ship."

"Where is Alba?"

"In her suite. She asked for a meeting with Quest, but he refused."

Omar shook his hands to restore the circulation. "Are we in Madeira?"

"Yes, we arrived earlier than scheduled."

He chugged the bottle of water. "What time is it?"

"Ten o'clock. We must get to Dex soon. While we take the ship, Mr. Narvik will rescue Alba."

"I am truly sorry, Hakim." Omar summoned his martial arts training and felled Hakim in a series of brutal blows. He removed his victim's weapon and placed it in his own empty holster. He retrieved the handcuffs and placed them on Hakim's wrists.

He cautiously slipped out of the door and closed it, then proceeded toward the seventh level.

"Should I go to Alba's suite now?"

"No, Matt, wait for Hakim to return, then you can go. Once you have her free, start for the security office. That's where we will make our stand."

"It's ten after now. Maybe Hakim can't be trusted."

"If it wasn't for Hakim, we would still be locked in that storage room."

Matt slammed his fist into an upper bunk. "I can't stand here and wait while Alba is in danger. Dex, you and I could take the security office by ourselves."

"No, Matt, I need some experienced professionals with me. You'll have your hands full releasing Alba."

Isabella curled up on the lower bunk and began chanting.

Chapter 87

Captain Auesnehmer played tour guide to Meaghan's group of friends and directed the driver to points of interest around the island.

"I'm so glad you came along, Captain. None of us speak Portuguese."

"It is an honor for me to be invited, Miss Meaghan."

Dave looked at the clock on the van's dash. "We want to be at Porto Moniz by eleven. We have reservations at a restaurant for noon."

"Very well." He leaned to the driver and whispered something in Portuguese, then added, "We will be there in a half hour, Mr. Carpenter. Relax and enjoy the scenery."

Alba, with her revolver in her hand, pressed against the wall behind the entrance door of her suite. A thump outside her door made her hands quiver. *Will I have the courage to kill Quest?*

The door opened slowly and her grip on the revolver tightened. As a figure entered the room, she pointed the gun toward it. Her eyes closed involuntarily. A sudden blow sent the gun to the floor, and she opened her eyes to see Omar.

"Oh, Omar, I thought you were Quest. Your face, what has happened to you?"

"Quest's apes roughed me up. Help me drag this one into your room."

Alba stepped around the door and saw a guard lying motionless on the floor. She grabbed one of the man's arms as Omar grabbed the other arm, and they dragged the guard into her bedroom. Omar used an electrical cord to bind the man's hands.

"We must hurry," Omar said. "We need to be at the meeting place at noon."

"It is only one half hour to Calheta."

Omar stared at her in disbelief. "Did Mashal tell you the meeting place in the letter?"

"He didn't need to. Your brother and I parted there. It is a fitting place to be reunited. The marina was new then. He boarded his yacht and sailed away. I've not seen him since."

"This time you are to meet on the beach. He is afraid that you will be followed."

"How will we get off the boat?"

"We must exit thru the grand foyer and walk across the gangway."

"Go wash the blood from your face and comb your hair. We can't afford to draw too much attention."

"Hakim is a half hour late. I'm going after Alba."

"No, Matt, you leave this room and our entire operation could be jeopardized."

"This isn't an operation to me. This is about the woman I love."

"I order you to wait here for Hakim."

Matt's face twitched with anger. "You fired me, Dex. That means I no longer take orders from you. I'm going."

"No, Matt!"

Matt shoved Dex onto the bunk. Dex bounced back to his feet and grabbed Matt's arm. Narvik felt the rage that was becoming more familiar to him. He slammed his fist into Dex's forehead, sending him to the floor.

"Stay out of my way, Rubino!"

Matt entered the corridor and stared at the security camera for just a moment. Its lens pointed in the opposite direction and made no movement in response to his presence. "Still off," he muttered.

Matt walked to the nearest elevator, then realized it only went to the third level. In frustration, he left the elevator and began climbing the stairs. When he reached level four, he encountered a crew of men loading cargo onto a forklift. He decided to take the outside stairs from deck to deck.

Arnan was jogging on deck five, but Matt avoided detection by crouching behind a towel locker. As he continued, he nearly collided with a small man descending the stairs. He avoided eye contact and in a few minutes, he was on the seventh level. He crossed the balcony overlooking the grand foyer and saw Quest ascending in the glass elevator. He ducked into a restroom and held the door ajar so he could see down the corridor.

Quest left the elevator and pulled a key card from his pocket. Matt quietly walked behind him until Quest stopped at the door of Matt's suite. Quest turned his head and looked at the door of Alba's suite. He put the key card back into his pocket and crossed the hall to her door. There he pulled a security card from his pocket and opened the door.

Matt heard voices coming from the bedroom and watched Quest move toward it. As Quest pulled a pistol from his shoulder holster, Matt pulled the Ruger from his pocket. Using both hands, he aimed the gun at Quest's back.

Chapter 88

At Port Moniz, the small group of Meaghan's friends gathered and began singing Amazing Grace. Captain Auesnehmer stood near the stairs carved in the volcanic rock. He watched the proceedings with the interest of an anthropologist studying the practices of an obscure tribe. When Brother Jeffers stood in the pool and began preaching, his heavy accent caused the captain to strain to understand.

Several passersby stopped to witness the goings on. Some pointed video cameras at the strange black man in the water. Meaghan Miller, wearing a sheer white dress over an orange bathing suit, walked down the stairs into the pool. She stood beside Brother Jeffers who smiled broadly at the young woman, revealing his two gold teeth.

In his faulting English he asked, "What is ya nam, child?"

"Meaghan Marie Miller."

"Does ya know Jesus as ya personal Savior?"

"Yes, I do. I admit that I am a sinner and believe that He is the Son of God. I confess him as the Lord of my life. He has forgiven me of all my sin and made me a new creature."

Brother Jeffers placed his left hand on her back as he cradled her hands in his callused right hand. "Magan Mallar, because of ya statmant of faith, I baptize ya, ma sister, in da nam of ta Fater, ta Son an ta Holy Ghost." He gently laid her back into the pool, submerging her.

"Buried together wit Christ," he said, then lifted her back to her feet. "Raised agin to eternal life."

Her friends began to applaud and several tourists joined in. Meaghan left the water and embraced Dave.

"Hold it right there, Mr. Quest. Drop the gun."

Quest froze but retained his weapon. He turned his head to see who dared challenge him, then smiled. "Mr. Narvik, you should put that gun down. I am here in my capacity as head of security." He started to turn toward Narvik, when the bedroom door opened.

Omar stepped into the doorway and pointed an automatic pistol at Quest. "Release the weapon. I need no further incentive to kill you."

Quest let his gun fall to the floor. "You will regret this insubordination, Omar."

Matt entered the room and closed the door. He lowered his gun and approached Quest. He grabbed him by the shoulder and spun him around, pushing him into an upholstered chair.

"Why did you throw me in that room with Rubino?"

"You are a security risk, just as Rubino. How did you get out?"

Matt turned to Omar. "Where is Alba?"

A voice called from the bedroom. "I am here Matthew. Are you injured?"

"No, I'm OK.

Omar held out his hand. "I'll take that gun, Narvik."

"I don't think so, sonny."

Alba intervened. "Matthew, do as he says. Omar is here to rescue me."

"I'm here to rescue you. Omar is supposed to be helping Dex take the ship."

Alba squeezed past Omar and entered the living room. "Matthew, you do not understand. Omar is taking me to meet my true love, Mashal."

"Mashal?"

"Mashal is Omar's older brother. Today Mashal and I are to be reunited."

Matt felt as if his soul was sinking into a dark sea. "But you never—. I came on this cruise to be with you."

Quest chuckled. "This whore was never interested in you, Mr. Narvik. You are but a pawn in her sick game. Now the tide has turned against her. She will never get off this ship alive."

Omar pointed his pistol at the man. "Silence!"

Quest laughed again. "You are about to die, pup. There is only one way off this ship, and my men have orders to shoot you on sight."

Alba shot an icy stare at Quest. "I have no reason to fear these men. I am the heart and soul of Windswept. Once Mashal and I are reunited, we will take over the corporation. You and that old witch will be eliminated."

Matt looked at her in despair. "These men are hired killers, Alba, but there is another way off the ship."

That caught Omar's attention. "What?"

"I saw cargo being unloaded on deck four. You'll have to ride the forklift to the dock, but security won't be looking for that."

"That is brilliant, Matthew," Alba said. She stood on her tiptoes and kissed his cheek. "I am sorry to hurt you like this, but Mashal is the only man I could ever love."

"You will never escape," Quest said. "Even if you evade my men, I will hunt you down."

Alba snorted in disgust. "You have no power. Perhaps you can return to being my aunt's driver."

Omar took her arm. "We should hurry."

She nodded at Quest. "What about him?"

Quest stood up, and Omar sent a lightning fast blow to the man's temple. The head of security crumpled to the floor.

Chapter 89

Dex felt the cool wetness of a cloth stroking his face. His eyes opened to see an anxious Isabella caring for him. He struggled to his feet and checked his watch. "Eleven o'clock! I have to get out of here."

He grabbed the Glock and, despite the protestations of Isabella, charged into the corridor. *I must get to the armory. Perhaps Omar and Hakim misunderstood my orders.*

Before he reached the stairs, he heard the voice of Jeanblanc echo off the metal walls. "Stay where you are, Rubino. Drop your weapon or I will dispatch Hakim to the next world."

"I see you've recovered from your mysterious illness."

"As have you. Put down your weapon. I am not bluffing." Jeanblanc pointed his pistol at Hakim's head and forced him into the corridor as a shield.

"Mr. Dex, please do as he says," Hakim said. "Omar overpowered me and took my gun. My hands are bound. Our plans are ruined."

"Let him go, Jeanblanc. We only want to take the ship's armory until the authorities arrive and rescue us."

"I am the authority, Rubino. Drop your weapon and no harm will come to you, or your comrades."

Dex reluctantly laid the gun on the floor and slowly approached Jeanblanc. "What's your game?"

"This is by no means a game. This is a deadly serious business. I need to find Doctor Zhan."

Dex smiled. "Doctor Zhan is in the infirmary."

"I think not. The man in the infirmary is much larger than Zhan. I have collected samples for DNA testing. I will have the results by tomorrow morning."

"He's the only Doctor Zhan I know, though he did mention the name Anton Carmella."

"Then where is Zhan? Give me the answer Rubino or your friends will die."

"I honestly don't know, but I think I know who does."

Meaghan's group left the pools and walked to the nearby restaurant, Cacholote. After Meaghan and Brother Jeffers changed into dry clothing, they all enjoyed a terrific seafood lunch. While the captain held the rest spellbound with tales of the sea, Meaghan and Dave strolled the walkways around the pools.

"Isn't it wonderful the way the Lord works things out? I thought if the large pools were closed, the trip would be for naught."

"I think using the small pool was a better choice. Maybe God caused the waves to overlap the large pool so we could have a more intimate experience."

"So what's next? I feel as though I should be doing something, something meaningful."

"Well, you and I work well together. We enjoy a lot of the same things." He looked into her eyes as he spoke. "And I'm hopelessly in love with you."

"I love you, too, Dave, but I'm not my own anymore. I want to serve the Lord, and I don't know how I could do that on a cruise ship."

"The Lord can use you wherever you are."

"You don't understand. I have this overwhelming desire to serve God."

"The truth is, I've been hiding in piano bars for the past few years. I've come to think of them as the belly of my whale. I know the Lord has something for me to do, but I'm damaged goods."

"Isn't ours the God of second chances?"

"You mean you'd even consider . . ."

"I need time. I feel like I'm taking baby steps. I'm not ready to commit to a marathon, not yet."

"So we'll wait and see?"

"No, we'll pray, and wait to see what the Lord wants for both of us."

Chapter 90

Matt led the way to the cargo loading area. Omar assisted Alba, who had changed into a fashionable dress and stiletto heels. Matt paused at the glass door nearest the loading operation.

"Hurry! When they unload that pallet from the forklift, we'll throw an empty pallet on the forks and have the driver lower us to the dock."

"Matthew, are you sure this is safe?"

"Safe enough. I used to ride a forklift like this where I worked. If he can handle a pallet of produce, he can handle three humans."

"You stay here, Narvik. I will take Alba to the rendezvous point."

"No way, junior. I'm sticking with her until she says to go. Take off those shoes, Alba. We'll have to run."

"Yes, Matthew."

"Ready, set, go!"

Matt led the other two across the deck. He pushed the safety barrier aside and grabbed a pallet, then pushed it onto the forks. The crewmembers looked on in confusion. When Alba hesitated, Matt shouted at her, "Come on, Alba, before security sees us."

Alba warily stepped onto the pallet. Omar joined her. As Narvik stepped onto the makeshift platform, he shouted to the crew to radio the operator to lower them to the dock.

"Matthew, they do not understand." Alba then spoke the same order in a calm, Spanish voice and the pallet began to rise off the deck.

"Oh, we are moving." Alba threw her arms around Omar and shut her eyes.

"Sit down so you don't fall off," Matt said as he crouched low on the pallet. "Just keep your hands in the clear. Omar, draw that cannon of yours. We may need it."

As Omar drew his weapon, he looked down and noticed the Haitian girl running toward the gangway. "This is not safe, Narvik."

"It's safer than dealing with Quest's goons."

The pallet slowly descended and set them on terra firma. Omar led Alba by the hand. "The car is this way."

The three raced to a Renault convertible. As Omar opened the driver's door, Alba stopped him and said, "I will drive, Omar, I know the way."

"Stop, Narvik!"

Matt turned to see Arnan running toward them and vaulted into the back seat. "Let's roll!"

Omar ran around the car and jumped into the passenger's seat as Alba got behind the wheel and started the car. She had trouble with the gearshift, and as they jerked forward, Arnan jumped onto the deck lid and slid into Narvik. Matt greeted him with a powerful right fist. The two giants began fighting as Alba pulled onto the roadway. A panicked look swept over Arnan's face as the force of the turn caused him to fall to the roadway. As they sped away, Matt saw his foe tumble into the curb.

"You knock, Rubino. Hakim's hands are not free."

"What do you hope to accomplish, Jeanblanc? The man in the infirmary isn't the one you are hunting."

"Madame Adolphe will know where Zhan is hiding, as well as where the funds he stole are located."

Dex reluctantly knocked on the door and in a few seconds it opened. "Well, hello, Cyn."

"Dex, what are you doing here?"

"I'm fine, Cyn, but before we exchange pleasantries, I should tell you I'm here to see Helene."

Jeanblanc shoved Dex into the room, then wrestled Hakim ahead of him. "Where is Madame Adolphe?"

Cynthia gasped when she saw Jeanblanc pointing a gun at her. "She's in her room getting dressed."

"Get her out here, now!"

"Yes, sir." Cynthia knocked softly on Helene's door. "Helene, you have guests."

A muffled voice came from the next room. "Who is here?"

Jeanblanc pointed his gun at Dex, who nodded. "It's Dexter Rubino. Get out here. We have business to discuss."

Helene burst from her room in a robe and slippers, her hair half done. "What the—" She stopped short when she saw a weapon pointed at her. Candace walked out of the room after her and said, "Oh, Auntie Helene, you have, like, really interesting friends."

Chapter 91

Alba sped eastward on the Rapida to Calheta Marina. She came to a screeching halt in the parking lot.

"Where is Mashal? Where are we to meet him, Omar?"

"You are to wait on the beach. I am to go to the chandlery and wait."

"Did he not tell you where he would meet me?"

"Yes, he said on the beach. Go there now and wait for him. We are several minutes late. You can wait here in the car, Narvik."

"No way. I'm not taking my eyes off Alba until she meets your big brother."

"Matthew, you go with Omar. I will be fine."

Alba watched as Matt followed Omar to a strip plaza that ran along the beach. When they stepped into a store, she walked onto the manmade beach. She remembered Mashal telling her that the sand had been imported from Morocco. It felt warm beneath her bare feet. The breeze gently lifted the hem of her skirt, and she wished she had brought a hat. Several families with children were enjoying the beach and the water that was shielded by a massive breakwater. To her left the masts of sailboats waved in the clear sky.

Will Mashal take me away on his yacht?

She turned to her right and saw a kite far above, just below the cliffs. As it came closer, she realized it was not a kite but a hang glider. A man piloted the craft in her direction, making graceful loops above the sea.

"Mashal? It is Mashal." She waved at the glider. "Mashal, I am here!"

When Matt and Omar entered the chandlery, a young girl stood behind the counter reading a magazine. She smiled and gave them a warm welcome in Portuguese. Matt said "hello" in English. The girl frowned and returned to flipping pages in her magazine.

"What's the plan now, Omar?"

"The plan was for me to wait here. You were not included in any plans. I told you to stay on the ship."

"No offense, but I don't trust you or anyone else involved with Windswept."

"Then walk away, Narvik. This is none of your concern."

"I can't do that. Hey, what's that?

"Where?"

"That shadow on the sand." Matt stepped closer to the plate glass window and peered into the sky. "Some guy is landing his hang glider on the beach."

Jeanblanc waved his gun as he spoke. "If the ladies will please be seated on the sofa, the gentlemen will sit in those two chairs."

"You make a great cruise director, Jeanblanc."

"Silence, Rubino, you are a failed security agent. You are fortunate to still be alive."

"That's me, Mr. Lucky."

"Be quiet! Now, Madame Adolphe, where is Alba Cologne?"

"I believe Alba is in her suite."

"I want her here. You, little girl, you will go and bring her to me. If you warn her or inform anyone else of your aunt's position, I will kill her."

Candace rose, left the room, and a moment later returned. "No one is there."

Helene seemed perplexed. "She must be there. She is supposed to be under guard."

"There was no guard," Candace said.

"Don't you have a security card, Helene? You can get into any cabin with a security card."

Helene gave him an evil look. "Yes, in my desk, I'll get it."

"Stay where you are. Which drawer?"

"Second drawer on the left."

Jeanblanc opened the drawer and removed a pearl-handled revolver. "A weak attempt, Madame. Where is the security card?"

"It is in that same drawer, on the side. I had forgotten about the gun."

"Yes, here it is," Jeanblanc said and handed it to Candace. "See if anyone is there. If you fail to return in three minutes, your mother will pay the price of your tardiness."

Candace's hand shook as she took the card and left the room. In less than a minute, she ran back into the room, shrieking. "That creeper Quest is in there. I think he's dead or something."

Chapter 92

Alba ran to Mashal as he released the harness. He swept her up in his arms, and she giggled uncontrollably. Three men who had appeared to be beachgoers ran to his glider and began securing it.

"Is Omar here?" Mashal asked.

"Yes, my love," Alba replied. "Which boat is ours? I can't wait for you to take me away from here."

"Alba, we must take your ship to your island. I need to escape from al Qaeda."

"I just escaped from the boat. My great aunt has kept me there as a prisoner."

"Now we will return and imprison her. Soon after the ship leaves the dock, we will take over all of Windswept. Sunset Cay will make a good base of operations."

"Then why did I escape the boat? You could have come there to rescue me."

"I needed to be sure you would leave it all behind to be with me."

"Mashal, I will do anything to be with you." She fell into his arms, and they kissed.

Omar bolted from the chandlery and ran to his brother. "Mashal, the mission is a success!"

"Not yet, brother. We must return to Alba's ship and leave this island. Once we are at sea, we will depose Helene Adolphe and Windswept will be ours."

"Must we return?"

"You can stay here if you wish. I must go to Windswept's island in the Turks and Caicos." Mashal pointed at a man walking toward them. "Who is this man?"

Alba answered. "He is Matthew Narvik, a close friend of mine. He helped me escape the ship."

"Is this the American you told me of, Omar?"

"Yes."

Matt approached and held out his right hand. "Hi, I'm Matt Narvik."

Mashal threw Alba to the ground and punched Matt in the stomach. In an instant, the three men who had been stowing the glider attacked Matt. They kicked and stomped him as he curled into a fetal position on the sand.

Omar helped Alba stand and addressed his brother. "Mashal, you need to leave here."

People on the beach retrieved their children and possessions and fled the conflict. Mashal pulled Alba to him. "Come, we must leave. Bounty hunters are pursuing me."

"There is no reason for you to beat Matthew. Stop them now!"

Mashal slapped her. "He has dishonored me. He has also dishonored you, but you are too foolish to see it. You will learn your proper role in time." Turning to his men, he said, "Enough. Leave this dog here and go before the police arrive."

"Did you close the door, girl?" Jeanblanc asked.

"Yes, sir."

"Good, we don't want anyone else seeing Quest's body. Madame Adolphe, you are the head of the Windswept Corporation."

Helene hesitated. "Yes, I am."

"You accepted an investment of four million American dollars in gold from a thieving dog named Zhan."

"Doctor Zhan made an investment of two million dollars a few months ago. I have not seen him since."

"You are lying, Madame. Zhan systematically embezzled funds from a Muslim charity and converted it to gold. He delivered that gold to Desmond Quest. Do not deny this. His mistress became quite cooperative after he abandoned her in Spain. She provided dates, times, and places where she transferred the gold to Quest. I have been retained to find Zhan. You certainly know where he is. You will share this information with me or I will begin killing the people in this room. To prove I am in earnest . . ."

He pointed his gun at Hakim. Dex flinched when he heard the dull thud of the silenced gunshot. Hakim fell from his chair, face down, blood streaming from the back of his head.

Candace screamed, and Cynthia pulled her close.

"Silence, child," Jeanblanc said. "You should be glad I do not practice ladies first. Now, Madame, tell me. Where is Zhan?"

"Zhan is dead. He died months ago. If you want me to return his investment, I will. It totaled a little over two million dollars. I can show you on my computer the dates the deposits were made."

"I know it was much more. I would not be surprised to learn that Quest has been stealing the gold before it reaches Windswept's coffers. The point is, my employers lost four million and they will want four million in return. The location of Zhan's body would be a goodwill gesture on your part."

Dex stared at Hakim's body. "You can't just kill us all, Jeanblanc."

"I can and I will, Mr. Rubino, unless I get all that I require. It is entirely up to Madame Adolphe."

Chapter 93

Alba drove back to the port, her face, and emotions, stinging from the slap Mashal had delivered. She noticed the police cars near the entrance of the cruise ship terminal. Blood stained the concrete roadway. When they reached security, she and Omar showed their key cards. Mashal pressed a wad of bills into the guard's hand and the guard nodded.

At the top of the gangway, the ship's security guards nodded to Alba but cast a wary eye at Mashal. Mashal pushed past them and continued on to the Grand Lobby. Six men ran to greet him. After a brief embrace, he led Omar and Alba on to the elevator.

"We must pay a courtesy call on your great-aunt Helene. I'm sure she will be pleased to see me again."

"Who are these men?" Alba asked.

"These are old friends of mine. Helene hired them as security for the casino. They will form the nucleus of Windswept's new leaders."

"You and I will lead Windswept."

"Do not worry about such things. Once we retrieve your father's device, we can return to Europe. You will look pretty on my arm."

"Mashal, I am not some harlot. I am the daughter of Philippe Ben-Balla."

Again, Mashal slapped her. "You are my woman. You will take me to Helene and keep your mouth shut."

Alba buried her face in Omar's shoulder.

"Stop hitting her, Mashal," Omar said. "She is a princess."

Mashal threw a brutal punch into Omar's face. "You will hold your tongue as well or I will cut it out."

Matt Narvik lifted himself from the sand as a kindly local directed him to a shower. The cool water helped clear his pounding head and wash away the blood that had spurted from his nose. He wandered through the parking area looking for the car that had brought him there. *It's gone. She's gone. Alba has abandoned me.*

A voice called to him and he looked around.

"Matt, it's Dave, over here, across the street."

Matt had trouble focusing on a group of people who appeared to be standing near a van. "Wait, help me. Please help me."

Seconds later, Meaghan and her friends surrounded Matt. They helped him cross the street and climb into their already crowded van.

Meaghan's voice broke as she touched his face. "What happened to you? You're bleeding."

"I'm not sure."

Dave asked, "How did you get here? You're just lucky the captain insisted we stop here so he could buy some wine."

"Alba. I came with Alba and Omar."

The captain shook his head sternly. "Did they return to the ship?"

"I don't know. She met some old boyfriend here. Then several big guys jumped me. I didn't see them leave."

Dave wiped away the blood that trickled from Matt's mouth. "We should get him to a hospital and call the police."

"No, we must return to the ship," the captain said. "Involving the authorities will only complicate things. Doctor Stuart will tend to Narvik and Madame Adolphe will determine the way forward."

Helene Adolphe sat at her desk, reluctantly typing on her laptop. "There, Jeanblanc, the transfer is complete. Leave us now before Hakim is missed."

"What is the location of Zhan's body?"

"He is at the bottom of an elevator shaft in Barcelona." She handed a business card to him. "This is the address. But he will be decomposed by now."

"As long as I can supply DNA evidence and perhaps a few snapshots, my employers will be satisfied."

"Just who are you working for, Jeanblanc?" Dex asked.

"It does not concern you, Rubino. You are a mere spectator to this transaction."

"You didn't have to kill Hakim. He was a harmless security guard."

"This man's death was not in vain," Jeanblanc said. "He helped me secure the embezzled funds in a timely manner. If Helene had continued to hesitate, you, Rubino, would have joined him. Go back to your rocking chair. This time stay there."

Madame Adolphe cast an icy stare at him. "Your bravery will not go unrewarded, Rubino. Hakim and Quest are dead. I will see to it that you are properly rewarded for your services." Jeanblanc roared with laughter.

Dr. Stuart shook his head as he lifted a sheet over the head of Dr. Zhan. "Sorry old man, I did all I could for you. Wish I knew who you really were. I'll go tell the old woman you're gone. I'm sure she'll be sorry to hear you died peacefully."

Chapter 94

Meaghan's group joined the crush of passengers filing through security. Dave and Captain Auesnehmer helped support Matt while the girls distracted the guards. At the gangway, Captain Auesnehmer began to bluster past security when one of the guards called him aside.

After a muted conversation, he turned to Narvik. "Alba Cologne has returned to the ship with Omar. She is with a male companion that seems very familiar with the casino security team. I am afraid we may be walking into a trap."

"I can't pretend this isn't happening, Captain. If Alba is in trouble, I have to help her."

"Alba may be the problem herself."

Matt felt his pocket. The Ruger and the stone from Gibraltar were still there. "Help me get to her suite. I need to know she's all right."

The captain said, "I will go ahead of you. My position will open many doors."

"Just remember to duck if things get rough."

"How do you think I managed to become an old man?"

"Please, Mashal, let me stop at my suite and freshen up before I see my aunt."

"Where is it?"

"Across the hall from hers."

"Very well, but hurry. I want to confront her before we leave the dock."

"Yes, Mashal."

Omar touched her arm and whispered. "Have you forgotten who we left in your suite?"

"We should let Mashal see how well you dispatched my adversary. Perhaps he will respect you more."

"What is all this whispering? Is this your suite?"

"No, mine is the next one."

"Open the door and fix your makeup, but hurry. I will not be kept waiting."

Alba unlocked the door and shoved it open. Quest lay on the floor as they had left him.

Mashal stopped and stared at the body. "Who is this?"

"Desmond Quest, the head of security," Alba said. "Omar killed him with his bare hands so that I could come to you. Omar is a powerful warrior and will prove to be an asset to us as we rule Windswept. There is another guard bound by Omar in the next room."

"Not as powerful as you think. This man is still alive."

A voice called from the hallway. "What's going on?"

Alba looked up and saw the doctor standing in the doorway. "Oh, Doctor Stuart, Mr. Quest has had an accident. We found him when we returned to the ship."

"Let me have a look at him." Stuart knelt beside Quest, rolled the man onto his back, and performed a preliminary examination. "He will survive, but he may lose that eye. Omar, call for an ambulance. He needs to be hospitalized."

"That will not be necessary, Doctor."

Stuart stood up. "Who are you?"

Alba answered for him. "This is Omar's brother, Mashal. He is joining the remainder of our cruise."

"Ms. Cologne, what happened to your face?"

"You ask a lot of questions, Doctor," Mashal said. "Omar, bring some ice for Quest. The doctor will provide him with first aid." He turned to Alba. "Come, your aunt will be anxious to see us."

"Yes, Mashal."

"Captain, we should go straight to Alba's suite," Matt said.

"No, Mr. Narvik, we must go to the security office and spread the word to every guard. We can isolate Mashal's supporters in the Grand Lobby. Then you and I will go to see Alba."

"What about the passengers?"

"We will announce an open bar on deck six. The only danger will be someone being trampled in the rush. Where is my friend Rubino?"

"I punched him out before I left the ship."

"Is he seriously injured?"

"I'm not sure, but we don't have time to look for him now."

Chapter 95

"I wish I could say it was a pleasure meeting you all, but I am an honest man."

"You have what you came for, Jeanblanc. Get off this ship."

"Alas, the mighty Rubino is spurred into action, even if it is only vocally."

"I'll track you down."

"I gave you good advice, Rubino. Return to retirement . . . if this old woman allows you to survive that long."

A soft knock interrupted Jeanblanc's farewell speech. He looked at Helene, then said, "Who is there?"

"Even I cannot see through doors. Open the door and find out."

Jeanblanc pointed his gun at Candace. "You, little girl, open the door."

"Oh, Mommy, no. I'm scared."

"Candace, you must be brave. Go open the door," Cynthia said.

Candace slowly rose from the couch and walked to the door. As she placed her hand on the knob, she stole a glance at Jeanblanc, who still had his gun pointed at her. She shuddered, then turned the handle and the door burst open, forcing her to step back. Mashal shoved Alba into the room, causing her to collide with Candace, and they both fell to the floor.

"Helene Adolphe, your days have come to a close!" Mashal said. "I have returned to take both Alba and Windswept from your clutches." He froze when he saw Jeanblanc's gun pointed at him.

Jeanblanc laughed. "Welcome, Mashal. It is true what they say. 'All good things come to those who wait.' "

"You!"

"Yes, Mashal, c'est moi. I am glad you joined us. I was planning on going to Gibraltar to apprehend you. You have saved me the trip."

"I have a small army on this ship. You will not take me alive."

"I recognized some of your cohorts earlier. They are rats who will abandon you as soon as soon as they detect the odor of defeat."

Alba stood and stared at Jeanblanc. "This is my boat. I order you all to get off of it!"

As she spoke, Omar charged into the room, knocking his brother aside. Dex saw the flash of Jeanblanc's gun and watched the bullet pierce the boy's shoulder. Omar's gun fell to the floor and Dex dove for it as Jeanblanc continued firing wildly.

Matt Narvik charged into the room, and Jeanblanc turned to fire, but Matt secured the man's wrist. The gun flashed again as Jeanblanc cried out in pain. Matt drove him into the wall with his shoulder. Jeanblanc, blood flowing from his thigh, slumped to the floor. Matt turned his gun on him.

Dex raised the gun in his grasp and aimed at Mashal. "Get your hands up!" Mashal, a perplexed look on his face, did as Dex ordered. "Nice work, Matt."

"Thanks, Dex. What do we do now?"

"Matthew, are you all right?" Alba asked.

"Yes."

"Then get these pigs off of my boat."

Candace sprang from the floor and ran to her mother. "Mommy, I want to go home."

"This is our home, dear."

Captain Auesnehmer stepped into the doorway. "I have five guards here in the hallway. Mashal's men are isolated in the Grand Lobby. Should I call the police, Madame?"

Helene sighed. "Ask Alba, she is the head of Windswept now."

Chapter 96

Alba smiled. "No, Captain, we will take care of things ourselves. Have the doctor come in here and tend to the wounded. Omar, do you wish to share Mashal's fate, or stay with Windswept?"

"I would like to stay with you, my princess."

"Very well Dexter, do you wish to continue employment with Windswept?"

"No, I want what's owed me—a fair share of your father's treasure."

Helene broke out in laughter. "There is no treasure, Rubino."

Alba smiled warmly at him. "I can offer you a mansion in Belize. We hold the deed on the property. I believe it is safely in Barcelona, isn't it, Aunt Helene?"

"Yes," Helene said. "You tell us where to get in touch with you, and we will send it there."

"I'll email you an address in the capital of Belize. Don't try to cheat me, Helene."

"Dexter, I wish to finally be rid of you. If I were to cheat you that would not happen."

Alba turned to Matt. "What of you, Matthew. What can Windswept do for you?"

"Windswept has done enough to me. I count myself lucky to be alive."

Helene interrupted. "We want nothing more to do with America or Americans. We will deed to you the remaining properties we hold in the US. I believe Dexter had you living in one of those properties. There is also a large farm that was given to us as an investment."

Dex said, "Take it, Matt. They owe you that much."

"All right, sign the properties over to me. Send the paperwork to my place in Florida."

Captain Auesnehmer stood aside to let the security guards into the room. Omar told the doctor he could wait, so the doctor began tending to Jeanblanc's wounds. Helene began typing on her laptop.

"There is a flight to London in three hours. If you both hurry, you can be on it."

Matt shook his head. "Quest took my passport. I'm stuck on this ship."

"I know where it is," Omar said. "Quest put your documents in his desk."

Dex grabbed Matt's arm. "Come on, let's get out of here."

Alba stepped forward and kissed him. "Goodbye, Matthew. I will never forget you . . . Honey."

"Nor I you . . . Honey."

"Come on, Matt, let's go!"

When Matt and Dex had gone, Mashal appealed to Alba for mercy. "If you ever loved me, you will let me leave this ship and return to the continent. I will not survive in prison."

Alba chuckled. "You are not going to prison, Mashal. Windswept takes care of its own affairs." She reached out and took Helene's hand.

Helene smiled at her niece. "Yes, Mashal, you will not spend a day in prison. There is no need . . . the Atlantic is dark and cold . . ."

Cynthia nudged Candace. She hesitated, then took Helene's other hand.

The women of Windswept stood united.

Matt looked around the port as he and Dex crossed the gangway. "Where are the police? They should have come to pick up Mashal by now."

"Don't worry about it," Dex said. "Response time is slow on any island."

Matt and Dex hailed a cab, and they headed for the airport.

"How will we buy our airline tickets?" Matt asked.

Dex grinned. "I have a Windswept credit card ... at least until Helene cancels it."

"Where will we go after we get to London?"

"I'm going to Belize." *If I tell him where to go, he may flip out on me again.* "You can go to anywhere you want, just stay away from me and stop taking those pills or you'll end up like Arnan."

"Why are you upset with me?"

"You didn't follow orders, I told you not to come on this cruise, and you did anyway."

"You fired me, leaving me to do what I wanted."

"Now you're free to do anything. Just don't do it around me!"

"What about your car? It's still in my garage."

"I'll send the title to you. I won't be needing it in Belize. Consider it your severance pay.

Epilogue

When Dexter Rubino landed at Heathrow, he slipped a note to the customs agent and nodded in the direction of Matt Narvik. He then quickly entered the terminal, ignoring the shouts of the panicked Matt. *That will keep Holy Joe out of my hair.*

Dex arranged for a flight to Belize, abandoning his partner.

Matt Narvik spent fourteen hours trying to explain how a knife he had never seen before had gotten into his carryon bag. Once liberated, Matt booked a flight back to Orlando. Fortunately, he had the cash to pay for it.

Arriving in Florida, Matt retrieved his Jeep and drove back to his Fort Myers home. *Madame Adolphe said it was mine now and some other properties as well.*

The baying of the neighbors hound greeted him and helped cover his shouts of anger as he entered the ransacked home. The few things he had left there were scattered about the floor, drawers, shelves. Even the garage had been recklessly searched. The doors, hood and trunk of the Crossfire were open, but it seemed unharmed. He went to the back porch and knelt to open the access door of the hot tub. The case of gold was still there. He plunged his hand into his pocket and removed his Ebenezer.

"God has brought me safe this far, and from now on I will serve him."

"Mr. Narvik?"

Matt turned to see a Lee County Deputy standing at the screen door of his back porch. "Yes, I'm Matt Narvik."

"I'm Deputy Beech. We'd like you to come down to the sub-station and answer a few questions for us."